SMOKE AND SURVIVAL

BOOK 2 OF THE BEST WISHES SERIES

A.J. MACEY

BLURB:

What do you do when your past comes back to haunt you? Fight back...

Life at Redwood Supernatural University is about as predictable as you could imagine a supe college would be— mean girls, douchebags, drama, and *a lot* of studying—but things are looking up. The Bitch Crew has started to leave me alone, and Justin has been expelled. With that nasty mess out of my way, it looks like I can finally focus on figuring out what is going on with my guys and our budding relationships and getting a hold on my powers.

That is until the nightmares that plague my dreams come to find me in my new life.

At least this time when I face my tormentor, I won't be alone. I'll have the support of my friends, a powerful supernatural, and six guys who are determined to keep me safe from my past.

I got this...I hope.

WARNING:

The Best Wishes Series is a WhyChoose/Reverse Harem saga featuring MMFMMMM meaning there is M/M content, and the female main character doesn't have to choose between her love interests.

This book contains references involving PTSD, sexual assault recollections, domestic violence, and other themes that some readers may find triggering.

Cover: JodieLocks Designs
Editing: Ms. Correct All's Editing and Proofreading Services
Formatting: Inked Imagination Author Services

Dedicated to:

My daughter, Evelyn Rose.
Just close your eyes and dream.

SMOKE AND SURVIVAL

BOOK 2 OF THE BEST WISHES SERIES

By A.J. Macey

1

November 1st
Thursday Morning
Lucienne

"Lucie baby." *His voice was soft in my right ear.* "You feel
so fucking good." *Muscled arms sat on either side of my
head as his lean stomach and chest pressed into my
breasts. I stared blankly at the ceiling, everything feeling numb.
He'll be done soon, I mentally chanted. He pulled back to look
down at me. His deep brown eyes were hard and cold, but his
mussed dark hair and hard face transformed into a black wolf. I
went from being naked on his plaid sheets to a formal dress on
damp grass. Screams ripped through me when the wolf's mouth
curled into a harsh snarl. When I tried to push away, sharp teeth
tore into my neck. My screams turned to flooded gurgling while
pain seared through me...*

I shot up, my body shaking and covered in sweat. The
sharp movement disturbed the wrap around my chest

which caused a painful pulling on the healing puncture wounds. Sucking in sharp breaths, I realized that Hudson and Dante were crouching in front of me, their hands openly stretched toward my shaking body. Both Dante's green eyes and Hudson's luminescent lavender eyes darted around the planes of my face, wide with fear. The rest of my guys were hovering behind them looking on with worried expressions. Running a hand down my face, I pushed the loose hair that had escaped my braid out of my vision.

"Lucie?" Hudson reached up and cupped my left cheek, his warm voice quiet and hesitant. The heat of his honeyed skin curbed the last of the tremble in my limbs.

"Sorry, I was having a nightmare." The words were scratchy from sleep as I looked around Dante's massive frame for my water bottle. Reaching around him to grab it, an involuntary wince scrunched my face as the bandage around my ribs tugged at the torn skin. He turned slightly before he snatched it off the floor and handed it to me. I gave him a tiny smile while I rubbed my injury to ease the pain. "Thanks, Dante." I took a big gulp of water, hoping the cool liquid would soothe the roughness in my voice.

"What was the nightmare about?" Cam asked once I handed my water bottle back to Dante. Carefully stretching before answering, my back popped satisfactorily in response.

"Noah, then he transformed into wolf Justin..." I hesitated, not sure I wanted to say anything else. I knew they were all struggling with what had happened last weekend.

"What else, Love? We know there's more than that. You were thrashing and doing this strangled scream." Logan glanced down at me with a knowing look, a brown eyebrow raised and his lips pursed. He crossed his tan arms over his chiseled chest and waited. Rubbing the back of my neck, I pressed my lips in a thin line. *These brats know me too well.*

"No one saved me this time, and he bit me," I forced out, the hard stare I directed at Logan clearly displaying that I wasn't happy about having to tell them the rest of the nightmare. "Getting your throat ripped out is not an awesome dream." I shifted to standing before looking at the clock. 8:45 AM. *Good, plenty of time.* "I'm going to shower. Cam, will you be able to help me wrap my gauze?" I hitched a thumb over my shoulder in the direction of the bathroom as I collected the socks that I had kicked off before falling asleep. Cam nodded as he moved toward my room to grab the first aid kit Dr. Ingress had prepared for me.

Slipping into my room, I opened the top drawer of my dresser and dug out a pair of black panties and a matching black bra. I heard my guys slowly shuffling about in the shared living room, most likely pulling out new clothes for the day. We had gotten into a routine the last three days of who showered when and whose turn it was to grab food for everyone. Next, I grabbed the rest of my outfit from various hangers: a pair of skinny jeans, my belt, a cami, and a plain, forest green sweater.

Once I had my change of clothes for the day, I headed back out through the living room and into the empty bathroom. The water warmed up as I unwrapped the current dressing around my breasts and ribs that held the gauze to my sternum. The puncture wounds were scabbed over, but Dr. Ingress wanted to keep them covered to reduce any irritation from my shirt or bag strap. Vicious red streaks surrounded the puncture wounds. The weight of his paw had left behind bruises in such dark, deep blues and purples that they nearly looked black on my fair skin. It wasn't as bad as I had expected, and I was surprised that the weight hadn't broken any bones in my chest. *It certainly felt like he was crushing me to death.* Stripping out of the rest of my pajamas, I quickly undid my braid and brushed out my hair before stepping into the steady stream.

My tense muscles relaxed slowly the longer the hot water poured down my shoulders. I made sure to keep my chest facing away from the water, having learned on Tuesday that it stung to have the spray hit my injury. I slowly worked my way through my shower routine of shampoo, conditioner, body wash, and a poor attempt of shaving my legs, taking my time not to rip open the scabs. After turning off the water, I dried my body and stepped out of the shower onto the plush bath mat. With my hair wrapped up in the towel, I pulled my panties up my legs and secured my bra around my torso before I knocked on the door to let Cam know I was ready for a new wrapping. I was stepping into my jeans when the door opened. *Me being bent over with my lace covered ass toward him was absolutely not on purpose. Nope, not at all.*

"Doll," Cam murmured, my nickname rough with heated desire. I slid the jeans up my thighs and looked at him over my shoulder as I buttoned them.

"Yes?" My question was filled with faux innocence.

Setting the medical supplies on the counter, Cam came up behind me. His hands were cool on my flushed skin as his fingers trailed around my sides to my stomach. The soft material of his shirt pressed against my back, his cock against my ass, rigid and confined in his dark jeans. I was mostly facing the mirror, able to look into his half-lidded hazel eyes as he stared at me. The multi-faceted irises were barely visible around the rapidly expanding pupils.

"Did you do that on purpose?" He leaned down slightly to be closer to my right ear. The warmth of his breath caressed my skin, and goosebumps formed under the soft heat.

"Do what?" I tried to continue my charade, but my lips twitched as I attempted to hide my triumphant smile.

"If you wanted my attention, then you've certainly gotten it." His long fingers gripped my hips tightly when I pressed my ass back into him, and his jaw clenched. A harsh exhale brushed my skin, and I felt him harden even more against me. He kept eye contact as he bent his head and kissed his way up my shoulder to my neck right over my tattoo. His left hand shifted to pull the towel off my hair, moving the damp strands to sit over my left shoulder. The tips of his fingers traced over the top of my breast as he nibbled my neck, the sharp point of his canines barely scraping my skin. I couldn't hold back my moan at the building heat in my core any longer.

Turning to face him, I let my fingers get tangled in his messy bed head. He pushed me up against the counter, gripping my hips roughly once more. His mouth pressed against mine urgently, moving with increasing fervor. I opened my lips and Cam bit down, not hard enough to break skin with his fangs, but the delicious sting drew a moan deep in my throat. He shifted his hips forward, grinding his cock against me as I slid my tongue against his. The restrained roughness in his movements urged me to push him past his control, to fully release the predator hidden behind his disarming glasses and parchment scent. I had gripped his hair tightly, intent to draw that animal out with a tug, when a knock sounded on the door.

"You two almost done?" Sadie questioned through the door, her words slurred slightly from sleep.

"Almost," I called out, trying not to smile. Cam's face was flushed, his eyes twinkling while he watched me. His soft lips pressed against mine briefly before pulling away and pursing in an attempt to hold back a laugh.

Stepping back, he grabbed the gauze squares off the counter, layering them on my puncture wounds. I held them in place and lifted up my elbows allowing him to wrap the bandage around my back until it was tight enough to hold everything in place. Once it was secured, I pulled on my black cami. When Cam held out my sweater for me, I couldn't stop smiling at the sweet gesture. Taking it with a soft 'thanks', I slid it on. I headed out of the bathroom first with Cam trailing right behind me. I smiled brightly at Sadie, my dimples prominent on my cheeks as she glared at me, cranky about being up.

"Good morning," I drawled.

"Mhm," she mumbled an agreement, "I'm sure it is." Her glare turned into a nosy look with a narrowed gaze and a smirk. *Clearly, she knows what I was doing.* I chuckled when her eyebrows wiggled suggestively, before turning back into my room to toss my dirty clothes in the hamper. Quickly grabbing my knee-high boots out of the closet, I dug out a clean pair of socks before going out to sit on one of the open armchairs.

The twins were lounging back in the loveseat like always while Nik headed into my room to change. Grigori fluttered off his usual perch of Nik's shoulder to land on the back of the couch cushions when Nik walked past the twins. Dante and Hudson were packing their backpacks as Cam leaned against the arm of my chair, his parchment scent calming me as I pulled on my socks and boots, moving slowly to not disrupt my wrapping.

"All right guys, I'm ready. Did we want to go grab breakfast?" Huffing, I leaned back in the seat. I looked around my guys and couldn't help but smile. They hadn't left my side since Dante had saved me from Justin.

"Hell yes, I can always eat." Landon hopped up with a jump and a boisterous clap. Logan followed, albeit more calmly, while Nik came over to help me out of the chair, Grigori shifting again to sit on his right shoulder. A blush spread across my cheeks and down my neck at the close proximity to Nik. So close that I could feel his power crackling as well as the hard planes of his cut torso brushing against my chest. I looked up between my lashes, enjoying my up-close view. His angular face was soft instead of cold and closed off, and a small tilt curled his lips. I suddenly became very aware that his hands were still wrapped around my own, his thumbs rubbing small delicate circles on my skin.

A thud from somewhere else in the room broke the spell, but his smile remained as he squeezed my hands before stepping back and letting go. I internally shook myself the rest of the way out of the stupor I was in before calling out to let Sadie know we were heading toward the dining hall and that I'd see her later.

The air was chilly, the small breeze cutting through my jacket despite having a sweater on as we made our way across the quad. Shivers ran down my spine and arms with each gust. Hudson was walking next to me with his hands in his pockets, so I slipped under his right arm, leaving it draped over my shoulders.

"I'm cold." I looked up at Hudson and pouted my lip out while giving him my best puppy dog eyes. He laughed and held me tight to his right side, his body warming me.

"I'll always keep you warm, Princess," he admitted happily, sounding fully back to himself after the several weeks he had spent under the influence of the emotion-altering rune. I rubbed my cheek against his wool coat and let my head cuddle into his shoulder. I knew he was still struggling with what had happened, with everything he had said and done even though it wasn't technically him. I wanted him to know I didn't blame him. I had missed the hell out of him these last few weeks and being curled up against him felt like coming home after a long, tiring day.

Gazing around the quad, I noticed the campus was slowly waking up for the day as more and more people filtered out into the grassy area. Most students didn't have classes until ten like us, so the only people on the quad were people who had early classes—*cue internal shudder*—and those who were getting food. We filed into the dining hall, the smell of breakfast and coffee filling the nearly empty space. Quickly shuffling around the tables toward the kitchen and buffet lines, we filled our trays. I grabbed only a banana and small oatmeal since I wasn't feeling hungry after my nightmare while the guys stacked their trays much fuller than mine.

"That is all you are getting, Babe?" Nik questioned from behind me in line, and the gravelly nickname brought a smile to my lips despite the increasing roughness of his voice, the sound like sandpaper had scored his vocal cords. I nodded and turned to look over at him, his dark brown brows dipped low over his clouded glassy eyes. Grigori's feathery head was tilted in question, his beady eyes staring intently at my tray.

"I can't ever really eat after I have a nightmare." I shrugged, unsure what else to say. *It's just been that way for so many years that I haven't given it much thought.*

"How often is that?" Dante asked as we weaved our way through the room toward one of the larger tables in the back. The few students who looked awake enough to form coherent thoughts glanced at us as we walked past, their eyes lingering on my injured face.

"How often do I not eat or how often do I have nightmares?" I asked quietly, sitting between Cam and Hudson and staring at my tray to avoid the looks I knew would be waiting.

"Well, nightmares was what I meant, but how often do you not eat? I know you told me about it briefly earlier in the semester, but I thought it was something you were working on?" Dante's brows drew together when I glanced up through my lashes. All my guys were looking at me with sad expressions except Nik whose blank face gave me nothing to go on. *Ugh, pity, I hate that.*

"I have nightmares nightly, so I don't have breakfast, and if I do, it's like this where it's something small and easy on my stomach in case I get sick. For other meals, it usually depends on how my anxiety is or how many flashbacks I have. It was pretty bad those first few days of the semester because of all the changes, but I *have* been working on it. I've been pretty consistent with lunch and dinner recently since my anxiety hasn't been too bad, but..." I paused, remembering the text I had gotten last night. I hadn't read it fully because I was half asleep when I went to bed. My heart raced as I dug out my phone. *Please don't be what I think it was.*

"But what, Love?" Logan prompted, looking concerned at my sudden change of demeanor. I ignored him, my sole focus on checking my phone, and wound up fumbling with the device, almost dropping it when I finally got it out of my jacket pocket because my hands were shaking.

Unknown Number: hello, Lucie baby

My phone slipped from my numbing fingers as my vision blurred, and the noises around me started to sound far away. *Oh god no...*

"Hello, Lucie baby..." His voice was cold as his hand wrapped around my throat, the pressure cutting off my air...

Logan

Lucie's phone slipped out of her trembling hands, dropping to the table with a thud. Her eyes widened with fear as her pale skin took on a sickly sheen with a green hue. Hudson and Cam immediately snapped into action, assessing her and how bad her panic attack was.

"Whatever she's seeing isn't here." Hudson's voice echoed through my head, keeping his observation to only us at the table so those around us wouldn't hear. I reached over and snatched up her phone. Cam's voice echoed within my head with another observation, his head tilted as he discreetly sniffed the air.

"Whatever she saw terrified her; the smell of fear is wafting off of her in nearly suffocating waves." I unlocked her cell while Hudson and Cam attempted to soothe Lucie out of her flashback. I felt my blood boil at the words I saw on the screen.

Unknown Number: hello, Lucie baby

Fury burned through my veins, knowing instinctively who it was. I felt my lip curl back in a snarl as I stared at the text. The pinpricks across my scalp and fingers, signifying the growth of my claws and horns, shot through me the longer I glared at the words, my Rage drowning out everything else. The smell of sulfur and smoke filled my nose, the acrid scent snapping me out of my haze. The Rage pulled back, my ears no longer ringing in the midst of my meltdown. I had accidentally conjured my hellfire, the slip-up betrayed by the blackened handprint burned into the top of the table. I took several deep breaths, my eyes falling shut as my daemon claws retreated into my human looking nails.

When I opened my eyes, everyone was looking at me with wide, fear-laden eyes. It was rare when Landon or I would use our hellfire, but it wasn't impossible, especially when The Rage was close to the surface. *Get control of yourself,* I lectured, *Lucie needs you, not a daemon in Rage.* She was slowly returning to herself when I looked at her, Cam coaching her through breathing and grounding exercises like the ones that Charlie had done early in the semester.

"It's him," I ground out between clenched teeth. The tension around the table climbed to staggering heights at my announcement. Landon's hands flared with hellfire, his daemon side coming forward, enticed by my words and the strength of my still-lingering Rage. Grigori squawked in anger, and Nik's face became hard, his blank expression giving way to stone. Cam's fangs were on display as he snarled in my direction, and Dante was curling and uncurling his hands into fists, his muscles rippling with the urge to shift. Hudson's lips curved into a severe frown while anger burned in his eyes.

"He always called me Lucie baby or babygirl." Lucie's voice was small and trembling. She was back with us and out of her flashback, her pale skin coated in a light layer of sweat and her eyes glistening with unshed tears. "That came in last night, but I didn't really read it when I was changing into my pajamas since I was so tired. I only remembered because you asked about my eating."

She looked at her food and pushed it away from her as she dry heaved. She threw a hand over her mouth and squeezed her eyes shut. *Someone as amazing as her should never have to suffer, especially not like this,* I thought, holding at bay my instinctive urge to tear apart the room.

"It's all right, Firecracker, we're here. We're going to keep you safe. We need to go to Dean Renaud's office. He needs to be notified." Dante slipped seamlessly into his unspoken role of leader, his words steady with authority despite the continuing rippling of his muscles.

Anger had my own stomach unsettled, turning what I had already eaten into a lead weight. Dumping Lucie's and my trays, I grabbed our bags. She curled under Cam's arm, her face pressed into his coat while Nik held her hand. It was some of the only physical contact he'd had with anyone other than Cam in years, and it didn't escape my notice, even in my anger, that he slowly walked closer to her with each step. Grigori had shuffled away from his normal perch, down Nik's arm, and over to Lucie's shoulder.

The familiar rubbed a feathery wing against her cheek to comfort her. *Grigori cares about Lucie just as much as we do,* I noted with surprise. He hadn't sat on anyone else's shoulder other than hers, and that included us. Hell, he didn't let anyone touch him other than Nik, and now Lucie. It spoke volumes of how much Nik cared about our girl. Lost in my internal musings, trying to distract myself from my anger, it didn't take long to reach the front door of the Administration building.

"Good morning, boys, how may I..." The older gentleman at the front desk trailed off when he saw Lucie crying between Cam and Nik. "Oh my goodness, Lucie, I'll call Mr. Renaud right away, so he knows you're coming." His wobbly, creaking voice was frantic when he glanced at the beautiful girl who looked defeated between them. I nodded my head and responded with a quick 'thanks' as I followed Landon toward the stairs. Lucie, Cam, and Nik trailed behind us with Dante and Hudson bringing up the back of the group.

When we reached the fourth and final floor of the building, the dean's office door flew open, Dean Renaud standing on the other side. My steps faltered with how terrifying he looked: light blue eyes burning, feet apart, shoulders pulled back, and the hand not holding the door open was in a white-knuckled fist. His power audibly crackled in the air as he shifted out of the way and waved for us to enter. Once we were inside the spacious office, he closed the door firmly and walked to the front of the group, standing near his desk.

"What happened?" His voice was clipped but not overtly angry, his power softening to a dull hum, likely so he wouldn't scare Lucie. I handed him Lucie's phone for him to see the text himself. As he read it, his brow furrowed. His eyes scanned the screen multiple times before responding. "Is it safe to assume this is Noah?" He looked at us, watching intently as I nodded an answer.

"Yes, it came in last night, but no one read it until this morning at breakfast. Lucie told us that was what he always called her. We came straight here," Dante explained.

Dean Renaud ran his free hand through his gelled hair, messing it a bit. He nodded slightly, lost in thought while still looking at the phone. His jaw tensed every few moments, the quiet growing around the room as we waited for his response. It was easy to remember how powerful he was when his eyes burned in fury.

"All right," he finally said in the tense silence. "We're going to do what we discussed this past weekend. You will keep close to her. If these continue, then we'll have one of you with her at all times, but for right now just stay close." He turned his attention to her. She had stopped crying and was standing up straight. "Lucie, will you be all right with the same phone number, or do you want me to get you a new one?" Her jaw was set, and her hands were fisted at her sides. Her eyes hard with determination. *There's our Lucie.*

When she spoke, her voice was strong and precise. "I'll keep this number unless it gets worse. If it does, I'll look into getting a new one. We can monitor any incoming messages or calls if I keep this phone active." She didn't avoid Dean Renaud's eyes as everyone else did; in fact, she honestly looked like a shorter version of him in her stature and determination. "I'll let my mom and my best friend who's at UW know to keep an eye out for him."

"That sounds like a good plan, Lucie," the dean praised proudly as he looked at her with a small smile, his anger receding the longer she spoke. "How are you handling all of this?"

"I had a flashback when I read it and looking at my breakfast almost made me sick, but I'm all right now," she answered softly, her eyes shifting to one of the many book-shelves in the office.

"Do you mind telling me about the flashback?" He sat down in his highback office chair as he motioned for her to sit in one of the leather chairs. "I'm not a professional, but I would like for you to think of this as a safe location to talk about what had happened. Together, we can try to work through some of your anxiety."

Before she started talking, she took the seat in the right chair as the rest of us got settled. Dante claimed the left one with Hudson perching on the arm. Nik took his usual pref-erence of leaning against something, this time against one of the many shelves, positioning himself behind Lucie's chair.

Grigori shifted off Lucie's shoulder when Nik stepped back from her. Landon and I kneeled on either side of her while Cam stood behind the chair where Dante and Hudson were seated. I took her left hand in mine while Landon put a hand on her knee.

She took a deep breath, her hands trembling ever so slightly as she started explaining. "He had just moved into his apartment. I don't remember what he was upset about, but he came up to me and said, 'Hello, Lucie baby' and he..." She swallowed hard, shadows flashing in her eyes. I squeezed her hand reassuringly, trying to keep my anger under control. *Don't burn Lucie.* Whatever she was mentally telling herself was working, and her spine straightened like she was physically gathering her strength. "He choked me until I passed out."

"That fucking bastard," Landon sent over our mental link.

"I'm going to kill him," I sent back. I saw Landon nod in response, his Rage boiling so close to the surface that his eyes filtered between normal and blacked out.

"Very good, Lucie, you're doing well. I know I've told you before, but my office is always open for you." He nodded at her approvingly. "That goes for you too, gentlemen. If you need anything, you're more than welcome to come to me at any time." His attention moved from Lucie to my brothers and me. It felt odd to have such a powerful supe being so personable. *Not saying that most supes aren't personable, but this is one of the most powerful supes around.*

"Is this weird? This feels weird, right?" I mentally shot to Landon.

"Having a Transcendent basically telling you that you can come to his office whenever we want? Hell yes, it's weird. I don't think I've ever heard of him being so accommodating," Landon responded.

I nodded slightly, turning my attention back to our girl. Her skin was finally starting to look normal, the sickly green tint fading. She glanced at her phone during the lull in the conversation and climbed to her feet, essentially cutting off any more discussion.

"Thank you for everything, Alex, but we have class soon, and we have our debate today." She gestured to Dante, Cam, and Nik. The dean stood and led her to the door with his hand lightly resting on her upper back.

"I completely understand. Thank you for coming to me with this as soon as you were aware. Let me know if it continues or escalates." She nodded and turned to him before passing through the door, and my brothers and I stood behind her, waiting to exit the room. "I'll make sure you're safe, Lucie," the dean told her with a small smile as he held open the door for us, each of us saying goodbye as we left. We filed down the four flights of stairs with Lucie leading the way, her stride filled with determination, her back straight and head held high. She strode confidently through the lobby with a wave and warm smile to the front desk clerk.

"Bye, Jonathon, I'll see you tomorrow morning." His face wrinkled in a smile, and he sent a croaked 'be good' as she pushed open the front doors. The weather was still chilled, but the sun had poked through the clouds as we made our way to our respective classes. Hugs and waves were exchanged before we went our separate ways throughout the quad.

2

November 1st
Thursday Morning
Lucienne

The first debate teams were closing their second rebuttal. Professor Crest reminded us at the beginning of class that this was more of a practice debate to get a feel for how the process would go. Learning how to conduct research, the steps of the debate, and getting a feel for the time limits to help prepare us for our larger debate that would occur during the spring semester. We had a speech that we needed to write and present to the class individually before winter break started to help us 'learn to persuade others.' I wasn't looking forward to that one since it would only be me instead of with a partner, but there was nothing I could do about it. We were picking out topics for those speeches at the end of class today.

The other debate finished quickly, so Cam and I, along with Dante and Nik, moved to the front of the classroom and sat at our respective tables—Affirmative for Dante and Nik, Negative for us. Dante was the first to go for their team. His deep, melodic voice carried through the room with confidence, his head high with his shoulders drawn back. The dominant, alpha vibes I was getting from him captured my attention as well as almost every girl in class. I pulled my attention from my blatant staring to get focused on our portion of the debate and not on the sexy, tanned shifter addressing the class. *Head in the game, Lucie, focus and don't drool.*

"Our debate today is on the topic of whether supernaturals are superior to humans. My partner and I have come up with multiple reasons why this statement is true. First would be that the majority of supernatural creatures have some type of power or powers. These skills give them the ability to perform feats that humans would never be able to duplicate.

"An example would be that it takes a fairly large group of human firefighters to stop and put out a fire, as well as to save someone from the destruction. It would take one, possibly two, water or fire elementals to extinguish the fire and a supe with the ability to fly or reach high locations to save the person trapped. The group of human firefighters are not always able to achieve the end goal. Sometimes fires continue, and sometimes they are not able to save that individual. This is because the fire is too much for humans to control, while it would be easily contained by supernaturals."

Dante continued with several different examples of situations where supernaturals' powers would be more effective than what humans could do. I jotted down bulleted points of what he was saying so Cam and I could create our rebuttals during the intermission. Once Dante had reached his five-minute time limit, he sat back at their table next to Nik. I was presenting the first of our points, so I collected my notecards and stepped up to the podium. *Deep breath.* I inhaled deeply before speaking, willing my voice to be steady.

"As Dante said previously, we are discussing whether supernaturals are superior to humans. My partner and I have several points which will show you this statement is false. Throughout our society and our history, both human and supernatural, we have multitudes of differences: hair colors, sexual preferences, powers, skin tones, intelligence levels, athletic ability, artistic ability. The list goes on.

"Why would one of the differences be superior to others? Those who are great artists are held in high esteem, and their stories and art are carried through generations, propelling that piece of history, but that does not mean they are superior to others who lived during those times. Athletes, both human and supernatural, are in a similar situation. They are placed in the spotlight due to their efficiency and athletic ability in whatever sport they compete in. They are looked up to by children as role models. These children want to follow in their footsteps, but that does not make these athletes better or superior to us," I explained. When I finally reached the end of my speech, I had only three seconds to spare before the five minutes were up. I smiled slightly at no one in particular before sinking into my chair, making sure not to plop down like I wanted to.

Nik explained their second point, essentially that an elitist view would be beneficial to the structure of society. I know it was just a mock debate and that none of my guys or any of my friends in the supe community felt this way, but my stomach rolled at the thought of anyone actually believing these viewpoints. I grew up in the human community and had spent my entire life, until five months ago, believing I was a human. I had gone to human school, had human friends, a human mom. *Well, a human adoptive mom, who turned out not to be my actual mother. She found me in the alley of her workplace one night when I was just a baby.* I still felt like an outsider in the supe community unless I was with my guys, Sadie, or Benji. Even Alex made me feel like I belonged, but I still got wide-eyed and speechless when someone did something significant with their powers.

I refocused on the debate as Nik finished his first point. His voice had to be spelled to be heard throughout the room. The longer he talked the more I saw him swallowing and drinking from a water bottle I'd never noticed before. My heart clenched painfully in my chest, the urge to take notes on what he was saying vanishing with the growing struggle he had with speaking. *Oh, Nik.* I quickly blinked away tears as he finished up his speech, Cam's movement next to me pulling me out of my stupor. Turning my attention, I scanned through Cam's notes on Nik's presentation so I could have proper counterarguments prepared. Cam made quick work of our next point which included that humans can do great things as well even without powers. *That famous storming on D-Day? Yup, all humans.*

Finally, over twenty minutes later, after Dante and Nik's final rebuttals came to a close, we were able to return to our normal table. *Thank god, I hate public speaking.* I slumped in my chair, exhaustion seeping into my bones. Along with my healing, the flashback this morning was zapping all my energy. It didn't help that I had noticed people throughout the room sneaking glances over at our table. The news of

Justin's attack had spread quickly over the weekend, but I had been holed up in my dorm since then so I didn't fully realize that I would be the center of the gossip. *Ugh.* I rolled my neck trying to loosen the knots that had gotten worse in the recent weeks. When I stopped, Cam's warm hand cupped the back of my neck, rubbing gently on the knots. A small groan rumbled in my throat catching the attention of my guys around the table.

"Feel good, Firecracker?" Dante's voice was low, laced with heat as he looked at me. I groaned again when Cam massaged a particularly painful knot. They chuckled at my non-response. Cam continued his circles until the end of class.

November 1st
Thursday Afternoon
Nikolai

Cam had a meeting with one of his professors for a potential project in the spring semester, so the dorm was empty as I set my bag down on my bed. I soaked up the silence, the stress of the day dragging my shoulders down under an enormous amount of tension. A few large pulls from the water bottle I had for speaking occasions did little to bring relief where I needed it most. The overwhelming burn in my throat intensified, spreading outward, and I scrubbed my sleeve over my useless eyes to dry the gathering tears. *Do not think about that,* I scolded. Grigori squawked at me in response.

"I know, I know," I murmured, nearly inaudible in the silence as I ran my fingers over his head and down his tucked wings. Ruffling his feathers, he smacked me in the ear, followed quickly by the little asshole nipping my fingers before hopping off my shoulder. "I am not unappreciative of you; it has just been a hard day." My rough whispers sliced through the heavy silence. The burn and skipping of my voice had me unscrewing the cap to my bottle once more.

Sinking down onto the plush material of my bedding, I sat still, trying to decide what I should do until we were gathered later for game night. Homework? *No.* Practice down at the range? *Possible.* Lay about and be a lazy log? *Definitely sounds appealing.* My thoughts shifted from one idea to the next, attempting to decide, when a soft knock sounded on the door.

My body responded instinctually, adrenaline flooding my system as I grabbed the small bag of prepared potion and spell capsules I always carried before approaching the door silently. I hesitated before walking fully in front of it, my left shoulder pressing into the wall next to the door frame. A faint trace of vanilla hit my nose through the crack between the door and the wooden frame.

The tension dissipated from my body when I heard Lucie shuffling restlessly on the other side, the sound of her usual jacket and boots rustling with each movement. I tucked the small bag into my sweatshirt pocket before opening the door, the warmth of her power blanketing me as her vanilla scent assaulted my senses. Grigori shot out of my room and onto my shoulder, preening under her attention as she smiled at him. *Asshole.* My thought resulted in another 'accidental' wing slap to the head.

"Hey, Nik," she mumbled, her lip worried between her teeth as her gemstone eyes turned to me. *Say something!*

"Hi, Babe." My voice cracked painfully with my welcome. Clearing my throat softly, I tried to speak again, that wretched burning growing with each word. "Are you looking for Cam? Because he has a meeting..." I trailed off as her brows drew together. *Ah, of course she would be disappointed he is not here,* I thought bitterly. Another feathery slap thudded my ear.

"Uh, no. I'm not looking for Cam, I came by to see you." Her fingers fiddled with her bag strap, her words soft as she spoke. *Wait, what?* I had to think through what she said before it registered properly. *She is here for me?* Grigori preened at the thought. "I was wondering, uh, if you would want to take a walk with me? I know it's kind of cold out, and I understand if you're busy right now." She stumbled over the last of the words, her eyes dropping to the ground as she trailed off. I laid a hand against her forearm and waited until her eyes met mine. *Well, until she looked up toward my face.*

"I would love to," I whispered, and thankfully none of my words cracked. I stepped back so she could come into my dorm. Grigori abandoned me to hop on her shoulder, but I could not fault him because I would do the same if I were him. My magic brushed out around me telling me where things were at so I did not trip or run into anything as I leaned into my room and grabbed by coat off my desk. I slipped it on before rejoining Lucie in the living room area, thankful that I had not yet taken off my shoes. She was smiling softly at Grigori who was puffing up his chest. I rolled my eyes. *Show off.* I made sure I had my keys to the dorm as well as my phone before following Lucie into the hallway. We walked silently down the hall and staircase before slipping outside. I wasn't sure where she wanted to walk to or if she had a destination in mind, so when she turned down a narrow dirt trail toward the woods, I followed. As we walked, Grigori took off, soaring in a wide circle before settling down on my shoulder so I could fully see where we were going.

The breeze shifted quietly through the trees and brush, the rustling accompanied by the sounds of small wildlife fluttering in and around the branches of the evergreen trees. The smell of pine, dirt, and fresh air grew stronger the farther away from the quad we walked. Thankfully, Grigori was focused on the path and not on the beautiful girl to my left or I would have tripped on the barely visible root sticking out of the dirt. Lucie, unfortunately, was not so lucky, and the toe of her boot snagged it just enough for her to stumble forward. I reached out, my right arm wrapping around her stomach to stop her from falling, while my left hand curled around her slender fingers. When she finally regained her balance, her cheeks were pinkened in the slightest flush, her hand tightening around mine.

"Thanks, Nik." My focus fell to her beautiful pink lips that quirked up in a small smile as she addressed me. "Don't worry, we're almost there," she reassured me, her quiet timbre meshing well with the calm surroundings of the forest.

"I trust you," I croaked. *Damn these useless vocal cords!* She smiled again, leaning softly against my arm.

"I know you do. You don't have to talk, hon, I don't want you to hurt yourself anymore." I scrunched my face at her. *How did she know it hurts? I did not tell her that... did I?* Before I could say anything, the trees parted into a small clearing. The area was mostly flat, the only break in the soft grass a little pond surrounded by stones. The sounds of students had disappeared when we broke through the trees, Lucie walking straight toward one of the longer, more worn rocks. I strayed behind her, listening and feeling everything around me.

The clearing was undisturbed by students, only some of the grass dented with Lucie-sized footprints. The calming lull of the atmosphere coaxed the tension out of my body with each woodsy inhale I took. The sound of Lucie's bag opening drew my attention. She pulled out a small cookie tin and two thermoses as well as some outdoor cups. I felt my head tilting in confusion as I watched her, the bite in the air giving her pale cheeks and small upturned nose a red flush. When it appeared as if she finally had everything out of her bag, she waved me over. Closing the distance between us in three long strides, I sank onto the cold rock next to her.

"What is that?" I whispered, thankful that it was quiet enough in the clearing for her to hear me. She twisted open one of the thermoses, and a wave of rich chocolate, cinnamon, and spice hit me. She poured a small amount into one of the cups, holding it out for me before answering.

"It's my mom's hot cocoa recipe." I brushed her fingers as I took the cup, the silky skin soft under the rough pads of my fingertips. "I always have it when I'm sick or when my throat hurts. I was thinking maybe it could help you too." Her statement was gentle and her intonation went up at the end making it sound like an unsure question. I brought the cup to my lips, inhaling before taking a sip. The hot chocolate was delicious, the warm liquid quickly easing the sting in my throat.

"It is delicious. Thank you, Lucie." I was able to say the words at a more normal volume, the gravel, cracking, and roughness slightly softened. Smiling, she poured some for herself and opened the cookie tin.

"I tried to pack my mom's softer cookies that she sent. I didn't know if rough food hurt your throat or..." Her words trailed off when I cupped her face softly with my right hand.

"How did you know?" The question was whispered, not

because my throat hurt, but because this was not a topic I approached lightly. Her sapphire eyes focused on me instead of the cookie tin in her lap.

"Well, the roughness in your voice has been there since I met you, but today it seemed to get worse. I could see you struggling with talking, and you kept taking drinks out of that water bottle that you've never carried before," she murmured, her slight shoulders shrugging. "I didn't want to make assumptions, but I wanted to see if this would help"— she gestured around us—"some hot cocoa and cookies and just hanging out in the place I come to just *be*, you know? Somewhere we can just listen to the breeze and the little animals and hang out, no talking required." She chuckled to herself. "Well, clearly I've done lots of talking, but my intention was to come out here and just relax until later."

I was speechless for probably the first time in years. *Who is this girl? How does she know that this is exactly what I need?* Questions filtered through my mind as I just stared at Lucie. Her blonde hair was up in a bun on the crown of her head, stray strands fluttering in the breeze. Power crackled across my skin, radiating safety and... *love?*

Say something! Grigori mentally squawked at me, cutting off my inner thoughts. I had never been good with words. Being from Russia and struggling with English when I was younger resulted in a lot of bullying. After everything that had happened to my vocal cords, it did not get any easier, so I acted on instincts instead.

Leaning forward, not too quickly as I did not want to scare her, I gently pulled her face to mine. Her lips were soft, warm, and slathered in an unscented chapstick. She tilted her face, allowing me to deepen the kiss, the spice and chocolate of her mother's recipe coating her lips and tongue.

Pulling back, I smiled down at her, her eyes sparkling as she looked up at me.

"Thank you, Babe," I whispered against her skin as I pressed my lips to her forehead. Her smile widened as I wrapped her under my right arm. Each of us taking a soft sugar cookie from the tin, we lapsed into a companionable silence, the sound of the wind and animals the only noise between us.

3

I walked across the quad early while the sun was still behind the horizon, and the only color in the sky was a soft glow transitioning from blue to pink as the day began. The wind blew lightly, causing the dew on the lawn to shift. I was thankful I had changed out my jacket for my wool, thigh-length pea coat. It was a deep navy blue with a belt around the waist. I fell in love with it when I found it at the small boutique during mine, Benji, and Sadie's dress shopping excursion two weekends ago. My messenger bag was cross-body, slightly hitting my hip as I walked, but the thick layer of gauze under my wrapping kept the strap from rubbing against the puncture wounds. I was almost to the administration building when my phone started to vibrate. I pulled it out and realized it was a call.

"Hello?" I was greeted with white noise, like the wind was blowing against the microphone of the cell. "Hello?"

With no response other than static, I pulled my phone from my face to make sure it was still connected. "I can't hear you, so bye," I drawled out before hanging up. I stuffed it and my hands back into my pocket, my fingers freezing despite my gloves.

My phone didn't ring again by the time I reached the administration building. *Must have been a wrong number.* The blast of warm air tingled my cheeks as I walked into the lobby and saw Jonathon standing behind his desk trying to grab something off one of the upper shelves that his slightly hunched back and frail body wasn't able to reach.

"Here, let me help." I hurried around the desk when he wobbled slightly on the step stool he was precariously perched on. I caught his arm gently to steady him before helping him step down.

"You don't need to do that, Lucie dear," he declared as he flopped into his desk chair adjusting his polka dotted bow tie. I gave him a look out of the corner of my eye before turning to the bookshelf.

"All right, Jonathon, what were you trying to get?" I asked as I perused the shelf, my hands settling on my hips.

"That grey box on the top shelf, the one with the black label." His hands shook as he pointed a crooked finger at the box. I nodded that I had heard, stepped on the stool, and reached up. I was a few inches too short to reach the box, so I decided it would be a perfect opportunity to practice my powers. I focused on the shelf the box was sitting on and visualized it curving down toward me so the box would slide easily into my hands. Once I had fully pictured what I wanted to happen, I held up my hands and pushed that visualization onto the locked target of the shelf in my mind. It did exactly what I wanted it to, and I caught the box with ease. The shelf slid back into its original form as I stepped down.

"Here you go." I handed the box off to Jonathon with a smile, proud that I was able to do something nice for him after he lit that fire within me at our lunch a few weeks ago.

"Thank you, dear! You head on up to your work with Mr. Renaud, Lucie." He shooed me from behind the counter, and I couldn't help but chuckle in response. I was closing the small door to enter behind the counter when several voices echoed through the room.

"Oh, look." Madison's southern twang was snotty as she crossed her arms in front of her chest. The rest of the Bitch Crew gave me looks varying from disdain to hate. I rolled my eyes and walked the rest of the way around the counter.

"Ladies." Jonathon's voice was low in warning as he addressed the Bitch Crew. Their attention barely flickered to him before returning to me.

"Don't worry, we aren't going to cause any issues for the star pupil," Brittney sneered, even going as far as to do a head bob. *Oh, brother.* I scoffed at her assumption.

"Brittney, shut up. Everyone knows how you and your friends manipulated Hudson, so don't try to play like you aren't a complete bitch." Gabe and Elijah walked around the four girls, causing a break in the flow of traffic in and out of the building. Elijah's arrogance was nowhere to be seen. He didn't walk with a swagger, and he didn't ogle as he reprimanded them, his voice biting as glared. They moved their glares from me to them.

"Oh, so you're fucking her too then?" Claire's perfectly plucked eyebrow raised. "Everyone knows you're a man whore, but it's beneath you to fuck a slut." My fists clenched as they all cackled at her insult.

"Miss Loren!" Alex's voice was harsh, his very expensive,

shiny dress shoes clacking on the stone as he stepped off the stairs to the tiled floor. *Jonathon must have called him.* "You will mind how you talk to other students while you are on my campus. Now, I believe you have a meeting with the Assistant Dean for your punishment." He turned to the side, sweeping his arm up the stairs to show them where they needed to go. They looked properly chastised and left without any further comments, but I wasn't so convinced that this drama would really get better anytime soon. I shook my head at their backs.

Seriously, what did I do to them? I looked over at Gabe and Elijah and gave them a small nod. "Thanks, guys, I'll see you later?" I asked as I walked toward the stairs.

They waved and smiled warmly at me. "No problem, Lucie. You going to the Kohl game tonight?" Elijah asked as I reached the bottom step.

"Yeah, I'm going with my friends if you want to sit with us," I offered. *Look at me making friends!* I internally squealed happily. They both agreed before heading to the elevator. I followed Alex up the four flights of stairs without talking. I could tell he was angry, his lips pressed into a thin line. He held open his door for me, and I immediately dropped my bag into my usual chair. "Are we heading back or are we staying here?" I asked him while he closed the door.

He gestured his arm toward the hidden set of rooms behind the bookshelf. It had become a sort of game the last few Fridays for me to try and remember which book opened the shelf. I reached up and grabbed a dark brown volume with a faded gold script on the spine. It pulled down with a soft click, and I pumped a fist in the air with an excited 'yes.' Alex followed behind me with a warm, honeyed laugh. I bounded into the practice room in a half skip/half run.

Despite all the shit that had gone down recently, I was feeling pretty good today.

"I'm glad to see you in such a happy mood this morning, Lucie. I know it's been a tough couple of weeks." Alex followed me into the practice room. "Have you gotten a chance to work with your wish granting?" I shook my head, but before he could continue, I remembered I still had a wish bond.

"Hudson made a wish during power testing, but we haven't gotten a chance to fulfill it."

"What was the wish?" Alex unbuttoned his suit jacket and took it off. He had added a hook to the wall next to the door so he could hang it up during our sessions, and it had become a start-of-session ritual.

"A date," I mumbled, fiddling with my ear and trying to cover my reddening face.

"Ah." Alex nodded once with a disapproving expression on his face. My eyebrows furrowed slightly at his response, but I couldn't focus on it because he continued, "When did he first make the wish?"

"First power testing session," I admitted, my cheeks growing redder.

"So, not necessarily long enough for any negative effects," he murmured with an absent nod before his head tilted. "One thing to note though, Lucie, is that if you're under an extreme amount of stress whether physical, psychological, or emotional that could affect the wish bond."

"Like with Noah?" I barely muttered his name, my mood quickly plummeting at the turn of discussion.

"Unfortunately," he agreed. "If it continues, it'll more than likely accelerate the wish wear side effects." I sighed defeatedly, my shoulders curling inward at the thought of more nightmares. It wasn't that I was opposed to a date with Hudson. I mean, I had liked him for a while, but I would rather do it when it felt natural instead of forcing it. "I wouldn't worry about that right now though, Lucie. We'll handle that if it comes to it, okay?" I tried to give him an encouraging smile to reassure him that I wasn't going to focus on it, but the tightening of his eyes made me think I hadn't quite managed. "Today, I would like to test some of the boundaries of your wish granting. Nothing big, I don't want to put you at any more risk, I just want to see what exactly some of the boundaries are."

I nodded, took off my wish token necklace, and dropped it onto his open palm. We spent the next hour seeing what would happen with different wishes. We conjured a five-dollar bill, a bottle of water, gave him the ability to hold fire for thirty seconds, and conjured a pair of glasses that were gold and so hideous I laughed until I cried. Alex was dressed in his typical sleek suit pants, button up, and black tie, and when he had a pair of gaudy gold eyeglasses, I couldn't hold it in. Unfortunately, my giggles became contagious, and then neither one of us could focus, so Alex called an end to our session after that.

Grabbing my bag on my way out, I headed out of his office and walked down the stairs. I was going to say goodbye to Jonathon, but he was helping a student. His back was to me and he was hunched over his phone while looking something up on the computer. I waved to Jonathon on my way out to avoid disturbing him. After receiving a wave back, I pushed the door open to the quad and dug out my phone to call my twins.

"Lemon Drop!" Landon shouted in the background before Logan had a chance to say hello. My breath puffed out in front of me as I laughed.

"Hey, guys." I smiled as I walked.

"All done, Love?" I hummed a quick affirmative to Logan's question. "That was quick, does that mean you're heading over early?"

"I need to stop by Dante's and Hudson's to drop off their portion of the cookies my mom sent first, but then I will." I curved down the path toward the guys' dorm room.

"Don't be a fool, wrap his tool! Practice safe sex! Don't do anything I wouldn't do, oh wait..." Landon shouted in the background causing me to burst out laughing. Several people around the quad turned to look at me, and I could feel my face turning pink as I quieted my laughter.

"That isn't going to happen," I scolded.

"You never know," Logan said in a sing-song voice. "Love, you know you can, right? We talked about everything with the rest of the group, and nothing like that shit show will happen again." I was still hesitant, but I felt the tightness ease in my chest hearing that they would be all right with it. *We're all adults*, I reminded myself, *we can do what we want.*

"I don't know how you could be okay with that." I lowered my voice, trying to keep my conversation quiet as I typed in the access code to their building.

"Because we're family and we all want you. I don't get upset when you're with Landon, why would I be upset you're with any of my other brothers?" I paused at that. *That actually makes a lot of sense.* I huffed and continued up the stairs.

"I still doubt anything will come from it. I'm almost to his room, so I'll text you guys when I'm headed down, okay? See you soon, brats." I chuckled into the phone when I heard Landon still shouting ridiculous sex sayings like 'no glove, no love,' 'don't be silly, wrap his willy,' and 'wrap the rod then please her bod.'

"All right, Lucie, see you soon." Logan's husky voice filtered through the phone before the call ended with a soft click. I knocked when I got to Dante's door, pushing it open to head inside.

"Hey, boys!" I hollered out as I shut the door. My breath left my lungs when I turned around. Dante was standing in his doorway in only a pair of black sweatpants as he towel-dried his hair. The sweats hung low on his hips showing the cut of his hip bones, chiseled six pack, and broad shoulders. The muscles in his arms bulged as he rubbed his short-cropped black-brown hair. His dark tan skin glistened with water from his shower. I couldn't help but stare as a drop of water traveled down his chest and abs. *Fuck.* I swallowed hard. Realizing I was staring at his body, I shot my gaze to his and found a smirk curling his kissable lips. *No, Lucie, bad.* I tried to stop thinking about him washing up in the shower as I turned to drop my bag on the armchair next to the door.

"Hey, Firecracker," Dante greeted, his voice thick with desire as he dropped his hand and towel from the back of his head. "Are those the delicious cookies I've heard so much about?" His head tilted toward the tin I had pulled out before coming in.

"Uh huh." My voice squeaked, as I was still struggling to form coherent thoughts with his bare caramel chest on display. "Do you want one?" I held out the tin for him. *Distraction, I need a distraction.*

"I do," he hummed, laying the towel over the back of the loveseat before striding over to me, his black sweats inching lower with each step. I started to loosen the tin lid after finally prying my eyes away from his shifting muscles, but his warm, calloused hands covered mine. "But"—he took the tin from me and laid it on my bag—"I want something else first." I was staring straight at his chest, my breath quickening as I felt a throb between my legs. His right hand came up and gently lifted my chin, his thumb brushing up to my lip and across my unbruised cheek. His cologne and musk scent filled my nose as he stepped closer, his broad chest brushing the front of my sweater.

"What about..." I hesitated briefly as his thumb continued to trace the planes of my face. My eyes fell back to his neck and chest, unable to look him in the eye as I admitted my worry. "What about the others... I mean, are you sure?" I couldn't stop myself from whispering the question, afraid that the reality of what I was bringing up would ruin the bubble of need around us.

"Lucie, I'm sure," he promised. His tone was low but determined as he reassured me. "The guys and I are more than all right with this as long as you are. I wouldn't ever pressure you into something you weren't comfortable with."

"I promise I'm okay with it," I murmured warmly, feeling the hint of a flush creep onto my neck as he nudged my face up lightly to look at him once more.

When I finally met his eyes, they were tracing my face as if Dante was memorizing every little detail before stopping at my lips. My left hand was on top of the armchair, steadying me as my head spun with desire. I lifted my right, lightly placing it on his hip, half on the soft fabric of his sweats and half on his warm skin. Need poured through me when he closed the distance between us, pressing his lips to mine.

He tasted like coffee, and his kiss was gentle at first but grew deeper when I leaned into him, smashing my breasts firmly against his chest despite the tiny throb of pain from my bruises. The heat from him seeped into my wrapping and bra, my nipples pebbling against the fabric. His tongue slid against the seam of my lips, and when I opened, he swept in tasting every piece of me. My breath caught at the amount of time he spent gently caressing me. His fingers lightly ran over my skin, sending goose-bumps trailing after his touch and shivers radiating through me. His other hand went to my waist, pulling me against his hard cock. I gripped his hip, digging my nails into his ass.

Dante's tongue was soft against mine as he deepened the kiss, his fingers running along my jaw to the back of my neck before burying into my hair. Turning my head to angle it away from him, he placed light kisses down my throat until he reached the top of my sweater. I pulled it up over my head to leave behind just my cami. He grabbed my hips as he started walking backward, kissing and nipping at the dip where my neck met my shoulder. I wrapped my arms around his shoulders and brushed my fingers over his muscled back, his body shivering under my touch. When we stepped into his room, his warm hands slid up under my cami, smoothing over my stomach until he lightly brushed over my wrap and breasts.

"I don't want to hurt you," he murmured against the skin under my ear followed by a small nibble to my earlobe. I moaned and dug my fingers deeper into his back.

"You won't, Dante, it's only wrapped to keep any irritation away." I ran my fingers under the waistband of his sweats, the dark trail of hair tickling my fingers. His hands wrapped around my back and pulled me tight against him once again. He kissed me deeply before pulling away to look down at me.

"Only if you're sure."

I smiled up at him, no longer feeling any pain in my cheek when I did.

"I promise I'll tell you if it hurts." I leaned in and kissed his stubbled jaw before pulling my arms up so he could remove my cami gently. My teeth nipped his pec as he unbuckled my belt and jeans. Making my way down his chest slowly, I slipped my hand under his sweats. *Holy fuck, how is that going to fit?* I thought as I rubbed his hard cock, circling my fingers around his length. My kisses continued to trail down his body as I fell to my knees and pulled his sweats and boxers to mid-thigh. I licked the bottom of his shaft from the base to the tip and watched his eyes fall closed, reveling in the soft moan that left his lips. His hand tangled in my hair, but not in a painfully tight grip.

Empowered by the pleasure blatant on his face, I circled his head with my tongue as I curled my fingers around the shaft. My lips slid firmly around him, and I took him into my mouth as far as I could. I pulled back and sucked him in again as he groaned, his head falling back. After a few more passes he shifted his hips away from me and pulled me to standing. He slanted his lips against mine as he softly laid me on the bed. *I didn't expect someone so dominant to be so gentle.* His kisses skimmed down my neck, skipping over my wrapping to my stomach. His warm fingers brushed my thighs and calves as he pulled off my jeans and panties.

He positioned himself in between my legs, my thighs resting on his broad shoulders. I was already soaked but seeing him between my legs caused another pulse of heat to shoot straight through me. He placed several kisses and a few nibbles on my inner thighs as he worked his way in. When he reached my core, he kissed my clit, lightly sucking in. My muscles contracted as the stubble rubbed against me, a rough contrast to his wet tongue that dipped and circled. I couldn't keep watching, my eyes automatically closing as my moans became more frantic. My back arched as my orgasm built.

"Dante," I gasped as waves of desire pulsed through me, my body shaking slightly at the tremors wracking my body. When I finally came down from that high, Dante took my right leg and turned me so I lay on my side facing toward the other half of his room. He nestled himself behind me, kissing my shoulder. Running his fingers in between my thighs until he reached my slick center, he pushed one finger in. My thighs parted, allowing him better access as he added another finger. Before he coaxed another orgasm from my ignited body and tingling nerves, he stopped. Burying my face in the pillow, I tried to muffle my groan of frustration. The tearing of a condom wrapper sounded behind me.

"Patience, Firecracker. I wouldn't leave you hanging like that," he whispered in my ear, the sound sending an eager shiver through me. Lifting my thigh to place my calf over his leg, he shifted his hips forward, bringing his cock from being pressed against my ass straight to my entrance. His right hand held onto my inner thigh, while his other arm was propped on the bed to support the weight of his upper body. He entered me slowly, pushing in and out until he was completely inside me. My head fell to rest on his arm, my body wracked with a panting need once he was in fully. *He's fucking big.* He shifted his hips out before pushing forward. Each pump of his hips was slow and languid, rocking at his own leisurely pace.

His hand in my hair tightened just slightly angling my head back up toward the ceiling. I couldn't tell what fell from my lips as he continued his rhythm, my thoughts lost to the bright flame building inside me at lightning speed.

The hand on my thigh shifted to my hip, fingers digging in while he increased his pressure and speed. My orgasm ripped a strangled moan from me, my hand strangling the sheets, the roughness of his stubble running lightly across my shoulder. He groaned my name as he pumped hard a few more times before reaching his own climax, shudders shaking his body. I went limp on the bed, warmth and the feeling of being cared for filling my chest as I focused on slowing my frantic breaths. Dante leaned forward and placed a long kiss on my neck, his leg nestled between me; I could feel him growing soft before he pulled out.

"Want that cookie now?" I joked, trying to quell the building emotions that quivered in my chest as I rolled back to look up at him. His laugh melted me from the inside out, and a sense of connection and closeness bloomed with the already pounding heat of our round of sex. I popped up to my elbow and gave him a kiss, my hand cupping his strong jaw.

"Hell yeah, I want that cookie now. Need my energy for the game tonight and someone used it all up," he teased. His lips curled into a small smile, and he pressed a soft kiss on my injured cheek before shifting to get up. He held out his hands to help me stand before bending down to hold open my panties. I was more than sure that I didn't hide the surprise on my face as the skin around his eyes crinkled even more when his smile widened. His shoulder was hot under my fingers while I steadied myself before stepping into the lace. Jeans followed quickly, his hands stopping when they reached my hips.

"Thanks." I smiled at him, pulling on and buttoning my jeans and belt. I tossed on my cami and sweater, the room's cool temperature chilling me quickly.

"Of course, if I take it off of you, you better believe I'll help you get it back on." Dante held me against his chest, arms wrapped around my hips. I ran my hands up his muscled arms and chest to rest on his shoulders. "Unfortunately, I need to go get checks done for our uniforms down in the locker room and get prepped for the game. You're coming, right?" I narrowed my eyes at him.

"That's a dumb question, Dante, you know very well I want to be there to support my guys." I stood on my tiptoes and kissed him. Pulling away, I grabbed my coat and bag off the chair, making sure to leave the cookie tin. "I'll see you after the game?" He chuckled and nodded, holding the door open for me. When I slid by him, he pulled me to a stop and kissed me once more before pulling back. A triumphant smile brightened his face before I found myself staring at the wooden door of his dorm room. I felt my cheeks redden when I realized there were several people in the hallway staring with raised eyebrows. I tucked my head down and texted the twins, heading down one flight of stairs to their dorm.

4

November 2nd
Friday Midday
Landon

"Hey, guys," Lucie called out from the shared living room. I came barreling into the room and slid to a stop in front of her.

"Lemon Drop"—I smirked at her, quirking an eyebrow—"you were gone for an awfully long time to be dropping off cookies." Her eyes widened slightly, a flush immediately rising up her neck and face. She opened and closed her mouth a few times without actually saying anything.

"Dante finally got some, huh?" Logan's face mimicked mine as he teased our girl. Her face turned even more red as she started to fiddle with her hair.

"Told you," I sang to her. I laughed at her expression which fell from embarrassment to a slight glare. "What, Lemon Drop? I did, did I not?" I turned to ask Logan who hummed his agreement. My teasing banter melted into a wave of seriousness as I continued. "Don't worry, Lucie. As we said, everything is fine. Please don't be embarrassed." I pulled her into a hug; her normal vanilla scent still held hints of sex and Dante's cologne and musk. My cock harden in my jeans as I buried my nose in her hair, and my heart rate sky-rocketed thinking of her spread out in front of me.

"Yeah, yeah, yeah, you two were right, blah, blah, blah," she mumbled against my Henley, but I felt the smile on her beautiful face.

"Damn straight, Lemon Drop, don't you forget that we're always right." I ran my hand down her hair, holding her to me. She burst out laughing, her thin shoulders shaking against my arms.

"Yeah, I don't think so, Landon, nice try." She pulled away to smile at me, her adorable dimples appearing on her cheeks. "Let's watch our movie until you have to go to the field for game prep." She jumped onto the loveseat and patted the seats next to her for us. *I could get used to this*, I thought to myself as I sat down, her weight settling against my chest.

November 2nd
Friday Evening
Lucienne

"So hungry," Sadie whined pitifully, her hands rubbing her stomach as we waited for the hostess. I rolled my eyes at her dramatics but couldn't stop the laugh that bubbled out of me.

"We literally just had ice cream," I reminded her, "because *someone* wanted dessert first." I looked pointedly at her. She waved me off with a smile, and the hostess leading us to a booth cut off her retort. We ordered as soon as the waiter stepped up since we always ordered the same when we came to the Indian restaurant on Main Street.

"So," my roommate started, her head tilted as she attempted to get her lemonade straw in her mouth without the use of her hands. *One of these days she'll realize they aren't just for painting.* "How's life in Lucie land?" My skin started to flush as my mind immediately thought of Dante and our earlier rendezvous.

"Uh..." *Smooth response, Lucie, very smooth.*

"I feel that there is something you haven't been sharing," she teased, leaning forward on her elbows so she could prop her chin in her hands. Her white with burgundy polka dotted nails were quite the contrast to her usual neon color or glitter. I hesitated a moment too long, and her eyes narrowed in suspicion. "You had sex."

"Shh," I shushed her, shooting forward so she didn't have to practically shout it to a room full of strangers. "Yes, okay?" I huffed in a whisper. "When I went to drop cookies off at Dante's... we kind of..." I trailed off in a mumble.

"Did the hanky panky? Horizontal tango? Bumped uglies?"

"Oh god, please, for the love of my sanity, stop." I laughed, covering my bright red ears and cheeks. "Yes, we had sex," I muttered in embarrassment. Not by the fact I had sex with Dante, because it was amazing, but because we were talking about it in the middle of a crowded restaurant.

"Did he treat my girl right?" she demanded, picking up a fork. "Cause if not, I'll gladly tell him to do better at the forking." I groaned at her phrasing and the dramatic way she stabbed the air a few times with the metal utensil. I was saved from having to respond by the waiter bringing us our food, the scent of spices surrounding me in a bubble of deliciousness. We dug in, focusing on our meals before continuing any kind of conversation.

"How's life in Sadie's world?" I asked with a groan when I was too full to even look at my plate. Pushing it away, I slumped back in the vinyl of the booth.

"Not bad, prepping a collection for a Yule exhibit at the college my dads work at. Other than that, haven't done too much. Except..." Her eyes sparkled as she leaned forward again, having moved her plate off to the side a few minutes earlier. "Harlem and I have been talking, and by talking I mean flirting, and by flirting I mean sexting." She waggled her eyebrows suggestively which made me laugh.

"That's the piercer, right?" She huffed and gave me a half glare for not remembering. I threw my hands up. "Just checking, I'm awful with names, remember?"

"Too true," she agreed with a laugh. "But we have a date coming up which I'm super excited for." I smiled optimistically. Sadie had spent a lot of time working hard on her art and studying, and she deserved a night of fun.

"Good, but if you're coming back to the dorm to have fun, tell me so I can stay somewhere else," I chastised playfully. She rolled her eyes, two pink stains blossoming on her cheeks.

"Trust me, if we're doing anything, we'll be going to her house. She has quite the toy collection, if you get what I mean." Her brows went up and down a few times. I face palmed and groaned at the exaggerated movement. *She's so dramatic.*

"Yes, I know what you mean, but girl, as much as I love you, I do not need to know that kind of stuff." I shook my head at her as she waved me off again, intent on ignoring my advice about the situation. "But I'm happy for you. What are you guys doing on your date?"

At the question, Sadie lit up and immediately started rambling about all the things they had talked about wanting to do. While she went off on about ten different tangents, I paid the bill, and we headed out down the sidewalk toward the stadium. My cheeks hurt from how much smiling I was doing, happy to have had a girls' dinner with Sadie before the game.

Now to support my guys.

————

The cheers filled the stadium as the game slowly came to an end. We were leading 6 to 4 with only five minutes left in the last quarter. I was standing between Sadie and Nik with Cam on the other side of Nik. Benji, Austin, Elijah, Gabe, and Hudson were on the bench behind us, Hudson directly behind me with his hands massaging my tense shoulders. A timeout was called, so I pulled my phone out of my pocket to check it. I didn't have any texts. *Not surprising since all my friends are right here and Char is working.* But I did have two emails waiting in my inbox.

Unknown: Lucie baby, you know you can't run from me.
Unknown: Your new coat looks sexy as hell on you, babygirl.

My heart seized. Reaching out with a shaking hand, I got Nik and Grigori's attention. Nik's glassy eyes looked toward me in a questioning expression, but his smile slid away when Grigori saw the look of terror I knew was blatant on my face. I shoved the phone in his hand and took an unsteady breath.

"You okay, Princess?" Hudson's baritone was close to my ear, helping me fight off an impending panic attack.

"It's him." My voice was shaking, catching Sadie's attention even though I had tried to be quiet.

"Like *him* him?" Sadie bit out, her voice hard. She was slipping into her angry chihuahua mode, but with the fear icing my veins, I couldn't find the humor in her mood shift. I nodded silently, unable to answer in any other way. The timeout ended, and cheers signaled the resuming game. Despite the atmosphere of excitement and happiness surrounding me, I found myself untouched by anything other than the numbness that was spreading from my chest to my arms and legs. Even though my heart raced and my breathing shortened, I knew my panic attack wasn't as bad as it could have been. When the worst of my attacks hit, my vision would completely dim and the sounds around me would fade away as if muffled by something.

"Let's go, Princess," Hudson suggested, keeping his words calm as he nudged me.

"No," I commanded firmly, that fire within me growing at the thought of running away.

"No?" From next to Nik, Cam's disbelieving voice reminded me that he was here for me too.

The numbness was pulling back, and the fire and determination that rose in its wake pushed me to answer them. "Yeah, no. He stole four years of my life, took everything from me. My life, my friends, my independence, *everything* that I was. I saved myself, and I will not let him take over my life again," I explained sharply. My hands curled into tight fists. The thought sliced through me like a knife—*he's here on campus.* I checked the emails again. One was from earlier in the day, and one was right after the game had started. *That bastard!* I whipped my head around the crowd. It was a sea of nameless students, no familiar faces other than those from a few classes. "He was here," I hissed as I continued to scour the crowd.

When I couldn't find him, I turned back to the game, refusing to let him steal my guys' victory from me. It was less than ten seconds until the buzzer and Dante had gotten the flag, earning our team the final score of seven to four. I clapped, but my mind was racing. I could see my guys and Sadie all closing ranks around me, eyeing the crowd discreetly. Before the students could filter out of the seats, we filed out of our row and up the stairs to make our way toward where the team comes out of the locker room.

I knew I should be worried about sticking around in the dark knowing he was here, but I felt safe with my guys. Sadie, Benji, Gabe, and Elijah all stayed with us as we went to our usual spot to wait for Dante and the twins. I was curled against Nik's solid chest with his arms wrapped around my torso keeping me warm, and Grigori was propped on my right shoulder, rubbing his feathery head on my temple.

Ever since the party, Elijah had kept his arrogant playboy attitude to himself, and I was finding out he was more like Gabe: quiet, polite, and friendly. I was having a nice conversation about several upcoming movies that we were excited about when the team started to come out of the locker room entrance. Nik dropped his arms with a gravelly laugh at my excitement, knowing what was going to happen next. My tradition of jumping into the twins' arms before being spun around continued. When Dante came out, he curled me in his arms and kissed me hard. My guys, the rest of the team, as well as all my friends gave loud whoops and hollers at the kiss. When it ended, my face was bright red, and I chuckled at the triumph on Dante's.

"I've wanted to do that since our first game, Firecracker." His deep voice was quiet, and his bright white teeth nearly glowed in the dark as he smiled down at me. I smiled back at him and started back toward our guys, our hands intertwined.

"Cover your stump before you hump," Landon sang under his breath when I walked by him. I laughed, punching him in the arm with my free hand.

"Shut it, brat, I already told you you were right, stop rubbing it in," I chastised.

"Holy shit, is it the end of the world? Landon Anson was told he was right about something?" Hudson's voice was filled with fake disbelief, his hand pressing against Nik's chest next to him. "And pray tell, what was he right about?" He raised an eyebrow at me. I opened my mouth, but nothing came out. *How do I explain that?* I was glad that only my guys were listening to this conversation, Sadie and Benji still deep in conversation with Gabe and Elijah about movies a few feet away.

"That she and Dante would sleep together today." Logan sounded proud of their prediction, both of their chests puffed up and their hands migrated to their hips giving them the look of mighty importance.

"Oh, really?" Nik's eyebrow raised, matching Hudson's expression, and Cam was looking over at my and Dante's joined hands with a smirk.

"Is that a problem?" I challenged with my own eyebrow raise as I looked at each of my guys so they knew I was serious. A round of nopes and nos went up, satisfying my worry that there would be jealousy.

"Come on," Dante directed with a head tilt, "let's go back to the room and get into game night. It's cold out here."

———

An hour later we were gathered around the coffee table playing a round of Life. I couldn't help but laugh as Dante got hit with yet another space telling to pay up. Based on the way the game had been going, Hudson and Logan were in the lead with the most money, with Cam right behind. Dante and Nik were near the bottom while Landon and I were in the middle of the pack.

"This is totally rigged," Dante playfully groaned as he tossed a couple of the brightly colored bills toward Landon, our banker for the evening. "One of you cursed me, I just know it."

"The only one who can curse you is Nik and you know he wouldn't do that," Hudson challenged through his bouts of laughing. Dante flipped Hudson off with a smile but didn't comment to give me a chance to go. Taking my turn, I felt light and happy at being surrounded by the normalcy of our usual game night even after that scare at the game. I moved my pieces, which had somehow grown from one car to two because I had three sets of twins in the family section of the board game, and crossed into the retirement section, meaning I was officially done.

Counting my fake money and my Life Tiles, I tallied my total while the guys all finished their trek through the game. Somehow, Dante wasn't in last after we all announced our winnings.

"I lost?" I huffed. "How did I lose? I wasn't even near the bottom!" I exclaimed, but Logan's quiet effort to avoid eye contact caught my attention. I held my hand out. "Cough them up," I commanded playfully.

"I didn't do anything!" He tried to claim innocence, but I knew that little light in his blackened coal eyes. I held strong and continued to stare until finally he grumbled under his breath and dropped ten more Life Tiles into my waiting palm.

"Damn cheater." I laughed, bumping into his shoulder as I added the stolen amount into my total. With the increased amount, it put Landon in last place.

"Sorry, dude, I tried," Logan told Landon from the other side of the table. I balked and glanced between them as the room laughed at the scene playing out.

"You two are so mean to me," I whined, playing up the situation by pouting out my bottom lip. They both pressed their hands into their chests in time with one another.

"You slay us, Love," Logan added at the same time Landon complained about my pout being cruel and unusual punishment.

"Not my fault you cheated!" I tossed one of the little cardboard tiles at each of them but turned my attention toward the rest of the group as they cleaned up the board game. "We done already?" I asked, my brows pinching in confusion. We typically played games until really early in the morning, and it was only nearing midnight.

"No," Cam answered, "we're going to play something else."

I perked up. "Battleship?" It was more than overdue for me to crush Hudson and Nik since the last time their team had completely destroyed me. Hudson and Nik both chuckled, knowing where my thoughts had gone to when I gave them narrowed eyes.

"Nope, we're going to play Truth or Dare," Dante explained as he took the box from Cam's extended arm to put away in his closet. Half of Dante's closet was used for its designated purpose while the other half was piled with a huge amount of boardgames, cards, and other activities the guys and I liked to do at least once every other week, if not more. My interest was piqued at the thought of playing Truth or Dare. *This could go either way, fun and playful or really, really bad*, I thought, knowing how the twins loved to prank people.

"Logan, truth or dare," Dante asked as soon as he sat back down. Logan hummed for a brief second before answering.

"Dare!" he practically shouted in excitement. *Why does it not surprise me that he loves this game?* I chuckled to myself.

"Sing the chorus of 'Barbie Girl' in the most girly voice you can," Dante dared with a big smile, pulling out his phone and holding it up as Logan stood. Clearing his throat, Logan began fluttering his eyelashes and doing some weird hip shaking as he obnoxiously sang the Aqua song. I could barely keep my giggling under control as he attempted to shimmy his shoulders and ended up shaking his whole body instead, making it look as though he was about to have a seizure. At the end, he gave a low bow to the rounds of laughter and claps that echoed through the group.

"Lucie, truth or dare." He nudged me in the shoulder urging me to answer faster when I hesitated.

"Dare?" I questioned, unsure as I gave him a skeptical stare. *He better not make me do something crazy like drink out of the toilet or something.*

"Give Landon a makeover!"

Landon balked at being thrown under the bus, but I was relieved that was all I had to do. Grabbing my overnight bag, I dug out my small makeup bag and got to work. At first, I tried to make him look somewhat normal, but by the end he had eyeliner smeared in a fashion reminiscent of a racoon and fire engine red lipstick in a Joker-esque smile.

"Smile!" Hudson cheered as his phone suddenly

appeared in our peripheral vision. Landon tossed an arm over my shoulder and pulled me close as we smiled up at the camera.

"Cam!" I pointed through my laughter. "Truth or dare."

"Dare," he challenged with a predatorial glint in his eyes. Smirking, Cam leaned forward until his arms rested on his knees and his intense hazel eyes centered on my face practically daring me to give him the best I could. I matched his smug smile when the perfect action popped into my head.

"Demonstrate the sexiest place you love to kiss on someone other than me...*or* Nik." A round of 'oos' went up at my dare. Cam tilted his head in agreement before scanning the room. The level of sexual tension grew as he leisurely took everyone in. Shifting, he strode confidently over to where Dante and Nik were seated. I almost rolled my eyes at the fact that he picked Nik despite the one rule, until I realized he had crouched in front of Dante. *Actually, straddled might be more accurate since he was practically in his lap.*

"There are two places I love," he murmured, his normally low tone heated and smooth and confident as he kept his eyes on Dante's green gaze. I felt my breath hitch as Cam leaned forward, gripping the back of Dante's neck and head as he fused his lips to Dante's pulsing carotid artery. Everyone was silent, staring with quickly heating gazes as Dante started to heave heavy breaths, his lids falling when Cam's jaw shifted slightly, dragging his lips down Dante's neck as he pulled away. Cam shifted back to look at Dante, whose breaths had turned to shallow pants.

"The other place is, well," he shrugged nonchalantly as he put his weight on his knees. As he shifted, I noticed the hard bulge Dante was sporting and felt another rush of heat pulse through me. Pushing the hem of his basketball shorts up, Cam bent over to kiss his inner thigh before nipping lightly. *Holy shit*, I breathed as I squeezed my thighs together. *I haven't ever seen two men together, but if this was what it was like... hot damn.*

"Holy..." the twins muttered under their breaths, their eyes locked on the display. At their words, I glanced around and noted that every single one of us was entranced by the display. *Have they... have they done this kind of thing together before?* I wondered silently as Cam finally moved back, his hand slowly resituating Dante's shorts to cover his leg back up. Before anyone could say anything, Cam darted forward and gave him a quick peck on the lips, patting his cheek lightly before moving back to his seat.

"Lucie," he continued on with the game despite that that entire interaction had left everyone completely silent and half-gaping. "Truth or dare, Doll." He flashed me a cocky smile, soaking up the attention. Shaking my head slightly to try and clear the naughty direction my thoughts had taken, I answered.

"Truth," I practically squeaked, still drowning in the sexual tension in the room.

"How do you feel about us?" he questioned. His question threw me for a loop as I glanced around the room. All the guys were looking at me with curious glances, including Dante, even though he was shifting slightly in his spot.

"I like you guys?" My statement went up at the end like a question in my confusion.

"Close your eyes," Cam commanded softly. Narrowing my eyes, I tried to figure out if he was about to prank me, but I reminded myself that this was Cam and not the twins. Finally, after a couple seconds in suspicion, I did. I heard some shuffling, and despite the urge to open my eyes, I wanted to show I trusted them.

"You can open your eyes now," Nik's rough voice caught me by surprise, but I obliged him regardless that I was so lost as to what was going on right now. The twins held a large piece of poster paper with different boxes of candy taped to it. As I read through it I realized the boxes of candy were strategically placed so their names completed the sentences the guys had written. A few were scribbled on to help them make sense, but the words made my heart flutter.

Just be-TWIX us, we realize we're BIG HUNKS and all, but there are so many RIESENS we still don't know how we SKORed with an ALMOND JOY like you. And everything about you is RED HOT! Every day with you feels like a PAYDAY, full of SNICKERS when we see you, SWEETART. If you'll let us, we promise to always ROLO with the punches and TAKE-5 to spoil you. U-NO we care about you to REESES PIECES, and we want you always, NOW AND LATER. You're worth 100 GRAND in our eyes, and we're STARBURSTing to know, will you be our girlfriend?

When I finished, I glanced over at them wondering if I was really seeing what I was reading at the bottom.

Will you be our girlfriend?

"Princess," Hudson took over before anyone could say anything. "We all care about you. We all want you, and we know you have asked about multiple partners in the past." I gave Cam and Nik the side eye, both looking unperturbed at being outed about sharing our private conversation. I hummed in response, waiting for him to continue. "So, we were hoping you would like to be our girlfriend?" Hudson finished, his hands wringing in front of him with a look of worry on his face.

"Like, all of you?" I gestured around the circle for clarification. They all nodded. My heart soared. *My guys.* I squealed, "Yes, yes, yes!" I bounced up and down in my spot, too happy to care if I looked ridiculous. They burst out laughing and converged on me in one big group, my heart warming at the thought of being part of their misfit family.

"We have the prettiest girlfriend of all," Landon sweet talked as they pulled back. My face flamed under six gazes focused on me, but I couldn't stop the bright smile that took over my face.

"So, let me guess," I started as everyone settled back into their spots, "the twins came up with the idea?" No one answered right away as they all laughed. My eyes widened when everyone pointed to Hudson. "You came up with it?" I was shocked, completely and utterly dumbstruck.

Hudson.

My sexy fae.

"Yeah, I just," he stuttered with a shrug, two patches of pink blooming on his cheeks as his hands wrung together in front of him, "wanted to do something sweet for you. I know you like kind of cute and corny types of things and love candy, so..." He trailed off in another shrug, his pink blush having darkened to a deep red that started to creep down his neck and up to the tips of his ears. I got up and sank into his lap, overwhelmed with fuzzy tingles of excitement.

"It's perfect, Hudson," I reassured him, pressing a quick kiss to his cheek. "Thank you guys. I couldn't have asked for a better way to be asked out." They beamed before we fell back into our usual fun and games. I spent the rest of the night soaring on cloud nine with my *six* boyfriends.

5

I sat at my normal table for studying, my book and notebook spread out in front of me, several colored pens and highlighters scattered around the table. My gaze skimmed over the materials strewn before me, and I realized I needed to grab two books from the shelves for my assignment for Supe History. I snagged my phone and wallet and stuffed them in my sweatshirt and jean pockets before heading toward the History section. Having worked at the library for the last five months I was able to find the two books I needed quickly.

Sending a quick text to the group thread with the guys, I let them know where I would be sitting. If I remembered correctly, they were going to be heading to the library shortly. Nik and Cam had just returned to campus from Nik's competition today meaning they'd be joining the study group. I got excited at the thought of Nik's archery since I planned on going to his next local competition in a few weekends. I had been wanting to go to one, but he had to travel on a jet for the last few, so I stayed on campus.

Curving back towards my table, I made sure to step around students' backpacks through the study area of the library. I plopped down at my seat and set my books on the wooden tabletop. I attempted to ease the slight throb in my bruising the books that had been pressing against by rubbing my sternum lightly, but it was no use. *Note to self, don't hug books to your chest when you're injured.* I had just opened the first one to the proper page when someone I didn't recognize came up to my table.

"Excuse me? Are you Lucie?" the small, mousy girl asked. Her voice was very quiet, nearly inaudible, and she avoided looking at me. My brows knit as I stared at her.

"Yes, I am," I admitted hesitantly, a lot of red flags flying right now.

"I was told to give this to you." She held out a folded piece of paper for me to take.

I knew instinctively it was from Noah, but I took it anyway with a trembling hand. I didn't want anyone in the crossfire of his wrath, so maybe I could at least keep this girl safe even if I might not be able to protect myself. I thanked her and placed it on the table. Once she turned away from me, I packed up my bag with every effort not to draw attention to myself. I knew he was here, watching, so I focused on breathing in slow inhales and complete exhales, schooling my face into a bland mask. When I had my bag completely packed up, I took the books I had grabbed and placed them in the return cart, saying bye to Muriel as I passed the front counter. With the note clutched tightly in my hand I dialed the first number I found.

"Hey, Doll. We're heading over to the library now." Cam's voice resonated through the earpiece.

"Change of plans," I sputtered quickly into the phone. "Meet me at Alex's office." My breathing was changing, coming in shorter pants as panic threatened to overtake me. *Stay calm, Lucie,* I commanded myself with little success.

"What happened?" I heard quick shuffling on the other end, and his voice was hard as he responded, a slight growl in his question.

"Just meet me there, please," I pleaded. I had just pushed open the door to the Administration building when Jonathon noticed my panicked expression. Picking up the desk phone, he called Alex.

"Of course, Doll. We're almost there. See you shortly." I voiced a goodbye and hung up. The little grip I had on my anxiety was slipping away the longer time went on, and I was quickly losing control of my breathing. I had run up the last two flights of stairs when it started to become too much and saw Alex fling open his door as I reached the fourth floor. I shot into his office, my vision finally starting to dim while my ears fuzzed over. My messenger bag slid off my shoulder onto the floor just before Alex grabbed my upper arms. *Oh god no.* I ripped away from him with a strangled cry.

His fingers dug into my upper arms, holding me in place despite my attempts to pull away from his harsh glare. I could feel his grip pressing into old, still healing bruises causing me to cry out in pain.

"You do not get to leave me." His voice was cold and rough in my ear as he whispered. "You are mine, Lucienne Marie Envie. You will never be with anyone else but me." When he finished his

tirade, he shoved me into the wall making the hanging pictures of us shake with how hard I collided with the wall.

"I wasn't leaving!" I yelled, hunching into a ball in an attempt to make myself a smaller target. My arms automatically came up to protect my face, leaving my ribs open. He seized the opening, and with a swift punch to the ribs and a sharp kick to my leg, I crumpled to the ground. After that, it was a haze of a boot stomping toward my curled form, smashing into my torso, leg, and arms over and over...

Camden

"How was the competition? Did you win?" Landon peppered Nik with questions as I double checked I had everything I needed for studying.

"It was the same people; Liam was being his normal asshole self." Grigori squawked at the mention of their main competitor who always gave Nik a hard time. "And yes, I won. Now I need to make it through the quarter and semi-finals. Championship competition is set for the first." Everyone congratulated him with pats on the back or high fives as we filed out of our room and into the hallway. Our group took up a large portion of the carpeted area slowing the traffic of students through the dorm on our way out to the quad. Logan and Landon were in an intense discussion with Dante and Hudson about something, but I was too busy mentally running through my list of things I needed to get done today and attempting not to think of Lucie. *You have to focus,* I told myself, a clear reminder that I had an additional research project for several professors for a display they were working on for after the holiday break.

"You all right?" Hudson's question pulled me out of my mental tallying, his lavender eyes concerned. I ran a hand through my hair haphazardly, a tired sigh working its way through my body.

"Yeah, I'm good. Just have a project for the school involving this rare artifact display they're doing for next semester. Need to collate five specific pieces, their background, lore and myth around it, and any important history. Basically, collect all the important stuff in a file for Professor Hans so he can take it to the dean." My words sounded tired even to me. A soft ding radiated from Hudson's phone, matching a buzz coming from my pocket. He checked it quickly before responding.

"She's at her normal table in the back corner by the windows." Shoving his phone in his pocket he turned his attention back to me. "That sucks, when does it need to be done by?"

"End of semester. The faculty who are working on the project are going to be finalizing the pieces for the display over winter break and will be pulling it out of storage after the new year before the semester starts on the seventh. I'll probably be asked to help with that," I informed them, but my next statement was cut off by a steady buzzing from my pocket. Pulling it out, Lucie's name and a picture from the All Hallow's Eve dance displayed on the screen.

"Hey, Doll, we're heading over to the library now." I smiled involuntarily, but at the tremble in her voice, my smile faded.

"Change of plans. Meet me at Alex's office." I could hear the wind whistling in the background accompanied by her increasing breathing. My heartbeat skyrocketed, thudding painfully in my chest knowing she was alone. I threw my second backpack strap over my shoulder and started to jog toward the Administration building, the rest of the guys picking up on my change in mood and quickly following.

"What happened?" I tried to keep the anger from filtering into my words, knowing that her anxiety would already be causing issues and not wanting to frighten her even more.

"Just meet me there, please." Her statement was full of fear. Hearing the sound of a door in the background let me know she was nearing the dean's office, and the panic that tightened my chest eased ever so slightly.

"Of course, Doll. We're almost there. See you shortly." I hung up after she gave a small goodbye. My jog turned into a sprint as I saw our destination on the crest of the hill.

"What happened?" Dante demanded, years of athletics and shifter genes allowing him to keep pace with me. I couldn't talk, I couldn't focus on anything other than reaching Lucie. The stares of students and staff around the quad didn't faze me as I pushed through the front doors.

"She's in Mr. Renaud's office," the front desk worker, Jonathon, called out knowing exactly why we were there. My steps didn't falter as I shot up the steps, the thundering of the other guys' shoes echoing in the staircase. A high-pitched scream filtered down the last flight of stairs toward us. *Lucie...* I pumped my arms harder, pushing the last of my enhanced agility into my strides. The wood of his door snapped open as soon as my foot hit the fourth floor. Dean Renaud waited on the other side of the threshold with Lucie curled on the ground at his feet.

"I'm not leaving!" she shouted, the words muffled by her arms curling around her head. Her screams cracked with fear as the dean crouched in front of her. Hudson closed the door behind us in a poor attempt to keep what was happening within the room. My jaw hurt from the amount of force I was using to clench it shut.

When I get my hands on that bastard...

Lucienne

"Lucie!" a honeyed voice called through the haze of pain and yelling. I could feel my voice starting to give with the intensity of my screaming. The tears began to subside, my vision clearing to the room in front of me, wanting to find the source of that calm voice. The gazes of my concerned, angry, and worried guys stared back at me. Looking around slowly, I realized I had dropped to the ground and was curled into a ball against one of the bookshelves. The edge of the two bottom shelves dug painfully into my back. I dropped my arms from around my head to my sides as I took shaky breaths. Alex was crouched down in front of me, his open hands stretched tentatively toward me like I was a frightened animal. *Which I guess I am.*

"Lucie?" His voice was hesitant and cracked softly with emotion.

I had frightened them.

"I'm back," I croaked. My rough throat protested even that short answer, stinging with every word. Cam handed me a bottle of water from his backpack which I sipped slowly to not aggravate my throat. "Thanks, Cam," I told him quietly when he took back the plastic bottle. Shifting forward, Alex grabbed my hand to help me stand, steadying me when I wobbled slightly.

"What happened, Babe? I do not think I have ever run so fast as I did when I heard you screaming." Nik's gravelly voice was filled with relief as he angled his face down toward me, and the skin around his eyes was tight with tension as he fiddled with the hem of his shirt. I uncurled my fist and, with shaking hands, opened the note.

Lucie,

You always look so cute when you focus and nibble on your lip. I remember how good those lips taste. Tell your "boyfriends" to back off. Don't forget what I said baby girl, you're mine.

N

I felt my stomach roll as I held it out for someone to take, Alex finally plucking it from my fingers. My free hand came up in front of my mouth, my focus solely on trying not to throw up.

"When did you get this?" Alex's voice was hard as he handed the note to my guys who had all crowded around Hudson to read it.

"I didn't read it until just now. I packed up my stuff and came straight here after some strange girl gave it to me in the library. I was doing really well with keeping my anxiety and panic down until I started climbing the stairs," I admitted, waving a hand toward the door of his office.

"What set off your flashback, Love?" Logan asked quietly, bringing his hand to my back to rub soft circles through my coat.

I looked quickly at Alex before dropping my gaze. "When you put your hands on my upper arms." I didn't want him to think it was his fault, so I forced myself to push out some kind of explanation. "He, uh, did that a lot. I had to wear long sleeves pretty much all the time because of all the bruises," I mumbled.

"I'm sorry, Lucie, I didn't even realize." Despite Alex's caring tone, he looked ready to murder someone. *Probably Noah.*

"It's all right, you all know now. My flashbacks aren't usually that bad." I pointed to the spot where I had curled up against the bookshelf. "I typically just get tunnel vision or blackouts and fuzzy hearing. If it's a particularly bad flashback, I get sucked into it, but I don't usually physically react like that."

"You screamed that you weren't leaving, and then just this long scream until you came out of it," Landon explained, his eyes haunted as he replayed what happened. I nodded and rubbed my hand down my face.

"That was the day that he broke my ribs. The day that I decided to tell my mom and Char about everything. I was here two days later," I murmured.

"Oh, Princess." Hudson wrapped his arms around my shoulders, pulling me into his chest. I threw my arms around his hard stomach. Rubbing my face against the softness of his hoodie, the feeling of safety washed through me. He placed a kiss on the top of my head, his cheek coming to rest on my hair.

"What did he mean by 'boyfriends'?" Alex's voice was suspicious as he eyed me in Hudson's arms. My face flushed. *Talk about embarrassing.*

"Uh, we're dating—I'm dating them," I stuttered.

"Them?" His eyebrows raised, and his voice turned disapproving. *He better not think he gets to dictate who I date.* I turned the rest of the way out of Hudson's arms to face Alex. I crossed my arms in front of my chest.

"Yes, them. These are my boyfriends, Alex," I challenged. "Is that really any of your concern?" His head came up as he looked down at me, thinking. His face turned from disapproving to considerate.

"No, Lucie, I just want to make sure you're all right," he reasoned, which seemed to irk the guys because they all straightened. Alex's attention shifted from me to them, his face stoic as they glared back.

The tension between them made my skin itch, my arms

crossing over my stomach in discomfort. "We would never hurt her," Landon's harsh statement cut through the silent standoff.

"That's not what I was insinuating, Mr. Anson," Alex bit out, his tone stern as he lectured them. "I take the well-being of all my students very seriously and with the current situation, my main concern is Lucie's safety against Noah, not you." He glared at Landon as he finished his statement, but when Alex turned to look at me before continuing, his words were no longer angry or harsh. "Lucie, do you have a photo of Noah or could you describe him enough for someone to identify him?" I pulled out my phone. Once it was unlocked I scrolled through my photos until I reached the ones from high school. Finding one, I felt my chest tighten as I saw his face. He and I were together at one of the high school football games, but before I could be sucked into another memory, I held my phone out for Alex to take.

Hudson

After Dean Renaud had taken the phone from Lucie, he emailed the photo to himself before printing several copies so he would have them to give to security. He also called for a meeting with the Head of Security and Assistant Dean Mastersen in a few minutes down in one of the conference rooms on the second level. As the printer fired up, Dean Renaud asked Lucie more questions about her piece of shit ex-boyfriend.

"What's his full name? Age, birthday, basic descriptors." He looked from the computer to Lucie expectantly, his fingers poised over the keyboard.

"Noah Hunter Montgomery. He's 19 now, his birthday is December 11th, 1998. Six feet tall with dark brown eyes, dark brown almost black hair that's usually all messy. Strong jaw, sharp cheekbones, he's lean, slightly muscled. Not overly tan, but not pale either. Uh, usually wears black jeans, darker colored shirts, and black boots. Drives a silver Ford F150 that has a small lift on it." She was staring off, her head slightly shaking when she reached the end. "I can't really think of anything else that would help identify him." She shrugged tiredly, and her pale skin had a green tint to it.

She was doing better than I had anticipated. *That scream though...* I shuddered. That sound, along with the scream from her attack, unfortunately, was going to haunt my sleep for the rest of my life. I felt my anger simmering, knowing he'd been on campus, and I wanted to find him. Based on the anger prevalent on my brothers' faces, they agreed.

"All right, do you want to be present for the meeting with the head of security?" Dean Renaud asked Lucie, pulling me out of my thoughts. She shook her head.

"No, I just want to go and relax for the rest of the day." She opened her mouth to continue, but a buzzing sounded from her pocket. Her brows scrunched slightly as she dug her phone out of her pocket. "Hello?" she greeted. Pausing, she waited for a response but only silence emanated from the earpiece. "Hello?" she tried again. When she was ready to hang up, a deep voice echoed through the room's waiting silence. She ripped the phone away from her ear and put it on speaker. Her hands shook as she held it out for us. Reaching out, I laced my fingers with her empty hand.

"Babygirl," a man's voice rang out, the voice taunting and cruel. "I know you're listening. I just wanted to introduce myself to those freaks you call boyfriends." A sneer laced his words.

"Noah?" Her voice was surprisingly steady despite

looking as though all her strength had fled with his first spoken word. "How did you find me?"

"Lucie, Lucie, Lucie," he chided, "I told you that you don't get to leave me. Let's just say I will *always* find you, Babygirl. I suppose I should also say hello to the dean of that freakshow you call a university."

"Leave me alone, Noah, we aren't together anymore. Never again will I be yours," she ground out. Lucie's voice rose in volume as she spoke, her anger pressing against my mental barriers. I was struggling to keep my own anger under control, and her addition strained the little grip I still held. The twins had lost most of theirs, fists blazing in their hellfire, black claws dark in the center of the red and white flames. With the smell of bonfire permeating the air, the dean kept one eye on their hands while focusing most of his attention on the phone call.

"You'll always be mine, and you will pay for running away from me." Noah's tone turned from lecturing to hard and clipped with anger. She didn't say anything else, just ended the call and dropped the phone on Dean Renaud's desk. As soon as the phone call was over, the dean picked up his desk phone and hit a button on speed dial.

"I emailed you and the rest of the security team the information and a photo of a man who needs to be secured as soon as possible, high threat level to one of the students. If it escalates, one of your guards will need to be with her at all times," he rushed through, giving an affirmative response before hanging up. "Lucie, you will be with one of them at all times"—he held a hand out towards us—"classes, when you're at the games, library, dorm, doesn't matter. You will have at least one of them with you at all times, understand?" She nodded her head, staying quiet. "If this escalates, the security guards will be added to your security detail. Now, it's been a stressful day so far, and I want you to go relax, all right?" She stood up when he did, the rest of us following.

"Thank you, Alex." She shouldered her bag.

"Anytime, Lucie. Here's my personal office number and cell number, as well as the direct line to the security team on duty. I want you all to have them programmed into your phones, memorized if you can. I have a bad feeling about all of this." He murmured the last part while rubbing a hand through his gelled hair.

"Thank you, I really appreciate it. I never had anyone to help before," she mumbled, looking at the card with the added numbers on it.

"Now you do, Princess, and we will always be there to help you." I pulled her to me, placing a soft kiss on her temple. Her vanilla essence calmed me as she snuggled closer. *Our Lucie.* I still couldn't believe that she wanted to be with us, although I was most surprised that she wanted to be with me after all the shit that had gone down. My heart soared every time I remembered she was our girl. "Come on, let's go get some snacks and continue our new TV show marathon." I nodded at Dean Renaud and shuffled Lucie toward the stairs, her arm wrapping around my waist as she cuddled into me. Dean Renaud said a quick goodbye and closed the door behind us. Now that I knew what this asshole looked like I kept an eye out around the quad as we stepped out into the cold air, but all I saw were a few students I recognized from my freshman and sophomore years on campus.

Come out, come out wherever you are.

6

November 5ᵗʰ
Monday Afternoon
Lucienne

I slid into my desk between Landon and Logan for Supe Society. Feeling Logan's fingers brushing the outside of my thigh under the table caused a small blush to flare up my cheeks. I could see people from around the room eyeballing me. *Ugh.* Professor Rasmussen entered the room, interrupting people's staring.

"Good afternoon, students!" Professor Rasmussen greet cheerily. "How are we all feeling?" She smiled wide at the class, her young face a deep coffee color and her hair a halo of tight curls offsetting her brightly colored dress. A murmur of answers sounded throughout the students. "We left off last week on talking about Otherworldly Creatures. We're going to be finishing that topic before moving into the discussion on the parallel world, Fae. If you have not gotten your schedule set for our trip to Fae on the seventeenth, then I suggest you do so. If you are unable to go, come speak with me and we will discuss other options for earning credit."

She turned to step back toward her desk, grabbing a stack of papers that we had written previously on vampires and different types of mental powers usually associated with them. "I have finally graded these so pass them around. They are in the correct order as to how you normally sit, so please don't take someone else's paper," she chided, handing the stack to the end of every row working her way up the steps. "We also have a special guest coming to speak to you today about the rarest types of Otherworldly Creatures. As some of you probably know Dean Renaud is a Transcendent." *A what?* I tried to scour my memory of my textbooks on what that was but came up blank. "So, I would like to welcome our dean for this portion of the lecture." Alex strode in with confidence and a soft smile as he waved to the students.

"Good afternoon, as most of you know I am Dean Alexandre Renaud, and as Terra has said, I am a Transcendent. Does anyone know what that means?" A few hands shot into the air, and he gestured for a guy I didn't know the name of in the second row to answer.

"A god-like being. The powers usually associated with Transcendents can include ethereal manipulation, healing, immortality, reality separation, resurrection, teleportation, and telekinesis." He shifted his glasses as he finished his list.

"Very good, Mr. Yewlin. As for me, I have reality separation, probability manipulation, teleportation, and healing. I am not a full immortal, but close. I can only be killed through a few means. As I'm sure you understand, I will not be going over those in this class." His comment was met with chuckles throughout the class, but my mind was still too busy trying to catalogue the powers he'd just listed.

Reality separation? Is that like reality warping? I had abandoned taking notes to listen to him speak. "Does anyone know what probability manipulation is?" When no one raised their hands, he continued, "How about reality separation?" Again, no one responded. I was sure several people knew the answer, and despite Alex's warm and friendly demeanor, he was still the dean. Alex started to pace back and forth in front of the seats.

"Probability manipulation is the ability to manipulate luck in its most basic definition. I can increase or decrease the amount of luck. I tend to not use this power because anything I alter has to affect something else, so if I increase good luck for one person then a certain amount of bad luck happens to another, or if I continually cause bad luck for someone, then that negative karma will come back to me. This is similar to the Rule of Three most Magick Users follow. This goes for almost all powers that can manipulate chance—wishes, luck, and so forth. The scales between using the advantage have to balance, and more than likely it's balanced by the person who uses it, resulting in physical fatigue, poor sleep, bad luck, and the like.

"As for reality separation, I am able to create a void known as the Omnilock. It's a separate entity from reality, its time and space are different than reality, essentially making it a parallel dimension." Alex continued to discuss the different types of rare Otherworldly Creatures including Demi-Gods and Goddesses. He ended up taking up almost the entire lecture time, so Professor Rasmussen let us out of class early. Packing up my bag, I headed out of the lecture hall with my twins, my thoughts whipping around Alex and his powers.

Logan

I stood in Lucie and Sadie's living room as my brother and I waited for her to finish changing. The colder weather that had swept in today chilled her to the point of needing more layers. Landon was fiddling on his phone, his tongue barely sticking out of his mouth as he concentrated on his game. Sadie wasn't back yet; her door had been left open, and no streaks of bright colors were fluttering around in her room. Lucie slipped out of her bedroom quietly, her cardigan and shirt changed out for a sweater, thick jacket, and her coat. A light grey scarf wound around her neck and a matching hat was pulled over her head, her blonde hair tumbling around her shoulders. Landon continued to focus on his game, and my hand clasped his elbow to help him steer around students as we followed Lucie out of her building and toward the library. There was a close call with another student who was huddled in his sweatshirt when I barely pulled Landon out of the way of getting run over.

"You know it would be easier to avoid people if you actually looked around you," Lucie teased my brother, her cheeks pink from the wind. Landon's left hand came up, his index finger extended to plead one more minute. I rolled my eyes and turned my attention to Lucie. I nudged her gloved fingers, an unspoken question if she'd be willing to hold my hand. I smiled down at her as she intertwined her fingers with mine.

"How was your day, Love?" I questioned, her shoulder brushing my arm lightly. Landon pumped his fist silently before slipping his phone into his pocket. *Guess his game is done.*

"Not bad. I thought Alex's lecture was really interesting. Other than that, not much has happened, thankfully." She shuddered, and I was unsure if it was because of the wind or the thought of Noah. I gently squeezed her slender fingers when Landon joined the conversation.

"What were you saying, Lemon Drop?"

She chuckled before looking over at him. When he realized she was holding my hand, he slipped around to her right side and tossed his arm over her shoulder.

"That you're amazingly wonderful even though you clearly suck at paying attention to your surroundings." Her face was flat as she answered him, pulling a laugh from me. Landon feigned hurt, his free hand pressing into his chest.

"I don't know whether to be happy or insulted, my little lemon drop." Leaning in quickly, he snuck a light kiss on her cheek. "But I forgive you for the insult part since I'm amazingly wonderful like that." We laughed at his antics, my arm pulling open the door for her. She shed her layers, piling them into her arms after they were off. My brother and I followed suit before walking toward the study area of the library. The rest of the guys were lounging in a cluster of the leather chairs near the front of the space.

"Hey, guys, Princess." Hudson noticed our approach first, popping out of the chair to wrap Lucie in a soft hug. "So, what do you want to show us?" he asked cheerfully. When he pulled back, Lucie answered as she gave the other guys hugs.

"Follow me." Her head tilted toward one of the walkways between the bookshelves. My brow furrowed when we took a turn to the left toward the back corner of the building. A door reading 'Employees Only' shifted under Lucie's push, her pale fingers holding the door open for us as we piled into the little area. I looked around quickly, seeing a few closed doors, a couple of wall sconces, and similar carpet to the main area of the library. Before closing the door, she eyed the area around it. My heart clenched painfully as I watched her take such precautions, knowing full well how necessary they could be. A set of keys jingled, bringing me back to the present as she placed one in the lock of one of the doors. *Where are you taking us, Love?*

The guys all held matching expressions of confusion and curiosity when the door finally opened silently on its hinges. A light green room with dark purple accents greeted us. The bed was bigger than the dorm room's twin-sized mattress and there was an attached bath as well as a closet. *Her room in the library*, I realized suddenly.

"No shit," Landon's voice echoed in my head. The asshole just couldn't resist listening in on my personal thoughts. As much as I strengthened my mental barrier, he could always get into mine and I could get into his. *"Not my fault you were thinking so loud, dude."* I quickly gave him the side eye before Dante's voice broke through the silence.

"Why'd you want to show us this, Firecracker?"

"In case everything that's happening escalates, you need to know where it is," she explained, her voice and face somber. My jaw clenched at the severity in her statement. Her fingers twitched ever so slightly, giving her away.

"What else, Love?" I prompted, my signature eyebrow raise making an appearance as I stared at her. Her luscious lips pursed, her jaw tensing under my scrutiny.

"If something happens or if you can't find me, you need to know where to check first." Landon, as well as Hudson and Cam opened their mouths to protest when she cut them off. "No, guys!" Sharpness in her words had everyone's rapt attention, mouths snapping shut. "I need you all to understand the reality of what's going on..."

"I think we understand just fine, Lucie," my twin snapped, anger pulsing off him. *He must be seething if he used her name instead of calling her Lemon Drop.* Her eyes softened as she looked at him, a mix of sadness and grim acceptance blanketing her features. My fingers itched to hold on to her, to remind her she wasn't alone. *Never again.*

"No, Landon, you don't. Do you trust me?" I knew my face matched Landon's as we stared at her, shock and surprise leaving us speechless.

"Of course we do, Babe," Nik answered for us, our brains still struggling to comprehend why she would think we didn't.

"Did we make her think we didn't?" I shot to Landon, hoping he could tell me that she was wrong, but a shoulder shrug was his only response.

"Then you need to trust me when I say you *need* to know where this is. I know exactly how dangerous he is, and one day I'll be able to talk about it, but not today."

A wave of hopelessness washed through me at her tone— defeated, disheartened, and sad. *So much sadness.* I wrapped my arms tightly around her, careful of her still bruised chest, willing my determination to deal with this piece of shit into her. *Come on, Love, we can do this.* Her slender arms wrapped around Landon and Hudson who had stepped up to my sides, hugging both of us in a tangle of limbs. Dante, Cam, and Nik all surrounded us last, covering her back in an arch of people, the sense of rightness settling over us.

"We'll be all right, Lucie. Thank you for showing us," Dante murmured, and a round of agreements hummed around us. A contented sigh passed through her lips before her back straightened, the determination seeping back into her demeanor. *There's our girl...*

November 5th
Monday Evening

Lucienne

The door closed with a soft thud when I stepped into my room, and I shucked the millions of layers I had adorned before showing them my other space. The mood had lightened slightly, but not completely by the time we had finished eating in the dining hall and made our way back to my dorm. Sadie had already passed out and was snoring loudly in her room. I tossed my extra layers into the hamper while the guys shuffled around into their normal seats for movie watching out in the living room. My lips curled at the thought that they'd all be here tonight. I was glad Sadie didn't mind having them here. She wanted me "surrounded by hotties at all times"—her words, not mine— until this situation was over.

I grabbed one of the several boxes of candy the guys had given me on my candy gram and made my way back out into the living room. They were arguing about what movie we should watch, their voices slowly growing louder until they were practically screaming. After today, I couldn't handle my guys yelling at each other, so I took a deep breath and got their attention in a loud shout.

"Hey! I will pick the damned movie!" I stomped over to the pile of movies and chose one I hadn't watched in years, the last time being with my mom when we binged on ice cream and hot chocolate after her and her latest boyfriend had broken up. "We're freaking watching *The Notebook*. Nope," I cut off their protests, "you guys couldn't decide like adults, and I can't handle anyone fighting right now." They grimaced at my reminder of how certain things could trigger me, including loud screaming during fights. "So, we're going to watch this together and then you guys can pick, okay?" I bargained, feeling bad for having completely overridden their choice.

"Sounds good to us," the twins agreed in unison.

"Yeah, Firecracker, whatever you want," Dante added, glancing to Hudson and Nik who both nodded. Cam agreed with a warm smile, taking the DVD case out of my hand to put into the DVD player.

Feeling frazzled after the ups and downs of the day, I wanted comfort. I wanted one of them to cuddle with me all while attempting to avoid another arguing match, so I quickly made my decision. Empowered by the choices I was able to make, especially after feeling so hopeless only a few hours earlier, I grabbed Cam's hand and walked over to where his empty seat was. Looking at me with a surprised expression, Cam sank into the chair with me following into his lap. His lean muscled arms wrapped around my waist and pulled me tightly to his soft t-shirt. No one commented on the fact that I had picked to sit with Cam, and no one complained again about my movie choice as we started it up.

After a while, I shifted in Cam's lap, my jeans growing increasingly uncomfortable. Finally, I couldn't handle it any longer and let Cam know I was going to change. As I stood up, I had to bite back a chuckle as I noticed wayward tears on the guys' faces as they watched. *So cute.* I smiled to myself as I stepped into my room and over to my closet.

When I was changed, I decided to quickly double check my materials for tomorrow's classes in case I fell asleep. I had just emptied some random trash out of the bottom of my messenger bag when I saw a corner of something poking out under my notebooks. I pulled it out, my smile falling into a frown. *An envelope? Did I get this from one of my classes when I wasn't paying attention?* I opened the flap and noticed a small stack of photos. I slid them out, instantly feeling my chest tighten.

"Guys?" I croaked. "Guys!" I called out, my voice slightly hysterical in my growing panic. They were 4"x6" photos in color of me from the last several weeks. A few from me in my room, working in the library, studying, walking across the quad, coming down the stairs in the Administration building waving at Jonathon, in classes, a couple even from getting our piercings done and shopping with Sadie and Benji for our dresses. *He's known since before the dance. He saw Justin's attack,* I realized, eyeing the photo of me pinned under the giant wolf.

One of my guys was talking to me, but I couldn't process what was being said. I couldn't even breathe as my stomach seized. I dropped in front of the trash can next to my desk and lost my dinner. Rough hands pulled my hair back quickly as I continued to dry heave despite my stomach being empty. When my tremors subsided, a tanned hand held out an open bottle of water. I took a few sips before moving to stand, my lightheadedness making me stumble.

"What happened?" Cam stood next to me when I got my bearings. I held out the stack of photos that had gotten slightly crumpled during my bout of sickness. Cam took the photos, his face growing hard while his lip curled back in a harsh snarl. He handed the photos to Hudson and the rest of the guys after he flipped through them all. His hand pressed against his mouth almost as if he was trying to keep in his reaction as the guys got their chance to look through the photos.

"He was here," I whispered, my throat still raspy from throwing up. "He was here when Justin attacked me." I felt my stomach roll painfully at the thought, knowing he would have enjoyed seeing it.

"Why didn't he help?" one of the guys asked quietly, probably not even realizing they had spoken out loud.

"Because he probably got a kick out of it. He wouldn't have given a shit if I was getting hurt at his hand or someone else's. As long as I wasn't killed..." I trailed off, raising a shoulder slightly before letting it drop. I looked around my guys, their eyes burning with fury as they stared at the photos, lips thinning into tight lines. "Can someone hand me my phone?" I asked as I went to my windows to make sure they were locked. Dante caught on to what I was doing and went over to Sadie's room to check the window. Landon jogged out of the room at the same time and jogged back in right after, my phone in his hand. I hadn't memorized Alex's number yet, so I scrolled through my contacts until I found it.

"Were they here in your room when you found them or in your bag that you brought in?" Nik asked as Grigori was shuffling about the desk.

"It was on my desk under my notebooks for classes tomorrow." I watched Nik lean down and sniff the desk.

"No chance that it was slipped in last week and you didn't see it?" Hudson asked as Nik straightened, but before I could respond Nik shook his head.

"No. Does Noah wear cologne?" he asked. Looking toward me with his glassy eyes, it was hard to remember he couldn't physically see me with his own eyes.

"Yeah, a spice scent. I don't remember the name, but he wore it every day." Nik nodded.

"Thought so, he was in here when he left the photos." He turned back toward the desk and waved his hand at the top.

"How do you know?" Logan's brow furrowed.

"I can smell the cologne on the chair, around the notebooks, the uh..." he stopped, glassy eyes flickering to me before whispering, "bed." *Oh, god.* My hands started shaking. I finally clicked Alex's name, and ringing sang through the earpiece.

"Hello?" I heard something banging in the background, like cooking pans. *I interrupted his dinner.* I winced at the thought.

"Alex?" My voice wavered, my nerves fraying.

"Lucie? What's wrong? What happened?" The banging stopped as his worry bled through his quick questioning.

"I found an envelope of photos on my desk. Nik said he smelled Noah's cologne here around my room." I had to throw my hand over my mouth when I dry heaved again. I heard Alex talking, but my phone was pulled out of my hand.

"We're all here," Landon said, then another pause as he listened to Alex's response. "I agree, what about changing locks?" More silence from our end of the call. "Security guards?" Landon directed the question at me. I shook my head. I didn't want any more attention right now. "No security guards, we'll keep her safe, and if it looks to be getting worse, we'll call you and security." There was one final bout of silence before Landon said goodbye and hung up. I didn't want my phone back in case there were any texts or emails. I didn't even want to be in my room anymore, the sense of safety tainted knowing Noah had been in here. So, I shakily pushed out of my group of guys into the living room and collapsed onto the mattresses on the floor.

"What did he say?" Hudson asked Landon as he came to sit next to me, his hand rubbing gently up and down my back after he got situated. Cam sat to the other side of me, his hand holding mine. Finally, Nik sank into the chair behind me before rubbing my shoulders gently.

"Starting tomorrow you'll be working on self-defense with us. Some of the guards, Troy and Bill, will be on call." I nodded, glad to be working with someone I knew. "They'll be changing the lock to your door tomorrow and only you, Sadie, us, and a select few necessary people will have it. Let's lie down, Lemon Drop," Landon suggested as everyone got comfy in their spots. We had been rotating who would sleep on the mattress each night, and I would usually try to make it to my own bed so more of them could fit on the makeshift bed on the floor, but tonight I needed to be with my guys. Once we were all bundled up together, Dante turned off the light, and with the heat of my guys surrounding me like a warm blanket I lulled into a dreamless sleep.

7

November 6th
Tuesday Afternoon
Lucienne

My sneakers squeaked on the gym floor as I walked with Cam and Hudson. Nik and Dante were busy grabbing pads at the other end of the room where the floors were covered in folded mats. The twins were still in their Energy Manipulation class for the next hour and a half, with plans of meeting us over at the dorm buildings when we were done here.

I had missed my workout clothes; the comfortable, wicking fabric of my tank rubbed against my torso while my leggings gripped my legs tightly. I hadn't gone for too many runs this semester, especially not after the All Hallow's Eve Dance due to the wrap on my chest. Dr. Ingress didn't want me to go for runs until it was healed. Apparently a crazy ex-boyfriend overshadowed that suggestion. *Not that I'm complaining.* I had been getting too restless without my outlet.

Glancing around, I noticed Dante was wearing only a pair of basketball shorts and his tennis shoes, his caramel torso on display under the gym lights. Memories of his tanned shoulders between my legs shot through me, waves of desire building the longer I thought about his gentle caresses. I swallowed hard watching his back, muscled from years of Kohl, bulge and shift with his movements. Moving my attention away from the handsome Kohl captain, my eyes landed on an equally handsome Nik. He was wearing a tight black tank top and sweats, his lean arms flexing as he helped Dante lay out mats. He might have had less bulk than most of the guys other than Cam, but they both had cut muscles that bulged deliciously when they moved. I felt my jaw drop as I watched them work.

"Like what you see?" Hudson asked quietly. We were still far enough away that Dante and Nik didn't hear his heated question. Cam, on the other hand, chuckled at my blush.

"Yes, you're all hot," I responded haughtily, refusing to be embarrassed. I gave him a big smile and bumped his shoulder to try and get him to focus on something else. Cam burst out laughing at my blunt response which caught Nik and Dante's attention.

"What is so funny?" Nik's rough gravelly voice called out as we neared them.

"Lucie was just admiring the view; she thinks we're hot," Hudson half quoted with a teasing smile. Dante and Nik turned to look at me, matching smirks and eyebrow raises on their faces. Nik's face turned a light pink with a blush. *That's so cute.* I gave the same response to them that I did to Hudson, a wide smile showing off my dimples.

"I can't admire my boyfriends?" I questioned, trying really hard not to laugh, my lips twitching at my effort. Nik shot forward and lifted me up with ease, his lean muscles strong enough to prop me up on his shoulder. Unfortunately, my upper body rubbed against the hard planes of his back and I winced a little at the contact. Nobody noticed and I didn't want to make a big deal out of it. He was so playful, and I didn't want to ruin the moment, but blood rushing to my wound and my head was disorienting. "Put me down, Nik!" I tried to keep my voice light and cheery despite the throbbing in my chest. Chuckling echoed through the gym.

"What? We can't admire our girlfriend?" Cam parroted back in a teasing tone as Nik smacked my ass with his free hand eliciting a gasp from me. The sting melted into a strange wave of pleasure, and a shiver worked its way up my spine. *What the hell was that?*

"You can, but we have shit to do, guys," I stated matter-of-factly in an attempt to distract myself from my body's odd reaction and the increasing ache in my upper body. Nik slid me down until I was standing, and I winced as my chest ran against his shoulder. This time he noticed, a tiny frown curling his lip.

"Did I hurt you, Lucie?" I waited until the dizziness passed and then popped up on my tiptoes to give him a quick kiss. I inhaled sharply when I realized what I had done but a bright smile met me as I lowered my heels back to the ground. The happiness on Nik's face eased my worry, my pain fading into the background.

"No, I'm fine, Nik," I reassured him, the throbbing lessening with each passing moment. He wrapped an arm around my shoulder and led me to the mat while the rest of the guys followed behind. No negative reactions, no jealousy. *Huh...*

Once we all gathered on the mat, Dante took over the beginning of our training. "All right, Firecracker, we're going to start with the basics. Do you have much experience in self-defense or fighting?"

"I have a bit, but it's been a while. I did most of it over the summer just to have some self-defense skills," I responded, swinging my arms around to loosen knots in my shoulders.

"Let's just start with some punches and blocking to warm up before we get into some more fighting." After I put on the MMA gloves Dante had tossed me, we started going back and forth, warming up with some light punching followed by running and stretching. Once we were warmed up, we went through some different techniques to get out of holds with a small amount of grappling. By the time we were done I was dripping in sweat and huffing in short breaths. *Damn, I am out of shape,* I thought, hunching over with my hands resting on my knees. My chest throbbed painfully at the amount of exercise I had done during practice, the twisting, turning, ducking, and other movements aggravating the puncture wounds and bruises that littered my pale skin.

"All right," I huffed, "I'm out. No more. I'm too out of shape for any more today." I straightened up. "I haven't gone for a run in almost two weeks."

"You run?" Logan was walking across the gym with Landon by his side. I was too busy trying to catch my breath to notice them come in.

"Yup." Popping the p in a very Sadie fashion, I circled my head around to check out my twins as they came toward us. "I love to run and do yoga. I meditate sometimes, but I haven't done that since the beginning of the semester." I started my stretching, being careful to not increase the pain I felt gripping my torso as the guys wiped down mats and put away the pads.

"We'll have to go for a run sometime. Oh, I know!" Landon clapped, emphasizing his exclamation. "You should come play on the Kohl team next year!" I side eyed him as I moved through another stretch.

"Hell no," I drawled out. "I might like to run, but hell will have to freeze over to get me on that field." Landon and Logan clasped their hands in front of their wide chests, pouted out their bottom lips and giving me puppy dog eyes, all in a synchronized display with one another. I shook my head, a smile creeping on my face as a laugh escaped. *They're so adorable.* I chucked my messenger bag over my shoulder as I walked toward the doors with my guys. I made sure to discreetly hold the strap away from my chest so it wouldn't rub against the wrapping around my ribs and chest.

"I thought you two were meeting us at the dorm?" Dante directed his question at the twins.

"We figured we'd come here; never going to pass up an opportunity to see Lucie all hot and sweaty." Logan winked at me, his lip twitching slightly with trying not to smile, but he didn't do a very good job as I saw it quirk up.

The cold air cooled my sweat coated skin as we stepped outside, the other guys fighting their own eye rolls and chuckles at Logan's response. I dug into my bag to grab my jacket, hat, and gloves before pulling them on as fast I could with my sore muscles. I heard my phone start to ring right as I adjusted my second glove. I was apprehensive to check it, anxious that it could be Noah again, but he hadn't contacted me today, and it ended up being Char.

"Hey, girl," I greeted cheerily, "how's it going?"

"Lucie, I have some shitty news, boo." I stopped walking, the guys turning to look back at me with concern etched on their handsome faces. *Please be okay.* "Noah showed up at UW today and tried to talk to me." *That fucking bastard.*

"Are you okay? Did he hurt you?" I turned, hurrying toward the Administration building, my guys following behind me.

"I'm fine, you know very well I'd beat that boy into the ground if he came after me. Pretty sure he just wanted to scare you by coming here. I was heading to class, so he couldn't corner me," she explained as I pulled open the glass doors to the building. Jonathon immediately picked up his desk phone. *At this rate, I should just move into the building.*

"As long as you're okay. Is he still there?" I could feel my muscles straining on each step after the almost two-hour workout.

"I don't think so. I notified the security on campus about him and gave them a picture so they'll be on the lookout if he comes back. I scoured the parking lots after my biology class and didn't see his truck anywhere. I think he left when I went into class." She sounded calm which helped keep my anxiety down. When I reached the fourth floor, Alex once again opened the door right as we stepped up to the top step. *How does he do that?*

"All right, Char, let me talk to the dean here. I'll let you know what he says, okay? Stay safe, love you, girl." She returned the sentiment and we hung up as I plopped into my usual chair. I knew the guys were worried, I could see it on their faces.

"What happened?" Alex jumped straight to the point, leaning back behind his desk.

"Noah went to UW and tried to talk to my human best friend Charlie." *Still feels weird making that distinction.* "She said he tried to talk to her when she was on the way to class, so he didn't get a chance to really say anything." I explained everything else that Char and I had discussed over the phone to Alex, each additional detail making his frown more severe.

"Would she be up for coming to campus this weekend to talk to our security team?" I shot a quick text to Char, thankful that she responded almost immediately since she wasn't working tonight.

"She works Saturday, but she can come Sunday. She said she could be here at ten."

"And what do we do in the meantime?" Logan hissed, the whites of his eyes blackened into his daemon eyes as he questioned Alex.

"Mr. Anson, I understand you're upset..."

"No, I don't think you do, Dean Renaud. Lucie is just a student to you, but to us she's everything," Landon interjected, his eyes also black as night, a hazy ring of red replacing the crisp burning coal irises they usually held.

"Gentlemen, I think you are forgetting yourselves. What Lucie needs is calm heads right now, not Daemon twins ready to burn the campus down." His voice was stern but understanding.

"Dean Renaud, we mean no disrespect to you or your efforts, it's just that they seem a little lax given the danger he currently presents," Hudson supplied calmly. I could feel something flowing from him which seemed to affect the twins a little. Their tense shoulders eased, and their fists uncurled. After another few moments, Logan and Landon's eyes shifted back into human looking eyes, the black receding until they looked normal.

"Do you give permission for a little leeway? Not a lot, just enough to make it possible for us to do what we see fit should the need arise?" Dante took over the direction of the conversation. Alex seemed to be considering his question scrupulously before nodding his consent.

Alex and I spent the next little while working out the rest of the details before giving Char and Alex each other's numbers so he could coordinate with the head of security.

"I am having Bill and Troy sent over to walk you back to your dorm. I know you'll all be staying together, but I want them with you guys since it's now dark. The locks were changed this afternoon, so here's your new key. They already gave Sadie hers." Alex handed a small gold key to me. I dug out my key ring and hooked it on there after taking off the old tarnished one. He took the original key and put it in the top drawer of his antique desk. After a few minutes had passed, his desk phone rang once. A very short conversation followed upon answering it before he returned it to its cradle. "They're in the lobby, Lucie, boys. Go get some rest and keep an eye out. Have you memorized those numbers yet?" I shook my head.

"I will tonight though," I reassured him. Knowing Noah was willing to go to Char to scare me was that final push I needed to memorize those numbers. *He's not going to stop until he's caught... or gets me.* I felt sick but being in Alex's office with my guys helped keep the knot in my chest at bay.

"Good, hopefully you are able to get some sleep, Lucie." Alex held open the door for us like he always did as we filed past him and headed to the lobby.

Bill and Troy were chatting with Jonathon at the desk while he was filing papers. Troy was a bit younger, in his early 20s, and wore his shoulder-length black hair pulled back out of his face in a hair tie. His olive colored skin was warm, sun-kissed glow under the lights while the thick muscles under his shirt strained against the sleeves of his security uniform. Bill was in his early 40s, his pale complexion shiny on top of his head where he had waxed it. He had a stocky build and was shorter than Troy with wider shoulders and chest.

"Hey Bill, Troy." I smiled and waved to both as I reached the front desk. They had always been nice to me since that night where the security system in the library went haywire after an update. Smiles were prevalent on their faces as they turned to me.

"Hey, Luce." Bill stuck his hand out. *Always the handshake man.* The calluses on his rough skin encompassed my lean fingers and palm.

"Lucie! Good to see you all healed up after that shit storm at the dance." Troy's eyes sparkled as he looked at me. When he noticed the guys behind me, his smile faltered slightly before sliding back in place, but his eyes no longer sparkled. "And who are these gentlemen?" His voice was cool as he eyed each of my guys.

"This is Dante, Hudson, Landon, Logan, Cam, and Nik." I introduced them one by one Vanna White *Wheel of Fortune* style. I held my arm out for Grigori who had been shuffling down Nik's arm toward me, ruffling his feathers in irritation at being left out of introductions. I chuckled when he hopped from Nik to me and crawled up to my shoulder. "This is Grigori." His usual head boop hit my left temple, showing me he was pleased to be considered as special as my guys. He settled when I started to pat his feathered head. Bill greeted my guys warmly with handshakes for everyone, but Troy seemed off-put that they were there.

"Ready to head out?" Bill questioned when introductions were done. I nodded and waved a goodbye to Jonathon who gave me a wobbly goodnight. The air was cold and the breeze shifted the hair in my low ponytail. I stuffed my hands in my pockets just in time to feel my phone vibrate and ding with a notification. I pulled it out of my pocket to check it and ground my teeth in response.

Unknown Number: You always look so sexy after your workouts.
Unknown Number: Don't think surrounding yourself with freaks will keep you from me.
Unknown Number: It's unsanitary to have a bird sitting on your shoulder you know.

Rage flooded my system, anxiety and panic having no time to take root as I stopped and looked around the mostly empty quad. I didn't see anyone on the grass, so I focused my attention on the sides of the buildings, doors, trees, and anywhere someone would be able to see me without making it overly obvious. Cam took my phone from my fist after uncurling my fingers from their death grip. I heard him curse as he handed my phone off to Bill and Troy. Refusing to be intimidated again today, I rolled my shoulders back, not even wincing at the sting of my wound, and I held my head high as I continued to stroll down the path to the dorm. *He doesn't own me anymore.* Hearing my phone ringing in Bill's hand, I didn't have to look to see who it was. Taking it back, I answered and immediately placed it on speaker, my steps stalling. There were no other students near us on the quad to overhear the conversation.

"What, Noah?" My voice came out flat and bored.

"Hello, Babygirl, you look sexy when you're mad." His voice held a sneer as he addressed me. I rolled my eyes. *Can he just take a long walk off a short cliff right now?*

"Cool, now if you'll excuse me, I have shit to do." Starting to walk again, I watched several eyebrows raise in surprise from the gaggle of men walking with me.

"What? Going to go fuck one of your freaks?" I gritted my teeth again at his continued taunting that my guys were freaks. *Here he is, chasing after me, who is also a supe. Hypocrite much?* I mentally scoffed.

"Well, they are my boyfriends, so I'll fuck whoever I want, whenever I want, and there's nothing you can do about it," I jeered into the phone, my confidence building from finally talking to him the way I had always wanted to. "Now if you'll excuse me, I have shit to do and men to fuck. Bye." I sing-songed the farewell and hung up the phone. Silencing it, I slid it into my messenger bag not wanting to hear him call again.

"Damn, Princess, that was..." Hudson trailed off, and I finally saw all the expressions around me. Raised eyebrows, wide eyes, and surprise blatant on every single one of them.

"Fucking badass is what it was," Landon cheered coming out of his stupor. When he threw up his hand for a high five, laughter bubbled out of me as I hit his hand with mine.

"Or really dumb," Troy chided, looking at me like a parent that was about to lecture a five-year-old who did something they shouldn't have. "He is clearly escalating, and we still haven't gotten him. I called the head of security and the guards on duty, but that might have just pushed him over the edge to do something extreme." I whipped around to face him, my face contorted with fury at the comment. I was still riding the high of my anger and subsequent freeing feeling of standing up for myself. I didn't need to be lectured at how dangerous he was.

"Don't you dare tell me what I'm up against. I was beaten, manipulated, raped, and nearly killed for four years of my life. I got myself out, and I started over. I finally have my life back, and I will not let him control me anymore regardless of if it's physically or this psychological warfare bullshit I know he loves. I know it's your job to keep me safe but keep your patronizing lectures to yourself." I was breathless at the end of my tirade, the fading adrenaline leaving trembling limbs in its wake. I took a step back and stuffed my hands in my pockets to hide the shaking. I couldn't stand to see the looks of pity from everyone around the group any longer, so I turned on my heels and continued my walk to the dorms, chastising myself for my outburst the entire way. I hung back to let the guys enter the building ahead of me so I could pull Troy aside. Not wanting to draw attention from the students in the entertainment area right inside the door, I mumbled an apology.

"I understand, Lucie, I didn't mean to make it seem like how it came out. I just want to make sure you're safe." Unsure of what else to say, I thanked him and headed into the building, exhaustion overshadowing anything else.

8

November 9th
Friday Afternoon
Lucienne

The wind was light against my cheeks, but the coldness it carried stung, causing my normally pale skin to become pink. It was odd being in the Kohl stadium while it was empty aside from Benji and me. I was able to hear the calls and shouts clearly from the field even though we were still at least ten rows up.

The team was working in rotations to practice, the Enforcers and the Raiders alternating on the field to work through miscellaneous traps. The Enforcers focused on defending their castle and other players, while the Raiders practiced how to get from one end of the field to the other where the opposing team's flag was located. The only players who were on the field the entire practice so far were the Guardian—a lean muscled guy with long dreads that were pulled back in a ponytail at the nape of his neck— wearing a number '20' jersey, and Dante, who practiced with each part of the team. He was in his element on the field, and his ability to convey directions and solve problems—especially under pressure—blew me away.

"What are they doing there?" I directed my question to Benji, my chin jutting out toward a set of moving stone steps. The moving slabs reminded me of the same set that was used in the first Kohl game I had watched. Dante, as well as three Raiders, were in a huddle at the base of the obstacle. Benji's eyes lit up as he looked toward them. He had been unbelievably happy last night when I'd asked if he'd want to watch their practice, and his squeal of excitement had made my ears ring. His perceptive eyes scanned the field before turning to me.

"It looks like Mia, the one with the wings"—a pale finger pointed toward a girl with black hair and a '17' on her maroon practice jersey—"is going to fly Rick up to the first step while Alexa, the redhead, attempts to slow the obstacle's movement to allow him to get to the suspended bridge." I watched closely, trying to keep their numbers, hair colors, and names straight as I observed. Benji had been right, Alexa, number 12, stood braced on the turf as Mia's taupe-colored wings carried her and Rick toward the first step. Rick dropped, landing in a roll as Mia continued to fly toward the other side of the field. Benji's voice caught my attention as he continued talking. "Alexa's the co-captain and a witch. Rick is a tiger shifter, and he has enhanced senses and agility even when he isn't shifted. See how he's able to move from one slab to the next?"

I was enraptured by the display on the stone steps, when the other two Raiders caught my attention, their coordinating movements looking like a dance. *A violent dance, but still.* Number 18 was punching his way through heavy objects being launched at him like they were nothing while player '19' was... *Did his arm just lengthen?* His limbs continued to grow, stretch, and maneuver around twisting ivy vines that attempted to attach themselves to the two supes.

"That's Lincoln and Zane, they're brothers. Zane's the one who's turning those things to dust in '18', and Lincoln is the Mr. Fantastic down there in '19'." Benji turned his pink-tinged face toward me, his light brown eyes sparkling. "I'm having fun, thanks for bringing me." I wrapped my left arm around his thin waist as the weight of his arm settled on my shoulders. In his very Benji fashion, his phone appeared, the front camera on and waiting to take our picture. Our cold faces were reflected in his phone's screen, large smiles appearing right before the clicking of the shutter sounded.

"Of course. As much as I like watching the game with everyone, I feel like I really understand it when I'm with you," I explained quickly, my arm squeezing him while he tucked his phone away. "If that makes any sense," I tacked on the end, realizing I was being emotionally rambly.

"Yes, it does. We should go see one of the professional games sometime when they're in Seattle."

"Oh, yes!" I exclaimed before changing topics. "So, how's it been lately? We haven't had some just Lucie/Benji time in a hot minute," I prompted. As soon as I asked, he seemed to perk up even more before launching into a cheery response.

"It's been so good lately. Austin has been thinking of possibly enrolling here since he's been able to save up enough from working at the mechanic and body shop, so that would be really exciting. We've even talked about moving in together if he does, although it probably won't be until the summer semester so he can save up enough to have a nice cushion for us. He's always been that money conscious responsible type," Benji gushed, his hands waving in front of him as he talked.

"That'd be awesome," I agreed. "Any idea what he wants to study? You still looking into writing?" I added, randomly remembering that he was taking a lot of English composition and literature classes with the hope to write a book while working as an English professor. I knew I wouldn't ever be able to teach anything, too much anxiety with being up in front of a crowd, but I'd noticed Benji slowly crawling out of that shy exterior over the last few months, finally growing into that social butterfly he wanted to be.

"Austin could do whatever he wanted with his telepathy, so I think he's just going to decide after he gets a feel for classes and everything. As for me, I'm hoping so, but this freaking Shakespeare class might just kill the plan for me. I mean, it is absolutely awful," he whined. "If I can make it through, then that is still the plan. What about you? Any ideas yet of what you want to do?"

"Hm," I hummed, trying to rattle my brain for an idea, but still came up blank. *How could I pick what I want to do when I'm still learning how to be a supe?* "I could follow in my mom's footsteps and be a baker, maybe have Nik teach me some potions or whatever to put in them. You know, like a sleeping tart, stress less cupcake, or an energizing breakfast bar."

"Can I be the taste tester?" Benji asked brightly. He bounced excitedly in his seat causing me to laugh, but I couldn't deny him with that enthusiasm.

"Of course," I assured, nudging his shoulder. A quick tinkling jingle signified his alarm going off meaning he needed to go get ready for his date with Austin. Hugging me quickly, he shifted to stand.

"You stay safe, I don't want to have to go all Kitsune on

anyone's ass, got it?" he commanded, his lips twitching in a poor attempt not to laugh. I nodded, a chuckle bubbling up at the image of his little double-tailed fox form attempting to stop anyone. With a final wave, he was off, jogging quickly up the steps toward the entrance of the stadium, leaving me to meet Dante and the twins down on the field on my own.

Leisurely paced, I walked down the rows toward the turf. The entire team stood in a group on the field, and I glanced at the time on my phone. Their practice should be over shortly. The iciness of the railing bit through my coat sleeves bringing goosebumps and a single shiver to my body as I waited for them to finish talking. I didn't have to wait long before the majority of the team went to the locker rooms, Dante and my twins splitting off to make their way to me instead.

"Hey, Firecracker." Dante's tanned face was coated in a thin layer of sweat, his hair glistening in the afternoon sun. I dipped down, my face only a few inches higher with me standing on the steps. "But I'm all sweaty," he protested, leaning away from me. I scoffed, grabbing his jersey tightly and yanking him to me. His lips crashed against mine, molding to me when he realized I wasn't letting go until he kissed back. After a few moments, I released him. His eyes were half-lidded and dazed with heat as he stared up at me.

"I don't care if you're sweaty," I murmured, a soft smile curling my lips. Landon hopped up and down excitedly, his blackened blood red eyes sparkling when I turned to him. His calloused hands tangled in my hair, giving a soft tug at the roots as he kissed me fiercely before stepping back. Logan took his place, his languid and unhurried kiss a direct contrast to his twin's. Running the back of his fingers against my cheek, the naughty daemon nipped my lower lip sharply when he pulled away. An unintentional whimper sounded in my throat, and his smile became absolutely sinful, knowing full well what he did to me. *Damn naughty daemons and handsome shifters, I need a cold shower,* I thought, desire pulsing in my lower belly. Heat thrummed through my body despite the cold weather.

"Come on, Lemon Drop, let's go wait in the locker room common area and out of the cold." Landon motioned for me to hop over the fence. Stepping up, I swung a leg over before Dante's large hands snatched me off the chain link. He grabbed my hand and pulled me in the direction of the locker room area, the soft turf of the field sinking under my boots. Our pace was slow going, so slow in fact, that the twins burst past us in a race, their shouted obscenities echoing in the empty stadium. I couldn't help but laugh when Logan jumped on Landon's back causing him to stumble.

The twins were panting, slouched on one of the couches in the team's common room when we walked in. My eyes flitted around the room quickly taking in the spacious area. Couches and chairs were scattered in clusters much like the library and common areas of the dorms. There were two doors, one to the men's locker room and the other to the women's. A small kitchenette with a fridge, sink, microwave, and a couple of cabinets stood between the two doors.

"Have a seat, Firecracker. Do you want something to drink or nibble on?" Dante's deep melodic voice caught my attention as he directed me to a chair across from the twins.

I'd like to nibble on you, I thought as I shook my head silently.

"All right, if you get thirsty, there's water, energy drinks, stuff like that in there." He gestured to the stainless-steel appliance before continuing, "I'm going to shower real quick." After a quick kiss, he strode into the appropriate room, leaving me with the twins, both of whom had that mischievous glint in their eyes as they stared at me. My eyes narrowed at them, the little smirks they wore making me suspicious of what they were thinking of doing. Thankfully, the boys' locker room opened, interrupting Landon as he opened his mouth. The tiger shifter and the Guardian of the team exited before they spotted us seated in the common area. Making their way over, they nodded to the twins before the Guardian stuck out his hand first, his teeth bright against his dark skin.

"Hey, I'm Titus," he introduced himself, his skin calloused and rough against my palm as he gripped it lightly and stepped back.

"Lucie, it's nice to meet you," I responded. Somehow my voice stayed steady despite my nerves I felt radiating through me.

"Rick." The tiger shifter stuck his hand out next. His eyes caught my attention and I couldn't look away. They were bright gold, the pupils in a cat-like slit. It took me by surprise when I noticed there were flecks of orange, red, and even some light green.

"Wow..." I breathed. When the room chuckled, I realized I had actually said it out loud. Feeling the heat of a blush on my cheeks, I tried to save face with a smile even with my mind just echoing *'Here lies Lucie, death by social awkwardness.'*

"Don't worry, I get that a lot," he reassured me. "The eyes run in the family. So, what's a pretty girl like you doing hanging out with these two losers?" Rick teased, light-heartedly tossing a thumb toward the twins. Both stuck their tongues out, their hands coming up to flip him off.

"She's our girlfriend, you ass," Logan retorted, but his laughing betrayed his harsh words.

"Of course she is, no idea how you two crazies are able to hold onto any girl for longer than two seconds. I would lose my damn mind if you were my boyfriend," Rick joked turning his attention to me. "So Lucie, you thinking of joining the team?"

"See!" the twin's both exclaimed loudly, waving at Rick.

"No," I said with finality, shaking my head. "I would not be a good addition to the team"

"You never know who would be good until you actually play," Titus added. "I'm only a junior, so I plan on playing next year too. If you do end up thinking about it, I can help you practice if you wanted. I'm sure those two and Dante would help too." I gave him an appreciative smile, but Rick's talking stopped any response I would have given.

"Well, I'm a senior so you're more than welcome to have my number after I'm gone if you end up being a Raider."

"Fine, fine," I finally gave in. "I'll *think* about it, how about that?" I compromised, looking to the twins who cheered and did a happy dance, all without leaving their chairs. Right as they calmed, the girls' locker room opened and two of the female players joined us in the common area. It was the red-headed co-captain, *Alexa*, I remembered, followed closely by the one who could fly. Mia's wings were tucked back, and I couldn't help but examine them. The taupe wings held flecks of white, grey, and dark brown throughout the soft looking feathers. Alexa's eyes lit up when she saw me. Mia's, on the other hand, looked suspicious as they flickered between me and the twins.

"Hey! You must be Lucie," the co-captain exclaimed, her slender hand extending toward me. "I'm Alexa, but you can call me Lexa. I'm happy to finally meet the girl who's had Dante's head in a tizzy." I shook her hand, unsure of what to say in response to that.

Come on, you've done well for the last few months being normal. Hell, you just had a good conversation with Rick and Titus, say something.

"That's me," I chirped. My smile felt fake, but I was hoping it looked sincere to these girls who didn't know me. *Yup, so normal, Lucie,* I chided.

"Hey now," Landon started, his face feigning indignation and drawing Lexa and Mia's attention away from me. A quick wink let me know he knew I was uncomfortable being a part of a conversation with someone new. He and Logan moved at the same time, one brother sitting on either side of me on the arms of my chair. Rick and Titus chuckled at their antics.

"Don't forget about us," Logan finished for his twin. Lexa joined in the laughing, giving me an eye roll as if to say she was used to their playfulness.

"I thought she was Dante's girlfriend?" Mia finally chimed in, her voice husky. The smokey quality added to the don't-mess-with-me vibe she was currently giving off with crossed arms and hip jutted out.

"She is," Logan started.

"But she's also ours," Landon continued. His hand came to rest on the back of my neck, his fingers tangling lightly in my hair mimicking what he did on the field.

"She's also our brothers'," Logan rounded off their verbal back and forth. His smile was soft as he glanced down at me.

"Wow, that's a lot of dick to handle, no wonder you're the center of the gossip mill." Mia's dark brown eyes rolled as she strutted out of the common room and into the cold weather. Her snarky statement left everyone in a state of shock. *Did she.... Was that supposed to be an insult?* My confusion scrunched up my brows, and I pursed my lips in thought. Coming out of the stunned silence before anyone else, Lexa gave me an apologetic smile.

"Sorry about that, Mia's a bit..." She trailed off, head tilting as she thought of how to phrase her next statement.

"Of a bitch, clearly." Dante's normally melodic words were short and clipped in anger, his eyes hard as he stared at Lexa. In my shock I hadn't even noticed Dante walking out of the locker room, but he must have just in time to hear Mia's snide remark. He stood stoic and angry next to Titus. The twins nodded their agreement, jovial attitudes falling into irritation while the other two men had scrunched faces and disbelieving expressions, as if they truly couldn't believe she had just said that.

"I'll talk to her." Lexa seemed sincere as she talked with Dante.

"See that you do," he snapped. Lexa gave me another apologetic smile before excusing herself, the door to the common room closing quietly behind her.

"No idea what the hell that was about," Titus started, shaking his head, "but sorry you had to be on the other end of Mia's very, uh, opinionated attitude. It was great to meet you, Lucie, but we've actually got to get going." His hand waved between him and Rick. "We have plans to watch the Seahawks play today."

"We'll see you around, I'm sure," Rick added before waving and following Titus out the front door.

"We'll be back, Love." Logan dropped a kiss on the top of my head, Landon following suit before they headed to the locker room leaving Dante and me alone. Dante was still standing where he had been when he had addressed the Mia situation, his jaw clenched tightly. Realizing he wasn't really paying attention to what was around him, I got up and walked over to him.

"Hey," I murmured, my hand resting against his corded forearm that was crossed over his chest. "You all right?" My voice startled him from being lost in his thoughts, and his arms dropped with a heavy exhale.

"I'm sorry, Lucie." Exhaustion was thick in his words. Sliding my arms up his biceps and around his shoulders, I hugged him tightly even though it hurt to do so. My body automatically popping en pointe with how tall he was. The smell of his cologne and a small hint of soap surrounded me when he wrapped his arms around my thin waist.

"Why are you apologizing?" I whispered, my fingers gently massaging his knotted shoulders. His face nuzzled into the crook of my neck despite needing to lean down to do so.

"Because you have enough to worry about, and you don't need one of *my* teammates treating you like that." His breath was warm on my skin, goosebumps rising at the heat.

"That isn't your fault, you don't need to take the blame for everything everyone does. You didn't make her talk to me like that or give her the attitude problem. She did that, Dante, not you." I pulled back, my deep blue eyes finding his emerald irises. The shadows that passed over his face and eyes told me everything I needed to know. He carried around the weight, of the world of things he couldn't possibly be responsible for, the tension clear in his drooping shoulders. "I'm all right, hon, I promise. I don't care what anyone says about me; nothing they say will make me feel like being with you guys is wrong or make me less than I am." For the first time in years, the sentiment felt sincere. Confidence in my decision to date them, to just be myself, flowed through me.

"Fuck, Firecracker, how did I get so lucky?" His black brows dipped low over his eyes as he spoke, his question quiet enough that I don't think he realized he said it out loud.

Grazing the back of his neck with my nails, I nudged his head down to mine. This wasn't like the other kisses I had gotten. This one was full of promise, of safety, of connection, a hope of something more. The thought made my heart pound painfully in my chest, from nerves or anticipation I wasn't sure. His lips were soft but sure as they moved, hints of coffee on his tongue as it traced against mine. Pulling back, he kissed my forehead softly, his arms still hugging me to his chest. My eyes fell shut at the contact, Dante's exhale ruffling my hair gently. The sound of one of the doors opening caught my attention, but he didn't let me go, his warm smile against my forehead feeling a pink tinge heat my cheeks.

"We're all done," Logan announced. Landon stepped up to the side of us, his arms wrapping around both Dante and me before squeezing.

"Awe, look at us. One big happy family!" he cheered happily, content to be the comic relief after the strained conversation with Mia that had played out and the intense emotions stirring inside me. My laugh was echoed by Dante's and Logan's as we fell into a line heading back into the cold. Confidence in our relationship solidified as we walked, their synergy around me calming the years of psychological shit I'd suffered from Noah.

My family...

9

November 11ᵗʰ
Sunday Morning
Camden

I held open the door for the conference room for my brothers and Lucie. Lucie's vanilla scent wafted past as she gave me a small smile, her pink lips curling ever so slightly before moving deeper into the room. Scanning the space, I didn't see Charlie seated at the large wood table. Only Dean Renaud, Head of Security Gerry Hanson, and the two security guards from the other night—*Bill and Troy, I believe*—were situated in various cloth-covered chairs. I took a seat between Nik and Lucie, leaving the seat next to Lucie empty for Charlie. Unfortunately, these weren't the best circumstances to be meeting her under, but I couldn't help but look forward to finally meeting Charlie. I was excited to get a glimpse into Lucie's life from when she was a human. *I can't believe he actually went to her best friend,* I mentally growled at the nerve of that asshole.

My brothers and I were struggling with not being able to

get to him as more and more texts and calls continued to come in. At this point, Lucie had left her phone on silent, only checking it once, maybe twice a day for the last few days. Of course, the guys and I checked it nightly to report to Alex, but we also wanted to make sure that the texts weren't escalating from just stalking to threatening. Although the stalker aspect was creepy, he hadn't taken it any further. Yet. We'd also noticed other side effects of Noah's stalking; she was barely eating, her already thin body starting to look a bit gaunt, and the purple smudges under her eyes had gotten worse with every night due to her increasing nightmares. While her flashbacks hadn't made too many appearances, she'd been jumpy and anxious.

Doll... My heart cracked a little more when I looked at her sitting next to me. Her hair was tossed in a messy bun on the crown of her head, no makeup on her beautiful face, her sweater looking a bit looser than it used to while her belt was one notch tighter to hold her jeans in place. Those plump lips had been permanently downturned since the beginning of this shit show. On a good note, her fighting has gotten better in the last couple of practices, showing she was a quick study. *A psychopathic stalker is great motivation,* I thought darkly.

The door opened, showing a woman with coffee colored skin and black curly hair. She was dressed similarly to Lucie in skinny jeans, knee high boots, and a sweater, although Charlie was wearing a thick cardigan instead of a jacket. Lucie was thinner than her best friend, but they seemed relatively the same height. She didn't look uncomfortable in a room of strangers, confidence shining through as she walked to the table. Lucie stood and gave her best friend a hug, her head dropping down to Charlie's shoulder as she sniffled. I had to sit on my hands to stop myself from reaching out and curling her into my arm. *She has only seen Charlie once this semester, she sees you every day,* I reminded myself.

When Lucie pulled back, her eyes were red and tear tracks streaked her sunken cheeks. She smiled at Charlie and sat back down next to me, and I immediately scooted her chair over to me and threw my right arm around her holding her trembling body to mine. She rubbed her cheek on my shoulder and settled in. I dropped a quick kiss on top of her head before pulling back, my arm still holding her to me. Charlie gave Lucie a look with a raised eyebrow and a small smile. *Apparently, Lucie didn't tell Charlie we were together.* The more I thought about it, the more I realized that multiple partner relationships weren't normal in human communities. *Makes sense.*

"Charlie, it's a pleasure to meet you, I just wish it could have been under better circumstances. I'm Dean Alexandre Renaud, this is Head of the Security Gerry Hanson, and two of our security guards who are on-call for Lucie's safety around campus, Bill and Troy." Dean Renaud gestured to each person as he introduced them. "These gentlemen are Lucie's boyfriends." No judgement colored his statement this time as he went down the line giving Charlie our names. "Can you please explain to us what happened with Noah?" Charlie continued to eye us as he listed out names, but at Dean Renaud's question she focused back on topic.

Over the next hour, we went back and forth about the details of Charlie's encounter with Noah. Her voice was warm, and a slight accent I couldn't place colored her words. She repeated much of the same story that Lucie had the other day, but she did say that Noah had changed his appearance with a ratty baseball hat and UW sweatshirt. She had been able to take a photo of him which she had printed out so she could give us a copy. Lucie refused to look at the picture but the rest of us did. He wasn't what I expected but then again bullies never were. It also explained why she couldn't pick him out of the crowd after she got out of class. Hell, he might have changed his appearance again, making the photo Charlie gave us useless. Nobody said he was stupid, just a fucking asshole. After sharing the photo with us, Alex and Mr. Hanson asked a few final questions before the meeting was concluded.

When it was finally called to an end, I led the way out of the room, Lucie's hand curled in mine. Charlie followed her trailed by the rest of my family. Dean Renaud and the security guards stayed in the room to continue talking.

"So, boo." Charlie gave Lucie a sassy 'give it up' expression with pursed lips, arms crossed, and a hip pushed out. "I feel like you've been holding out on me." Lucie started to slowly turn pink, her hand squeezing mine slightly. She coughed quickly into her free hand before addressing Charlie.

"Uh, yeah, about that," she muttered, fiddling with the zipper on her jacket. "These are my boyfriends." She ended her statement with a small shrug. "Sorry I didn't tell you; I've had a lot on my mind recently." An apologetic smile creeped onto her face.

"Boo." Charlie's voice was chilled, her mouth thinned into a tight line. "I'm so jealous!" She burst out laughing and clapped her hands. "You have six boyfriends! Where can I find six sexy guys for myself?" She threw an arm over Lucie's unoccupied side, and Lucie's arm circled Charlie's waist as she laughed with her.

"I know two somebodies you seemed to like," Lucie teased, poking Charlie in the waist. "If you want, I can talk to them." My brow furrowed in thought, unsure of who they were talking about.

"Gabe and Elijah," Hudson must have read the confused look on my face because his voice echoed the names in my head. I gave a slight nod to let him know I understood.

"We'll see." Charlie shrugged, a small smile curling her lips. "Let's grab those cookie tins you collected since I last grabbed them. Your mama's on my ass about the fact that she's running low again, Miss-Cookie-Tin-Hog." Lucie's warm laugh filled the area around us as we turned toward her dorm building. The quad wasn't overly busy with students since it was lunch time, but there was still a small amount walking this way and that. The girls continued to chat as Dante typed in the code for the building, the common room bustling with students watching TV or playing games. The guys talked amongst themselves while I trailed behind with Lucie and Charlie, the two lost in their own little world.

The dorm room was empty after Lucie unlocked it, Sadie having a lunch date with a girl she was gushing about the last few days. It had been five days since Lucie's locks were changed and yet we weren't confident in the idea that he couldn't find his way in again to leave any surprises. Thankfully I didn't see any envelopes or colored photos of Lucie. The girls split off from us and slipped into her room, and the clanking sounds of the metal tins clashing together filled the air. My brothers sank into their usual spots: the twins on the couch, Nik against the wall, and Dante and Hudson in the chairs. I remained standing to walk Lucie and Charlie to the parking lot. They emerged from her room, their arms filled with colorful tins that she set on the coffee table. Her dark brown eyes zeroed in on Hudson, narrowing slightly.

"Charlie." Lucie's voice was soft but firm, having caught the look on her best friend's face. "Don't," she urged. The quiet command pulled the attention of the rest of the guys out of their conversations, gazes falling on Charlie who waved off Lucie's warning.

"You treatin' my girl right?" Charlie's accent grew thicker, her Creole roots becoming more obvious as she squared off with Hudson. "Because if you don't, I'll kick your ass to the moon and back like I did your ex-ho." A slender finger poked Hudson in the chest, the force strong enough to make him wince. The guys' brows shot up at the not-so-subtle threat. "That goes for the rest of you as well." Her finger swung around the room, her eyes making contact with each of us as she talked. Lucie's reddened face was buried in her hand, and a groan rumbled in her chest before she glared up at her friend.

"Charlotte Ava Hauser," Lucie's voice was sharp, "you mind your manners, or I'll tell your mom you're threatening people. Hudson was under the influence of some dark magic those few weeks, so he didn't know what was happening." Charlie's hand fell to her side the longer Lucie explained. "They're not who you should be worried about, okay?"

"Oh." Charlie sounded surprised, dark eyes darted to Hudson once more. "Sorry 'bout that." Her voice was humble as she apologized, and then she turned and addressed Lucie again. "But boo, you can't blame me too much, I mean, I *am* your best friend. That means I have to let them know what'll happen if they break your heart." Her smile was wide, a subtle glint shining in her eyes as she justified herself. Several of us chuckled at her, and Lucie shook her head, unable to hide the tiny curl of her lips.

"Let's go," Lucie directed as she bent down to scoop up

half the cookie tins, "before you decide to start throwing punches or kicking them in the shins, you crazy person." I took the tins from Lucie as she tried to pass me, her mouth opening to argue, before my stern look silenced any protests. Charlie followed suit before turning to address the room.

"It really was nice to meet you guys." Her smile was sincere as Lucie held the door open for us. Lucie gave them a quick 'we'll be back' as we filed into the hallway. Lucie took half of the tins Charlie carried, the walk to the guest parking lot short since it was right by Lucie's dorm.

Their conversation continued, the topics bouncing around from current happenings to stories from their youth. It was nice to see Lucie so lighthearted, her carefree laugh echoing through me. Her and Charlie really did have a special bond. *Sadie would fit in well with them,* I thought as I observed their interactions. *Charlie's pretty much a blend of Lucie and Sadie.* After loading the car with the tins, Lucie gave Charlie another hug. I said goodbye, giving a small wave before curling my fingers around Lucie's hand. We turned away from the parking lot, intent to have a relaxing afternoon.

November 12th
Monday Morning
Lucienne

My feet hit the floor, slowing into a walk as we finished our pre-training workout. I took the small towel I had been bringing with me for training and wiped the moisture beading up on my forehead. It was just me, Cam, and Nik today in the gym because Dante and Hudson had their early morning Statistics class. My twins were assisting with set up for a class because they had gotten in trouble with their energy manipulation professor for "horsing around" on Thursday so they couldn't join us. I followed Nik to the mats and noticed Cam break off toward the locked storage cabinets where weapons and practice props were held. He unlocked one of the cabinets and reached in. When he pulled back and relocked the door, he was holding a wooden knife and rubber gun. *Oh god.* Regardless of them being obvious fakes, my stomach lurched uncontrollably.

"We are working with weapon defense today, Babe." Nik dragged my attention from staring at the weapons, his rough words filtering through the air. I nodded meekly, still feeling several memories creeping up.

"You all right, Doll?" Cam's eyebrows furrowed as he looked at me, and I felt my skin paling, becoming clammy. Goosebumps creeped across my arms and legs with the memory of staring down the barrel of Noah's handgun, hearing the hammer click as it was pulled back. I shook my head sharply, as if shaking my head enough would dislodge the memories.

"Uh, kind of," I stuttered, rubbing my hands up and down my face a few times, wiping away the clamminess of my skin. I knew there was no way they'd let me get away without answering, so I tried to get it over with as quickly as possible. "Just reliving a few of the times Noah held me at gunpoint, but I'm good now, so let's get going." Nik and Cam went still as stone, hands curled into fists as their eyes burned.

"He did what?" Nik's rough voice trembled with fury, ending his question with his jaw crushed tightly together. The gravel in his voice grew thick in his anger.

"Yeah, like I said when I first told you guys about him, he

did a lot, and I only gave the basics." I shrugged, not making eye contact with either of them.

"I know you brought this up last Tuesday, but the, uh, sexual assault," Cam stuttered out, struggling with bringing it up. It was the first time I had ever seen him uncomfortable during a conversation. *He is always so articulate and well-spoken.*

"Yeah, he didn't always force it. But even when he didn't, I knew my choices were to give it up or deal with the beat down that came with disobeying," I murmured, worrying my lower lip between my teeth and feeling the flashbacks clawing to the front of my mind. "Can we get on with fight training, please? I don't want to think about any of that." Bouncing from one foot to the other on the balls of my feet, I worked to keep my muscles loose. They didn't appear happy with my abrupt change of topic, but neither argued. I knew they would be there for me when I was ready to discuss it. They didn't have to say it. I could see it in their eyes and feel it in their soothing touches and warm embraces. They cared about me—all of me—even the broken pieces.

After almost an hour, I was able to keep my flashbacks and anxiety away by reminding myself that Noah was a very real threat. *I can protect myself. I can save myself.* Sweat dripped into my eyes as I disarmed Nik, the rubber gun steady in my hand despite the tremble in my sore arms and tightness in my chest from my injury. While the wound was still healing, it was taking longer and longer with each practice we had.

Cam clapped once, calling an end to the training. "All right, I think that's enough for now on those, you've gotten good at disarming. We'll work on it again tomorrow after classes."

I handed off the gun to Cam, and Nik's bare chest brushed my arm slightly as he gave Cam the discarded wooden knife we'd used earlier. I couldn't help but stare at Nik's chiseled torso and the drop of sweat that slid down his cut abs and onto his sweats. *Fuck.* A throb of desire shot through me as I looked up at him and saw his glassy eyes boring into me. The corner of his lips turned up as he shifted closer and the air crackled with his power. His fingers lightly gripped my chin, keeping my head tilted up toward him, his thumb brushing against my lower lip. Power and magic sparked and tingled across my skin with each pass. A shiver slipped down my spine at the pure sinfulness he was exuding, the thick sexual tension in the air bringing a throb to my core.

"I want to spread you out on this mat, Babe. I want to see all of that porcelain skin on display for me." His words were heated as he whispered them into my ear, and I found myself leaning into his chest the more he talked. My breathing was hard, my heart thumping erratically in my chest as heat poured through me. I turned my head to look at him, my lips brushing his strong jaw. Desire built within me at the touch, and I found myself unsure of what to say. Instead, I nipped him lightly on the jaw causing a sharp intake of breath.

"Keep that up, Doll, and you'll see exactly what we want to do to you." Cam's voice was soft as he stepped up behind me, his warm torso pressing against my back. Two pale hands curled around my hips tightly. A kiss pressed on my neck, two sharp points lightly grazing my skin as Cam's glasses brushed against my hair. Nik closed the space between us, cupped the back of my head, and pressed his lips to mine. *Holy shit*, my jumbled brain murmured, *I can't believe this is happening.* I moaned quietly when Cam's cock pressed into the curve of my ass while Nik was hard against my hip. Nik sucked in my lip and bit down, not hard enough to hurt but with a teasing sting that had me arching my back so that my ass rubbed against Cam while my breasts pressed against Nik's naked chest. This wasn't like being with the twins, when it was just for fun, this was us in a relationship. They were a unit, and they were willing to have me join them. I wanted to panic, but at the same time I wanted to give a girly squeal. Shoving away those thoughts, I focused on feeling their hands and mouths on me, losing myself in the sensations.

"My, my, my," a husky voice called out, "look at you, Love, sexy as can be between two equally hot guys."

I chuckled, recognizing the voice and nickname. Logan and Landon were heading our way from the door, satisfied smirks curling their lips.

"Cockblocker," Nik growled at them, the hint of laughter in his voice the only thing giving away that he wasn't truly upset. "We were busy here, thank you very much." They both rolled their eyes.

"Clearly not practicing what you should have been," Landon teased. "How has it been going? You know, other than interrupting your chance at sexy times." Cam gave me a quick kiss on my hair and stepped back to grab his stuff off to the side of the mat. Nik's hand slid from around my neck and fell to his side as he shook his head, a small chuckle bubbling out as he started to wipe down the equipment.

"Not bad. Lucie did well on her weapon's defense." Cam handed the straps of my messenger bag to me before slipping his backpack onto his shoulders.

"And your injury, Lemon Drop, is it bothering you at all?" Logan asked, eyeing my injury laden chest.

"It stings a little but nothing too bad. At least not while I have my mind occupied with other things..."

"Like Nik and Cam's naked bodies?" Landon interrupted as Cam snickered. I couldn't fight the blush that I felt; luckily my face was already red from the workout. We put all the equipment away and headed out into the quad, but all I could focus on was needing a cold shower.

Ugh.

10

November 14th
Wednesday Evening
Lucienne

The quad was quiet and empty as my guys and I strolled down the walkway. The air was misty and cold, and a small shiver slid down my spine as I pulled my hat down over my ears. The only noise around us was Dante and the twins discussing the upcoming Kohl game. I jogged the last bit of the walkway when the door came into view, their laughs echoing against the stone of the building as I left them behind. *So cold.* I punched in the access code as quickly as my frozen fingers would allow and rushed inside leaving the guys locked out. *They know the code,* I reasoned. Ripping my wet gloves off my hands, I blew into them. The warm air of the building common and entertainment room seeping into my bones.

"Jeez, way to leave us out there, Babe." Nik poked me in the side playfully when they had finally filed into the building.

"I'm freezing, not my fault you weren't right behind me. Let's go, I need to change into sweats and bury myself in blankets." I shivered in my wool coat. When we reached the second floor, I had finally started to warm, and the shivering subsided. I slid the key into my door knowing Sadie was working late on a project for one of her classes in the library. I pushed the door open with my hip and slid my hand against the wall to the light switch. The door hit something on the other side with a thunk bringing me to a stop. Confused, I flipped the light to see what blocked the entrance. My lungs seized as my eyes darted around the area of the room I could see through the crack in the door. The shared living room darkened and tilted, my legs giving out. Strong arms slid around my back as everything went black.

Dante

Lucie's brows drew down as the door stopped with a thud, and she reached in and flipped the light. Moments of silence passed as Lucie stood unmoving before suddenly falling sideways. Nik caught her before she made contact with the carpeted hallway floor, cradling her to his chest and stepping out of the way from the door. Logan shouldered the door open, knocking whatever was blocking it out of the way with a loud crash. Logan muttered a curse as he eyeballed the room. Landon whipped his phone out of his jeans pocket and dialed a number while peering over his twin's shoulder at Lucie's dorm. My adrenaline ratcheted up as I saw the tension in their shoulders and fisted hands, black claws lengthening at the tips of their fingers. I slipped around the twins and into Firecracker's dorm.

I walked in on a complete disaster—chairs overturned with ripped cushions, the stuffing strewn about the floor.

The TV was smashed and lying screen up, the doors open to all of the rooms. The bathroom was in ruin with a destroyed shower curtain and bottles everywhere. Sadie's room seemed relatively unscathed with only her bed overturned. Her art supplies and in progress pieces were untouched. *Thank goodness.* I wove around the chaos and headed toward Lucie's room. *Please don't be too bad,* I internally pleaded.

Seeing the state her room was in had bile rising up the back of my throat. Everything was cut or torn, furniture flipped and broken, and there were several dents and holes in the walls and door. I stared hard at the holes next to me trying to identify what caused them. *There aren't any objects by the wall*, I thought, glancing around. After a few seconds I put my fist up to one of the chest height holes, and it fit perfectly. The holes toward the bottom of the wall lined up well with my boots. *He literally beat the shit out of her room.* I shook my head, the knot in my stomach growing with each thought of what would have happened to our Lucie had she been here alone.

In one last sweep of her room I noticed an envelope on top of the upturned mattress. I shifted a few things out of the way and plucked it off the top. I strode into the living room where the twins and Hudson were righting the loveseat and cushions. Lucie was still unconscious in Nik's arms, Cam in front of him rubbing a hand across her forehead and brushing her hair out of her eyes. A thunderclap sounded in the hallway, and Dean Renaud stepped up to the door. His light blue eyes took in the destruction of the dorm. While he continued his perusal, assuming Landon filled him in on the details when he had called, I turned my attention back to the envelope.

I flipped it around and pulled open the seal. As I suspected, another stack of photos peeked through. I tilted the envelope, the pictures sliding into my palm. They were of Cam, Nik, and Lucie during training earlier in the week. It started with their warmups, into the weapons defense, and several were of Lucie sandwiched between Nik and Cam getting hot and heavy. The last few were all of them talking with Logan and Landon. There was one picture out of the stack that didn't match the rest. This one was of a younger Lucie whose beautiful face and body were covered in harsh bruises and cuts while blood splattered on her sickly pale skin. This one was the only one that had writing on it. *"Babygirl, you know what happens when you act like a slut."*

I couldn't look at them anymore, so I walked over to Dean Renaud and shoved the stack into his hands. Lucie was slowly stirring, her eyes squinting against the overhead lighting. *Focus on something else,* I commanded myself. I went over to where Nik was setting Lucie down from where she had been cradled in his arms. She leaned into him with Cam supporting her other side, her legs trembling as she finally shifted to put her weight on them.

"How are you feeling?" I took one of her hands and rubbed her soft skin with my thumb hoping to comfort her. She coughed lightly, eyes darting around the room fully taking in the state of her stuff.

"Peachy." Her voice was flat and tired, her lips turning down into a harsh frown. "Please tell me Sadie's stuff is untouched? I couldn't stand it her art was damaged because of me." *Oh, hell no.* My nerves frayed with that last statement.

"Her stuff is fine, but don't you dare think this is your fault, Lucie." My gaze bore into hers, her sad deep sapphire eyes staring back. "This is solely because of Noah and no one else. You did not destroy the room, you did not force him to come here, and you didn't make him into the fucking psycho he clearly is. You are not to blame, understand?" My voice was hard, willing her to listen and doing its best to hide the turmoil that stirred inside me. Her head tilted up and then back down slowly in a tiny nod. I leaned forward, unable to help myself, and placed a soft kiss to her equally soft lips, about to deepen it until Dean Renaud's cough broke up the moment.

"All right, Lucie, I'm going to have you move into your other room. I'll also have Sadie placed in a room in Administration Housing with two security guards, so she'll be under watch in case Noah tries to go after her, but based on the destruction in here it seems it was mostly targeted toward you." His words were clipped in anger as he walked out of Lucie's room. Turning to look at me and my brothers, he continued, "One of you will continue to stay with her at all times. Her secondary room is smaller, and I'm not sure all of you will be able to stay the night, so I'll give you a couple of rooms in the Administration Housing. That way you're right next door instead of across campus until this situation is dealt with. I'll let you sort out the details."

"What about your archery competition this weekend?" Lucie murmured, her eyes fixed on Nik.

Dean Renaud's hand raked through his hair, his lips thinning the longer he thought. "Is it a local competition?"

Nik nodded, his face stone hard, but the whipping crackle of his power gave away how angry he was.

"Unfortunately, I don't think it would be wise for you to go, Lucie. Campus security only extends so far, and while I know you wouldn't be alone, I'm not sure it would be safe for you." The dean's face flashed quickly in an expression I couldn't place when Lucie's face fell, but it smoothed into his professional demeanor before I could identify what it

was. "I'm sorry, Lucie." She dipped her head in acknowl-
edgement before he continued with her safety plan. "I'll be
having Bill and Troy on duty rotations with the Head of
Security, Mr. Hanson, consistently, so you won't be without a
guard. No one other than us, Muriel, and your security
detail know of your secondary room, and the library security system was upgraded yesterday. You still have the
majority of your things there, correct?" She nodded silently.
"Very good, Mr. Hanson will be taking the morning shift,
Bill with the overnight shift, and Troy during the afternoon
and evening shift. Go on down, Troy is waiting in the hallway. I will handle this."

"Wait." She looked up at him seemingly defeated. "What
about my trip to Fae? That's coming up soon too." A small
bubble of anger popped inside me. Noah was ruining her
life again, and he hadn't even laid a hand on her.

"That should be doable what with Portal Patrol and
Gerry going along. I'll forward the picture Charlie gave us
and any other pertinent information to their head office so
they will know to be on the lookout. It would also be best
not to discuss any trips, events, or gatherings that you might
be attending while outside my office or your rooms. We
don't know for certain how he is getting his information,
and there are eyes and ears everywhere. The less he knows,
the safer you are." Dean Renaud's hand fell lightly onto her
shoulder and with a small, encouraging squeeze he turned
and exited her room.

We filed out into the hallway, Troy falling into formation
behind us when we reached the lobby. All of us were quiet,
lost in thought. I could tell based on our body language that
we were all shaken up about how real Noah's threat was. *Not
that we didn't know it before, but this time he got too close to our
Lucie.* I kept thinking as we made our way back to the

library. Regardless if Dean Renaud thought the room was too small for all of us, I knew none of us would leave her side tonight. Lucie went through her nighttime routine as the guys situated extra pillows and blankets around the room. After emerging from the bathroom in pajamas, she gave each of us a quick kiss and a mumbled good night before sinking into a deep sleep, the events of the day catching up to her. There was a soft pop in my head of the mind link Hudson always kept open for times when we needed to discuss private matters.

"I'm going to kill him." Landon's voice filled my mind, his rage palpable in the biting words as he curled his hands into white knuckled fists.

"I second the urge, but our main focus needs to be keeping Lucie safe," I commanded.

"She'd be safe if he was dead." Landon's eyes flashed black as he stared at me from his seated position in the corner near her dresser, his horns curled out of his messy hair.

"We'll deal with how to handle Noah when we get him. For now, we need to figure out how to make sure Lucie is safe and as happy as she can be right now." My tone conveyed that the previous conversation was over.

"Make sure at least one of us is with her at all times," Cam tossed out, joining in the mental conversation.

"Having security nearby at all times will help," Logan added. The longer we talked the more Landon's horns and blackened eyes changed back into his human form.

"If it seems she's struggling too much, as a last resort I can try and soothe some of the fear and stress," Hudson suggested. His empathy not only gave him access to feel others' emotions, but he had another complementary power that allowed him to alter them. It was typically considered rude and was highly discouraged, but we couldn't rule out his power to

help if the situation was bad enough and Lucie gave her permission. I nodded in agreement, thinking through anything else we could do.

"*I could get in contact with...*" Logan started, before I cut him off.

"*No, absolutely not. You got out, and I'm not going to let you go back to that. Lucie's safety is a priority, but I'm not willing to risk you turning to any of them in the process,*" I bit out, my voice hard and cold as I addressed him. I got why he would suggest it, the twins knew a lot of people in not so great places, but their welfare was my responsibility, as was Lucie's. *I will keep my family safe,* I chanted internally, not allowing the words to filter into the telepathic link Hudson had opened.

"*I second Dante. As easy as it would be to turn to them, your safety could be at risk. I'll see if I can get in touch with anyone who can trace or track him,*" Cam added into the conversation, his eyes darting to Nik who nodded in agreement.

"*All right, Cam and Nik, see if you can find someone. Hudson, monitor her emotional state. We can't let it get too bad. If it seems like it's taking a turn for the worst, we'll talk with her. Logan, Landon, and I will keep an eye out for him or any suspicious students. Got it?*" Mental hums of agreement and physical nods went up around the group showing we were all on the same page. I nodded before we all started to shuffle into our designated sleeping areas. My arm curled around Lucie's tiny waist, her body heat radiating against me as she curled sleepily into Hudson on the other side of her. No matter how hard I tried to fall asleep, I stared at the pale olive walls until the early hours of the morning, *too close* echoing through my thoughts.

11

November 15ᵗʰ
Thursday Afternoon
Lucienne

The library buzzed with quiet activity; students filled all of the study tables and a majority of the leather chairs. I was seated next to Sadie with Benji across the table from her. Both were buried in their classwork, neither speaking after starting their assignments. Despite their protests against me being out of their immediate eyesight, the guys were tucked away in the library office with Alex discussing what to do with the Noah situation.

My attention darted around the room at the thought of Noah. I didn't spy his messy dark hair, but I spotted Troy. He wasn't in his uniform as he reclined in a leather chair right by our table, his gaze flittering around the room every few seconds. Feeling a quick burst of comfort at his presence, I tried to get back to some semblance of work. Books scattered around the shiny wood surface in front of us as I focused on my near blank notebook page, the topic for my persuasive speech the only words on the paper.

Do you think there should be more separation between supernaturals and humans within society? Why or why not?

My brain was short circuiting the longer I stared at the words, irritable and cranky with lack of sleep. *How the hell should I know? I barely know anything about what it's like being a supe within a human-dominated community.*

A bag dropped with a thud at the end of the table, and Elijah's fire red hair came into view. The waves of his hair flipped over his pale and freckled forehead. Gabe, in his typical plaid shirt, showed up next to me at the end of the table, sitting down softly into his chair whereas Elijah flopped like a dead fish into his before slumping over to his bag.

"Hey," Gabe greeted the table politely, his bright white teeth shining against his darker complexion. I flashed a friendly smile to both of them when Elijah sat up straight, a heavy textbook and notebook in his hands.

"Hey, guys, how's it going?" Benji looked up from his notes, his pen falling to the wayside. Sadie's head also popped up, her purple frames tilting crookedly on her nose at the sharp movement.

"Not bad," Gabe started softly.

"Speak for yourself, I have so much damn homework," Elijah interrupted, his pitiful groan making me chuckle.

"Maybe you should have worked on it throughout the week so it wouldn't be as bad," Sadie lectured, her eyebrow raising as she teased the ginger sitting across from me. I sat silently, listening to their back and forth banter, a smile permanently affixed to my face at their easygoing teasing. I forced my attention away from their conversation in an attempt to concentrate on my debate speech. At some point though, I must have spaced off because Elijah's hand waved in front of my face over the lined paper I was staring at blankly. I snapped my head up and looked at him, and a smirk teased his lips as he attempted to hide his laughter.

"So," he started, his forearms coming to rest on the table, his book unopened in front of him. "The other day I saw that friend of yours who punched Claire in the face. Why was she here?" Despite his head tilted toward the table, I saw Gabe peeking at me through his lashes waiting for my answer. Sadie and Benji were back in their homework world not listening to anything happening at the table.

"She just stopped by to pick up cookie tins for my mom," I fibbed, not wanting to get into the background of the real reason. "Why?" My eyebrow raised, my lip curling on its own accord as I leaned forward mimicking Elijah's position. "Do you *want* to see her?" A blush flamed on his cheeks almost as red as his hair, and he scoffed lightly playing off my question.

"Good one, Lucie. Nah, I was just wondering." He waved a hand in the air looking anywhere but at me. *Oh, he's got it bad,* I thought, turning to look at Gabe whose eyes had lit up at the topic of my human best friend.

"What about you, Gabe? Do you want to see her?" I ignored Elijah who was shooting looks at his best friend trying to keep him from talking. Taking a deep breath, Gabe answered.

"Yes, I wasn't sure if she liked us or if she would be open to something like you and your guys have." His words were soft, not wanting to pull attention from those around us. I gave a large triumphant smile to him and Elijah.

"Good thing for you guys," I taunted quietly, my dimples

strong on my cheeks with how wide my smile was. "She wants to see you two as well. She gave me permission to give her number to you two if you wanted it." They both went slack jawed as they stared, stunned by my news. I held out a hand waiting for one of their phones. Elijah recovered first, unlocking his phone and handing it over for me to program in Charlie's information before doing the same with Gabe's.

"Thanks, Lucie." Elijah's voice was filled with sincerity as his fingers flew over his phone screen. Gabe echoed a similar sentiment.

"No problem, now let's actually get homework done," I chided Elijah in particular since he hadn't done any work in the last half hour he had been sitting there. His groan had me chuckling, but internally I agreed as I stared at my topic. *Ugh is right.*

November 16th
Friday Morning
Lucienne

My sneaker clad foot hit a root that was sticking out of the moist dirt. I stumbled, wasting precious time, before I righted myself and continued my sprint, the sound of steps closing in behind me on the trail. I pushed harder, my breath coming in hard puffs of clouds in front of me. Cold, rough fingers brushed against the back of my neck...

My alarm sounded startling me from my vividly real nightmare. Arms shaking with adrenaline, I pushed to a sitting position, my heart racing in my chest. Hudson's warm arm slid down my side onto my lap as I moved. He didn't stir despite the continued dinging of my alarm. I shut it off and gently moved his arm off my hip and onto the spot I had just vacated. I slipped silently into the bathroom, immediately brushing my teeth and turning the shower knob; the sound of the running water filled the air.

Steam from the shower billowed out of the bathroom as I collected my clothes for the day. I quietly pulled the bathroom door closed and undressed, removing my bandage so I could check out how my wound looked before the mirror fogged up. I was relieved to see that it was healing nicely despite all the exercise I'd been doing. I probably wouldn't need the bandage anymore since it no longer bled, but I wanted to check with Cam to be sure. The bruise was dark in the center, but the edges had started to shift from the deep blues and purples to more of an ugly yellowy brown. The scabs on the punctures were starting to itch more and more, and I had to force myself not to rub them throughout the day. My focus turned to my face; the bruised cheek had healed quicker than my chest since the bruising had been less severe and was almost completely gone. The checking on the progress of my healing complete, I stepped into the shower.

The hot water chased away the last of the effects from the nightmare. I pushed through washing my hair and the rest of my routine, fighting the urge to stand under the hot stream for the remainder of the morning. *Have to get ready for work,* I reminded myself. I turned the fogged-up handle to off and slipped the towel off the bar. As I rubbed the soft material against my skin I heard Hudson rustling around in the bed. I was one step out of the tub when a light knock sounded on the door.

"Come in," I shot out, pulling my second foot out of the tub making sure the towel was secure around my chest.

The door squeaked open, and a sleepy-eyed Hudson poked his head into the bathroom. His black hair was sticking out in the most adorable way, his honey-colored chest barely visible through the crack of the door. His eyes zeroed in on the striped towel that I had tightly wrapped around me.

"Good morning, sunshine." I leaned over and pressed a quick kiss on his cheek, but he was still staring at the towel. *Clearly not a morning person.* I chuckled at his dumbfounded expression. The kiss seemed to jolt him out of his stupor.

"Good morning, Princess, when did you get up?" The usual warmth of his voice was thick with exhaustion. He pushed the bathroom door open the rest of the way and stepped into the quickly dispersing steam cloud.

"About twenty minutes ago. You were still passed out, and I didn't want to wake you. I only got up so early so we both had time to shower." I spritzed my leave in conditioner onto my hair and ran a brush through the long strands. Hudson reached behind the shower curtain and turned the shower back on. The steam started to build again as he stretched up toward the ceiling, his back popping. I stored my brush back in the medicine cabinet and turned to face Hudson. A sense of peace filled me at the normality of our morning routine.

This is what normal is like. A bubble of hope filled my chest chasing away the darkness that had seeped in the last few weeks of the fucked up game of cat and mouse Noah had been playing. *Is it too early to love someone?* I immediately pushed the thought down. *You haven't even been with them for two weeks yet,* I chided myself. I placed a hand on Hudson's warm chest, and he brought his lips to mine in a soft kiss before I headed back into my bedroom, pulling the door closed behind me.

A half hour later, Hudson and I exited my room into the back hallway meeting the Head of Security outside the

"Employees Only" door. I gave a small nod and a quiet 'good morning' that still seemed to echo around us. The library was fairly empty in the early morning since most people were still sleeping. I sat behind the desk and signed into the system, taking over for Muriel who was shuffling around in her office. Hudson plopped onto the stool next to me and flipped through one of the books for his classes. Once he reached the page he needed, he hunched over his notebook and started taking notes. My phone vibrated, and panic seized my chest as I pulled my phone out of my pocket, only easing when it read Cam instead of Unknown Number.

"Hey, Cam," I greeted softly, not wanting to disturb the couple of students spread throughout the study tables.

"Hey, Doll. We're grabbing coffee and breakfast from Coffeeology, what do you want?" The bustling in the background gave away that he and the rest of my guys were shuffling out the door.

"Just tell Em it's for me, she'll know what to get me," I responded. Turning to Hudson, I asked, "What do you want from Coffeeology?" After relaying his order, I hung up, ignoring the thirteen unread messages. The guys knew if they wanted to reach me to either call or contact whichever guy was with me. It had been odd last night having only one of them stay with me. Every night leading up to that they had all stayed, but sleeping cramped around my small room was too difficult, so they finally gave in and took the temporary rooms in the Administration Housing building.

"Lucie, hon." Muriel's grey hair and wrinkled face poked out from the office door. I spun on my stool to look at her. "I have several rare books that need to be returned to the basement. Would you be able to take those for me? Stairs no longer get along with this frail old body." She chuckled as I rolled my eyes. She knew very well my thoughts on her "frail body." *She's one of the nimblest people I know.* I took the three books in their protective coverings from Muriel's age-spotted hands and squeezed around Hudson on his stool.

"Hudson, you want to come with?" I asked, pushing open the half door that separated the study area from behind the desk. He closed his textbook and slid it under the raised section of the counter.

"Where are we headed?" he whispered, peeking around my shoulder at the books.

"The basement." I turned down the aisle we took earlier out from my room.

"The library has a basement?" Eyebrows furrowed, his question was colored with surprise. My lips curled into a smile at his reaction. I nodded and looked over at him.

"Yes, it does, it's where all the rare items are kept. I overheard Muriel talking with several professors about a special exhibit for the spring semester. I'm sure I'll be getting roped into coming back from winter break early to help with set up since Muriel and I really are the only ones who can navigate down here," I explained, turning on the light switch at the stop of the stairs after we had slipped back through the "Employees Only" door. The first door wasn't locked, but the steel door at the bottom of the stairs was accessed with a key card. I swiped my employee badge and pushed the heavy door open with my shoulder after I heard the click. I flipped another switch illuminating the large, crowded basement. Display cases, locked storage cages, large bookshelves housing rare books in protective covers, like the ones I was returning, and randomly placed concrete columns cluttered the open space.

"Wow." Hudson's exclamation was breathy, jaw open, eyes wide as they darted around the basement. "This is amazing." He took more in-depth looks at the display cases trailing behind me as I wove in and out toward the bookshelf where these books called home. "Cam would love this, Nik too."

"Why's that?" I questioned, finally seeing the shelf in the sea of objects.

"Cam's aunt and uncle are historians, and they work fairly closely with Nik's parents who are archivists and curators for museums around the world." His explanation caused my eyebrows to raise.

"What about Cam's parents? Are they in the same field?" I slid the first book into its slot. Silence greeted me, and when Hudson didn't respond I turned to see him rubbing the back of his neck as he stared at the ground. "What?" Worry wormed into my chest at his expression.

"Cam's parents were killed when he was little; his mom's brother and his wife adopted Cam after it happened. He was five, so most of his memories are of growing up with them. He grew to love history like his aunt and uncle." My heart felt like it had been ripped from my chest. I had completely forgotten when Cam had talked about his parents. I squeezed my eyes shut to will away the tears that built. I thought it was bad not knowing who my parents were, but I couldn't imagine what it was like having them and then losing them. *I would be absolutely devastated if I lost my mom.* I didn't know what else to say as I slid the second book onto the shelf, so I remained quiet. "Can I ask you something completely random that has nothing to do with all of that?" His voice was quiet, and he avoided looking at me when I turned to him clutching the third volume to my chest.

He's so nervous. "Of course, Hudson." I made sure my voice was friendly to ease the tension in his shoulders. My eyebrows drew low over my eyes as I watched him fiddle with his jacket zipper.

"I know we're all dating and everything, but I was wondering," he hesitated, shuffling from one foot to the other. "Well, I was thinking we never did get to go on that date I wished for, and I was wondering if maybe you would want to go on a date with me on Sunday? I know you have your trip to Fae tomorrow, so I was thinking we could go get some dinner and spend some time together." He sped through the rest of his statement in a hurried string of words.

"I would love to go on a date with you." I put the final book away and strolled back over to him. My arms wrapped around his waist, and his circled behind my shoulders. The worry that had been etched on his face melted into a wide smile. He pressed a soft kiss to my forehead, a happy sigh falling from my lips as that feeling of love warmed me. I pulled back to look up at him. "Let's head upstairs. I'm sure the rest of the guys are here with coffee, and I'm in need of my morning lifeline." His baritone laugh echoed throughout the basement, our fingers linked as we made our way back up to the main level.

November 16th
Friday Evening
Lucienne

The crowds were loud in the stands as cheers and yells sounded from the sea of students. The game was going to be starting its fourth quarter shortly, and while I was bundled up and squished between Sadie and Benji, my guys behind us while Elijah and Gabe were in front of us, I was still freezing. I hopped in line at the concession stand with Austin who was grabbing a snack for him and Benji to share. I had seen Troy on and off throughout the game, but right now he was nowhere to be found, lost in the bustling group of students going to and from the stands to the concessions and bathrooms. Cam had broken off from me and Austin to run to the bathroom, with plans to rejoin us in line. Thankfully the line wasn't long with only two people in front of us, and it was moving quickly. I stepped up and ordered my extra-large hot chocolate—*never can have too much hot chocolate,* I hummed to myself—and paid. I took my drink and headed to wait behind the lines for Austin and Cam.

While blowing off the steam I felt the hairs on the back of my neck stand on end, and a chill that had nothing to do with the weather slid down my spine. My eyes flitted around the crowd of students seeing nothing but nameless faces. I was about to stop my perusal when I saw *him* leaning against the fence near the entrance. Noah's cold, deep brown eyes locked on me, his lips curled into a cruel smirk. Blood thudded through my ears as he pushed his weight off the fence and took a step toward me, causing me to drop my full cup of hot chocolate. A warm glove rubbed my lower back, scaring me away from our staredown. A startled yelp ripped from my lips as I jumped away from the hand. Cam pulled his hand back, palms facing me with open hands.

"It's just me, Doll." His hazel eyes scoured my face before his lips thinned into a tight line. "What's wrong? What happened?" he demanded.

"He's here, he was against the fence over there." I waved with a shaking hand toward the fence where he was no longer leaning. "He had just pushed off the fence when you came up." My voice was low, trembling with the amount of adrenaline pulsing through my system.

"Where's Troy?" Cam's head was whipping around us looking for my security detail. I shrugged my shoulders.

"I haven't seen him since I came up here. Austin was

waiting on his order when it happened," I explained. Troy finally moved back into view, and I pointed him out to Cam. Austin had walked up to us, and Cam whispered in his ear gesturing to me before he pulled back and headed toward Troy, leaving Austin to loop his arm through mine to lead me back to our seats. The rest of the game was spent in a haze of panic, unable to relax after having seen him so close to me. He had changed his style—outfit and hair—since the photo Charlie had given us, but those eyes, I'd know those eyes anywhere. I had stared into their cold depths too many times to ever forget them.

It had been easy, for the most part, to be ignorant to how close he actually was when I hadn't seen him, but that bliss came crashing down tonight, fear settling deep into my stomach. The guys closed ranks around me while we waited for the others. Alex and a large group of security guards had scoured the crowds as soon as Troy had alerted them to Noah's presence, but they didn't manage to find him in the crush of spectators.

When we finally got back to my room, I was a shivering mess. I couldn't get the image of Noah coming toward me out of my head. God only knows what would have happened if Cam hadn't shown up when he did. All I wanted to do was sleep for days, but I was terrified of what nightmare I would be sucked into if I did. I didn't even feel it when Logan helped me out of my wool coat, or when Landon sat me down and removed my boots. I couldn't stop shaking. I wanted to scream, I wanted to run, I wanted to crawl out of my skin. I felt so stupid for thinking that I would be strong enough to face him. He knew that I would cave. He had beat the submission into me. I felt Logan wipe tears I didn't know I was crying from my cheek.

"Lemon Drop, I know what you're thinking, but you're

wrong. You are brave; you are strong. You can't see it, but we can. You stayed when you could have run despite being scared." Logan's words were soft and reassuring, urging me to listen yet giving me a quiet moment to try and come back to myself and them.

"Love, I know you're scared. I know you think that you'll never escape him, but you did once, and you will again, and this time you have us. You're not alone. You'll never be alone again."

I looked at my twins. *So sweet, so caring.* I wanted so much to believe them, so I did. If only for tonight, I would believe. They laid me down between them, their warmth and soft breathing lulling me to sleep.

12

November 17th
Saturday Midday
Lucienne

I was seated next to Logan on the right hand side of the bus with Landon across the aisle, the window seat next to him empty. The greyhound bus had left campus a half hour ago toward the nearest portal to Fae. It was situated outside of Seattle to avoid major traffic from the city and was halfway between the large city and the campus. As we neared the portal, the bus pulled to the side and was boarded by a tall man. His long hair was pulled back into a braid showing off his pointed ears. He collected the roster of names and quickly walked the length of the bus. When he had verified we didn't have any stowaways, he disembarked and the bus was rolling again. Going through the portal was an odd sensation, like being wrapped in a blanket of static, light shocks running over my skin causing goosebumps to rise.

When we reached the other side, the cloudy sky had

transformed into a sunny day. The portal we used took us to the Spring Court, the grassy rolling hills spreading into the distance, budding trees and flowers randomly splashed through the greenery. The road was paved, but more rural with only two lanes, rather than the large interstates that dominated the human world. I watched countryside slowly turn into a small town. I remembered Professor Rasmussen explaining that Fae was a blend of historical aspects, such as smaller towns and villages with modern technology, but it was different to see in person. It was as if we were transported back in time.

The people around the main town center looked to be wearing peasant style clothing. Women were adorned with long skirts and tucked-in flowy blouses, some with leather tie vests around their chests. The men sported britches tucked into knee-high boots, loose shirts that were either under leather belts that held small leather pouches, or vests. There looked to be a market off the main street, different booths and stands holding fruits, vegetables, and a range of other food and goods. On closer inspection, not everyone was wearing peasant inspired clothing, some were in jeans and shirts, and there were a couple cars parked at the other end of the market. There were other modern touches as well including street lamps that held light bulbs instead of oil-fueled flames. We drove through the town without stopping, watching a few of the locals wave at the passing bus with cheery smiles.

On the outskirts of the town a stone building stood with a large set of wooden doors and a sign above it reading "Spirit's Tavern." One woman walked toward the door but stopped before going inside. She was shorter, with coppery ginger hair styled in a long bob. She turned her head and seemed to be talking to thin air. Her black leather pants and boots, as well as a loose top under a leather jacket, stood out in front of the historical face of the tavern. She turned and headed inside as the building moved out of view from my window.

After another forty-five minutes of driving through similar towns the bus finally pulled up to the main gate of the capital city, Frondescentia. I rested my head against Logan's shoulder as we went through the verification process with the gate guards. We had been briefed before we left that we would be taking smaller groups in rail cars through the city since larger vehicles weren't allowed due to the narrow cobblestone roads. We filed off the bus, my twins and me standing with Mr. Hanson, who had insisted that I call him Gerry.

We wouldn't be with anyone else per Alex's instructions. He had pulled me aside after the game yesterday and expressed his concerns that someone was working with Noah. Alex didn't think he'd be able to get as close as he had, especially after no evidence of someone picking the lock or forcing their way into our dorm, without help. I knew without a doubt it wasn't one of my guys, Sadie, or Benji, but I wasn't willing to risk doubting him. Alex had told me he was personally taking a look at any and all security guards, any mutual friends with other students on campus, or other potential issues. He also told me he had been in contact with the human police for not only the investigation but to also press charges for his previous domestic violence and the current charges of stalking and destruction of property.

My attention was brought back to Fae when Gerry started walking toward the streetcar. The rest of the students were splitting their attention between looking around them and staring at us. The personal security I've been sporting recently combined with all the rumors going around had drawn a large amount of attention to me through campus. *Ugh.* I slipped my hand in Landon's and took a few quick steps to catch up to him. I pushed the thought of being the center of the gossip mill out of my mind as I climbed into the car, with Logan close on my heels. The buildings passed by the open windows, moving from smaller, closely-packed houses to more shop fronts, and finally to the city center where taller buildings, the courthouse, the capitol building, and more extravagant homes littered the blocks.

The warm breeze and shining sun were a stark contrast to the cloudy, misty, cold weather of campus. I took off my cardigan and shoved it in my bag, leaving me in a pair of yellow skinny jeans, a dark blue blouse, and nude colored flats. My hair was tossed up in a messy bun like usual on the crown of my head. The twins were wearing their typical dark wash jeans, but instead of their coordinating graphic tees, they were sported white dress shirts which were buttoned and tucked into their jeans to show off their black belts, and then topped off with black ties. We had been told to dress nicely, but we were not required to wear formal wear. The twins had actually gelled their hair up and out of their faces in a very Nik hairstyle. I had been sneaking peeks at them all morning, unable to keep my eyes off their handsome faces and tanned forearms that were on display under the rolled-up sleeves. We got off at the Capitol when we reached the front of the building.

The outfits of the people moving up and down the steps around us were similar to the historical style from the smaller towns on the drive in—women in fancier dresses and men in higher end coats and pants and shined shoes. Some of the women had parasols or larger hats like what one would see at a horse race. We walked up the marble steps to the ornate doors, no one paying attention to us. *Probably because they get visitors fairly frequently,* I surmised as the twins pulled open a set of double doors for Gerry and me. I smiled and gave a small thanks when I walked by.

The lobby of the capitol building was bustling with different creatures, some appearing human, while there were also elves, giants, dwarves, and a few with wings. The clopping of footsteps and hushed conversations echoed off the marbled floor and walls. Marble was everywhere around the building including the columns and detailed ceiling, decorated in a foil filigree that was reminiscent of the Music and Arts building back on campus.

We were all going to meet in the lobby, and since we were the first ones there, the twins and I took a seat in one of the empty sitting areas off the front doors. After the rest of the students filtered in, Professor Rasmussen signaled for us to follow her. She went over the history of the building and the functions, hands waving around animatedly. I found myself taking in the details around me, her voice fading into the background the more I focused on the day to day goings on flitting around the lobby. I knew I shouldn't stare at the different creatures that were scattered around the room, but even though I'd grown up in a world where supes and humans coexisted, it was still a reality I couldn't wrap my head around. *I'm one of them.*

The group started toward what looked to be the main staircase, footsteps clopping on the smooth stone steps. The professor turned off the large hall through a similar set of ornate wooden doors to the front of the building. Large canvas portraits surrounded by golden frames adorned the walls. I dragged my eyes away from the very realistic faces as I headed into a room that seemed to be smaller than the lobby, but just as extravagant. A golden throne sat at the head of the room, and long benches faced the small dais, filling the majority of the space. Landon sank onto the bench near the far end, and I followed suit with his hand curled around mine. Gerry stood at the end of the row next to Landon, his hands tucked into his slacks as he eyed the room.

"All right class, I have a special surprise for you." Professor Rasmussen's voice bubbled with excitement, her eyes wild. "Queen Lily Attwell has agreed to meet with us."

Gasps, jaw drops, and wide-eyed stares met her statement, including my own. *The queen?* My fingers intertwined with Logan's, holding both of my twin's hands in mine as I processed what she had said. *Holy crap, the queen.* My brain blanked as a tall, lithe woman breezed into the room. Her tan skin and warm golden hair had a slight glow to them, but it was her green floral crown and wide smile that caught my attention. She was wearing a silk dress in a light cream, and her golden tan was warm against the light, shiny fabric. She sat on her throne, her back straight in regal elegance.

"Hello, students." Her voice was tinkling yet strong in the quiet room. "I'm so happy that you came to visit us here in the Spring Court. I do love seeing young faces come through, and I hope you are enjoying your trip so far." She looked around the room, her eyes bouncing from student to student until her light pastel green and golden streaked gaze met mine. Her eyes widened slightly, but her friendly demeanor slid back into place fast enough for me to question whether her reaction had even happened in the first place. "What are all of your names? Oh! What year of schooling are you on?" She clasped her hands in front of her, twinkling eyes sparked with excitement. Professor Rasmussen started the line of introductions when no student spoke up, inviting each of the students to stand and speak respectfully when it got to them. We were near the back. *So many names I won't remember,* I found myself thinking. Logan and Landon stood at the same time on either side of me.

"Logan Anson, freshman." He dipped his head as Landon introduced himself.

"Landon Anson, also freshman." He gave her a small smile before they both took their seats. *All right, you can do this.* My internal pep talk was not quite soothing my building anxiety, and my legs felt weak as I stood.

"Lucienne Envie, freshman," I answered, my voice wavering slightly as I nibbled on my lip when I was done. Her eyes were speculative, burning with curiosity before flicking to Gerry.

"Gerry Hanson, Head of Security at the university." He gave a slight bow to the queen. Her smile still on her face, the energy that shone through her made her look young despite the few wrinkles that crinkled around her eyes.

"Wonderful! Does anyone have any questions?" She called on a girl on the other end of the benches, the questions and answers flowing between the queen and the students after that initial volunteer. I tried to focus on what was being said, but exhaustion weighed on me heavily. *Don't fall asleep.*

Twenty minutes later, Professor Rasmussen thanked Queen Lily before leading the students out into the hallway to view the paintings. I stood with my twins and Gerry, waiting for the rest of the class to go ahead of us so we could avoid the gossip-hungry eyes that had been following me since the dance. Landon's thumb rubbed over my knuckles softly, the small gesture warming my chest. *I'm not alone.* I took a deep breath before eyeing the paintings.

"Love," Logan called back softly, having moved a few

paintings over. "Come look at this." It didn't escape my notice that multiple students looked at the painting then looked to me with raised brows or slight frowns. My breath and calm whooshed from me when I looked at the painting. *That can't be...*

"Wow, Lemon Drop." Landon's voice was filled with awe as he stared at the portrait. A woman smiled down at us, her pale skin wrinkle-free. Her light brown-blonde hair held a slight curl, pulled in front of her right shoulder. Dark blue eyes sparkled even in the painting, but what caught my gaze was around her neck. A gold medallion with a fleur de lis in the middle.

"She looks just like you." Logan's voice matched his brother's, his gaze bouncing between me and the woman. I felt my heart drop from my chest painfully. *Is she my... Is she family?* I looked down the gold plate under the portrait. *Mireille Bonheur, 1940 -*

"She's still alive?" I found myself asking quietly. Wrapped up in staring at the painting, I didn't notice the class had filtered farther down the hallway.

"No one knows where she is," a tinkling voice came from behind me. I let out a startled yelp as I whipped around, my hands coming up to guard position until I realized I came face to face with the queen. *Holy cannoli.* I dropped my hands as quickly as they had gone up and bowed my head.

"Your Majesty." I continued to stare at her shoes. *What the hell does one do when face to face with royalty?*

"You don't have to bow." Her tanned hand came to rest on my arm, and I think my brain fizzled out of commission as my gaze raised to meet hers. "Mir is a close friend of mine, and she's quite the famous woman around here." Her eyes held the tiniest glint of something I couldn't place as she shifted to stand beside me, and Logan moved to stand with Landon on my left. "On the day of my coronation she came in during the celebration and materialized a full ballroom of living, animated plants that danced to a song she had commissioned for me." Her voice filled with wistfulness.

"How did she do that?" I asked quietly, staring into the deep sapphire eyes of a missing woman.

"Her wish token. She was able to conjure such wonderful treats with her coin. She's one of the most famous Djinn, but she's been missing for almost two decades." Her sorrow was palpable in the quiet hall.

"She's a Djinn?" I whipped my head to the queen forgetting momentarily that she was royalty and I was, well, a nobody.

"Well, yes." Her voice was hesitant as she eyed me. "I thought she was your grandmother or great grandmother." I felt my heart squeeze painfully at her thought.

"I was adopted as a baby, and I don't know who my family is." I fiddled with my necklace chain, my eyes on the coin in the portrait. "Is this her token?" The cold coin settled into my palm as I held it out for her to examine.

"Yes, it is." She smiled down at the coin before looking at me. "You may not know who your family is in its entirety, but you have at least one person," she said warmly as her right hand waved out toward the painting. "I will let the Dean know if I hear anything from her or find out what happened to her if you would like." The portrait wavered through unshed tears as I launched myself into her arms, squeezing her tightly around the waist.

"Thank you, thank you, thank you," I mumbled, a sob breaking through my words. The emotional rollercoaster of the last few weeks tumbled out with my tears. Her warm arms wrapped around me, a hand rubbing up and down my back gently as I continued to cry.

"It's all right, Love, everything will be all right. You're safe," Logan and Landon both cooed softly, their husky words comforting me. "We'll keep you safe." I pulled back when I finally realized what I was doing.

"Oh my god, I'm so sorry," I stammered, my hand covering my mouth when I saw a water stain on her silky dress. "I've had a really, *really* hard time the last few weeks, and I think it finally caught up with me," I rushed to explain, embarrassment flooding my cheeks.

"It's all right, little one." Her hand resting on my shoulder drew my eyes up to the pastel green irises laced with golden shimmering streaks that stared down at me. "One does not fully live if one does not feel. It is what separates those who merely exist and those who truly thrive." Her heartfelt words radiated through me down to my very bones, as if she was my mentor and not a queen. I nodded slightly, a loose strand of blonde hair falling into my eyes before I tucked it behind my ear.

"Thank you." I bent my head forward, grateful for her willingness to help me. Professor Rasmussen's voice broke through the moment, calling us back to the group at the end of the hall. Students stared shamelessly as I stepped back from the queen. *Great.*

"Of course, Lucienne, I look forward to seeing you in the future." She patted my shoulder gently before she turned and walked back into the throne room. I inhaled a shaky breath as I wiped my eyes, and Landon and Logan took up their usual positions on either side of me.

"Look at you, Lemon Drop, making friends with a Fae Queen." Landon's tone was teasing, his arm wrapping warmly around my shoulders with a gentle squeeze. A slightly hysterical laugh bubbled up through me, echoing against the marble and mixing with the increasing volume of my fellow students' conversations. The rest of the trip passed with no more bouts of uncontrollable crying or thoughts of Noah, my mind focused solely on Mireille Bonheur and who she was to me.

13

November 18th
Sunday Morning
Lucienne

I eyed the outfit Sadie had picked out for me; a slinky navy blouse, a black pair of skinny jeans, my cream chunky knit cardigan sweater, and a simple pair of cream colored heels. My heart stuttered in my chest as I thought about going on an actual date for the first time in years. Sadie had taken what had been coined 'Lucie Duty' this morning after I had asked her if she'd help me get ready for my date. *I don't think I can do this.* My stomach turned with a surge of nerves.

"All right, girl, take a seat." She waved her hand at the wooden chair she had dragged in from the main library. I sank into the hard seat and focused on my breathing. "Anything in particular you'd like me to do?" I shook my head, my hair shifting on the back of the plushy robe I was wearing. "I think since you have your hair up most of the time we should leave it down, or mostly down." Her brightly painted fingernails peeked out between the blonde strands as she ran her fingers through my hair. I nodded again, willing to let her do as she wanted.

She spent the next half hour curling large, loose curls, shortening my hair up to the middle of my back. She worked quietly, focusing solely on my hair, and my music filled the silence. I didn't have a mirror in front of me, so her moving my hair from my face was the only indication she was styling it.

"I'm so excited! Now time for your makeup." Sadie clapped her hands sharply after she slid in yet another bobby pin. I tried to channel some of her excitement, but I was filled with too much anxiety. *What if this goes terribly? I don't know how to even act on a date! What if he doesn't want to be with me after this? What if Noah shows up?* Fears filtered through my head at a dizzying speed. My breathing started to pick up, eyes tunneling.

"Lucie." Warm hands cupped my face, bringing me back to the moment. Sadie's blue hair was pulled back out of her face, her purple glasses winking in the lamp lighting. "What's going on in that head of yours?" I took a deep breath, and her hands dropped from my face.

"I'm nervous," I mumbled, my finger worrying my lip. "I've never really been on a date." She stood straight, her hands fisted on her hips as she smiled down at me.

"Even if it goes terribly, none of them are going anywhere." Confidence shone through her statement. *At least one of us feels good about tonight.* "They love you too much for that."

"We've only been together for like two weeks, how could they love me?" I scoffed, but despite my protests, hope swelled in my chest at her words.

"Trust me, they've got it something fierce. I know it's

nerve wracking, but just try to have fun. You deserve it." She wrapped her arms around my shoulders, and I squeezed her waist tightly, glad we hadn't started makeup or it would have smeared everywhere. I pulled back and swiped my eyes, quickly drying the tears that threatened to escape.

"Thank you, Sadie, now let's get makeup on before I want to cry some more." Happy laughter filled the air, my nerves settling as she started on my eye makeup.

November 18th
Sunday Late Afternoon
Hudson

I took a deep breath, my heart thudding behind my tie and dress shirt. I rubbed my free hand on my jeans, drying the sweat that had accumulated on my palm. Raising a slightly trembling fist, I knocked softly on her wooden door and stepped back after hearing shuffling on the other side. My jaw went slack when she opened the door. *Holy shit*. Her deep blue shirt brought out her eyes which were played up with a mix of brown shadows and black eyeliner. Her hair was curled, the top half pulled up and out of her face and knotted in a fancy bun. She had a small bag in her hand and a sweater folded over her arm. I adjusted my quickly hardening cock that grew stiffer when she turned to close and lock her bedroom door, and I got an eyeful of her denim clad ass. *Fuck me, those luscious curves.* I held out the small bundle of roses I had picked up from the small shop on Main Street.

"You look beautiful, Lucie," I murmured, unable to take my eyes off her. Her sapphire irises sparkled as she took the flowers from me, a bright smile and flushed cheeks lighting up her face.

"Thank you, they're beautiful." She sniffed the flowers, her eyes closing as she took a deep inhale of the fragrant red bulbs. "You look very handsome, hon." She looked me up and down, and I was glad I went with the blue dress shirt and black tie. I cupped the back of her head gently and placed a soft kiss against her pink lips. She tasted like cherries, her vanilla scent swirling around me in a blanket of delicious sweetness.

"Ready, Princess?" I wrapped my arm over her shoulder as we made our way through the library, sticking close to the stacks and away from the main study area. She hummed a soft agreement and curled under my arm, roses cradled close to her chest. "We can leave the roses in the car if you would like? I figured we'd drive since it's supposed to be cold out later." I pushed open the front door to the library and held it open for her. She pulled on her sweater, wrapping it tightly around her before cuddling back under my arm.

"I'd love that. Besides, my muscles are so sore from all the working out and walking around Fae yesterday, so I think walking would be a bad idea. I kind of like my feet to be functional." She chuckled, the click of her heels on the cement emphasizing her point.

"How was your trip?" I asked, opening the passenger door to my car. Her dimples appeared when her smile grew wide at the gesture.

"It was really fun." She paused her response for me to get in on my side. Once we were both buckled, she rushed through her words. "Walked around the main buildings, had lunch with the twins, met the queen, learned about my family."

"Wait, what? You met the queen? And what do you mean learned about your family?" My brows drew down, the campus fading in the rearview mirror as I pulled out onto the main road.

"Our professor set it up. She came out and answered our questions for a while and when we were in the hallway with all these portraits, I found a woman who looks exactly like me; she even had my wish token." I flicked my eyes over to her, seeing pale fingers clutching the coin around her neck.

"Who is she?" I had to admit, I was dying to know more about her. *A family member in the Spring Court capitol building? Impressive.*

"Mireille Bonheur. She was born in 1940, but she disappeared and no one knows where to. The queen confirmed that these were her wish tokens and said she hadn't heard from her in almost two decades. She was a famous Djinn." I heard the smile in her voice as she continued to stare at the token.

"The queen confirmed it? You had a private conversation with the queen?" *She really is just full of surprises.*

"Well, not fully private, the twins and Gerry were there, but yeah. Lily Attwell, the Queen of the Spring Court, told me about my grandmother or great grandmother. Hell, she even let me hug her when I started crying. Honestly, now that I'm thinking about it, it was pretty surreal." She smiled at me, her dimples and white teeth drawing my attention. I found myself smiling back at her, unable to fight the infectious joy in her face.

"That's amazing, Princess, I'm glad you could learn about your family." I looked back at the road, turning into the nearly empty restaurant parking lot. "But why did you cry?"

"I think the stress of the last few weeks just overwhelmed me and learning about my family was, I don't know, the final straw?" Her words tilted up, making it into a question. "I'm all right now though. I'm excited for food and our movie. You're staying tonight, right?" I nodded before getting out of the car, my shoes quiet on the pavement around the car. "Speaking of you staying, where is Troy?" Her head looked around us toward the parking lot.

"They did their shift change when I picked you up, so Troy should be here somewhere." I locked the car and held my arm out for her, and thin fingers curled around my elbow in response. My lips pressed against her temple as we walked across the parking lot, the smell of the restaurant growing strong in the cold air. I greeted the hostess politely and relayed the reservation information. She motioned for us to follow as she grabbed two menus. I nudged Lucie to go first, my hand resting on her lower back.

The small booth was off to the right against one of the walls, but not near a window. A tealight candle on the table flickered next to the single rose in a small glass vase. The white tablecloth was smooth under my hands as I slid into the booth, Lucie sitting on the side opposite me. We scanned the menu in silence before telling our orders to the waiter who kept sneaking glances at Lucie as he jotted them down. Lucie seemed completely oblivious to his attention, even when his fingers brushed hers as he took the menu from her. I ground my teeth at the nerve of this asshole while Lucie's face scrunched in confusion as he walked away.

"So, sweets," she started, her attention shifting to me as she crossed her arms in front of her on the table. I had to force my eyes to stay on her face and not at her recently unwrapped chest that was being propped up on her arms. "Tell me something about yourself." Her eyes twinkled in the soft lighting. I smiled and mimicked her stance, the leaning bringing me close enough to smell the way her signature vanilla scent mixed with the fresh rose that sat between us.

"Let's see... I'm a junior at the university, my favorite color is green, and I have two little sisters. One is in middle school and the other is a sophomore in high school." I chuckled as I thought about them.

"What are their names?" Lucie's voice was excited, her chin resting on her palm as she looked at me.

"Ella and Aria. Ella is the sixth grader and Aria is the high schooler. They love to help our parents at their jobs when they get a chance, pretty sure they'll follow in their footsteps." A soft smile curled my lips as I saw Lucie's eyes widen slightly in excitement, her full attention on me and what I was saying despite the fact that the waiter had just walked by with another glance at Lucie.

"What do your parents do?" she asked, face lighting up with a broad smile.

"My mom's a vet, and my dad is a park ranger. They're both really into outdoorsy stuff and gardens," I explained. "One of my mom's favorite things to do is go to The Garden in the Spring Court with Dante's mom."

"What's The Garden? And your mom's friends with his mom?" Her brow wrinkled in thought, probably trying to organize all the new information in her mind. It was sometimes hard to remember that she had only been with us for the last couple of months, not the years that we'd all known each other. Before I could answer, the annoying waiter returned with our drinks, setting my iced tea in front of me and a soda in front of Lucie. She gave a quick 'thank you' before her eyes returned to me despite the waiter's attention solely on her face. After a few awkward moments, he mumbled something I couldn't hear and walked off.

"The Garden is the Spring Court's official botanical

garden. It's over 250 acres and has pretty much any flower and plant you could think of in it. It even has different biosphere domes to allow plants that flourish in the other courts to thrive in a new climate. A lot of fae who go to school there visit it for a field trip." Pausing quickly, I took a drink of my tea, then continued as I added in two packets of sugar. "Miranda and my mom love to go and just walk through it or sit in the greenhouse cafe and enjoy tarts and tea." Lucie's eyes were bright; the longer I talked the more interested she became.

"Can we go some time?" she exclaimed excitedly, her arm that was propped up falling to the table as she asked. Chuckling, I nodded, knowing full well I had wanted to take her there before she even asked.

"Maybe we can make it a weekend trip. There's a little bed and breakfast nearby that I love. They make the best pastries." At the mention of pastries, Lucie moaned lightly. I knew she loved any type of baked goods, but the moan had my thoughts traveling in another direction. In an attempt to distract my thoughts, I started asking about her. "Tell me about you, Princess."

"Well you already know I grew up believing I was human," she began, her eyes dropping to her glass. "I know I said I was adopted, but that was a lie." I reared my head back at the news. *Lucie lied?* "I was found when I was a baby outside the restaurant my mom worked at. My birth mother left a note saying how she and I weren't safe." Her voice was soft, keeping the conversation between us. "I didn't know until the day before graduation. Before that though," she perked up, "I would help my mom bake for her catering jobs or for the holidays. I usually handled the cooking because, while my mom can bake with the best of them, she sucks at cooking." I laughed at the admission, the scent of our food interrupting her stories as the server set them in front of us. My seafood dish looked delicious, and by the expression on Lucie's face, she was really looking forward to her pasta.

"What else?" I prompted before taking a bite. She finished chewing, giving another moan at how good it was before continuing.

"Charlie and I have been best friends since we were really little. We used to get into *so* much shit. Mainly Charlie's ideas but I tagged along for the adventures." She laughed, her fork twirling the fettuccine around the tines. "I was on the cross country and track teams when I was in middle school, decided in high school to focus more on school work because the races were almost every weekend and I was taking advanced classes." She shrugged, a small smile curling her lips. "That's about it, I was just a normal kid." Even though she didn't say it, I heard the unspoken words *until Noah*. I swallowed down the bite I had in my mouth that had turned to lead at the thought. To my surprise, I was thankful when the waiter stopped at our table again, pulling us away from the spiral our conversation could have taken. We slipped into easy conversation for the rest of dinner, me doing most of the talking to keep any mention of Noah far away.

Lucienne

I curled under Hudson's arm, my shivering hitting him in the side as we walked toward his car. The movie had been fairly empty, only three others and Troy in the theater with us. Thankfully none of them were Noah. He also hadn't shown at dinner, which was a very pleasant surprise, but I was still worried throughout the night. Hudson held the door open for me once more, and I sank into the freezing leather seat, the cold seeping through my jeans. The revving and radio filled the silence, and his warm hand scooped up mine and let our intertwined fingers rest in my lap. We didn't talk on the drive, but I felt safe and comfortable with him, the soft rock through the speakers calming me. When the car was parked in the lot by the library, Hudson ran around the car and opened the door for me. Making sure to grab the bundle of roses from the backseat beforehand, I took his hand and stepped out.

The library was empty, Muriel having gone to her room an hour ago, leaving me alone with Hudson. Bill was waiting near the 'Employee's Only' door, starting his shift since Troy had left when we reached the front doors to the library. Instead of turning down the way to go to my room, Hudson gently tugged on my hand, pulling me toward the reference section. My curiosity grew as we reached one of the aisles. We stood in silence for a few moments, Hudson's lavender eyes seeming to glow in the dimmed overhead night lighting.

"A little over three months ago, I had to stop at the library to check out a book I needed to read before the next semester started. I was checking the stacks when I heard the scraping of the roller ladder a couple aisles over. When I turned the corner, there was this beautiful girl with blonde hair near the top of the old rickety piece of wood. She somehow was able to stay on the ladder while juggling these giant ass books, much to my surprise. When she tried to reach for the last book, I felt my breath leave my lungs. Not only was this girl beautiful and hard-working, she was powerful as well and she didn't even know it."

He turned his attention to me from the area of the shelves I recognized from that day we met. "I just knew I had to talk to her." My heart thundered in my chest as he spoke, his eyes soft as they looked down at me, and his free hand moved to my cheek. The slight roughness of his skin brushed gently against my face, a mere whisper of a touch that made me wish he'd never let me go. "I will never regret the choice to talk to you, I just wish we had gotten together sooner. I'm truly sorry, Lucie, for everything that happened with Brittney. I just want you to know you're the girl for me." A flush crept along my skin as his head dipped down, his breath warming my skin.

When his lips brushed against mine, a shiver ran down my spine. I set the bundle of roses on the shelf next to us and leaned into him. I put everything I had into our kiss, wanting desperately for him to understand I didn't blame him, that he was perfect just as he was. My tongue traced his lower lip, and his hand let go of mine and wrapped tightly around my waist, holding me in place. I gripped his tie tightly in my fists, wrinkling the satin material as we drank each other in. He pulled back slightly, his luminescent eyes searching my face. Willing my heart to still, I looked up at him.

"You're perfect, Hudson," I started, "you and the others make me so happy. It doesn't matter to me that we didn't get together right away. All that matters is that we're together now." The smile he flashed me was full of happiness, for once his overt sex-on-a-stick attitude overshadowed by this handsome man who needed a reminder that he was valued, that he was cared for despite any mistakes. He dropped another quick kiss before handing me my roses, the scent filling my nose and reminding me of all the good memories of the night.

"Let's get some sleep, Princess, don't want to have Dante on my ass for keeping you up too late on a school night," he teased. I laughed, the sound loud within the silent library.

The weight of his arm settled on my shoulders as we strolled slowly toward our room, my heart full from our perfect date.

As soon as the thought echoed in my mind, a wave of electric static started at my chest, thrumming softly in a rhythmic pattern. Each beat grew stronger, so much so that my steps faltered, my hand rubbing my chest. The strange feeling rapidly spread to my arms and legs, a sharp throbbing between my legs as it reached the crest between my thighs. A gasp left me when the tingles almost became too much to bear throughout my body, the pearlescent bond connecting Hudson and me pulsing brightly in the darkened library. An audible snap echoed slightly through the stack we were in as the magical string dissipated.

"Holy shit," Hudson panted, a light sheen of sweat over his forehead as he heaved. "That was, uh, intense. You okay, Princess?" I nodded, unable to talk as I adjusted to the feeling of being free of any wish bonds.

I felt lighter as a weight I hadn't even realized was resting on my shoulders had lifted, leaving me giddy. A smile spread over my face, unable to stop myself. Before I knew it I was giggling, clutching onto Hudson's toned arm to keep upright as I lost myself in the feeling of having started new and fresh.

"You all right?" Hudson smiled down at me, happy but seemingly unaffected by the resolution of our wish bond.

"Apparently the wish wear had been really pressing on me, and I didn't even realize. I feel like I could do absolutely anything!" I cheered gleefully, spinning around playfully. My hair flared around me as I came to a stumbling stop. Thankfully, Hudson was close enough to catch me before I tripped and fell.

"I'm happy you're feeling better, Lucie. I'm sorry my wish

was causing any negative side effects," he murmured softly, staring down at me. His golden skin was warm and sensual in the cozy atmosphere of the empty library. I pressed my fingers against his lips lightly to stop him from apologizing anymore.

"No more of that." I smiled up at him, feeling my dimples appear on my cheeks and my eyes crinkle at the edges from how wide my smile was. I suddenly became aware of his soft lips under my fingers, my body dizzily shifting from lighthearted and fun to a different kind of warm emotion buzzing through me.

"Lucie? Hudson?" Bill called out from somewhere near the corner of the room. "You guys get lost in here?" I couldn't stop the tiny conspiratorial chuckle at the direction my thoughts had taken while in my place of work. Hudson's lips quirked up under my fingers making that heat flare again, but his hand grabbing mine from his face stopped me from taking it any further. We walked with our fingers tangled together, our shoulders brushing with each step.

"Nope, we're right here," Hudson responded when we finally rounded the end of the aisle near my room. "We were just wandering around for a bit."

"All right, just wanted to make sure you two were okay." He gave us both a tiny grin and a small respectful dip of his head that we both returned as we headed past him into my room.

I set my roses on my dresser before grabbing my pajamas quickly from the drawer and making my way into the bathroom. Pulling off my clothes, I found myself nearly bouncing on my toes. This newfound sensation had me excited to curl in bed with the hopes of having a night terror free, but the sound of Hudson shuffling around in my room had me glancing out the crack in the door. His muscled back shifted and rippled in the lamp light, his jeans slung low on his trim hips as he unbuttoned them. Unable to stop myself, my eyes trailed the curve of his ass and his muscled legs as he slid them off. The surge of heat built as I watched him stand up to fold his jeans.

Without realizing what I was doing, I opened the bathroom door the rest of the way and leaned against the wood while I waited for him to look over at me. When he did, his lavender eyes flared, dragging slowly down my nearly bare body, lingering on my lacy white bra and matching panties. My face heated, not in embarrassment, but in this sense of empowerment. Right now, it was just my sexy fae and me, and I wanted to fulfill everything promised in his half-lidded gaze.

"Princess," he breathed, barely audible even in the quiet room. Taking a step forward, I hit play on my music. One of my jazz songs started playing through the speakers as I made my way over to Hudson. Wanting to savor the moment, I placed my palms on his chest before slowly bringing them up his pecs and neck to tangle in his silky black hair. My gaze roamed up his body until I finally looked him in the eyes and pulled him to me without a second thought.

The heat from his toned torso brushed against me as his body pressed to me, our lips colliding in a kiss full of passion and fire. His hands gripped my ass roughly, Hudson's tongue tangling with mine as we deepened the kiss. I couldn't hold back the moan as he maneuvered my hips to grind against his hard cock. That heat within me built, leaving me breathless as he trailed frantic kisses down my neck until he reached the edge of my bra. Only pausing for a moment, he removed the thin barrier between us before his mouth was back on me, nibbling at the curve of my breast.

Gripping his hair tighter, I lost myself in his circling tongue as he sucked my sensitive nipple into his mouth. A sharp gasp left my lips when he nibbled just enough to sting, but the slight pain melted as he lapped the stiff peak once more. When Hudson had decided my chest had received enough attention, he worked his way down my stomach until he sank onto his knees. My arm shot out to brace myself against the wall when his tongue darted out, barely licking the edge of my panties. He continued to tease over the lace with the lightest brush of his tongue across my throbbing clit to the other edge of my underwear.

Wanting more, I pulled his head closer, and when he realized I didn't want teasing— that I wanted his mouth on me—he fused his mouth to my pussy. Circling his tongue, he shifted the lace around on my sensitive skin. The rub of fabric had me shaking, the roughness of the material mixed with his hot kisses pushing me closer to that edge, but I wanted his mouth on me utterly and completely. For his tongue to circle, dip, and fuck my aching pussy without my panties in the way.

As if he read my mind, his fingers hooked into the waist of my underwear and pulled them down and off my legs where he left them discarded on the ground. Before returning his attention to me, Hudson maneuvered my right leg up onto the bed. Knuckles circled my slick entrance, only stopping when he licked my juices from my swollen lips. Stars burst in front of my eyes and they rolled back, fire burning me from the inside out as he seemed to do exactly what I wanted when I wanted.

"Oh, fu—" I didn't even get my words out as my orgasm slammed down on me. Hudson's expertly swirling tongue continued its ministrations until the aftershocks subsided and I was only still standing because of his support on my legs and hips.

Suddenly, he stood and picked me up with ease before depositing me in the middle of my bed. Nestling himself between my thighs, he rocked his hips and his cock rubbed over my pussy dragging a low moan from me. I was coming apart against my sheets without him even being inside me, his hips rolling in a steady pace in just the right spot on my clit, causing my climax to build once more.

"Are you ready for me to fuck you, Princess?" he whispered roughly in my ear, his fingers running through my hair until he held my head steady.

"Please," I begged, almost whimpering to feel him inside me. At my plea, he pulled his hips back enough to line up. The head of his cock pressed had into my entrance when he stopped.

"If you want a condom, Princess, you have to tell me now," he murmured, shaking as he held himself back from sliding home.

"I'm on the pill," I whispered, hooking my legs over his hips and pulling him into me. Goosebumps raised on my skin as he pushed in slowly, the sensation of being stretched rippling through me in a wave of delicious need. Hudson didn't wait until he was seated fully before pulling out, the crown of his thick head passing over my entrance. I couldn't stop the slight whimper at his retreat, but before I could direct him forward he slammed in to the hilt.

"Hudson," I moaned, the sound mixing with his hips meeting mine in a slow but deliberate pace. Without ever picking up the speed of his thrusts, my release grew in a wave of near painful tingles, and when he started moving harder, I came apart in his arms.

"That's right, Princess, come for me." His heated whispers filled my ears, making me tremble as another aftershock flooded by body.

"I want to taste you," I murmured, rubbing my palms down his muscled back. With a scrunched brow, he shifted back before sliding out. Sitting up, I pushed him back enough to drop to my knees like he had. My hand wrapped around him, his cock slick with my arousal, before taking him into my mouth as deep as I could.

Power filtered through me at his moans and the look of pure pleasure on his face as I bobbed my head. That freeing feeling from earlier, mixed with a the surge of confidence, pushed me on until I was able to nearly take him completely in with each pass.

"Lucie, I'm going to come." His words were breathy and broken, as if he could barely get them out. I sucked, my cheeks hollowing around him, and that was the final straw. His cock twitched, and several spurts of his cum shot into my mouth. Waiting until he finished, I rubbed him with the hand that still wrapped around his length. I swallowed quickly before standing. "Holy shit." I couldn't stop my laugh at his dumbfounded expression.

"What?" I shrugged, unsure why he was looking at me like that. "I wanted to return the favor."

"It was amazing is what." He chuckled, coming out of his surprised stupor to wrap me in his arms. "Although, Dante is going to have my ass in the morning for keeping you up so damn late."

"Oops?" I sassed with a smile. Hudson kissed me passionately, a bright smile appearing as he pulled back.

"Let's get into bed, Princess. Actually into bed. For sleeping," he prodded with a light poke in the side, as if to blame me for our extra plans.

"I would never seduce you when we should be sleeping." I flashed puppy dog eyes that made him laugh once more, and with that we crawled into my bed. Curled against him, I fell into a deep, dreamless sleep for the first time in a long while.

14

November 21st
Wednesday Midday
Lucienne

"**I** got it done at least!" Elijah balked, his eyes widening as he stared at Sadie who was pointing at him with a sparkly fingernail. I rolled my eyes as I took another bite of my burger. They had been going back and forth for the last ten minutes on the importance of getting homework done, the same thing they had argued about in the library last week. *Or anytime they were together*, I mentally grumbled.

"Yeah! Literally the minute before class started!" Sadie shrieked, her loud voice catching the attention of tables around us.

"Sades, babe," Benji started, his quiet voice directed at my huffing roommate. "Dial it back about five notches, I don't want to get yelled at for disturbing the peace or whatever." She scoffed in response before turning to me.

"Whatev, Eli. Fail for all I care." I choked on my burger

when I tried to laugh with the bite still in my mouth. Gabe hit my back a few times as I coughed up a lung. "You good?" Sadie asked with a tiny smile, chuckling at my reddened face as I nodded. "Good, what are your plans for Thanksgiving?"

"Charlie's going to pick me up, and we're going to have our usual family get together on Saturday," I explained after taking a large drink of water.

"Don't you guys do something on Thursday?" Benji asked, his light brown eyes fixed on me. I shook my head, picking at the fries on my tray.

"No, Charlie's dad usually has rotations at the hospital that day, and this year Char's working, so it makes sense to have it on Saturday. Also helps my mom get time to make cookies for it since she usually gets a big order for Thanksgiving from a few of her repeat customers." Heads nodded around the table at my explanation. "What about you guys?"

"I'm not doing anything this year, we're waiting until winter break," Sadie responded while she attempted to catch her straw with her mouth, once again forgetting she had hands.

One of these days, I chuckled.

"Austin and I are getting together for a date," Benji cooed, his face wistful as he drifted off thinking about it.

"We're going to his house." Elijah hitched a thumb over at Gabe. "My family doesn't really do much for Thanksgiving, we celebrate Samhain and Yule more. But I'll celebrate if it gives me a chance to scarf down some of his family's cooking." Laughter greeted his admission, and when Gabe opened his mouth to say something, he was cut off by a familiar nasally voice.

"Oh great," Khloe sneered looking over at us, her eyes focusing on me. The rest of the Bitch Crew stepped up around her, holding matching containers of depressing premade salad in their hands.

I sighed. *Here we go.*

"What?" Sadie scoffed, her eyes rolling at Khloe's dramatics. "We're in the middle of eating, if you don't mind."

"Yeah, maybe it was good we interrupted," Madison's twang filled with snark as she eyed Sadie's body, a cruel smirk curling her lips as she turned her attention to Sadie's face.

Oh, hell no. I ground my teeth at the nerve of these bitches.

"Fuck off," Elijah cut in before I could say what was on my mind. "Everyone knows a little extra to hold onto in bed is the best." He threw a wink, receiving a grateful smile in return.

"Well if that's the case, then I don't see why anyone is with this skeleton. No one would want to fuck a stick." Brittney waved a manicured hand toward me, but it was my turn to smirk.

"Hudson and Dante seem to love it," I remarked, a slight smug smile taking over my face. My friends whooped and hollered at my statement while the Bitch Crew gasped, horror masking their features. *Don't sink to their level, Lucie,* I reminded myself. But I had to admit that it felt good to put them in their place even for just a minute.

"Why are you here?" Gabe demanded. His face was hard as he stared at them, and his fist tightened around his silverware. "Clearly you aren't welcome at our table." I nudged his leg under the table with my foot, his grip loosening at my touch.

"We just came to ask why she was still here. You know, wondering why you have bodyguards and everything. It's not like they can protect you all the time," Claire finally spoke up, taking a half step in front of her cronies. Elijah's and Gabe's brow furrowed while Sadie and Benji joined Gabe in his stranglehold on their own silverware.

Great. I groaned knowing exactly where this was going. *Ugh.*

Landon

"Hurry the hell up!" I shouted, my head dropping back with a frustrated sigh. I was so incredibly hungry that I was bordering on hangry as I waited for Logan to grab his book for our afternoon class. I had shoved everything I needed haphazardly into my bag while Logan had to dig through one of his piles to find the right notebook. The guys were waiting in the lobby, and more importantly, every minute wasted was a minute less with our girl.

"Shut the fuck up, dude, I'm coming," he bit out, a glare aimed in my direction as he shuffled from his room. "Let's go, asshole."

Yanking the door open, I followed him into the crowded hallway and down the stairs. The guys trailed away from a few girls who were very poorly trying to flirt with Dante and Cam, the girls' faces falling when they responded that they were taken. I snickered softly to myself when we got outside.

"What?" Dante asked, his hand rubbing through his short hair. I eyed him, a small smirk on my face as I readied to mercilessly tease him.

What can I say? I get mischievous when I'm hungry.

"You"—I waved a hand at Cam—"and him attracting all the ladies. Poor Lemon Drop's going to have a whole gaggle of girls coming after her." The rest of the guys rolled their eyes as Dante glared at me.

"Not my fault. Besides"—he shrugged—"as soon as it

makes it around campus that we're all together, they'll back off."

"Hopefully. Lucie doesn't need any more stress right now," Cam added, his hand adjusting his glasses. "Let's hurry and get to the dining hall. With this Noah shit show going on it makes me jumpy when I can't see her." The mood sobered at the reminder of what was going on. It was easy to ignore it when we weren't dealing with his shit directly, like when he trashed Lucie's dorm, but when he was brought up, it weighed heavily on all of us. I could see it in my brothers' faces and stances—hunched or tightened shoulders, fisted hands, and severe frowns. Thankfully the dining hall was directly ahead of us, allowing me to focus on Lucie and not that asshole and everything I wanted to do to him when I got my hands on him.

The seating area of the building was packed full; only a few tables held extra seats as students filtered from the buffet lines to the door or their friends. Buzzing conversation filled the space as we all packed our trays full. Logan and I were the first through the line to pay and led the group toward the beacon that was Sadie's blue hair. My steps faltered when I saw Claire and her band of prissy bitches hassling Lucie and the rest of the table. Grinding my teeth, I closed the distance between us, Claire's voice finally reaching me as I drew nearer.

"We just came to ask why she was still here. You know, wondering why you have bodyguards and everything. It's not like they can protect you all the time." She paused, a catty eyebrow raised as she stared at Lucie. "I mean, you *are* endangering the entire student body by staying while Noah's chasing you around." I heard a growl to my left and saw Dante's white-knuckled grip strangling his tray in my peripheral vision. Knowing the rest of my family, they were as angry as I was. My claws extended sharply, the grey plastic in my hands cracking under the harsh points.

"Fuck off," Nik ground out. His power crackled audibly around him, and light sparks danced across his skin. The girls jerked their heads to look our way, not having heard us approach.

"You've caused enough problems," Cam snapped, cutting off Claire's retort. "I will gladly turn you over to the dean if you keep harassing our girlfriend and our friends."

"He doesn't scare us," Claire flipped her hair over her shoulder with her free hand. I had opened my mouth to snark back at her when a thunderclap sounded around us.

"Miss Loren," Dean Renaud's voice boomed in the suddenly silent dining area. His stern look shifted from Claire to Madison and Khloe, finally landing on Brittney. "Miss Summers, Miss Davis, and Miss Sansbury. I'm growing quite tired of your petty fights." Khloe started to protest. "Enough!" The dean's voice cut through anything she was about to say, his voice harsh enough to make several students jump in surprise. "Report to the Assistant Dean's office immediately if you wish to stay enrolled at my university." His threat hung in the air as they turned quietly and exited the room, every set of eyes on them before turning to us in curiosity. "I'm truly sorry about their behavior, Lucie, I'll take care of it." His hand rested lightly on her shoulder before he turned and walked out of the hall.

"What a bunch of bitches," Benji scoffed, his statement bringing a slightly hysterical laugh to Lucie's lips, essentially breaking the tension running through our group.

"How did he know to come?" Gabe questioned, his eyebrows furrowing slightly as he looked around us. A chuckle came from Hudson whose face sported a satisfied smile. When everyone flashed him questioning looks, he held up his phone. The device was unlocked, revealing his text conversation to Dean Renaud saying they were causing trouble with Lucie in the dining hall.

"Oh shit." I gaped at the message, a single 'K' response showing the same time he had appeared in the room. "That's fucking awesome!" I held up a hand, high-fiving Hudson as the rest of our group voiced their agreement around us. As we situated around the table, my hand finding Lucie's over the top of the formica table, Dante's voice echoed in my head.

"They're purposely taking chances whenever we're not around. To try and deter them let's not leave Lucie alone for more than a few minutes when we're on campus even if she's with Sadie or the others. Keep that stressful shit away from her," he suggested before continuing, *"and as much as much as I appreciate the dean taking care of this issue right now, this display just put a target on Lucie's back."* I kept my face straight despite wanting to look at Dante.

"How so?" Logan questioned before anyone else, his confusion clear.

"Shows he's willing to drop everything when she's having a problem," Cam answered, his voice somber. *"People will assume that with her own security, her Djinn coin, and now the dean seemingly at her beck and call, she's either dangerous, a favorite, or important enough to justify all these extra precautions."*

"But the security is for Noah," I explained, a sinking feeling in my gut.

"That will not matter," Nik whispered, even his mental voice carrying the strain of his damaged vocal cords.

"Doesn't matter. People don't think for themselves; they'll only think about the gossip." Hudson's voice was hard, no doubt remembering how kids rejected him in school for how his

family was. Despite our best attempts, they were relentless in their teasing of the kid with the 'hippy dippy' family. It only stopped after Hudson beefed up over the summer between junior and senior year.

"Regardless, she'll be all right," Logan exclaimed, determination lacing his words.

"Let's focus on Noah and that shit show first, but just keep this in the back of your minds in case it becomes a problem," Dante commanded before turning his attention to Benji's question about Kohl. As I took a bite of my food, my gaze scanned the area around us, taking in the whispers that filled the room and the eyes that refused to turn away. I caught Logan doing the same, his face grim as his attention turned to me, mimicking exactly what I was thinking.

This is going to be an issue...

November 21ˢᵗ
Wednesday Evening
Camden

"I'll see you guys later," Lucie said as she moved through the rest of the guys, giving warm hugs as they dropped kisses on her head or cheek. Sadie mimicked gagging when Lucie reached her. "Shut up." She laughed, her face going an adorable shade of pink. They hugged each other tightly before pulling back. Sadie and my brothers headed toward their temporary rooms in the Administration Housing as a group, the twins' boisterous jokes echoing as they drew farther from Lucie and me. The library was closing shortly, so Muriel was chasing all lingering students out from between the stacks and study area with a wave of her wrinkled hand. I continued to leisurely read the large manuscript laid out on the table in front of me. Researching for this additional project was slow going, but I had about a month before it needed to be turned in, so I wasn't worried.

The library grew quiet as the last of the students filtered out the front doors leaving Lucie and me alone aside from Troy—still seated in the leather chair—and Muriel walking the aisles. Books and papers straightened on their own as she passed, her power allowing her to take care of such a large space without too much hassle or help, at least when Lucie wasn't working. Muriel's green eyes sparkled as she neared us, a large smile growing when she noticed the book I was studying.

"Ah, Mr. Smith, *The Book of Knowledge: Myths and Legends,* good choice," she praised. "You two be good." She waved and made her way into the office and back into her own set of rooms. Lucie gave a warm smile and goodnight before returning her attention to her own books. Her expression was serene, her stance calm, no harsh frown marring her beautiful face as she scanned the text. I knew I should look away, but I couldn't stop staring. Her sapphire eyes flickered up to me when she felt mine on her, and her face squished up into an adorable look.

"What?" she murmured, her hand running over her hair. "Do I look funny or something?" I chuckled and leaned forward, my forearms resting on the manuscript.

"Or something is right." I smirked at her, the tip of my fang stabbing into my lower lip. The feeling I had grown used to when I was with Nik started as I stared at Lucie, my fangs aching as I took in her signature vanilla scent mixed with her unique pheromones. "Beautiful, amazing, absolutely perfect." I leaned closer to her with each word, trailing off at the end with my lips only a breath away from hers. Lucie didn't talk, just leaned forward ever so slightly, pressing a soft kiss to my lips before pulling back.

"You're such a sweet talker, Cam," she teased, but her twinkling eyes and the light flush on her cheeks gave away how she truly felt. "I don't think this is what Muriel had in mind when she left us alone... well, mostly alone." Her eyes darted to Troy before returning to me, her blush deepening from pink to red.

"You're right, I just couldn't help myself." I kissed the dimple that had appeared when she smiled then reclined back into my chair, not wanting to continue reading from the boring text in front of me.

"What are you reading about?" Her head dipped toward the large volume that had some of the smallest writing I had ever seen. After a while, I'm pretty sure my eyes had started to cross. I closed the book softly, not wanting the book to slam shut, and angled it toward her. "What's *The Book of Knowledge*?" Curiosity was brimming in her words, her hand barely brushing the cover.

"It's a book that's mostly legend; a lot of people don't think it exists," I explained, comfortingly slipping into my researcher role of stating fact and information. "I'm doing an extra project for the university, and I need to deliver files on five different artifacts, as well as information about them." I shifted the notebook from off to the side to in front of Lucie, turning to the page about the artifacts I was researching. "These are the ones I've decided on, now I'm just compiling information."

"Is this for that special exhibit showcase thing they're doing here in the library after winter break?" Her eyes scanned the page. My eyebrows went up in surprise. The professors hadn't talked to anyone other than other faculty, the dean, and me about the display. She glanced at me before smiling, clearly reading the confusion in my expression. "I heard Muriel and several professors talking about it.

One benefit of working in the library." She chuckled and shrugged. "Besides, I'll get roped into helping set up. Muriel and I are two of the only people who can navigate the basement."

"There's a basement?" This conversation just kept getting weirder and weirder, but I had to admit that I was loving these little surprises. Lucie stood and collected her books, stuffing them behind the checkout counter.

"Troy," she murmured walking up to him, "we'll be right back. We're just going to go check on something in the basement." He hesitated to agree but nodded, shifting his attention back to the library. He waved us off, and Lucie gently tugged me in the direction of her room. I wrapped my hand around hers and followed obediently, curiosity piqued as we turned to one of the doors opposite her bedroom. At the bottom of the stairs, Lucie pulled out an ID with her smiling picture on it and scanned it on a reader to the right of the door.

"What's down here?" I whispered.

The air was still, no noise except the unlocking click surrounded us. She smirked at me and pushed the door open. It was dark, only a few safety lights lighting the ground every few feet on the multitude of pathways. She turned to the left and hit a large lever, and the clunking sound of industrial lights turning on immediately followed. My jaw dropped as the space was slowly revealed, the yellow lighting cast over the large area filled with a wide array of shelves, cases, and grated storage cages. I immediately recognized several of the objects near us, famous daggers and swords laid out on velvet backing in clear glass storage cases. Lucie took my hand and pulled me toward another area of the basement.

Holy shit... there's so much history in this place. I was dumbfounded. Completely and utterly starstruck at the objects we passed, so much so I could barely comprehend what was around us. When she stopped, she pointed with a slender finger at a display.

"That should look familiar." She chuckled as I stepped forward, her hand still tangled in mine. It looked just like an old-timey broom, the handle made of worn, knotted wood, the bristles made of twigs held together by cracked leather ties. This wasn't just any old broom though, it was one of the first Witch's Brooms ever made, the kind that magick users used to fly on. I turned my head to gape at her, still at a loss for words. She had recognized it from my list of artifacts. I hadn't expected to actually see any of the items until the university started to set up the display. I found myself speechless at Lucie's thoughtful gesture—breaking rules, I'm sure—just to show me something she knew I'd love. My brothers always supported and looked out for me, but I wasn't used to anyone but Nik doing special things like this.

"You…" I couldn't think, I just moved, cupping her jaw in my free hand and molding my lips to hers in a passionate kiss. Her hand rested on my chest, fisting the material of my sweater as she kissed back. Her tongue battled against mine as I deepened our kiss, my hand dropping from her jaw to her hip and pulling her flush against me. The thudding of my heart filled my ears, her soft curves pressing against my chest as I nipped sharply at her lip, making sure to not draw blood. "You are absolutely one of the most incredible people I have ever met," I murmured against her lips, our heavy breaths coming out in sharp pants and filling the silence around us.

"You're not so bad yourself," she teased, shooting me a cheeky grin before pulling back and yanking me toward another part of the basement. "Come on, we can look at a few other objects before we head back upstairs. Or, if you want, we can check the archives down here for any information on your artifacts."

"Seriously," I whispered, sneaking another kiss before moving down the aisle with her at my side, "absolutely perfect."

For the next half hour, Lucie and I combed the shelves, locating several books for my research. When I didn't think my heart could be any fuller, it nearly burst when she grabbed a pen from a random shelf and started taking notes on a scrap piece of paper for me, intent on helping me with the workload. As soon as we realized we had abandoned Troy to his own accord and their shift change would happen soon, we returned the antique books to their proper homes and headed back upstairs, planning to sleep away the night. *Our Lucie is perfection,* I thought, quietly curling her in my arms when we slipped into bed.

15

November 23rd
Friday Morning
Lucienne

The vehicle swerved sharply off the interstate and into an abandoned rest area. My heart pounded painfully against my ribs, the sound drowning out the music flowing from the truck's speakers as the anxiety that gripped my chest constricted. His white-knuckled grip slipped from my sight, shifting to throw open the driver side door. My breathing seized. Please no, I mentally pleaded, my body frozen in place. His cold expression filled my window right before he yanked away the only barrier between me and him.

"Lucie baby," he cooed sadistically, his hand tightening on my upper arm, "let's go have some fun..."

Yelling and warm hands against my face pulled me from the memory, my vision watery when I cracked open my eyes. Nik's drawn face stared down at me, his rough hands stroking my hair away from my forehead. Logan's worried expression caught my eye as he knelt in a pair of grey pajama pants next to Nik on my bed. His hands trembled as they reached out for mine.

"Lucie?" he murmured, sighs of relief echoing through the room as the other guys pulled back from hovering over the edge of the mattress. "You awake?" I nodded slightly, just a small dip of my head, my breathing still ragged as I attempted to control the sobs that wanted to break through.

"Oh, thank god." Landon's husky voice shook, his hands raking over his face as if he was trying to rid his memory of something he'd seen. I shifted slightly, the sweat coating my body making it uncomfortable to be under the blanket. Nik and Logan realized what I was attempting to do and moved back enough to give me room to sit up against the head-board. Cam was waiting between the bed and the bathroom door with a small paper cup of water which I gratefully drank. The cool liquid soothed the roughness in my throat, and my brows scrunched in confusion.

Why is my throat rough? It was fine when I went to bed.

"What happened?" Rubbing my hand over my forehead to wipe away some of the sweat beading up, I took in their silent glances toward one another and waited for someone to explain. Dante knelt next to me, his tanned hand wrapping around mine.

"Were you dreaming?" His deep voice resonated within me, chasing the last of the dream away. I nodded, unable to keep my eyes fixed only on him. Instead, I continued to scan the room, making sure all my guys were here. Nik and Logan were still seated on top of the blankets, their hands resting on my legs. Landon stood next to Cam to the left of the bed between us and the bathroom. Landon's arms crossed tightly across his bare chest while Cam's hands were tucked into his sweatpants pockets. Hudson rounded out the group standing in front of my dresser, off to the side behind Dante's crouched position. Hudson's hands wrung restlessly in front of his plain grey shirt, his black boxer briefs tight against his thighs.

"You were whimpering and shaking and then started sobbing," Nik filled me in, his gravelly voice harsher than normal, as if sandpaper had ground against his already rough vocal cords.

"You wouldn't wake up," Landon continued, a shudder running through his body. I paled at his words.

"Like right away? Or....?" I trailed off, waiting for him to expand.

"Like at all, we've been trying to wake you for over ten minutes." Logan took over from his brother, his fingers tightening on my thigh. "We almost had to call Dean Renaud."

"I'm sorry, guys—"

"Don't apologize, Firecracker," Dante cut in. "It isn't your fault." His free hand reached out and gently turned my head to face him, his thumb tracing against my jaw. "You're awake and you're safe, that's all that matters." I nodded, trying to stay calm despite the tears that brimmed in my eyes and the remnants of the nightmare that clung to my mind. It was difficult to keep my cool when all I could see was the unbearable fear clearly written in their eyes.

"Thank you." I eyed everyone around me as I said it. I lost control at trying to push the tears back, several dripping in quick succession down my cheeks.

"For what?" Cam's hand came out to wipe my left cheek, the tears glistening on his palm.

"For being there for me." I tried to smile, but from the softening of Cam and Landon's eyes in pity, I'm pretty sure it came out more like a grimace. "What time is it?" I didn't want to keep talking about my shitty sleep. I wanted to focus on the fact that it was Thanksgiving weekend and we'd be all heading toward my hometown later today.

"It's a little after seven," Hudson responded, shifting out of the way of my dresser when he saw me shuffling out of bed. I nodded, a shiver running through me at the air hitting my quickly cooling body. "You going to shower, Princess?"

"Yeah, just real quick. We going to grab breakfast? I might not be able to eat much, but I want to at least try to keep something down." I piled everything I needed for the day into my arms from the dresser and closet before turning and making my way to the bathroom. *This room really isn't meant for seven people.* I chuckled, brushing against every one of my guys while attempting to get to my bathroom. They started to move, pulling clothes from the closet that they had stored there earlier this week. I left the door to the bathroom cracked open for them to come and go as they needed to get ready for the day. The water heated quickly, and I jumped in as soon as it was hot, my body covered in dried sweat and goosebumps until the stream washed over my skin.

I lathered my body wash on my arms when the first of the guys came in, a squawk echoing off the tiles followed quickly by Nik's murmurs, too quiet for me to hear over the sound of the water. The guys quickly rotated through brushing their teeth and getting dressed as I rinsed the soap from my body and shampoo from my hair before slathering the ends in a thick dollop of conditioner. Too lazy to shave this morning, I piled my hair on top of my head and stood under the spray, letting the heat melt away the tension in my shoulders.

My eyes trailed down my body as I relaxed. My ribs weren't sticking out, but I could tell my body had continued to lose what little weight and fat it carried due to stress and anxiety. I groaned. *This shit is really getting tiring.* Noah's texts and emails had become consistent over the last few weeks, but the silver lining was that he hadn't called recently, and I hadn't seen him since the Kohl game. Whichever guy was with me carried my phone, forwarding and screenshotting all texts and emails to Alex and the police detective that had been assigned to my case. She was compiling any and all evidence against Noah and working closely with the security of the university to try and catch him. I sighed, knowing I would need to meet with her after this weekend was over.

"Hey, Love." Logan's words pulled me from my internal musings, his head appearing at the edge of the shower. His eyes immediately dragged down my body and up before speaking, his smile sinful and full of mischievous promises. "Just wanted to see if you wanted us to grab food and bring it back or go get food from the dining hall together. I wasn't sure what the plans were for the day until Charlie picked you up."

"We can go get something unless some of the guys want to hang out here," I suggested, tilting my head back to rinse the conditioner, "or I can stay here with someone. It makes no difference to me." I looked at Logan whose eyes were half-lidded as he watched the water pour down my pale skin. He held up a finger signifying one minute and disappeared. I heard disjointed talking before the door was shut completely. I had reached behind me to shut off the water when rough fingers caught my wrist. Surprised, I turned to look over my shoulder, finding Logan's naked and chiseled body stepping into the tub. The water pouring over his head and shoulders brought my attention to every dip of his defined torso.

"I sent them to get food," he whispered, his lips brushing

my ear as he shifted my wet hair into his left hand, his hard chest pressing against my back. "So we only have so much time." Barely brushing the sensitive spot under my ear with his lips, he ducked his head down my neck, showering my skin in kisses.

"What did you have in mind?" My question was breathy with need, and his own arousal was obvious as his hard cock pressed into my ass. He used the hand that was tangled in my hair to angle my head back toward him, his lips moving desperately against me as he drew me closer.

"I haven't gotten my chance to taste you yet," he growled, his hand tightening slightly. A moan escaped at the tugging, a shot of desire curling through me at his words. "Bend that beautiful ass over, Love." His grip on my hair loosened enough for me to follow his command as I folded forward. His hand ran over my back and down to my ass, gripping tightly as he groaned from his place behind me. "Fuck..." He fell to his knees, my hair tumbling around my face as I propped my hands on the tile. I glanced over my shoulder and was captivated by Logan's eyes that burned with desire as his fingers massaged my thighs and ass.

My legs quaked under the intensity of his stare, gripping the wall harder when he shot forward. A long, hot lick trailed from my throbbing clit all the way to my ass. More moans echoed against the tile, his tongue swirling over my clit before dipping inside me, my own wetness mixing with the water dripping from us both. My breathing grew ragged at his relentlessly sinful tongue. *Fuck,* I groaned, feeling myself nearing my orgasm. The build was intense, and my limbs were trembling with anticipation. Logan's name was disjointed to my own ears as I shattered in release, my legs nearly giving out under the tremors.

Logan continued his ruthless pursuit, holding my thighs

tightly against his chest to keep me standing. My eyes widened when his attention shifted from my throbbing pussy and tender clit to my ass. My heart thudded erratically at the onslaught of new sensations. Despite my initial protests, the tension melted from my rigid limbs and left me panting. A hand shifted from my thigh and gripped my ass tightly as Logan stood. As I adjusted to try and stand, he held me in my current position. I opened my mouth to ask what was happening when I felt the head of his cock pressing into my entrance. Without prompting, I pushed back, Logan sheathing himself fully inside me. I received another tight grip at my movement, a responding moan nearly covering his words.

"Now, now, Love," he cooed, rubbing the curve of my ass, "you did the work last time. Let me take care of you." I bit my tongue at the feeling of him slowly pulling out before sliding back in. His torturous pace brought whimpers to my lips, my gaze darting back to him. The water poured around his shoulders, down his torso, and over where he pistoned in and out of me, falling into a hard but steady rhythm. Fire burned in my veins, my orgasm slamming down on me without any build up. I couldn't hold back the disjointed moans that ripped from my throat as he pounded into me.

"God damn, Love, you feel so good," he murmured, bringing a hand down on my ass. Though it wasn't a hard hit, the half slap turned into another grip that seared through me. I shifted my support just enough to slip one hand down to my clit, rubbing quick, hard circles in time with his thrusts, bringing us both to an explosive release. After the shaking subsided and my muscles were able to move, Logan stepped back and pulled me to stand against him. Our breathing was ragged as our chests heaved in an attempt to get more air.

"You taste even better than I imagined." He nibbled my ear lobe. "I could eat you for every meal of the day and still be starving for more." My used pussy quivered under his words, strong emotions building in my chest that pushed me to say something I wasn't sure I was ready for.

You can't think that yet, I chastised myself for wanting to blurt the words that danced on the tip of my tongue. Swallowing the sentiment, I turned, Logan reaching behind him to turn off the shower as it had started to turn cold.

"Hopefully we didn't scare Gerry." I giggled at the thought of how that situation would go. Logan reached out of the curtain, handing me my towel before quickly drying off in his, a humorous glint shining in his eyes. I stepped out of the shower, wrapped tightly in my towel to come face to face with Landon's devilish smirk and heated gaze. He was leaning his hip against the counter of my vanity, a hardened bulge straining his pants.

"Well, I see why you made them go get food." He cocked a brow at his twin before turning to look at me. "Trying to leave me out. I see how it is," he teased lightly.

"I didn't know he was going to come in the shower with me," I defended in a huff. "Besides, you could have joined too if it was such a problem." The red in his burning coal eyes flared, igniting my own flame again.

"Good," he said with finality before shooting forward and yanking the towel from around me as he kissed me fiercely. "Because listening to you being fucked is damn near torturous," he murmured against my mouth. Without any warning, he hooked his hands under my legs and hoisted me onto the counter.

"Holy cold," I squealed at the icy stone under me, but Landon's hands roving my flesh distracted me. His movements were frantic and rushed as he pushed his pants down to free his hard cock from its tight confines. As I was still dripping from my round with Logan only moments earlier, Landon was able to push in with ease.

"Fuck, you're so tight," he moaned, rocking in and out of me. I had no idea what fell from my lips as he moved, my mind a muddled mess of desire and need, unable to form any coherent thought as I slowly started my climb to release. I tightened around him, my pussy over-sensitive from the roughness of my previous romp. Lightning seared every nerve as I clamped down, falling into the blissful pool of my orgasm. Landon crushed his lips to mine, swallowing my loud cries, his hair gripped tightly in my hands as he reached his own explosive release.

"Think we have time for another round?" Logan questioned from his position right outside the tub, his own erection thick in his hand as he pumped it. Landon shook his head tiredly, his forehead falling to my shoulder as he panted. My eyes locked with Logan's as Landon caught his breath, the burning in his gaze searing me despite having both of them in the last little while. Logan pumped faster, the motion bringing my attention to his thick cock that was still slick from being inside me. I was near panting when he finally came, thick ropes of his cum falling over the head of his cock and down his hand.

"Like watching him jerk off to you, Lemon Drop?" Landon asked in a soft, sensual voice, his words whispering across my neck before he kissed my throat and stood upright again. I nodded, unable to speak as he slid out and helped me off the counter. "Good, maybe we can watch each other get off next time," he offered, and my mind ran wild with the thought of watching them jerk off while I masturbated in front of them. To try and curb the desire still pulsing through me, I turned and grabbed my brush to detangle the knots Logan's grip had caused.

"I'm going to go get dressed, Love. The guys should be back shortly," Logan said, dropping a quick kiss on my cheek before slipping out into my room. Landon's rough palms cupped my cheeks, his lips pressing against mine gently. He followed his brother to get dressed before the guys came back from the dining hall. I took a deep, calming breath as I picked up my dropped towel and slung it over the shower curtain. In the silence of my bathroom, unwanted thoughts and loneliness crept in. I tried to quell the raging emotions fighting for my attention, worry about the guys being upset, fear about Noah, stress of the entire situation we'd been in since he found me, and finally, the one I was most terrified of, love.

I stood up after sliding on my panties and hooking my bra, wiping the mirror of condensation to look at my gaunt face. As I stared into my own dark blue eyes, I knew without a doubt that I loved them. Turning away from the truth easily painted all over my face, I quickly slipped into my jeans and a thick sweater. *When did it happen?* I questioned myself. *Isn't it way too soon?* I didn't want to think about it at the moment, so I was thankful when the sound of the guys filled my room, their talking loud and boisterous. Steeling myself, I pushed out into the room to find the guys spread around the floor and bed passing takeout boxes between them.

"Hey, Doll." Cam's sweet demeanor washed away the loneliness.

I smiled and crawled onto the bed between Nik and Hudson. Grigori shuffled off Nik's shoulder and onto the bed, coming closer to me. I watched him curiously. *Where are you going, little guy?* I silently questioned him. A tiny squawk answered me, his talons heaving him into my lap as I stared wide-eyed at the strange bird. *Did he just... read my mind?* Another squawk, his beady eyes zeroing in on my face before he leaned into me, a feathery forehead booping my jaw. The guys were silent as I started to rub Grigori's wings, and several of their mouths gaped open as they tracked Grigori's movements.

"He likes you." Nik smiled at me, his words soft, his attention shifting to the bird. His next statement to Grigori was so soft, in fact, that I almost didn't hear him mumble, "Attention whore." In response, the hawk flicked a wing against Nik's hand making him drop his sandwich into his lap. I chuckled. *These two have quite the love/hate relationship.* I snatched up the dropped food and took a large bite, creamy peanut butter and strawberry jelly meeting my tongue. Laughs filled the room as we slipped into comfortable conversation. My phone started to ring, and immediately the contentment came crashing down. Dante reacted first, answering with cool politeness.

"Hello." The room was silent as we waited. The female voice on the other side was garbled from this far away, but it didn't seem like it was Noah. "May I ask who's calling?" More silence, Dante's face grew drawn, his naturally tanned skin fading into a sickly pale. "One moment," he said softly, holding it out for me to take. Reaching around Cam, I took the phone, the number reading that it was the hospital where Charlie's dad worked.

"Hello. This is Lucie." I willed my voice to be steady despite the dread filling my stomach.

"Hello, Miss Envie. My name is Stephanie Long, and I'm a nurse at Pinewood Drive Medical Center. I'm calling to inform you that your mother was brought in via ambulance about an hour ago."

My hearing fuzzed over. *My mom's in the hospital.* I couldn't believe it. I forced myself to focus. *Mom needs me.*

"Is she all right? What happened?" Almost as though he sensed the urgency building within me, Grigori shuffled off me without prompting. With him safely out of the way, I surged off the bed. I slipped on my tennis shoes, not bothering with socks, my phone secured between my shoulder and ear.

"She's currently being examined, but we don't believe there was any major damage. The matter is under police investigation, so I'm not privy to any information."

I took in a sharp breath. *Police investigation... examined...* My brain swirled in a thousand directions about what could have happened, but I knew. Deep down, I *knew* this was Noah.

"All right, thank you. I'm currently at my university, but I will be heading straight there. Call me with any updates." I hung up as soon as I received confirmation she would notify me. The guys had shifted to standing, waiting anxiously for me to explain. "My mom's in the hospital. They don't think there are any major injuries, but it's under police investigation." I hurriedly tossed on my jacket when my phone rang again, but this time Charlie's name flashed on the screen.

"Boo, I'm coming to get you. I'll be there in a bit, and we'll go to the hospital." I heard her car radio being turned down in the background and sound of her huffing as she balanced the phone while driving. I didn't question how she knew, figuring her dad was on call today and had let her know as soon as he was able to. Knowing I'd have my best friend by my side helped calm some of the nerves that were still bouncing around inside me.

"All right, I'll see you in a bit." I hung up and turned back to the guys. "I need to call Alex and let him know what's going on." Before I could dial his number that I did in fact memorize, Dante's hands covered mine, bringing my attention from my phone to his face.

"You ride with Char to the hospital. We'll leave in a little while after we pack up the overnight bags that we planned on doing today, all right? We don't want you to have to stress." He turned his attention to Hudson who was closest to the door. "Go talk with Gerry. Let him know what happened and that she'll be going to Enumclaw ahead of schedule." Hudson nodded sharply before slipping into the hallway. "Call Alex, Firecracker. We're going to start packing." He hitched his thumb at Logan, Landon, Cam, and Nik to head to their dorms. With quick kisses they filed out of the room, leaving Dante and me alone. I took a fortifying breath, trying to contain the panic attack that was brewing, and dialed Alex's number.

He answered after half a ring, his voice clipped. "What's wrong?"

Will we ever have a normal conversation?

"My mom's in the hospital. I don't know what happened, but Charlie is coming to get me, and we're heading there early," I rushed to tell him, growing tired of having to repeat the same sentence over and over. "She should be here in about five to ten minutes." I summarized the rest of the plan before he gave me an affirmative and a request for updates. I hung up and went with Dante into the main library. Hudson was still talking with Gerry, both sporting severe facial expressions.

"I'll wait with you for Charlie to get here. Hudson, go pack her bag," Dante directed, his hand on my lower back guiding me toward the front of the library. Gerry fell into step behind us, our strides purposeful and gaining the attention of the few students in the study area this early in the morning.

The bite of the cold air stung my cheeks, but I wasn't fazed. *Please let my mom be all right,* I pleaded as I spotted Charlie's car pulling up to the sidewalk. With a kiss goodbye to Dante, Gerry and I slipped into the car and were off to the hospital.

16

November 23rd
Friday Midday
Lucienne

Thanks to the lack of traffic and Charlie's innate ability to speed without being pulled over, we made it to the hospital within a half hour instead of an hour. The smell of cleaner, antiseptic, and the tang of blood lingered in the air of the Emergency Room. Charlie's dad Lucas met us at the ER desk, his white doctor's coat bright against his coffee skin as we entered the waiting room. His warm chocolate coloring was a shade lighter than Charlie's, and his eyes were a blue-green mix instead of brown. He straightened and walked out from behind the desk when he spotted us.

"Lucie." He gave me a quick nod before sticking his hand out for Gerry. "Dr. Lucas Hauser, Charlie's dad." Gerry introduced himself, Lucas not at all fazed by his presence, having been kept in the loop about Noah by my mom and Charlie. "Your mom is this way. We were able to examine her right after she was brought in, and she's just finished getting treatment. She's going to be all right. There was some bruising and a few cuts that required stitches, and she'll be staying overnight for concussion monitoring, but she's conscious and aware."

My anxiety drained from my body. *She's okay.* My eyes started to water with relief. Charlie grabbed my hand and squeezed, her touch keeping any lingering panic at bay.

"What happened?" I curved around a male nurse wheeling a crash cart, my steps quickening to keep up with Lucas' long legs.

"An attack of some kind, but I don't know any of the details. The police wanted to interview her before you arrived, so they wouldn't be in the way." I nodded, grateful for their foresight. We reached her room near the end of the hall by the emergency exit. "I have a surgery I need to prep for, you know my number if you need anything." I gave a quiet thanks and went in, Gerry taking up residence outside the door in the hallway.

My mom was lying in a large, bulky hospital bed. Her torso was propped up on the inclined mattress, her brown wavy hair disheveled. A darkening mark on her left cheek caught my attention, two butterfly strips holding a small cut together in the middle of the shadowed bruise. I quickly scanned for other injuries as I practically ran to the bed. Several small bruises on her upper right arm peeked out from under the hospital gown sleeve, the same bruises I used to carry around from him grabbing me. My fists tight-ened at the sight of the four-inch-long cut along her left forearm that had required at least 20 stitches to hold the wound closed.

"Mom," I choked out as the dam holding my emotions together broke. Sobs wracked my body as she reached out and pulled me tightly against her. She shushed lightly, her hand rubbing my back in soothing strokes. Despite my best efforts, I couldn't control my crying. Hiccups and garbled cries filled the room. This was because of me. Noah couldn't reach me, so he did something he knew would hurt me just as much as if he had hit me. I felt guilty and ashamed that I had caused the attack on my mother, and I couldn't control the sobs that wracked my body. Instead of consoling her like I should be, she was consoling me. Charlie stood quietly from the chair at the end of the bed and excused herself to stand in the hall, the door closing gently behind her.

"I'm all right, sweetheart," Mom whispered, her voice full of emotion but not damaged. "Nothing's too bad, just a couple of bruises..." She hesitated, long enough for me to pull back and look at her. My right hand swiped uselessly at my cheeks and the pouring streams that leaked from my eyes.

"It was Noah, wasn't it?" I whispered, a hiccupped sob following my statement. Her lips pursed, eyes shadowed at the mention of his name. *Definitely him then.* "I'm so sorry..."

"Don't you even start that, Lucienne Marie," she cut me off, her tone reprimanding. "This is not your fault. You got out and you got away, this is all on *him*. Do you understand?"

I nodded, my tears finally slowing. Her speech reminded me of Dante's the night Noah had broken in and destroyed mine and Sadie's room. The quick memory of that night made me realize that I hadn't checked my phone since leaving campus, and I made a mental note to do so as soon as possible.

"I've missed you, sweetie." She ran a hand down my hair, her warm palm grazing my cheek. "It's been hard having you so far away." I opened my mouth to apologize, but the look she threw me had me swallowing the words down. "But I'm happier you have a place you enjoy being, loyal friends, and your boyfriends." Her corny eyebrow wiggle made a giggle break through the tears. "Speaking of which, I still get to meet them this weekend, right?" I nodded, pulling my phone out to check.

Dante: We're all packed up, Firecracker, leaving now.

The text was sent over a half hour ago. Knowing how Hudson and the twins liked to drive, they'd be here within the next twenty minutes.

Logan: I've made a terrible mistake letting Landon drive. I fear we're going to die before we get there.

Scared emojis followed his text bringing another bout of giggles to my lips. The other guys had sent words of comfort that I responded to quickly so I could answer my mom.

"Yeah, they stayed behind to pack up their bags, but they're on their way now." I showed her the dramatic texts from Logan where he narrated their perilous journey in such an exaggerated way that we both burst into laughter. "Should be here soon." I started when there was a loud commotion down the hall. Jumping off the bed, I peeked my head out the closed door and saw Gerry assisting several nurses to secure and stabilize a combative patient. I pulled my head back and left the door ajar, so Charlie and Gerry knew that they could come back in when they were done. Charlie hadn't been in the hallway, so I assumed she had gone to see her dad while he prepped for surgery. I sat back onto my mom's left side, my knee propped up on the incline of the mattress.

"I'm excited to meet them." She smiled, her good-hearted glint that always shone in her blue eyes sparkling. Her eyes traced over my face slowly, taking in every detail of my puffy, red, tear-covered face. "They've been good for you, Lucie."

I felt my brow furrow at her statement. *How can she tell?*

"You had so many shadows in your eyes when you were home. So many that I wasn't even sure if I'd ever see your eyes sparkle like they used to, but I can see it now. I can see the laughter, happiness, and love radiating in you again. I know you've been working hard and making friends and growing into your powers, but I know they help you. They've helped bring my baby back to herself." Her hands cupped my cheeks, thumbs wiping the fresh tears that fell down my face. I leaned in for another hug, her warm baked sugar scent surrounding me.

"Is there anything I can do for you?" I finally stuffed the emotions and tears down, wanting to help her be as comfortable as possible. As she shook her head, the sound of the door opening and quietly closing shifted our attention to the other side of the room. I turned, seeing the male nurse I had tried to avoid earlier in the hall standing in front of the closed door, facing away from me, his long fingers curled around the door handle.

"Hello, Lucie baby." The fake nurse turned, cold eyes seeking me out. Noah's cruel smirk contorted his lips as he faced me fully. He was dressed in light green scrubs with black boots covering his feet. My heart pounded wildly at being so close to him. Adrenaline flooded my veins as I jumped to a standing position. The panic and anxiety were there, but my body forced them away, focusing on survival instead.

"You," I ground out, fists clenched tightly at my sides.

He chuckled quietly. The sound grated on my ears, and flashes of memories flickered to life in front of my eyes. Pushing them back, I took a defensive step forward, ready to punch the smug look off his fucking face. *I'm going to give him everything he deserves.* Rage flowed through me, increasing with every second he stood before me.

"Yes, Babygirl, me." He started to pace a few steps into the room before stopping. His strong jaw clenched giving away how angry he was despite his smooth tone and gait. "You have been increasingly hard to get ahold of." He curved his shoulders toward me. "But here you are, all alone." My mother scoffed.

"Not alone." She sat up fully, bare legs swinging over the edge of the bed. Before she could stand from the bed, Noah pulled his handgun from the waistband of his pants, aiming it directly at my mom.

My vision tunneled at the short distance between my mom's forehead and the barrel of his gun. *I need to get him away from here.*

"Shut up," he huffed, rolling his eyes like a petulant child. "I don't have time for your shit. Let's go, Babygirl. Out the door, to the left, and out the emergency exit." When I hesitated, attempting to form a plan, he cocked the hammer back. The clicking echoed in the utterly silent room. "Come now, I don't want to blow your fake mom's brains all over the wall, but I will if you don't move that sexy ass outside."

I took a steadying breath, taking a half step forward to the end of the bed. *Where is Charlie? Or Gerry?*

Focusing on the gun and keeping my hands near my waist, palms out, I stepped closer to the door. When I was nearly there, Noah closed the distance between us. His right arm held the gun swung down, pointing to the tile. His left hand reached across his body and gripped the door handle.

He peeked his head out before aiming the gun at my midsection, the cold metal brushing against my sweater.

"Now, Lucie baby, if you even think of making any noise or bringing attention to us, *I will shoot you.*" I nodded, smoothing my face into a look of compliance. When his head turned toward the hall, I moved. I shoved his arm to the left, the gun moving away from my stomach before I grabbed the barrel and twisted so he couldn't hold on to it. He groaned painfully at the sharp angle, trying to yank it back out of my hand. I kicked, punched, screamed as loud as my voice would go, anything to keep him from getting hold of the weapon or me.

The sound of thundering footsteps sounding out down in the hall. *Thank god!* I pulled back from his hand as he attempted to grab my shoulder, his grip strong enough to rip the material of my sweater. When the steps in the hall neared the door, he threw the door open the rest of the way and took off at a sprint toward the exit. Gerry continued until he reached the room, several security guards and two police officers barreling the last few feet down the hall past him and out the door. The moment felt like it had gone on forever, but the encounter had only really taken a minute. Gerry gingerly took the loaded weapon from my trembling hand before disassembling it.

"Are you both all right?" he asked, and my head whipped around to check on my mom. She released a large, shaky breath and nodded.

I ran around the bed and hugged her again, leaving Gerry's question unanswered. *So close. Too close.* We latched onto each other and didn't let go, the severity of what happened finally settling into us. Another collection of running footsteps filled the hall. The guys and Charlie anxiously entered the room, their faces telegraphing the worry that had caused them to sprint here.

"What happened?" Charlie questioned first, reading our body language. I had opened my mouth to answer when the smell of bonfire filled the air. Landon and Logan were facing the gun parts in Gerry's hand. Their claws and horns were out, and their eyes literally smoldered as they stared at the gun, the flames of their hellfire crackling dangerously.

"He was here?" Logan bit out, his chest heaving. "Where is he now?" The two police officers entered the door frame at that time, huffing after their chase.

"He's gone," the first officer stated, his beet red face matching his equally red hair. "Jumped into an idling car. Someone else was driving and was prepared to leave in a rush. We'll need your guys' statements, and we'll be posting an officer outside the room." The second officer had short blond hair, his skin tan under the lights. His eyes widened when he saw Logan and Landon's daemon form and realized that he was in a room with supes.

"We'll give you guys a few moments." The blond officer gripped the redhead's bicep, pulling him away from the room. Dante and the rest of my guys turned to me after shutting the door. Charlie sat next to my mom, her hand rubbing gentle circles on her back.

"Yeah, he was here. Tried to kidnap me," I forced out. The adrenaline was fading from my system fast, and spots formed in front of my eyes. My legs gave out under me, and blackness took over.

November 23rd
Friday Late Afternoon
Nikolai

Lucie's blonde hair was splayed out on the hospital's thin pillow. Her breathing was steady with long deep breaths that raised and lowered her chest. I could not take my eyes off her. Her pale skin was free of bruises or injuries, but knowing she was at gunpoint only a few hours ago had my jaw clenching and power crackling against my skin. The rest of my brothers were scattered around the space in various chairs we had dragged into the room.

Charlie and her mom were situated in the room next door with Lucie's adoptive mom, Abigail. I could hear their laughter every once in a while, their door partially open to allow Gerry and Officer Pearce to check between our two rooms. The officers had taken Abigail's statement after the nurse and doctor strapped Lucie up to an IV and checked her vitals. She had woken up briefly in a panic a while after passing out, only calming when we talked to her. After telling us what had happened and slight convincing from the doctor, she was sedated for a deep, restorative sleep.

Grigori scanned the room, ever vigilant of my family. Everyone had drawn faces, worry and anger radiating in their eyes. No one was really talking since we were all lost in our own thoughts. Based on their quickly changing facial expressions, Logan and Landon were communicating through their twin telepathy, but the silence of the room was heavy and oppressive. The opening of the door shook us out of our haze. Dean Renaud's sleek black pinstriped suit appeared, his hand reaching behind him to close the door. His eyes zeroed in on Lucie, and a pained expression passed over his face quickly before smoothing into his normally calm exterior. *Why is he so drawn to her? I am glad that he is on our side, but why does he care so much?*

"What happened?" he asked softly. His shiny dress shoes

clopped against the equally shiny white tile as he stepped closer to the foot of the bed.

"From what we understand," Dante started, standing up on the opposite side of the bed from me to look down at our Lucie. "Noah attacked her adoptive mom, trying to intimidate her into calling Lucie to come home. Abigail resisted, calling the police quickly enough that it scared him away. Apparently, he followed them to the hospital and stole a pair of scrubs, so he could blend in with the nurses and wait for Lucie to get here to see Abigail. Lucie said she walked past him on her way in and didn't realize it." He sighed heavily, rubbing his fingers on his eyes as if trying to banish the images I knew were plaguing him; it was the same for all of us.

"He created a distraction by drugging another patient into a frenzy," I explained. My throat throbbed with each word. "Gerry went to assist the nurses and security only a few rooms down." My voice cracked painfully at the end. Unable to continue, I glanced quickly at Cam who understood.

"Charlie had gone to talk with her dad to give Lucie some time with Abigail. When they were alone, Noah slipped into her room, the scrubs giving him the perfect cover." His quiet words were somber, the honey in his usual voice darkened. "Said how she had been hard to get to recently, and when her mom tried to get out of the hospital bed, he pulled the gun on her."

"On Abigail or Lucie?" the dean questioned, his eyes never leaving Lucie's sleeping form.

"Abigail, initially." Cam shifted his glasses up his nose before continuing, "Saying Lucie needed to accompany him out of the room and head out the emergency exit. Threatened..." He snarled, fangs winking in the dimmed lighting.

The predatory side of him surged forward with the memory of Noah's ruthless threat. Logan took over from there.

"He said, and I quote, 'Blow her fake mom's brain all over the wall' if she didn't go with him." He finger quoted Noah's words, disgust curling his lip. "This guy is seriously fucking insane."

"I can't wait to get my hands on him," Landon murmured, his eyes flashing dangerously. Dean Renaud waved his hand, cutting off his thoughts.

"We'll handle him when we get him," he commanded softly, looking toward Dante. "For now, though, what else happened?"

"When Lucie got to the door of the room, he came up and held the gun at her stomach saying if she made any noise he'd shoot her. When he looked out the door, she disarmed him. We had just walked by the front desk when we heard her screaming like a banshee." Dante smiled down at her as he recounted what Lucie's mom had told us. "She had apparently landed several solid hits, and when Gerry, a couple of officers, and several security guards neared, he ran out the emergency door. The cops and security ran after him but didn't get him. We showed up shortly after Gerry had disassembled the gun." Dante looked at the dean, his face harsh. "There was someone waiting in the car outside, so he was able to leave immediately. Whoever is helping him knew where they'd be and when." A small groan came from the bed, Lucie's face squishing up against the soft light in the room. Dean Renaud laid a soft hand on her blanket covered foot.

"Lucie?" he asked softly, her eyes fully open now. Shuffling, she inclined the back of the bed to sit up further.

"Fancy seeing you here while I'm confined to a hospital bed." She coughed a giggle, her voice thick with sleep. "This is starting to become a really shitty habit." Dean Renaud squeezed her ankle, the pained expression on his face obvious despite him trying to hide it. "I certainly hope this doesn't become a habit. How are you feeling?"

She shook her hand back and forth miming so-so. "Spent, exhausted. I feel like I want to sleep for the next week." Her face scrunched up as if she finally realized the dean was here. "Who called you?"

"Mr. Hanson reported an attack but didn't elaborate, and I wanted to come check on you and your mother. I also wanted to talk with you." He pulled his hand back to straighten his signature black tie. "I already discussed it with Abigail, but we think it would be best to go back to campus. I will be bringing in additional security for the campus as a whole."

She sighed, her shoulders dropping, but she agreed with a nod.

"I'm very sorry, Lucie, but we'll get him. I will be contacting a Tracker as soon as the one with the FSID is available." My eyebrows raised— finding Trackers who were not currently hired or under contract was hard and very expensive. They were highly sought after, most working on the wrong side of the law because of the amount of money they could make. The one that worked with FSID was a hard man to get, but if anyone could do it, I would assume it was Dean Renaud, especially considering his family's influence.

"It's all right, Alex." She gave a timid smile. "We'll get him eventually. Until then, I'll stay with them and security."

He nodded and lightly cleared his throat, seeming uncomfortable with not knowing what to say next. "I'll leave you to sleep then." He gave a single nod to us before heading to the door, pausing before exiting completely.

"Call me if you need anything, Lucie. You too, gentlemen." The door shut quietly behind him, and my hand found its way to Lucie's, intertwining our fingers.

"All right, boys." She turned her attention to us. "I'm fighting sleep really hard right now, so I'm going to try and rest some more. You guys okay?" She smiled warmly at us after we gave our assent. "Good, I'm so happy you're here." She snuggled down into the thin blankets, her eyes falling shut. "I couldn't imagine any better boyfriends than you six." Her words trailed off in a mumble, her breathing evening out. Despite the silence, the tension was not as thick as it had been. Each of our faces held a small smile as we looked from her to around us. *We could not agree more...*

17

November 26^{*th*}
Monday Midday
Lucienne

"Race you!" I shouted as I took off. My boots thudded against the wood flooring, my bag bouncing against my hip as I sprinted toward the power practice room. Hudson's long legs were right behind me and catching up quickly. His honeyed colored hand reached out, crossing the threshold of the room an inch before me. The sudden exercise left me bent over with hands braced on my knees as I gasped for air.

"I win," he boasted triumphantly. His chest puffed up, and he put his hands on his trim hips. Glaring at him from my bent over position, I tried to keep a straight face but I couldn't. I had been trying the last couple days to keep the mood light and fun. Distracting the guys from their agitation and urge to go hunting for Noah was tiring but necessary. They had been bogged down with the severity of what had happened, their shoulders slouching and frowns on their handsome faces since I had woken up in the hospital. And while I knew this wasn't over, diverting our attention to focus on us and school helped keep tensions down.

"Yeah, yeah rub it in." I chuckled, chucking my bag into the corner. From what I had heard, almost all the freshmen had been released from their power placement testing and practices, so I was crossing my fingers and hoping that my time would end today.

"I would never do such a thing." Hudson dropped his bag next to mine and leaned back against the single table pushed up against the wall. I gave a skeptical hum, watching Professor George enter the room in his usual disheveled manner, cutting off any response from either of us.

"Ah, perfect, you two are here already!" He straightened his crooked glasses; unfortunately, he just overcorrected it and made them tilt the other direction. "I have good news!" He clapped his hands and for the first time I realized he didn't carry his clipboard or papers. I waited patiently for the news, but it didn't escape my notice that Hudson's lip was twitching in an attempt not to smile.

"What's the good news?" I prompted when I realized the professor wasn't going to say without me asking. He jumped up and down slightly, his half-untucked shirt flapping underneath his sweater vest.

"You've officially completed your power testing!"

My jaw dropped, my brain sputtering out of commission. "What?" *Smart, Lucie, real smart,* I chided. I shook my head slightly to kickstart my brain. "For real?"

"Yes!" He clapped again, hopping from side to side. "You're to meet with Dean Renaud before your next class to go over your progress." I smiled, lost in my own excitement, as Professor George checked his broken watch and scurried quickly out the door leaving Hudson and me alone.

"Did you know?" I asked Hudson, my smile hurting my cheeks from how wide it was. He nodded enthusiastically before wrapping me tightly in his arms.

"I got notified this morning, and I've been trying to keep it to myself, but it was really difficult. I was just so excited for you, Princess." A kiss pressed into my hair as I curled my face into his soft dark grey sweater, a widening smile affixed to my face. "I have something for you, if you want to close your eyes." Suspicious but curious, I did as he asked. Once my eyes were shut, he stepped away from me, my arms falling to my sides. I heard some rustling of his backpack before it stopped and Hudson let me know I could open my eyes.

"Hudson," I breathed, feeling my heart flutter as I saw what he had pulled out. In his hands was a pair of earrings; the clear teardrop shape dangling from the silver hooks held a couple pieces of a flower. Looking closer I realized the flower was baby's breath, the white of the bulb and the green of the stem dainty in the nickel-sized earrings. "They're beautiful," I praised, a broad smile spreading as I looked up at him.

"I made them for you," he murmured, two tiny patches of pink spread on his cheeks as he talked. "Baby's breath isn't a flower Nik or I use very often, and I figured you would like them..." He trailed off shrugging slightly as if he didn't know what to say.

"I think they're gorgeous," I said happily, glancing back at the dainty flowers before focusing on him. "Thank you, hon. I can't wait to wear them. Maybe I will on our next date?" I added. With that statement, he perked up, the nervousness melting back into his confident self.

"I would love that." He gave me a quick kiss before pulling back. "Come on, Princess. Let's go to Dean Renaud's office." Hudson grabbed our bags, handing me mine so I could tuck the earrings away safely in the inside zipper pocket. When it was secure, I tossed my messenger bag over my shoulder and opened the door for us.

Gerry was waiting against the wall next to the door, his middle-aged dark skin wrinkled as he smiled at me. He fell into step near me, his muscled legs shortening steps to keep next to us. I watched him out of the corner of my eye. He had been around for the last month, but I hadn't really looked at him since the security detail had been keeping their distance until the shit show this last weekend. His buzzed black hair was barely visible on his dark chocolate skin, and his muscles were bulkier than Dante's or Bill's. The more I watched him, the more his build reminded me of Dwayne 'The Rock' Johnson.

The cold air outside hit my face when Hudson held open the door for me. The sudden chill pulled my attention away from the head of security to where I was walking. I slipped under Hudson's arm when he caught up to me, his sweater soft against the back of my neck since I decided to forgo the scarf today. We were quiet during our walk, eyes scanning the quad for any signs of Noah or suspicious people. Before I knew it, I was being greeted by Jonathon, his wobbly voice warm as he talked.

"Hello, Miss Lucie, Dean Renaud is waiting for you. Good Afternoon, Mr. Hanson, Mr. Nguyen." He smiled and nodded toward my company before waving his hand up the stairs. "You get to it now, don't want to keep him waiting." I chuckled before starting up the steps.

"I'll be waiting out here." Gerry's deep, booming voice echoed slightly off the walls of the stairwell as we neared the fourth floor. "Hudson, the dean wished to speak with Lucie privately. Someone will be by to get her before her afternoon class." Hudson's lips thinned, but he didn't argue.

"All right, I'll see you tonight, Princess."

I popped up on my toes giving him a brief kiss, his chapstick slick against my lips. I smiled as he turned to head back downstairs. As soon as my foot hit the top floor, Alex's office door opened.

Curiosity finally won over as I stepped into his office, and I blurted out, "How do you *do* that?" I pretended to ignore the fact that Gerry was chuckling out in the hallway at my question.

"Wards." Alex smiled down at me, his dark suit standing out against the warm wood bookshelves.

I nodded, understanding the basics of what he meant, but I wasn't going to ask how they worked because that type of magic was way too advanced for me. *He wouldn't tell you anyway,* I whispered to myself.

"Have a seat, Lucie." He waved his hand toward my normal seat, the plush leather chair on the right in front of his antique desk. I plopped down slightly bouncing on the rich dark brown leather. "Congratulations on completing your power testing. Professor George spoke very highly of you, and I know I have seen great improvement in our sessions."

"Thank you," I mumbled, my face burning under his praise. While I felt my cheeks glow, my heart leaped into my throat with excitement from knowing he was proud of me. His smile was warm, slight crow's feet appearing at the corners of his eyes.

"I would like to continue our sessions, but I think you deserve some time off. Would you be willing to start them up again after the holiday break?" He looked expectantly at me, and I nodded, knowing I wanted to be as good as I possibly could be with my powers. "Perfect, we will resume them January eleventh after the spring semester begins." He paused to make a quick note on his desk pad. His hand flowing smoothly with the fancy pen he picked up, the kind that came in an expensive wooden box. "Has Muriel talked to you about the exhibit we will be hosting in the library for the spring semester?"

"I heard her talk about it with several professors," I started. "Also, I was helping Cam with locating more references for his research."

"That's good, I was asked by Muriel if you would be permitted to come back to campus before the start of the semester to help assist set up."

I nodded excitedly; I did want to help because I was very curious about everything they wanted to set up. Not to mention, it would be a great opportunity to spend more time with Cam, seeing his eyes light up at each new discovery.

"Perfect, we will be starting setup Friday the fourth. If you want to stay in your room at the library, you're more than welcome, but I'm unsure how busy that area will be during the day. If you prefer, you will have access to your dorm room pending a more current update on the situation."

"I understand," I responded, my stomach clenching painfully at the implication of Noah and what it would mean if he was still out there by the New Year. His lips turned down ever so slightly catching my attention. "What?"

"That is another reason I wanted to speak to you today." He sighed, running his hand through his hair messing the gelled strands. Obviously aware of where my thoughts had drifted. "Are you aware of how many text messages and emails you've received since having your gentlemen carry your phone?" Despite the dark topic, I felt my cheeks heat at his words 'your gentlemen.' I shook my head, my growing panic clamping my jaw shut. "You've had several hundred of each and dozens of missed calls." My jaw dropped. *Holy shit.* I hadn't realized it had been that bad. The more I thought about it, the more the guys' solemn attitudes made sense.

"What do we do?" I whispered, hating how scared I sounded. His eyes softened at the obvious fear seeping through my words.

"I have something for the time being at least," he started, a soft knocking cutting through his words. My brows knit together. *Who is that? Why didn't Alex open the door as soon as someone approached his office?* He smoothly stepped around his desk and opened the door revealing Nik on the other side, Grigori perched regally on his shoulder. Now I was very confused as to what was going on.

"Dean Renaud." Nik dipped his head as he entered, his gravelly words soft and full of respect as Alex held out his hand towards the open chair.

"Have a seat, Nikolai." My brain struggled to keep up, even more surprised to hear Alex call anyone other than me by their first name.

"Hey, Babe," Nik whispered, leaning in closely to kiss my cheek. I turned just in time to catch his lips in a soft brush against mine. He smirked at me before sitting back into his seat. Alex's eyes were tight as he sat behind his desk, but he didn't comment on our behavior. *Even though I don't always understand it, it's nice that he's so protective.*

"As I was saying," Alex started, his hand waving toward Nik, "we have a temporary solution. Nikolai's archery competition is out of state, and we discussed you, Camden, and Gerry accompanying him." I perked up. *I get to go to the competition?* Alex chuckled at my blatant excitement. "I take it you would be all right with that?" I nodded enthusiastically.

"We will be leaving Friday afternoon and coming back Sunday morning," Nik supplied. Alex hummed an agreement.

"It'll get you away from everything for a few days, but before you go..." Alex hesitated. Leaning forward, he propped his elbows on the desk, his suit jacket straining against his shoulders. "I know you hid your wish token box, but I feel it would be more secure in my private safe."

"How did you know?" I felt my eyebrows raise in surprise. *I didn't tell him about that, did I?* My cheeks tinted when they both chuckled.

"Professor George included it in his power testing notes. Don't worry, no one else knows about it." I breathed a sigh of relief. *That makes sense,* I reasoned.

"I can bring it in, but I have to get it first. Can I drop it off tomorrow evening? We were planning on studying this afternoon." I glanced over at Nik. His ankle was propped on his left leg, arms resting on the leather chair. Grigori perched on his right shoulder, his beady eyes focused on me instead of Alex. I pulled my eyes away when I saw Nik's lip curl ever so slightly.

"That's fine, I'll be here." Alex stood buttoning his jacket. Nik and I followed suit, and I situated my bag on my shoulder. "I believe that's all I had. Is there anything else you need?" I shook my head, and when Alex looked over at Nik, he did the same. Nodding, Alex walked around his desk and opened the door. "I'll see you tomorrow, Lucie. Keep me updated if anything else happens." In the bustle of everything going on around me, I kept forgetting to tell Alex about my conversation with the Spring Court Queen. Not wanting to waste his time or let whatever he could tell me about Mireille potentially ruin my weekend if it wasn't what I wanted to hear, I decided to wait until we returned to bring it up.

"Thank you," I mumbled, my mind going a mile a minute. *I finally get to see one of Nik's competitions!* I internally squealed. Nik's hand grabbed mine, lacing our fingers together as we started down the stairs. For the rest of the day, I struggled through class and studying, my focus on our weekend trip.

November 27th
Tuesday Afternoon
Lucienne

"Hey, Lemon Drop," Landon greeted cheerfully, his bag falling to the ground. His arms wrapped around me tightly before I could ask what he was doing. "We get you all to ourselves for a while."

"Love," Logan hummed, pulling me back against his chest when Landon released me. "Where are we going now?" I felt a kiss on the top of my head before his arms dropped.

"Follow me, it's kind of a walk," I said quietly, not wanting to pull attention from the other students. We followed the flow of students through the quad but turned on one of the less used paths. When we reached the barely worn footpath into the woods, I quickly glanced around before starting to the edge of the trees. The twins looked around the surrounding area, whether out of curiosity or for trouble I didn't know, but the tension in their shoulders worried me. "So how was your energy manipulation class?" I asked trying to rid them of some of their worries.

"Not bad, we're working on some complex building and

deconstructing of structures. I built a multi-room doghouse," Logan explained.

"He freaking built his imaginary dog a bunker, but don't worry, I got it taken down," Landon prided himself. Logan rolled his eyes but continued on as if his twin hadn't said anything.

"We're going to be starting on studying energy manipulation uses in military and war next week. Once the book portion is done, we'll be working on actual application." Logan's arm wrapped around my shoulder as Landon's hand grabbed mine.

"Yup, then we have finals." Landon groaned pitifully. I chuckled, but internally I felt the same. I always got nervous during major tests, the worry of failing making the stress worse.

"We have a few weeks still at least," I pointed out, "finals week isn't until the twelfth, and we have a weekend in the middle of it." Landon grumbled inarticulately. "Got to look on the bright side, babe." I nudged his arm with my elbow, a happy smile taking over my face. I had missed the happy-go-lucky times we had together in the stress of the last few weeks. Landon grumbled a bit more, but he wasn't able to hide his smile.

"So, Love, what are we doing out in the woods?" Logan's voice was curious as he looked around us, the forest thick as we continued our walk.

"I need to bring my lock box to Alex's office so he can put it in his safe." I kept my eyes on the ground not wanting to trip on any roots like I had with Nik.

"Lock box?" they asked at the same time. *Oh yeah, I hadn't told them yet.*

"It holds the rest of my wish tokens. I had it when I was found." I sighed, realizing I needed to tell them about my mom and what had happened. If I wasn't focused on talk-ing, I would have giggled at their scrunched-up faces. Briefly I told them my story, and their eyes widened signifi-cantly. "And here we are. As instructed, my adoptive mom led me to believe I was human until college, and Adelaide was specific on where to send me. I think she knew Alex was the dean here or something, so my adoptive mom reached out, and they got me all squared away." I shrugged, not sure what else to say. Thankfully the path widened as we reached the little clearing cutting off anymore of the conversation.

"Woah," Logan breathed softly. Turning my attention to them I saw surprise and appreciation for the little space. I knew exactly how they felt; this place seemed almost sacred, something about the area and the serenity that permeated the space soothed any jagged shards inside me. I stepped away from them, their eyes darting around the greenery in awe. I headed straight for the stone pile, noting that none of the stones had been moved despite the couple of storms we had had since I placed my tokens out here. Making quick work of the makeshift lid on the hole, I reached in and wrapped my fingers around the soft material of the fabric wrapped around the trinket box.

"Is that it?" Logan had stepped up to my seated form, his blood red eyes full of curiosity as I unwrapped the box. I nodded, feeling Landon sit next to me on the rock. I grabbed my token and rubbed inconspicuously. It wasn't that I didn't trust the twins, I just wasn't sure I wanted *anyone* to know how to open it. The soft hiss and click of the box sounded in the quiet area. I opened the lid, the jingle of coins rattling together tinkling to my ear.

"Wow, that's cool," Landon added, his chin propped on my shoulder. "Think Mireille Bonheur made the box? Or had it commissioned?" I tilted my head looking at the hand sized box that nestled perfectly between my clenched fingers.

"I don't know. I can see if Alex can look into it, or Cam." I relocked the box and stood, tucking it and the fabric into my messenger bag. They nodded and resumed their positions on either side of me. "Let's get going. The guys will be getting antsy without their coffee before studying," I joked. They both scoffed.

"The only one who gets antsy without their coffee is you, Lemon Drop," Landon teased. He looked over at his brother. "Speaking of the guys, what are we getting Dante for his birthday?" I stopped walking, their forward momentum tugging on my upper body, but I remained where I was.

"When's his birthday?" I asked.

"December fourth."

My eyes widened. *That's in a week!*

"Why didn't anyone tell me?" I squeaked, my mind whirling with stuff I wanted to do for his birthday. They both looked at each other guiltily.

"Dante doesn't really celebrate his birthday." Logan shrugged, his attention shifting back to me. "We thought someone had told you." The nervous smiles on their faces practically pleaded with me not to yell at them for the slip-up.

"Okay," I said, my voice determined, "I need to text Sadie to have her meet us at Coffeeology." I started walking again, my steps purposeful as I planned. Landon handed my phone to me as I passed, and I blatantly ignored the texts from the unknown number.

"Love," Logan huffed, shuffling to keep up, "what's going on up in that pretty head of yours?" I hit send on the text and stuffed my phone back into Landon's outstretched hand.

"He might not celebrate his birthday much, but I want to do something special for him. It's the first time we're all together for one of our birthdays." I paused, tilting my head back and forth. "Well, first time I'm included, but still. We're doing something, and you two are helping me."

"What do you have in mind?" I chuckled at Landon's question, his eyebrow rising at my lack of an answer.

"You'll find out when we get to Sadie." I gave him a sly smile. They pleaded the entire way, but I wouldn't give them any idea into what I had planned. After twenty minutes of walking through the cold, the heat of Coffeeology blasted against my face when Logan held the door open for Landon and me. Sadie stood out among the small crowd, her blue hair a shining beacon after having been freshly colored and cut this last weekend.

"Okay, Lucie loo, what's with the secret Batman meeting?" she questioned as I sat down at the table she had saved. Her eyebrows rose as she looked to the twins for an answer, and they both shrugged cluelessly. I rubbed my hands together and smiled. *I love planning.* "Uh oh, you look like you're about to admit you want to take over the world through some weird means that will eventually be foiled by a superhero." I laughed, catching the attention of several of the students around us. I quieted, my cheeks flushing under the unwanted attention.

"Dante's birthday is coming up next week," I blurted out.

Her brow furrowed as her head tilted. "You have a plan, don't you?"

I nodded quickly, leaning forward as if anyone around would hear and tell Dante the plan. "We're going to throw a surprise party," I squealed quietly, "us four, and we'll invite the guys, Elijah and Gabe, and Benji and Austin." I started to list more guests when the twins' eyes lit up in under-standing at where I was going with this.

"The Kohl team," Sadie suggested, her hand disappearing into her bright red heart-shaped purse pulling out a small notebook and pen to jot down our ideas.

"Oh yes!" I pointed at her excitedly.

"Maybe not Mia," Logan suggested, his lips thinning as he likely thought back to how she reacted in the locker room. I waved away his concerns.

"Mia too." Landon started to protest, but I cut him off. "She might have been rude that one time, but she's part of the team, and he's the captain. I'm not going to exclude anyone just because of one bad interaction." They didn't look happy but didn't fight me.

"You leave it to me," Sadie mumbled, her pen scrawling quickly across the page. "We got this. You guys go study, and I'll head back to my room to figure out the place to host it." We all shared a conspiratorial smile before she headed out of the coffee shop leaving my twins and me to collect coffee for our study group.

"You're a little minx, Lemon Drop," Landon whispered in my ear, the sound sending shivers down my spine. "He'll never see it coming."

"Is it a good idea?" I questioned, suddenly nervous.

"It's perfect," Logan murmured. The warm excitement of the party filled me as we took the cup carriers to the library. Not even the cold air, upcoming finals, or thoughts of Noah could dim my happiness.

18

I double checked my small duffle bag quickly after pulling it from the trunk of the town car. I was excitedly jittery as well as nervous, having not been out of state or on a plane in several years. Gerry and Cam were already boarding the private jet stairs, seemingly comfortable with the whole situation. I, on the other hand, was freaking out. *Who owns a private jet?* I eyed the metal contraption with suspicion.

"You all right, Babe?" Nik's rough question was startling enough for me to yelp as I jumped to face him. My chest heaved, my heart thudding out of control. His eyebrows went up as Grigori's head tilted.

"I haven't flown in a really long time," I admitted quietly, securing my bag in my hand. "Just a bit nervous is all."

"It will be okay, the flight is only a few hours," he assured me as we started toward the jet.

"Where are we going again? And whose jet is this? I've never been on a jet, only commercial flights, and even then it was always in coach." I was rambling and I knew it, but once I started asking questions my mouth just wouldn't shut. I continued peppering questions without giving him time to answer as we ascended the steps. Only when we entered the plane did my questions cease.

The interior was cream and wood tones, and a mix of expensive looking chairs, tables, and couches filled the carpeted area. There was even a mini bar and small bedroom in the back that held a queen-sized bed. My eyes continued to dart around the space as Nik stored his bag and archery equipment into a closet. Cam chuckled at my expression, which I'm sure looked like a fish out of water, and took my bag to stow it with the others.

"Come on, Doll." He gently maneuvered me to one of the clusters of chairs. Two of the seats faced another set with a fold down table between them. I sank into the chair closest to the window, Cam situating himself into the chair across from me as Nik and Grigori sat next to me.

"To answer your question," Nik smiled at me, his glassy eyes angled toward me, "the jet is mine." My jaw dropped at his revelation, and all I could do was sit there stupefied.

"Technically, it's his parents' second jet, but they gave it to Nik when he was younger for competitions," Cam corrected matter of factly. His black frames winked in the overhead light as he leaned back against the headrest.

"To answer your other question, we are going to Phoenix," Nik took over for Cam, buckling into his seat.

"Arizona?" I knew it was a dumb question, but for some reason my brain wasn't processing information after hearing the fact that Nik's family was rich enough to have two, *two*, jets. They both smothered laughs at me as the pilot announced the preflight information and the plane started to taxi to the tarmac.

"Yes." Cam finally buckled his seat belt while responding. "Phoenix, Arizona." They continued to answer the multitudes of questions I had rattled off during boarding as we reached the runway. As soon as the plane took off, my attention had shifted to looking out the window taking in the Washington landscape. My eyes struggled to stay open after we reached cruising altitude, but I was lulled fully into sleep when the press of a warm blanket covered me.

———

Something nudged my shoulder, but grumbling, I burrowed deeper into the soft blanket I had curled around me. A masculine chuckle echoed and another shake rattled my body. My mind continued to float in the abyss of sleep, unwilling to wake.

"Babe," a familiar gravel tone pulled me closer to the surface, "we are here." I finally pried my eyes open, the bright sunlight through the window temporarily blinding me.

"Ugh," I groaned covering my eyes, black spots flashing in rapid succession in the dark. "Too bright," I mumbled. The sound of the shade closing reached my ears, and the light filtering through the blanket darkened.

"There Doll, come on now, let's go get checked in and drop our bags off." Cam nudged my leg with his knee. I yanked the blanket down and mustered my best glare. Cam's bright smile and Nik's smirk melted my fake anger into a fit of giggles.

They're too handsome for their own good.

"What's the plan for the day?" I asked, my words

sounding weird as I stretched before standing. Nik, Cam, and Gerry must have unloaded our stuff from the closets, as they were open and emptied when I passed them.

"We head to the hotel and check in," Nik shared while holding the door of the SUV for Cam and me. Gerry slid into the passenger seat, Cam crawling past the second row of seats to the third and plopping down. His hair splayed out against his forehead at the sharp movement before he brushed them back with an open hand. I crawled in behind the driver, Nik sitting behind Gerry and closing the door with a loud thud.

"That it for today?" I asked as I buckled my seatbelt. The SUV was quiet except for the soft classical music streaming from the speakers as we pulled onto the highway. Nik sighed, rubbing his hands down his face.

"No," he groaned, "have the Competitor's Dinner at seven. You do not have to go if you do not want." He turned toward me, leg propping up on the seat.

"Why wouldn't I want to go?" I questioned. *Did he not want me to go?*

"There's another competitor who's an ass and will probably try to talk some shit. It isn't that we don't want you there, but we weren't sure if you would be comfortable with that." Cam must have recognized the hurt I tried to hide on my face, but after his explanation I nodded in understanding.

"Is it a fancy dinner?" They both nodded. "I didn't bring anything to wear for *fancy,*" I mumbled, worrying my lip between my teeth.

"If you want to go, we got you something," Cam supplied softly.

The car pulling into a parking lot dragged my attention away from the conversation. The Camby Hotel's drive up entryway was filled with expensive town cars and SUVs, and I even spotted a few limos. *What kind of people go to these competitions?* My mouth was open, and I knew my eyes widened as I took in the extravagance of the hotel and its posh lobby. Everything screamed art deco and expensive tastes. I felt out of place in my skinny jeans, scuffed knee-high boots, and oversized sweater while people around us flitted around in designer labels and fancy suits. Nik stepped up to the counter, the concierge recognizing him immediately. The check-in process was seamless, only requiring him to take the keys with a quick 'thank you.'

Stepping into the elevator it was just the four of us. I was glad to be away from the mass of people and competitors collecting in the lobby, bar, and billiards room downstairs. Our room wasn't too far from the elevator, but far enough for me to get a good look around the marbled hall. Once the door was unlocked, I lost my breath.

The room was a suite, the bedroom behind an open set of double doors. The living room held a blue sectional, flat screen TV, desk, and a view of the desert mountains. I didn't want to touch anything. It almost felt like my middle-class-ness would somehow taint the expensive furnishings around us. I mean, *holy shit, how expensive is this room?* The bedroom and bathroom also blew my mind. A king bed seemed small in the space with a small table with two chairs that sat under yet another window with amazing views. I think I stopped breathing at the all marble bathroom. Not being able to take anymore, I stumbled to the bed in shock. *This is what Nik does almost every weekend?* I couldn't believe it.

"It is a lot, I know," Nik grumbled, flopping onto the bed next to me. Grigori had taken off when we arrived, not liking being trapped on the plane. Nik had assured me before we left that Grigori just needed to stretch his wings, but he would be back before dinner tonight.

"Is this what it's like every competition?"

He tilted his head back and forth as if unsure how to answer. "Sometimes it is a little more laid back, especially if it is a smaller competition, but yes, it is like this for the larger ones." He lay back, his gelled, chocolate brown hair a stark contrast to the white comforter.

"What do you mean larger competitions? Does that mean the number of people or...?" I was curious since Nik rarely talked about his competitions. Hell, Nik rarely talked at all. He was my silent companion, always there to help soothe any problem with a hug, kiss, and a feathery head boop.

"It is more for the big-name competitors." He turned his head toward me. "Bigger competitors, bigger sponsors, bigger prizes, bigger rewards." His voice cracked at the end. Clamping his jaw shut, he turned watery eyes to the ceiling. I laced my fingers with his; more questions brewed in my mind, but I didn't want him to hurt anymore. Cam finally shuffled off the couch from his prone position, having flopped face first into the deep sapphire cushions when we got to the room.

"So, you want to come with us to dinner?" I nodded, my eyes wandering down Cam's muscled body as it leaned against the door frame of the bedroom. His denim clad legs were straining against the material, his arms hanging loosely by his side as he slid his hands into the pockets of his jeans. He'd shed his sweater when we landed, leaving him in a forest green shirt that was tight against his chest and biceps. His lips curled in a smirk at my perusal, but he didn't say anything.

"I would love to go," I said happily. The bed was outrageously comfortable, but if I was going to go, I needed to get ready. "What's the dress code?" I shifted to sitting, my hand squeezing Nik's lightly before standing.

"Formal, near black-tie," Cam answered. "We'll be in nicer suits. Do you want to do your own hair and makeup or have someone else do it?" My eyebrows went up.

"I didn't know that was an option, but if it's that fancy, then I guess I'll have someone do it if we can even find anyone on such short notice." Cam waved his hand at me, dismissing my concerns.

"You going to shower?" Nik asked, his voice a near whisper. I nodded. "You do that and Gerry will take you to the salon. We made an appointment before coming."

"You guys," I started, my chest filled to bursting with warm and fuzzy emotions. My eyes watered and words escaped me. To express how I felt, I launched myself at Nik, wrapping him tightly in my arms. He smelled of fresh spring air and clean linens. His arms encircled my waist, holding me to the hard planes of his chest. I felt my tears soaking his black Henley before pulling away. He leaned down and pressed a soft kiss to my lips, dropping his arms to let me go to Cam. I closed the space between us, his parchment scent enveloping me as he folded me in his arms. "Thank you," I mumbled against his chest.

"No problem." Cam's hand rubbed gentle circles against my back. "We want you to be able to enjoy your weekend away." He pulled back and looked down at me. "Now, go shower and get ready." I gave him a kiss and grabbed my bag from the bed before heading into the bathroom, still feeling relaxed. My panic and anxiety had truly melted away for the first time in a month.

November 30th

Friday Evening
Lucienne

Holy shit. I stared at the dress the guys had gotten me. The navy blue was the same shade as my eyes, and the silhouette was reminiscent of the dress I wore at the All Hallows' Eve dance. Only this time instead of being a strapless sweetheart top, it was a halter. The halter portion connected in the back leaving most of my back covered except a sliver in the middle where the skirt portion lay and a small portion of my shoulder blades.

The dress was soft against my skin, and the gold and crystal diamond bib necklace they had left with the dress sparkled against the deep blue. I wanted to wear my token necklace, but I didn't want to keep it around my neck, so I did something I hadn't done in a while. I wrapped the chain around my wrist until it resembled a multi-strand bracelet and clipped it in place.

"You almost ready, Doll?" Cam's voice traveled through the crack in the bedroom door. Nik and Cam had had their garment bags hanging neatly in the living room when I returned from the salon, and neither of them were in the room so I could surprise them with a grand reveal.

"Almost, just have a bit left," I called out, sitting gingerly on the bed. I slipped on the simple gold heels, the straps wrapping over my foot and around my ankle to keep it in place.

"We're ready when you are."

I stood, double checking myself in the mirror one last time. My makeup was simple but classic with a soft smokey eye and nude lipstick. My hair was curled, the top half pulled back and set in a fancy knot like how Sadie had done my hair for my date with Hudson. Grigori fluttering into the room abruptly took me by surprise. Nik's familiar settled on the back of one of the chairs over by the window, his head tilted as he looked at me.

"You come to check on me?" I asked jokingly, his slight head shake making my brows creep up my forehead. "Well, if you aren't here for that, then why aren't you with Nik?" My question was low and hesitant, unsure if I was imagining Grigori responding to me, but when he gave a tiny squawk and glanced at the door, I knew I wasn't. With my curiosity piqued, I started toward the door cautiously. Peeking through the space, I felt a strange rush of heat flow through me at what I saw.

They were seated on the couch together. Cam's hand cupped Nik's jaw, his face buried in the crook of Nik's neck while his jaw shifted rhythmically. Nik's eyes were closed, his lips barely parted as Cam drank from him. A part of me was screaming to stop watching, that they were doing this in private, but the majority of me was entranced. Both by the intimacy of the situation and the almost erotic way Nik was reacting. *Does it feel good?* As soon as the thought popped in my head, Nik's eyes opened, his face shifting to look toward me. I huffed, glaring over at Grigori who was staring at me with unblinking eyes.

"Tattletale," I hissed under my breath. The familiar puffed up slightly before darting off his perch and into the living room where he landed on Nik's shoulder. I felt my face burn as Cam and Nik watched me, the former wiping his lip with his thumb to catch the smallest drop of blood that slid down his chin.

"Doll, you don't have to hide in the room," Cam cooed softly, giving a little wave of his hand for me to join them. I took a deep breath and opened the bedroom door the rest of the way. Now that I stood before them completely, I took in what they were wearing as they did the same to me. Both were sporting the same black suit, white dress shirt, and black-tie combination. Their dress shoes shone in the soft overhead light, and when they sat next to each other, my breathing faltered, unable to function with how handsome they looked.

"Wow," Nik's whisper was rough as Grigori's eyes trained on me to allow Nik to take in my outfit in its entirety. Cam's multifaceted hazel eyes sparkled.

"You look beautiful. Are you ready?" Cam asked shifting to stand. I nodded, still unable to speak after being caught watching something private. "Doll, it's all right, I wouldn't have fed in the room if I was worried you would see." His words helped ease that niggle of worry, but it didn't douse it completely.

"Promise?" I mumbled, slightly fiddling with my hair self-consciously.

"Lucie." Cam grabbed my hand, stopping my nervous movement to intertwine our fingers. "I promise. If you have any questions or anything, you can ask me at any time." I gave him a tiny smile before dipping my head in assent. Checking his watch, Cam nodded absently. "We should get going, the get together should be starting soon." Nik gave my lower back a soft brush of his fingertips as he passed me, stepping out into the hallway with Cam and waited for me to join them. They offered their arms, Cam on my right, Nik on my left, and once I tucked my fingers against their elbows, we headed down to the lobby.

The lobby and surrounding areas of the hotel still left me speechless as men and women, even children, were dressed to the nines. I couldn't tell which were competitors and which were sponsors as we made our way to the bar.

Cam ordered a round of sodas for us as Nik and I hung back.

Nik leaned down close to my ear. "You look beautiful, Babe." The gravel in his words brought a shiver to my body that I didn't try to repress. I had curved toward him to respond when a guy who looked to be our age stepped up to us. His light brown hair was slicked back, similar to Nik's style, and he wore a taupe colored suit. His dress shirt was red checker, and he wore a black skinny tie. His skin was tan while his cocky smile was slightly crooked. He was shorter than Nik and Cam, standing around 6' where my guys stood at 6'3".

"Nikolai." The guy's voice was deep, but not as deep as Dante's, and it held a Boston accent. I felt my skin prickle at his short greeting. The tension between Nik and this guy was thick, suffocating me in edginess. Nik's shoulders pulled back as he stood to his full height. Grigori seemed to be glaring at the newcomer, as well as a bird could glare, I supposed.

"Liam," Nik nearly growled his name. I tried to keep my expression smooth, but I couldn't help the surprise that flashed over my face at his harsh tone. The newcomer, Liam, turned his blood red eyes toward me. His cocky smile melted into a self-assured smirk.

"Who do we have here?" He held out his hand for me, I assumed to shake, but he turned my hand and kissed my knuckles lightly. I felt my back straighten, his action having set my teeth on edge.

"Lucie," I said coolly, not bothering with any other pleasantries.

"It's quite peculiar to see you with a woman, Nikolai." He smirked down at me once more. "Especially one this beautiful. Did Camden not attend this time?" His question seemed normal, but I could read the underlying sneer in his words.

"I'm right here, Liam," Cam responded, stepping up to my left. He held out our drinks for us, his resting on the empty cocktail table next to him before turning his attention to Liam. Cam's face was cold and stoic, a complete change from the smile and warm eyes he had given me. Liam raised a single brow as Cam's hand rested lightly on my lower back, his fingers brushing the sliver of skin revealed by my dress.

"Ah, of course you are." I clenched my teeth slightly, wanting to punch this guy in his snooty face. "If you'll excuse me, I have several others I need to see before dinner is served." His attention was solely on me as he spoke, his self-assured smile reappearing before he was lost in the crowd of people.

"Ugh," Cam groaned, his hand rubbing down his face. "I hate that guy." I had to agree with him, and I didn't like to hate anyone.

"I am sorry, Lucie, I did not expect him to approach us until tomorrow." Nik's voice was sad, the first I had heard it that way since I had met them. I turned to him, handing my drink to Cam after taking a sip.

"Don't apologize, Nik," I murmured softly, pressing my hand into his silky tie. "Even with that douche, I wouldn't want to be anywhere else tonight." Cam chuckled, his face warming to his normal happy expression. Nik blew out a breath, but he couldn't hide the small curl of his lips. "He's the asshole competitor, I'm assuming?" I took my drink back as we circled the table, content not to socialize with anyone else. They both nodded.

"He's been a thorn in our side since Nik started competing," Cam explained, grabbing two hors d'oeuvres from a passing waiter. "Want one?" he offered, but the cracker held some unknown meat and veggie spread, so I shook my head.

"He has been fighting for the number one competitor spot for years," Nik whispered to save his voice. I had to lean into him to hear him over the lull of conversation around us. "When I took a break from competing, he took over, but he has been even more of an ass since I came back two years ago, angry that I reclaimed the top spot." I nodded, Nik's explanation making me dislike Liam even more.

"Well, he's not important, let's just focus on having a good time." I perked up as I heard a dinging over the crowd. They both laughed and directed me toward the hotel restaurant that had been booked for the evening. I settled in between my guys, the smell of the food making my stomach growl. Our evening was spent with fun conversation that left me feeling warm when we collapsed into bed a couple hours later. Their cozy bodies and mixed scents surrounding me as I slept.

19

December 1st
Saturday Morning
Lucienne

I rolled over and shot up in bed, breathless. My heart pounded erratically, galloping at insane speeds. For once, I didn't remember my nightmare, making it easier to bring down my heart rate and breathing to normal levels. When I finally relaxed, I noticed only Cam was still in bed with me, his light brown waves fanned out over the pillow. He wasn't wearing his glasses, the sharp planes of his face smooth as he slept. I turned my attention to Nik's empty space, my hand rubbing along the bed and finding it nearly cold. *He's been up for a while then.* I noted the time read almost eight. We had an hour before the competition began, so I decided to curl back under the blankets, taking in Cam's heat.

"Mm," he hummed, curling his arm around me and pulling me flush against him. "He had equipment check at seven." I curved my head back to look at him; his amber irises with their flecks of blue, green, and gold were heavy with sleep, but that didn't mask the happiness in them. "I felt you moving around, and I didn't want you to worry about where he was." He gave me a sleepy smile while nuzzling my shoulder. "You hungry, Doll?"

"Not really, but I could definitely use some coffee," I said honestly, sleep clinging to me like dead weight. He chuckled.

"Ah, of course. How could I forget my doll's caffeine addiction," he teased, tickling my sides lightly. I laughed loudly, rolling away from him and jumping off the bed.

"Do you need to shower?" I asked. The weather today was supposed to be warmer than Washington, so I made sure to pull out a pair of jean cut-offs and a loose tank. I had washed my face and taken down the pinned knot in my hair the night before, so I didn't need to shower, especially since I planned to toss my hair in a ponytail and wear a baseball hat. He shook his head, stretching his bare upper body before shifting out of the sheets. His pajama pants hung low on his hips, no underwear in sight. *Fuck,* I internally groaned at the sight of his body. I quickly changed, practically prying my attention away from his lean muscles. *Not the time for that,* I thought, realizing I should probably have taken a cold shower before leaving. *Too late now.*

———

Cam and I joined the crowd of spectators on the padded bleachers. Gerry had been my silent shadow since we left campus, staying near but not coming within a few feet unless necessary. His body was covered in tactical pants and a black short sleeve shirt that was straining against his bulky body. He wasn't the only security around the group either.

Similar looking bodyguards were scattered throughout the crowd hovering close to their clients. I pulled my attention from scanning the crowd to the competition that was about to start.

A caravan of cars arrived at the competition site off to the side of the fields, Nik stepping out with his bow in his hand and quiver strapped to his back. Grigori immediately took off flying above Nik, but when he spotted me, he darted over. His large wingspan and sharp beak caused the few people near us to crouch in fear, their eyes wide as they spotted the hawk landing lightly on the bleacher in front of me.

"Hey." I giggled at the absurdity of the situation and at the looks people were giving me. I petted Grigori's feathered head and wings before jutting my chin to Nik. "Kick some ass today." He squawked and preened under my attention before taking off once more and diving right for Nik's shoulder.

Liam was only a few feet away from Nik, his eyes darting between him and us, the crowd's eyes doing the same. Nik was clearly sending a message to everyone else that I was his, and despite being at a distance, I could see the cocky smirk that he aimed at Liam and the crowd. Nik fully embraced the power he held over the competition. It was quite the change from his usual withdrawn, quiet behavior.

"Are these competitions mostly supes or are they a mix?" I leaned into Cam, his arm going over my shoulder and drawing even more attention and whispers of those around us.

"Usually it's a mix, but I think this one is mostly supes. There may be one or two humans," he explained, eyes scanning the crowd before nodding. "Jesse over there." He discreetly pointed toward a blond pre-teen standing and talking to another competitor. "Looks like he's the only human here." The sound of a horn blaring cut off the conversation around the field and bleachers. Competitors separated to their areas. Nik was competing in multiple events today starting with target archery. Liam followed Nik as well as a few other adult archers. Circular targets were placed at different lengths down the field for the different events.

From what Nik and Cam had explained to me, the competitions were usually held in rotations after being split into different competitor categories. Nik and Liam were both considered advanced adults whereas Jesse had moved to other younger teens. There was one beginner category that held a range of ages. Until they reached intermediate or advanced skill level, archers could compete against a wide range of individuals. Once the categories were split, they were assigned to their events. Nik was competing in all the categories: target, field, and moving decoys. The rotations meant competing in one event, then moving to the next after the event was finished.

Liam was the first to go, his arrows sinking into the bullseyes in quick succession. His clock still had most of the time left when the last arrow struck. I politely clapped, not wanting to seem snooty or rude. The other three adults went next, leaving Nik for last. Sweat beaded on my back from the sun bearing down on me, and we had only been out here for a half hour. *Thank god I put on sunscreen or I would be a lobster by the end of this.* Nik's shooting was a mimicry of Liam's, the only difference was his time spent shooting was shorter by a fraction of a second. The crowd, of course including Cam and me, cheered loudly in response.

The archers were allowed two more attempts, their best

one taken for scoring. Nik and Liam nailed their shots every time, both within the same time frame as each other. I could see the cocky smirks Liam kept throwing to Nik, his eyes darting to me in the crowd. I purposely continued to look the other way, but when I did end up catching Liam's eyes, he gave me a salacious grin.

"Ignore him," Cam whispered, his eyes hard as he flashed his fangs at Liam in a cruel snarl. They shifted to the next section of the grassy area, only one of the archers dropping back, not competing in the field event.

"What kind of supe is he?" I asked quietly, not sure if anyone in the crowd was here to support him. Cam's lip pulled back slightly when several people blatantly stared at us, their heads whipping around to face the field.

"He's a daemon." I nodded. *Guess that explains the red eyes.* The whistle to signify the start of the event caught my attention. The rest of the day continued in similar fashion. I asked Cam questions when I was confused, but for the most part I was able to follow along easily, enjoying watching Nik as well as other archers. Before I knew it, the competition came to an end, the blaring horn signaling the announcement of winners for each category and event. I clapped for each winner, anxiously waiting till they got to the final announcement, those who won in the advanced adult category events.

"Third place in the Advanced Adult Category," the man announced several times for different competitors in each category who won bronze. None of which were Liam or Nik. "Second place in the Advanced Adult Category, for all of the events," the booming voice paused dramatically, "Liam Knowl!" The crowd erupted in cheers including me. *Nik won first place in every event,* I realized with a start. "Finally, our grand prize winner in the Advanced Adult Category, Nikolai

Volkhov!" The cheers grew louder as Nik took the stage to take his medal and trophy. Grigori shot off his perch, landing on my shoulder in the crowd and once again taking their attention.

"Come on, Doll," Cam shouted over the screams and cheers around us, tugging my hand lightly to lead us down toward the stage. Other spectators were standing, but we were the only ones actively moving off the bleachers. I felt eyes on us, but I kept my head straight and eyes trained on Nik who jumped off the stage when I reached it. His free hand wrapped around the back of my head and pressed a hot kiss to my lips, the intensity of his movement making me arch backward into Cam's chest. More cheers, this time accompanied by whoops and hollers.

"I have wanted you here at my competitions since I met you," Nik whispered roughly in my ear, the breath of his words tickling my skin. He stepped back, his arm going around my waist. Cam took my hand and faced the crowd. Several photographers were shouting to us, their cameras flashing. I made sure to smile, feeling my pulse in my head at the wave of attention. Gerry appeared, standing in front of us with a stern look on his face as we turned to move toward the waiting line of cars to take us back to the hotel. I was too flustered with the attention to make sense of the questions the photographers and reporters were shouting at us. The cool air conditioning of the SUV dried the light sheen covering my skin, and I settled between Nik and Cam, my eyes drooping as the car started to move. I was asleep before we left the competition field.

December 1ˢᵗ
Saturday Late Afternoon
Nikolai

Lucie stood from the couch, hands brushing down the front of her flowy white blouse. She had showered quickly after returning to the hotel and changed into a pair of skinny jeans and heeled ankle boots. Cam and I had showered as well and changed into our usual clothes, not bothering with anything dressy. I debated ordering room service to avoid having to talk to anyone, but Cam reminded me it was Lucie's first competition, and she should get to enjoy the full experience.

The hall and elevator were empty save for us and Gerry, leaving me relieved. Grigori situated himself on Lucie's shoulder, the little asshole soaking up her affections. He purposely ignored my mental name calling as the elevator dinged, the stainless-steel doors sliding open silently.

The lobby was filled with familiar faces. I nodded politely to anyone I recognized—almost everyone who had been to previous competitions knew I did not talk. Lucie hovered next to me, her eyes darting around at all the activity. I squeezed her hand reassuringly, and her small smile made my heart pound harder in my chest. Cam stood on her other side, his hand on her lower back since she was still petting Grigori. We had just taken a seat at the practically empty restaurant, most people were in the bar next door before coming to eat, when Liam's asshole smile appeared in my range of view. *Breathe,* I commanded, not wanting to lose my shit in front of everyone, especially Lucie; she had enough to stress about.

"Hello again, Lucie." He bowed his head to our girlfriend, probably thinking the move made him look smooth. Cam's jaw clenched as he reclined in his seat, his position radiating the predator that he normally hid. I noticed Lucie's face was not frowning, but it was not smiling either as she eyed my competitor.

"Liam." Her low timbre was cool as she addressed him. It had not been missed by her that he had not greeted Cam or me. Liam smirked, the loud thundering of his heart reaching my ears as his eyes dipped down to Lucie's chest briefly. My power crackled against my skin despite my tight control over it, and his smirk grew ever so slightly, proud that he was pissing me off.

"I came to see if you would like to have a drink with me." He angled his torso slightly toward the crowded bar. Her eyebrow raised.

"I already have company for dinner," she countered, not swayed by his attempts to charm her.

"Ah, yes." He turned his eyes to Cam and then, finally, me, disdain dripping from his gaze and the words that followed. "I was hoping you would be willing to spend some time with another archer, one who didn't cheat." He smiled, but his statement held a bite. Her brows dipped low in confusion.

"Do you mean Grigori?" She gestured toward the hawk that had taken residence on my shoulder when we sat down. Liam nodded.

"Some of us don't have hunters to help us," he bit out, lips pursing at my familiar. "Besides," he turned his charm back on, "a woman as beautiful as you deserves someone who can actually hold a conversation with you." I surged forward, intending to punch him, but Lucie's hand shot out to rest on my forearm. Liam, however, did not realize she had stopped me and used his telekinesis to fight back at the perceived threat. A dinner knife hovered against my throat, the sharp tip mere millimeters from my skin. His gaze darkened, the black taking over the whites of his eyes, the red irises melting into a daemon's signature red haze. "Careful, Nikolai," he murmured, his voice radiating power.

"One doesn't need to hold a conversation to know who is worth my time and those who aren't," Lucie snapped, her eyes burning in anger as she stared at the knife. Without any prompting, the knife started to twist on itself. The metal whining softly under the pressure of tying itself into a knot. Liam's blackened eyes widened at the display before turning to Lucie, a predatory smile taking over his face.

"My, my," he hummed. His claws, horns, and daemon eyes retreated as he straightened his tie. "You surprise me, Nikolai," he taunted, "who knew you would be able to land a reality warper." Lucie stood sharply, stepping around the table to stand before Liam. My heart was thundering in my chest, and while Cam looked calm and collected, still reclined in his seat, I saw the tightness around his eyes as he watched Lucie.

"What I am or not," she snarked, "is none of your concern. Now, I suggest you leave me and my boyfriends alone." His eyebrows raised looking down at her.

"Boyfriends, huh?" He opened his mouth once more, but Lucie cut him off.

"Clearly, you don't understand what the topic of *alone* is, so let me show you." Crossing her arms, the floor between them started to stretch. The space growing until he was several dozen feet away from us. He chuckled before bowing.

"As you wish." He winked before turning and heading back to the bar. Lucie exhaled, the flooring in front of her shrinking and the knife on the table unfolding to its normal position. She sank into her seat, eyes purposely avoiding the curious stares around us. I internally groaned, Grigori squawking quietly in agreement.

This was going to cause issues for Lucie.

20

December 1st
Saturday Evening
Nikolai

Once the Liam situation was handled, dinner was a joyous affair filled with happy conversation and Lucie and Cam's laughter. Unfortunately, I could not shake the funk that had settled on me since Liam's shitty slights. Sensing something was wrong, Cam held Lucie's attention throughout our meal and back up to our room. I slipped into the bedroom, shedding my shoes next to my bag. I heard Cam talking with Lucie in the living area, but what he said next caught my attention.

"I'll be back in a little while," he murmured quietly, I assumed trying not to catch my attention, but my hearing caught it anyway.

"Where are you going?" Lucie asked just as quietly.

"Just down to the billiards room. Let you and Nik have some time, if you know what I mean." The sound of a soft kiss followed his words. I felt my lips thinning. I did not want to talk, and I doubted she would want to do anything else. Lucie's blonde head popped around the corner of the door after the sound of Cam's departure echoed through the silent room.

"Nik?" she asked hesitantly, walking slowly into the room. Her feet were bare, her navy painted toenails dark against her pale skin. I turned my torso toward her making sure she knew I was listening. "Are you all right?" My lips thinned even more. *Say something!* Grigori mentally shouted at me, my silence irritating him.

"I am fine," I whispered, the burning in my throat grating on my already thin nerves. Lucie's warm hand pressed into my back, her left leg leaning into the mattress as she turned to face me.

"That's the biggest load of shit, Nik," she countered. Her sharp tone had me whipping my head in her direction, Grigori focusing on her face. "Don't lie to me," she whispered, "please." I deflated, the emotion of dealing with Liam and her soft, pleading tone catching up to me. I turned and sank onto the bed, my head falling into my hands.

"It is not a big deal..." I started, turning my face back to her, but her finger pressed against my lips. Her eyes leisurely looking around my face before speaking.

"It's a big deal to me when you aren't happy." Her finger shifted, her palm cupping my jaw. "It's what Liam said about your voice, isn't it?" *How does she always know?* I nodded, mentally preparing to explain the story.

"I was fourteen," I sighed, taking her hand and wrapping it in mine. My fingers lightly rubbed her skin as I angled my face toward my lap. "My parents were inside making lunch. They had taken a break from their current work project, shooing me to go soak up some time outside instead of being cooped up indoors. It was a really nice day outside, the trees and grass were green, the flowers blooming throughout the yard. I remember the smell of the different bulbs and the feel of the wind on my face, how the sun filtered through the trees." I blinked away several tears that had built up in my eyes.

"We do not have a large house or overly fancy cars, but my parents are well known for their high-quality work in archaeology and curating for museums and collectors. They are paid very well for their jobs and their finds which is why I think they came to us." I took a shuddering breath, ignoring the burning in my throat. "A fire elemental and a witch attacked, wanting whatever expensive items or money we had in the house. I did not have access to most of my magic at that time, so I did what I could, but the fire and smoke inhalation damaged my throat and larynx. I somehow tapped into my magic during the fight and was able to bind them before my parents came out, but not fast enough before the witch's spell blinded me." I felt the tears pouring out of my useless eyes dripping onto mine and Lucie's combined hands.

"There was nothing they could do. I was very angry for a long time, but the guys never left my side despite my anger and outbursts. They helped me learn how to read braille and use my other senses. When I was good enough, they helped me re-learn to shoot my bow. I was almost seventeen when Grigori came to me." I absently petted the hawk perched on my shoulder. "It was another adjustment, but a welcome one." I focused into Grigori's sight, seeing Lucie's tear streaked face as she stared at me. "And now you know why I am damaged." She violently shook her head at my statement.

"You are not damaged." Her voice shook with repressed emotions. "You are my Nik. My silent protector who I know would do anything for me. Fuck what anyone says about you, especially assholes like Liam, you're a hero." My heart stuttered at her words, and I was helpless to stop the new tears that flowed at the look of determination on her face. *Our Lucie,* echoed through me as I released her hand to cup her face, her skin smooth under my rough fingers.

I closed the distance between us, shutting out Grigori's sight and once more focusing on the feeling of her under my touch. He fluttered quickly into the living room and out of sight, understanding what was about to happen.

Her lips were smooth and soft; she was not wearing chapstick since we were no longer in cold weather. Feeling her tongue dart gently against my lower lip, I opened tentatively to brush against her. Her shirt rustled as she pressed her palms into my chest, fingers curling to clutch my shirt tightly.

I shifted, and Lucie followed my movements, lying back against the down comforter. My hands combed through her ponytail, the silky tresses flowing smoothly through my fingers. Her legs fell open allowing me to nestle between her denim-covered thighs, my cock throbbing as I pressed into her. I leaned up, putting my weight on my legs, and reached down. Lucie's hands were hot against my bare skin as she pushed the hem of my Henley up my chest. My fingers brushed hers before I yanked the shirt over my head, dropping it carelessly behind me.

I heard Lucie shifting underneath me and felt her arms tucking into her chest. I traced my hands up her sides until I found her hands, fingers fiddling with the buttons on her blouse. I took over for her, making quick work of the small closures. I tucked my head down to her jaw, nuzzling into her neck as her vanilla scent filled my nose. I couldn't help but revel in the feel of her skin against mine. As I gently trailed my fingers over her trim stomach, my cock strained painfully against my jeans.

I nibbled her skin, her moans like music to my ears as I pressed against her in rhythmic pulses. Listening to her erratic breathing urged me on. I continued my kisses and bites down her neck and collarbone. The curve of her breast strained against her bra, teasing me with a hint of what had yet to be uncovered. I wrapped a hand around her back and up to the band of her bra, unclipping it quickly. She leaned up and shed both shirt and bra, tossing them to the side.

"Nik," she breathed, hands tangling into my hair and tugging gently. The move prompted a deep groan from me. I returned my attentions to her chest, my rough hands bringing her nipples to stiff peaks before sucking them between my lips. Circling the soft skin with my tongue caused more writhing from her underneath me.

My blood pounded in my ears with the need for her, so I pulled back and shucked my jeans as quickly as possible. I heard the zip of her pants as I kicked my jeans to the side. A sharp inhale had me pausing. She must have read the confusion on my face because she quickly answered me. "I didn't realize you didn't wear underwear."

Soft fingers wrapped around my throbbing cock, no longer painfully confined by unforgiving denim, dragging another groan from my lips. Her light strokes felt like lightning in my body, the pleasure building quickly. I grabbed her wrists, pulling them away from me so I could kneel between her thighs. The scent of her arousal was thick on my tongue before I even tasted her. Wrapping my arms around her thighs, I pinned them to my shoulders before rubbing lightly at her clit. At the same time, I circled my tongue around her entrance before dipping into her. My name fell from her lips in a prayer-like chant as I picked up the pace, the bedspread rustling under her erratic thrashes.

"Fuck, I'm going to..." Her strained voice trailed off in a loud scream, her orgasm freely flowing against my mouth and chin. I quickly reached into my bag right behind me and snatched out a condom, ripping into the foil wrapper before rolling it down onto me. Her body was still shuddering as I lined up, her warm skin slick with sweat. I slid in gently, her pussy wet enough to let me sheath myself in one smooth motion.

"Lucie," I murmured roughly, the pleasure of her wrapped tightly around my cock adding to the gruffness of my voice. Sliding out slowly before pushing in, my pace was leisurely and unhurried despite the urge to move faster. Our breathing, moans, and sounds of our bodies moving together filled the space. I was fully immersed in the moment, lost in scents, sounds, feelings, and building emotions.

Losing control of my tempo, I started to pound harder, faster. Her nails raked down my back and chest before burying into my hair and pulling harder than before, urging me even more. Crying out, I felt her clamped down around my cock. I surged forward, dampening her screams as I kissed her hard, my hands curling tightly into the bedding. Letting go, I hitched her calves up over my shoulders, my new position sending me deeper. She started to tighten around me, milking me toward my own release. I held her legs against my chest before rubbing her swollen clit. It only took a few more strokes before she came again, the surge of her arousal slickening the condom once more.

"Nik," she gasped, her voice broken up by the aftershocks of her orgasm. My name on her lips pushed me over the edge. For once, not caring about the rough pain my throat caused, I shouted out, emptying hard into her. My throat burned, but I did not pay it any mind as I shifted her legs gently from my shoulders to around my hips, leaning over her onto my forearms. Our breathing was hard as I kissed her softly. "Wow," she breathed, her arms rubbing gently against my chest. I felt the raised, irritated criss-cross lines that now covered my torso and back.

"That good, huh?" I teased softly, her laugh and the feeling of her nod reassuring me. "Good, Babe." I kissed her again before sliding out. I took the few steps into the bathroom and grabbed a towel for her. She thanked me and hearing the happiness in her words made me smile. Cleaning up myself was done quickly, before locating and pulling on a pair of sweats. I heard Lucie slip on her clothes before crawling into bed, and I followed, curling around her between the sheets, her body soft against me. The sound of the door unlocking sounded from the living room, and Lucie's spiking heart rate had me chuckling.

"I bring post-sex snacks," Cam called out, his hands rustling with chip bags and other goodies. I tuned back into Grigori's sight to see Cam's smug smile as he walked into the room. My familiar fluttered lazily onto the headboard giving me a bird's eye view of me and Lucie curled in bed.

"Ugh," she groaned, her face bright red as she covered her blush with her hands. "Did you really just say that?" She shot a playful glare to Cam who looked unfazed.

"Duh," he said as if it was obvious, "I purposely left so you two could get it on." He changed into sweats and slipped into the bed. "Next time though, I call dibs on being part of the fun." His joke brought a laugh to my lips as he tossed me one of my favorite snacks, dark chocolate covered cherries. Lucie wasted no time shoving a chocolate-covered mini donut in her mouth, apparently ravenous after our round of sex. I popped another cherry in my mouth, and I could not stop the smile that wanted to escape at remembering the feeling of her under me.

I cannot wait to do it again.

Lucienne

I licked melted chocolate off my fingers, my teeth grazing over my thumb and bringing my thoughts back to the night before with Cam feeding on Nik. Steeling myself, I blurted out my question. *I mean, he did say I could ask whenever I want.*

"What's it like feeding on blood?" My eyes stayed glued to the comforter, picking at a loose thread to avoid looking at either of them. The chip bag Cam was snacking on crinkled next to me as he pulled another one out before answering.

"It's nothing really all that different than drinking out of a water fountain," he explained easily, unperturbed by my random question. "It would be different if I didn't have Nik or the guys. If they weren't around, I would drink from a blood bag. I don't like to feed from strangers," he informed me, flashing me a warm smile when I glanced over at him.

"So you feed off the guys too? Not just Nik?" I found myself asking, somehow surprised at that admission even though I knew I shouldn't have been. He nodded, tossing another chip in his mouth.

"It has been a while though. I think the last time was over the summer when I had a weekend trip with my parents. The twins, if I remember correctly," Nik took over in a soft whisper.

"Do people taste different? Like does Nik taste different than Logan or Landon?"

"Yeah, it's not just because they're different people though. Supe type and powers are big factors. Nik has a spice note to his that reminds me of fall whereas the twins have an actual spice—a slight bite—to them," Cam explained, his free hand adjusting his glasses while his perceptive eyes took me in. "Is there a reason you're asking?"

"Would I taste different?" I blatantly ignored the question of what I truly wanted to know.

Does it feel as good as Nik made it seem like yesterday?

"Yes. Although I'm not sure how since I've never tasted a Djinn or someone who could manipulate reality." Cam's voice lowered, heating as he leaned forward slightly. "Do you want me to find out?" My heart jumped into my throat while a flood of excitement filled me. Absently nibbling my lip, I nodded. Cam smirked, the tiny peek of his fang pressing into his lip reminding me of what I was getting into, and the tiniest bit of fear slid through my veins.

"You do not have to be afraid, it does not hurt," Nik reassured me, his calloused palm resting on my thigh under the blanket. "If you do not want to, you do not have to though, Babe."

"I do, I promise. It's just something I never thought I'd get to do," I rambled nervously. Turning my attention back to Cam after having looked over at Nik, I looked him directly in the eye. "I would like it if you would... you know..." I shrugged, losing the brief moment of bravado.

"Bite you?" Cam finished for me with a grin. Bouncing my head, I felt my pack of donuts lifted out of my lap as Nik moved it. Cam shifted quickly to put his food on the end table before turning back to me. "It might sting for a brief second since you've never done this before, and if you want to stop at any time, tell me, okay? I'll stop as soon as you tell me to."

"Okay," I said lamely. "Uh, how do we do this?" I fumbled, waving my hands between us.

"If we stay in bed, it's easier when I'm on top of you so neither of us have to twist or move into weird positions," Cam explained, moving to his knees.

My heart thundered in my chest as I lay back against the fluffy pillows. Nik never left my side as Cam nestled his hips between my legs. Bending over, he braced his elbows on either side of me. Flashes of Nik on top of me only minutes before rushed through me. My sensitive pussy flooded as a surge of wetness slicked my panties. Looking up at Cam's position above me, I saw the hazel irises flare as he inhaled before feeling him hardening in his sweats. I had no idea how to ask if he could smell my arousal with his enhanced senses, so I just focused on turning my head the way his hands directed me.

"Remember, Doll, you can tell me to stop whenever you want. I won't take more than a little because I don't need very much," Cam assured me, his lips brushing against the skin on my neck. My heart thudded hard enough for the vein to press against his lips with every pulse. I hummed an agreement quickly, and as soon as I did, Cam's mouth opened, and his tongue circled the skin.

As soon as the two sharp points of his fangs sank into my neck I was gone, my eyes rolling back when he took his first pull. A feeling of sensual contentment filled me, a sense of warmth blooming in my chest as Cam fed. My arms circled his shoulders, my hand holding the back of his head to me. Unable to stop myself, a breathy moan escaped, and I rocked my hips up against him. The sound of rustling to my left caught my attention, my eyes cracking open enough to see Nik readjusting himself in his pants.

Reaching out, I fisted Nik's shirt and pulled, our lips

crashing together as he rolled into Cam and me. Feeling Nik against us had Cam grinding against me, Nik's hand coming to hold Cam in place with mine against my neck. Nik and I didn't bother with the sweet and tender thing this time around, our battling tongues sending another pulse of heat through me, my nipples pebbling against Cam's muscled chest. Cam continued to rock forward, shivers wracking my body as he rolled over my sensitive bud and pulled back. I whimpered when he licked over the wound in my neck, goosebumps rising as his breath barely teased my skin.

"Was it like you expected?" Cam murmured in my ear, mine and Nik's fingers still tangled together on the back of his head and holding him close. I moaned against Nik's mouth as he sucked my bottom lip in between his teeth for a sharp nip. "There's plenty of other places I could bite you, if you would like that. Places more..." He trailed off, his finger tracing the edge of my breasts before running them up my bare thigh. "Intimate."

I didn't respond as I turned from Nik, my lips peppering Cam's strong jaw until we were locked in a fiery kiss. His fangs nicked my lip, a bead of blood welling up before Cam sucked it off, groaning deeply within his chest. Shifting, Cam's hand ran up Nik's chest before pulling away from me to kiss him roughly. I panted under them as I watched their lips lock and tongues brush, Cam's hard cock still rolling against me. Without warning, Cam pulled back to sit back on his heels, cold air rushing in his absence.

"Nik, go sit in the chair next to the bed," he stated softly, but the command laced in his voice was strong within the quiet statement. Nik nodded before shifting to stand. "What was that, Nik?" Cam questioned with a heated and yet steely tone.

"Yes, King," Nik's rough voice was low but excited as he

continued to move without Grigori's help since the familiar had flown out of the room at some point when I wasn't paying attention.

"King?" I arched a brow at Cam as he turned a cocky smile toward me from his position between my thighs.

"That's right, Doll. I'm the King," he stated simply before folding back over me as Nik sank into the chair to the right of the bed. "And I'm about to make you feel like a queen." Before I could respond, he captured my lips again with a fevered passion that seared me from the inside out. Warm hands slid under my shirt as Cam worked it up over my chest, only breaking the kiss long enough to pull it over my head. "Do you want me to bite you in other places?" he whispered, shifting his kisses down my jaw and throat. Too lost in the feeling of his roving hands and hot kisses, I didn't respond until he pulled back. "Do you want me to bite you in other places, Doll? I won't do anything unless you tell me yes or no."

"Yes... King," I tacked on the end softly and unsure, but when he shivered and a near growl rumbled in his chest, a shiver of my own worked up my spine. I wanted to push him; I wanted that tight control he held himself under broken.

I wanted Cam to take me exactly the way he wanted.

"Then I want you to look over at Nik and make sure he's being a good boy," he murmured against my skin as he started his trek from my neck to my chest. Turning my head, I saw Nik sitting still, his hands resting on the arms of the chair as he waited. "Nik, I want you to listen to our girl as I feed from her, as I pleasure her, and I want you to wait until I give you permission to touch yourself."

"Yes, King," Nik said eagerly, his nails digging into the

arms of the chair as I sighed, Cam's tongue tracing the curve of my breast before sucking on my skin.

"Now, Doll, I want you to close your eyes, and if I think you've peeked, I'll stop." I nearly whined at the thought of being left wanting, so I did as he said. The absence of sight heightened my hearing and sense of touch, everything nearly deafening in a wave of breathing, rustling, and painful tingles at Cam's teasing. Before I could say anything, fangs sank into my breast. A sharp burn from the bite around my nipple melted to fire as he drank deeply and circled my stiff peak with his tongue.

I melted into a puddle of pure desire, my wetness soaking through my panties as Cam's fingers drifted under the hem of my clothes to rub my clit. After a few more pulls, Cam left a trail of kisses down my stomach until he was lying on the bed and his lips brushed against my inner thigh. Squeezing my eyes shut, I arched against the soft sheets and fluffy comforter as my mind replayed Cam between Dante's legs during our game night. A spark built within me as I played the memory over in my head.

"What are you thinking about, Doll?" Cam questioned as he dragged the edge of his fangs against my leg slightly, but not enough to break skin. The sharpness a match to the flame within me that continued to flare as he pulled my underwear off.

"Game night." I could barely speak, my words breathless and heated at all the overwhelming sensations. "When you were demonstrating your favorite place to kiss on Dante."

"Ah, yes." I felt his lips curl into a smile against me. "I've thought about that as well."

"Would you ever want to do that with him?" I asked quietly, feeling like I was about to combust as he continued to lightly nip at my leg. When he didn't respond, I finally gave in and looked down at him between my legs. His eyes were lit up in a mischievous glint, but he stayed silent, only answering me in a small slash of a grin before shifting his attention from my thigh up higher.

"Fuck, Doll, you smell so amazing," he groaned, inhaling against the seam of my hip where it met my pussy. "But before I taste you there, I have one more place I would like to bite, if you wish, but you have to close those eyes first."

"Yes, King," I pleaded in a barely audible voice, squeezing my eyes shut, stars flashing behind my lids at the extremely slow building orgasm that tingled throughout my body. As soon as my assent was voiced, Cam bit me a third and final time. While he drank from my inner thigh, one of his hands rubbed and teased lightly, smearing my arousal around his fingers before sinking into my core. Erratic cries erupted from me at the feeling of both the bite and his rhythmic thrusting until I finally fell into a blissful release that was nearly too painful to handle. Aftershocks wracked my body sharply as Cam sat up to crawl back over me, yanking his sweats down until his hard cock was free from behind the fabric.

When he was pressing into me, Cam rocked his cock against my lips eliciting another gasp as I continued my comedown from release. Without giving me time to settle completely, he slipped in slowly to allow me to adjust to his size. He was about the same length as Nik, but Cam was thicker, making me feel full to the point that it was nearly painful when combined with the sensation of my nerve endings being on fire.

"Doll," Cam murmured softly in my ear, leisurely pulling out before sinking back into me. "Will you let me direct you like I do for Nik?" I almost opened my eyes again, but another thrust from Cam had me squeezing them even tighter since I didn't want him to stop.

"I want you to do what you want with me, King," I said in a sultry voice, running a single nail down his spine. His rhythm faltered at the motion but didn't stop.

"Open your eyes then and go kneel in front of Nik."

My brow furrowed slightly, but I did as he asked. Cam moved off of me leaving me aching, and I climbed off the bed. The emptiness had me wanting to crawl back onto the bed and ride him, but I wanted to give him this experience, so I sank onto my knees in front of a panting Nik.

"He's been such a good boy that he deserves a reward, don't you think?" Cam asked, his fingers brushing against my shoulder blades as he stood behind me, looking down at both of us.

"Yes, King," I agreed, a flood of power filtering through me as I looked at Nik holding himself back, submitting to Cam. "I think he's been a very good boy." Nik's gravelly voice groaned painfully as he shifted, his hands white-knuckling the fabric of the chair's arms.

"Take out his hard cock and suck him off, Doll. Treat him for being patient and letting his King take his time with you." I hurried, wanting not only to give Nik that pleasure but to please Cam by following his commands. Cupping Nik's balls in one hand and gripping his shaft in the other, I raised up enough to be able to wrap my mouth around him.

"Oh god..." he moaned, his voice breaking under the heat as I moved faster.

"Very good, Doll," Cam praised from behind me, feather light kisses peppering my shoulders as he sank to his knees. "I think you deserve a reward too for sucking Nik's cock so well." At that his hands cupped my ass to angle it up, the head of his cock pressing into me before filling me up, fucking me as I swirled my tongue and bobbed my head on Nik's cock. Between the two of them I exploded into another orgasm, my vision darkening momentarily as Cam continued to pound into me at a fast, hard speed. Slowly, the tremors that wracked my body stopped, and Cam held me tightly to his chest, his cock fully inside me, as his free hand covered mine where it was circled around Nik. Stroking together, I watched Nik's jaw clench, his brows furrowing as he fought to keep his hands on the chair.

"Please, King," he begged softly, making Cam chuckle.

"Lucie," Cam whispered, "go lie on the bed on your left side." Following his directive, I pulled away from Cam, but before moving to the bed I shot forward pressing a quick kiss to Nik's lips. "Now, Doll. I don't want to punish you too," Cam hummed, rubbing his hands over my thighs and ass. A bite sank into one of my ass cheeks but not enough to break skin. Finally doing as he asked, I crawled onto the king-sized mattress and settled in on my side.

I glanced over my shoulder and watched Cam digging around in his luggage until he pulled out a small bottle. Uncapping it, he placed a little dab of whatever it was into his hand and started stroking Nik's cock. I bit my lip as I watched Cam smear the lube down Nik before doing the same to himself, and somehow, without talking, Cam crawled up behind me, Nik following him up on his other side. When we were all in a row, Cam pushed into me once more.

"Are you ready for this, Doll? I'm going to fuck you, and while you're filled with my thick cock, I'll be filled with his. Controlling the pace for both of you." His sinful words had me panting.

"Yes, King," I mumbled in my lusty fog. I knew the moment Nik had filled Cam; a rough groan sounded from the vampire between us as he adjusted to Nik's cock. And when he started to move in earnest? In hard, meaningful thrusts? I was totally and completely gone. Lost to the fire, desire, and Cam's hard as steel cock as he fucked me and controlled Nik's pleasure.

"Come for me, Doll," Cam commanded forcefully when I was nearing that ledge for the fifth time in one night. I was burning from the inside out, and at his demand, I erupted, clamping around him until he faltered. Cam pulled out right in time, streams of his cum landing on my ass and hip; both him and Nik groaning roughly as they reached their release.

"Holy..." I breathed, unable to string two words together after going two rounds in a night, especially with two of my sexy as hell men. Cam and Nik huffed a chuckle, both panting.

"I'm glad it was mind blowing, Doll," Cam teased, giving my cheek a quick kiss. Shifting, Nik and Cam crawled off the bed to grab towels to clean all of us up. My useless body was too tired to move, but I wanted to wipe off my hip and get dressed so I could fall into the deep sleep that was currently calling my name. I stood, gaping when I noticed my thigh and breast were completely smooth, no bite mark in sight.

"There is a healing aspect to Cam's saliva, so no scars are left behind," Nik explained, turning to look at me. Grigori had fluttered in as I stood looking like a fish out of water.

"We totally learned that in class, but apparently I've been fucked into stupidity," I blurted out before immediately feeling my face redden in embarrassment. *Why am I the way that I am?*

"You're not stupid, Doll," Cam said with a laugh, pressing a kiss to my cheek as he tossed the towels into the bathroom, "but I can't wait to fuck you again." He threw me a saucy wink, the sexy confidence in his actions a stark contrast to his usual quiet, book nerd persona. Shaking my head at him, I dressed back in my discarded pajamas and situated myself between them on the bed.

"So," I started, reaching around Nik to grab my snack off the nightstand. I gave him a quick kiss on his jaw before stuffing a donut into my mouth. "What else do we have before we leave tomorrow?" I asked behind my palm as I tried to chew.

"There's a Competitor's Breakfast tomorrow, but we don't have to go, especially after Liam today," Cam supplied.

"Can we just grab something quick to go before heading to the airport?" I asked, my question still muffled as I continued to eat my donuts. *Hey, a girl's gotta get her energy back somehow.*

"That would work," Nik agreed as he sank down to prop himself on his hand, his other popping another of his cherries in his mouth. We chatted and ate junk until we were all stuffed. When we finally couldn't fit anything else into our stomachs, we slipped down between the soft sheets and fell asleep, me nestled safely between Cam and Nik.

21

December 2ⁿᵈ
Sunday Morning
Lucienne

Having checked my bag already for anything we might have missed, I stepped into the hallway. I was sad to be leaving this gorgeous hotel but happy to be seeing the rest of my guys soon. I had been talking with them consistently on Nik's and Cam's phones throughout the weekend, making sure to send them lots of pictures. They had all freaked out when they saw me in my fancy dress, saying they were jealous of Nik and Cam who stood tall next to me in the photo. I tried to keep Noah from my thoughts, having kept him out of my head all weekend, but heading back to campus, where I knew he was, brought all the worries and stress back.

"You all right, Lucie?" Gerry asked, his deep voice pulling me from my internal worries. I nodded, shooting him a grateful smile as he took my bag.

"Just everything with the situation back at school." I

couldn't bring myself to say his name, the thought making my stomach rebel. He nodded sympathetically.

"I understand, don't worry though, all right?" He caught my eye. "We'll do everything we can to handle the situation. I know Dean Renaud is raising hell to find a Tracker so we can locate him." I knew I shouldn't be surprised to hear Alex was trying so hard, but I was. My chest filled with emotion, knowing he, along with everyone else handling everything, had my back. *I'm not alone.* I soared at the thought.

We met Cam and Nik in the lobby; they had come down ten minutes earlier to check out and turn in our keys. My cheeks heated when I saw the bright red claw marks peeking out of Nik's unbuttoned Henley. *Did he do that on purpose?*

"There you are," Cam greeted happily, leaning forward giving me a kiss, his arm wrapping around my shoulders. I grabbed Nik's free hand as Gerry handed my bag off to a bellhop to load in the waiting SUV. We quickly ran through the buffet grabbing things that we could eat in the car and on the plane. Moving toward the lobby, we ran into the last person I wanted to see. Liam's smug smirk was firmly in place, but his eyes held a hungry gleam.

"Well, hello again, Lucienne." My blood ran cold at my full name. "How's my favorite Djinn?" I couldn't breathe. *How did he know?* Nik's power erupted in bright sparks across his skin as he stepped protectively in front of me, Grigori hunkering down and preparing to launch himself at Liam. I expected that from Nik, but Cam's reaction surprised me. He leisurely stepped up to Liam, his shoulder partially covering me.

"I don't know what you think you know," he murmured. His tone was friendly, but his body was rigid with predatory energy. "But if you threaten our girl," he took a stalking step toward Liam before continuing, "or tell anyone about what she is"—another prowling step—"I will kill you," he whispered coldly, the threat blatant enough that Liam paled. He tried to play it off with a scoff and an eyeroll, but it was clear that Liam was shaken. His gaze darted to Nik, dropping long enough to notice the scratches on his chest. His blood red eyes found mine before returning to Cam. After a brief nod, Liam turned and walked away, unwilling to further the confrontation. I took a shuddering breath, my hand brushing against Cam's muscled back. He turned, his serious hazel eyes finding mine.

"Have you killed someone before?" I whispered. The way Liam had reacted, the blatant fear on his face, left me wondering. Cam's expression was somber when he answered me.

"Yes, Lucie, I have." His tone suggested he was waiting for me to leave him, and at first I hesitated, but then I thought it out. Cam would never hurt me or another soul without good reason. My guys would never stand by someone who hurt others in cold blood. Coming to the conclusion that it didn't bother me, I nodded and gave him a small smile.

"All right." I nodded my head toward the door. "That's enough shit for one day, and I haven't had enough coffee to deal with any more. Let's go home." I took their hands and dragged them outside. The heat of the Arizona weather washed over us, a stark contrast to the hotel's air conditioning. The ride to the airport was quiet but comfortable, the guys realizing I wasn't going anywhere because of Cam's confession. I settled in with my breakfast, my head leaning against Cam's shoulder.

I would ask him later about his past.

*December 2nd*
Sunday Night
Lucienne

I was curled between the twins while the rest of my guys were in their administration rooms. But try as I might, I couldn't seem to sleep. My anxiety levels were off the charts, tightening my chest painfully to the point it was hard to breathe. I lay still, the twins' deep breathing keeping me in place. I texted one of the guys to distract myself, hoping I wasn't waking them up. Making sure to keep the brightness down on my screen to not wake Logan or Landon, I waited for a response, and Cam replied almost instantly.

Lucie: Hey hon.
Cam: Hey Doll.
Lucie: Can't sleep?
Cam: No, is that why you're texting? Can't sleep?

I nibbled my lip as I responded, deciding to be honest. I didn't want to hide stuff from them.

Lucie: Too much anxiety, I was able to ignore it while we were in AZ, but now I can't. It's kind of a lot to handle.
Cam: I'm sorry Doll, I wish there was something I could do.

My heart squeezed at the sentiment.

Lucie: It's all right, why can't you sleep?
Cam: Worried about you, about what you found out.

My face scrunched involuntarily, confusion filtering through me at that response. I was trying to think of what he meant when another text came in. I nodded in understanding even knowing no one could see me.

Cam: about what I told you after asshole Liam.
Lucie: why would you be worried?
Cam: it isn't exactly normal to have blood on your hands.
Lucie: will you tell me what happened?

I waited, my breath holding in anticipation. Since we got back, the rest of my guys had been vying for my attention, and I hadn't gotten a chance to talk to Cam privately. I would be lying if I said I hadn't been thinking about it since the situation this morning. After another few tense minutes, my phone flashed a response.

Cam: can you let me in?

Nervous energy flooded me as I very carefully maneuvered out from between the twins. Slipping on my slippers and one of my hoodies, I headed out into the hall. Bill gave me a quirked brow as I stepped out but didn't question when I pointed to the library stacks and whispered about grabbing a book. I scurried through the empty library towards the front door making sure to disarm the alarm system.

Cam stood bundled in an RSU sweatshirt and a pair of black sweatpants, his breath puffing out in front of him as he shuffled from one foot to the other. As soon as the system showed clear, I opened the door for him and he darted inside with a chattering jaw. Quickly resetting the alarm, I waved Cam to follow me to the section opposite my room. I took a steadying breath as we reached the corner and turned to face my boyfriend. One of my boyfriends.

"I figured I owe you an explanation face to face," he murmured softly, and a hint of worry laced his words. "I was younger, eleven about to turn twelve, and my aunt, uncle, and I had traveled to Seattle for a weekend trip for them to study an artifact for a presentation they had to do at the college. I was out walking from one of the shops, and a human was attacking a woman in an alleyway, attempting to force himself on her." His jaw clenched tightly as he told the story, his eyes glued to the carpet.

"I wouldn't—couldn't—stop, after I got a hold of him. It only took a couple of hits before he was dead. I mean, it wasn't intentional, but it still happened. I can't deny the fact that I'm a predator regardless of if I wanted to, and when I see someone hurting someone else, I lose myself in that instinctual side of what I am."

"Why were you worried, hon?" I asked quietly. There was a tiny part of me that still thought I should be upset, shocked, or even the slightest bit outraged. But honestly? I couldn't bring myself to listen to that voice for even a split second knowing what it was like being at the receiving end of such an attack.

"Since you grew up in the human community and are used to the different standards they tend to follow, I was afraid that what I did was going to scare you away," he mumbled, rubbing the back of his neck, glancing up at me from under his lashes. I chuckled which surprised him. "What?" he asked, finally standing up fully. *There's my Cam.*

"Unless you're a psychopath, which I know you aren't, I'm not going anywhere. You're stuck with me," I reassured him, wrapping my arms around his waist. Snuggling in, I realized that a part of his statement didn't make much sense. "What do you mean 'different standards'?"

"That's a very in-depth topic of conversation, and it's already late. When we get a bit of free time, I'll tell you about it, how about that?" He sighed in contentment, his nose buried into my hair as he hugged me to his chest. His parchment scent calmed me, making my eyes droop in sleepiness.

"Okay, hon. I'm really tired." My words were muffled as I rubbed my cheek on the soft maroon fabric of his collegiate hoodie.

"You get some sleep, Doll," Cam said after we finally stepped apart and walked to the front door.

"I will if you do," I challenged playfully.

"Deal."

"But before you go"—I nibbled my lip, getting the courage to ask—"you never told me how I tasted."

"Like sweet perfection," he said with a beaming smile. "Goodnight, Doll." Cam left with a soft kiss, hustling down the sidewalk through the cold back to his dorm. Locking the door and arming the security system to the library, I made sure there wasn't any security breaches before grabbing a random book off the shelf, thinking it would be weird if I returned without one.

I slipped back between my twins without even looking at the book I chose, and I drifted off.

Camden

My shoulders sagged in relief. Talking about what I had done, even in the defense of others, was hard and I hated doing it. I didn't hate that I saved the woman from an awful fate, but I wouldn't have been able to stand seeing the look of hatred or fear in Lucie's eyes if she hadn't been all right with it. I was almost to the dorm when my phone buzzed.

Digging it out, I saw several texts from Hudson flashing on the screen.

Hudson: Don't forget, we gotta look into what I asked my mom about
Hudson: And we have to be careful with Lucie being in the library, don't want to get her hopes up if nothing turns up as we look through the archives.

Sending back a quick confirmation, I stepped into the building and darted up to Nik's and my room with a quickly growing list of things I would need to research for Hudson's surprise.

I hope she doesn't mind...

December 3rd
Monday Afternoon
Dante

"You're coming tomorrow, right?" My mother's question irked me. Sighing away from the phone, I tried to keep my irritation out of my answer.

"Yes, Mom." I was pretty sure it didn't hold as steady as I wanted, but there was nothing I could do about it now.

"You going to bring your girlfriend?" Gritting my teeth, I pulled open the door to the library.

"I still need to ask her," I huffed, weaving around the stacks toward the back study area where Lucie and Hudson were. Cam and Nik were grabbing our usual coffee orders and wouldn't be here for another little while. The twins were working on a project and would be back this afternoon. "I'll let you know what she says." I didn't want to bring Lucie, but I would ask her. I knew she'd be upset if I didn't.

"Good," she exclaimed, her voice cheerful from knowing she was getting her way. "I know Miguel and Sebastian are curious about her." This time I didn't bother to hide my groan as I reached the study area. Hanging back, I scanned the crowd for my firecracker. "Don't sass me, Dante James, we're all curious. Now, I need to go, Vera and I have plans to go to happy hour." I gave a quick goodbye before hanging up, stuffing my phone into my coat pocket as I reached Lucie and Hudson. I flopped down into the chair with a huff. *I don't know why I let them get under my skin.*

"Hey, dude, you all right?" Hudson's eyebrows crawled up his forehead. I huffed again.

"What's wrong?" Lucie's soft voice had me turning my head to look at her. Her eyes were worried as she took in my features.

"My parents want me to come home for a birthday dinner tomorrow." I rubbed my hands down my face. Hudson chuckled, understanding what that meant— dealing with my asshole brothers and my father with his too high standards.

"Do you not want to go?"

I tilted my head back and forth debating how to answer. "I want to see my mom, but dinner with my family can be a bit much." Looking over at her again I mustered up the courage to confess. "They want to meet you." Her sapphire eyes grew wide.

"What?" she squeaked, her cheeks blushing in the most adorable way. Hudson laughed again, finding this whole situation humorous because, for once, he wasn't forced to attend the dinner.

"Yeah, but you don't have to if..." I started, but she cut me off by pressing her hand to my lips.

"I'll go," she rushed, "you just surprised me is all.

When is it? And where?" She looked over at Hudson whose eyes were sparkling. "And why are you laughing like it's the funniest joke you've ever heard?" Her eyes narrowed.

"I've always had to go to his family dinners. Our moms are best friends, remember? It's just funny it's not me this time." He gave her a wide smile. Her eyes were still narrowed, but a smile curled her lip as she turned back to me.

"It's at my parent's house, tomorrow night," I answered so she wouldn't have to ask again.

"Where is your guys' hometown?" She looked intrigued, her eyes lighting up at our conversation.

"Issaquah, about half an hour northwest of here." Pulling my phone out, I texted my mom to let her know Lucie would be coming tomorrow. She replied almost instantly, meaning she had been waiting by her cell for my answer. "Dinner's at six tomorrow, nothing fancy or anything, they just want to celebrate me going through the Separation." Lucie's eyes lit up even more, reminding me of a curious and excitable puppy.

"The thing that happens when your animal mentally separates itself to be its own entity? Doesn't that mean you've reached 'shifter maturity'? I thought that usually only happened around the twenty-fifth birthday unless you're an alpha shifter." Her eyes blew outward as she realized what she had just said. "You're an alpha shifter? Does that mean you can radiate Dominance to other shifters?" Her words were rushed, questions blurring together in her realization. The way her eyes lit up as she got lost in her questions reminded me of Cam when he found something new to research. Suddenly, it felt like I could understand the way they connected so well. Inside our little firecracker was another born researcher, and I found her curiosity, her passion, endearing.

"My whole family is made up of Alpha shifters," I explained, my elbow leaning on the arm of my chair toward her. "Both my brothers went through the Separation at twenty-one, same as my dad, and grandfather, and so on and so forth. To answer your other questions, yes, I can do that now, but I haven't tried it." I could feel my griffin curled up in my mind, and it was odd no longer having his essence wound around mine. He was still there, obviously, and I was still tied to him, but I could now identify and separate my emotions and his. It had been a strange transition; I was going about my normal morning routine yesterday and all of a sudden it was like this weird out of body experience that didn't seem to end. Over the last twenty-four hours I had adjusted, but not completely, still feeling like I was missing something essential from my sense of self.

Reaching shifter maturity was considered a rite of passage into adulthood. The sooner you go through the Separation, the higher on the hierarchy of shifters you were. Alphas go through the process around their twenty-first birthday, Betas anywhere from their twenty-second to twenty-third birthday, and finally Omegas, or 'normal shifters,' when they turn twenty-five. This included shifters who didn't associate with packs, clans, or prides. It made it easier to identify who was the stronger predator for shifters and supes alike.

Lucie nodded enthusiastically, but instead of asking questions her eyes locked on Cam and Nik carrying coffee. Once the topic of my family dinner was on the back burner, we buckled down to focus on homework, but my mind continued to race with worries about how Lucie would handle my family. *Please let them not be their normal selves...*

December 4th
Tuesday Evening
Lucienne

Dante pulled up to a quaint two-story house with red brick and cream siding. The porch was small, the columns and railing a natural wood. There was a two-car garage attached to the left of the house and the front door was a bright red calling attention to the festive winter wreath. The wide driveway held two vehicles—a black SUV and a red sedan, both relatively new. Dante parked his truck on the curb, shutting off the car before turning to me.

"Just so you know," he said with obvious resignation, "my brothers might be a little extreme and my dad..." He paused with a grimace. "He's a bit of a perfectionist, so don't take anything he says personally, my brothers either."

Unsure what to say, I nodded, putting on a brave face despite the anxiety building at his words. *I can't believe I'm meeting his parents.* I swallowed the lump in my throat as he exited the vehicle, walking around the front to open the door for me. Happily taking his hand, I made sure to not squeeze too tightly in my nervousness.

The door opened as we neared the porch steps, and a short woman with the same caramel skin tone as Dante stood in a pair of jeans and a yellow blouse. Her feet were bare, her long black hair hung down her torso in soft waves. She was beautiful in an earthy way.

"Dante!" she greeted warmly, pulling him into a tight hug, her head only going up to the middle of his chest. "We've missed you, darling." He leaned down as she gave him a quick kiss on the cheek, his face reddening slightly in an adorable way. Her attention turned to me. "You must be Lucie." It was my turn to blush, and I didn't have enough time to speak before she gave me a warm greeting of my own. I spluttered when she pulled me into a hug, her head reaching my nose. She smelled like roses, fresh ones, not the overbearing scent of perfumed flowers.

"It's, uh, nice to meet you," I stuttered, nerves rattling through me. *Come on, you can be a normal human... supernatural... whatever.* She smiled invitingly at me, her coffee colored eyes focused on my face.

"Where are my manners?" she exclaimed, clapping as she stepped back into the house. "Come inside and make yourself at home." Her gaze shifted to Dante. "Your father and brothers are in the den." Her encouraging tone and the way her eyes crinkled conveyed that she knew he was nervous about seeing them. *Are they really that bad?* I looked at Dante and noticed his shoulders were tense and pulled back. His spine was ramrod straight as he kept his chin lifted, looking fully the part of an Alpha shifter.

As Dante led me through the house to the den, I looked around. The dark hardwood floors were well worn but not damaged. The walls held a soft cream color and were filled with photos of Dante and others I assumed were his brothers. The house smelled like delicious food, and the sound of masculine talking grew stronger as we turned the corner at the end of the hall.

There were two men standing around the room while an older gentleman sat in a leather chair. His skin tone was a shade darker than Dante's, and his black hair was in a military style buzz cut unlike his son's. Dante's hair was short but had grown long enough in the last few months that if he didn't comb it every morning, it looked unruly. The man wore slacks and a white button-up shirt, both of which had been starched and ironed, the creases perfectly straight. He held an alcoholic beverage in a glass that he swirled before sipping. His black eyes immediately locked on me when we stepped into the room.

The other two men were younger, both close to Dante in age at around mid-twenties. They had the same skin and hair, both sporting buzz cuts. They were more casual in jeans, one in a plain black long sleeve shirt, the other in a green flannel that was open to show a white undershirt. It was obvious they were related despite the little differences, like Dante's shoulders were broader than either sibling, but the one in the plain shirt was taller by an inch or two. They also looked at me when we entered, their eyes full of curiosity. Which didn't help my nerves at all.

"Father." Dante nodded his head respectfully. "Miguel, Sebastian, I would like you to meet my girlfriend, Lucie." His left hand gestured toward me, my hand slightly tightening against his at being the center of attention. "Lucie, this is my father General Alejandro Rodriguez, and my two brothers Miguel and Sebastian." Miguel was the tallest as well as oldest at twenty-five if I remembered correctly. He was the one in the plain black shirt. Sebastian was the one in the green flannel, twenty-three years old, and the same height as Dante.

"It's nice to meet you." I dipped my head, the steadiness of my voice surprising me since I was trying to not shake with nerves. His father stood, setting his glass onto a cork coaster before stepping up to me. He was tall, my head having to lean back to look him in the eye, and he held his hand out for me to shake. I made sure to get a good grip. He seemed like a man who judged people based on how they shook his hand.

"It is a pleasure to meet you, Lucie. You can call me Alejandro." His voice was deep and slightly rough as though he had smoked one too many cigars in his life. His handshake was firm, but his skin wasn't as calloused or rough as Dante's. "Dante has not told me anything about you." His gaze slid to his youngest son. Dante's face was stoic as he stared at his dad, hand gripping mine tighter.

"I wasn't sure she would be comfortable with me sharing." His tone attempted to stop any further arguing, but Alejandro didn't back down.

"Well, why don't we let her decide?" he suggested before stepping back. Miguel and Sebastian replaced their father in front of me.

"Nice to meet you." Miguel's voice was smooth like honey, not cold, but not friendly either as he eyed me speculatively.

"Wow, Dante." Sebastian laughed as he stepped closer, his eyes roving over me like I was a delicious entree available on a buffet. "Who would have thought you could have snagged up such a beautiful girl." He took my hand and kissed my knuckles.

Why do people keep doing that? I thought in irritation.

"Hands off, Bas," my boyfriend growled, yanking me back against him. Dante's muscles were twitching under his skin as he glared at his brother. Sebastian threw his hands up, palms toward us.

"Damn, all right." He nodded slightly and stepped away from me. "Didn't mean anything by it." His tone contradicted his words as he eyed me once more. *Do I have 'piece of meat' tattooed on my forehead? What's with all the guys lately?* The tension rapidly escalated as all three of the Rodriguez boys glared at each other.

"Come on, boys." Dante's mom, Miranda, stuck her head into the room. "You'll scare Lucie away." She waved her hand toward her. "Food's ready, come in and sit." The tension lowered as we followed his mom across the hall into an open dining room, kitchen, family room combo.

The kitchen was filled with dark cherry wood cabinets and speckled countertops, and the hardwood floor continued throughout the space from the hall. The dining table was a large rectangle holding six chairs and place settings. The living room looked cozy with large overstuffed sectionals and a large TV. Dante led me to the table, pulling one of the chairs out for me to sit. I felt my cheeks reddening as I smiled shyly at him. *He's so sweet.*

His brother Miguel sat across from me with Sebastian next to him. Dante's father sat at the far end of the table while his mom sat at the end near me. It didn't escape my notice that his brothers had shared a look and quietly laughed at Dante, teasing him for pulling the chair out for me. I ground my teeth to keep from saying something I'd regret. I turned my attention to the table where there was an array of traditional Mexican food including tamales, enchiladas, and empanadas that had my mouth watering. I couldn't even identify half of the dishes, but the scents and variety had me itching to dig in.

"Would you like something to drink, Firecracker?" Dante asked me quietly as everyone finished dishing some food onto their plates before passing the dish to the next person. More smothered laughter came from his brothers, but Dante's eyes focused on me. I shook my head.

"Water's fine, babe," I reassured him, my lips curling.

"Well, it is your twenty-first birthday, darling, you should share a drink with your father and brothers," Miranda suggested lightly, her eyes sparkling as she looked at her youngest. Dante nodded politely and poured some of the brown liquor into his glass. From what I could see of the label it was a bottle of scotch. His father raised his hand in toast, the Rodriguez brothers following suit. Miranda held her lemonade up, smiling encouragingly at me as I raised my water.

"To Dante," he gruffly stated, the light clinking of glasses filling the air. After taking a small sip, we dug into our plates.

"So, Lucie," Miranda started after a few minutes of silent eating. "What do you want to do when you finish college?"

I swallowed my bite, the delicious food turning to lead in my stomach. *Ugh, 20 Questions time.*

"I'm not sure yet," I said politely. I wasn't lying either; I had been too busy with all the changes in my life to focus on what I wanted to study and do when I graduated. "Right now I'm focused on doing well in my classes." She smiled brightly, pleased with the answer.

"What grade are you?" Sebastian asked, his empty fork pointed toward me. "You look pretty young." I swallowed the snarky response I so desperately wanted to give him and answered honestly.

"Freshman." His eyebrows raised before glancing at Miguel. The fact that they seemed to team up against Dante was rubbing me the wrong way. There was nothing wrong with how Dante was acting, so I didn't understand their poking and prodding. Then again, I was an only child, so maybe that was just how siblings were with each other.

"What type of supe are you?"

I felt my throat seize, but thankfully Dante answered for me.

"Bas, you know that question is rude." His stare was hard. Bas' lip quirked, eyes finding mine again.

"Well, if she's going to be sticking around, we'll find out eventually." He leaned forward on his elbows. "You *are* going to stick around, aren't you?" I knew he was goading me, and

Miranda shot a look to her husband, but he was staring at me as intently as Sebastian and Miguel. I leaned forward to mimic Bas' position, my face as flat as stone. I don't really understand what came over me, but whatever did steeled my spine.

"Yes, I am." I smirked. "But that doesn't mean you get to know things about me that I don't wish to share." I kept eye contact, unwilling to look away. A wave of static electricity brushed against my skin, a steady current of little shocks. The sensation wasn't painful, but it pushed against my stubborn thoughts, urging me to answer. Sebastian's eyes flashed as he pushed his Dominance onto me, but I didn't—wouldn't—give and finally his mother had had enough.

"Sebastian Antonio Rodriguez," she barked. He flinched at her harsh tone and broke eye contact, eyes dropping to the table. I sat back and lifted my chin slightly in victory. The electrified tingles stopped immediately after he had been reprimanded. *They might be Alphas, but I bow down to no one, not anymore.* Dante's hand found my leg, squeezing gently, and his lips twitched in an attempt to hide how pleased he was. Miguel was eyeing me with suspicion while his dad's gaze held a similar gleam to the one I'd seen in Liam's in the lobby. "I am sorry for my son's rude behavior," Miranda apologized, glaring at him again.

"It's all right." I smiled politely. I might not appreciate how he acted, but what I had said was true. I wasn't going anywhere, and I wanted to have a good relationship with Dante's family. *Well, as good I possibly could.*

"What do your parents do, Lucie?" Alejandro took over questioning, the wheels and cogs turning behind his dark, watchful eyes.

"My adoptive mom is a baker." I left it at that, unsure of what to say about my birth parents.

"Does she use magic to help with her creations?"

The question was innocent enough, but I was able to catch the fishing for answers in it. I shook my head, taking a quick sip of water to gather my thoughts before responding.

"She's human." His lips pursed. I was a puzzle he wanted to figure out, and at each turn I shuffled the pieces around. "I don't know who my birth parents are," I answered after hesitating a moment too long.

"What about other family members?" His smile was smug, a cat that had gotten the cream. *Damn it.*

"My great grandmother is Mireille Bonheur," I supplied evenly, fudging the truth just a bit. Their eyes widened at the name.

"The famous Djinn?" Miguel spoke for the first time since we sat down.

I nodded, growing increasingly uncomfortable at the turn of conversation. Fortunately, my phone started to ring in Dante's pocket, breaking the conversation. He pulled it out, silencing the ring as he read the name. My heart thudded at his look; the caller was Noah.

"Do you want to answer that?" Alejandro asked, and I shook my head quickly. "Why are you carrying her phone, Dante?" he asked in a demanding tone.

"No reason," Dante tried to play off, but his family knew him better.

"Is this the same reason there is an additional car out front holding a security guard from the university? What is going on?"

I paled.

Here we go...

22

December 4th
Tuesday Evening
Dante

I clenched my jaw at my father's questions. I would have really liked to throw my glass at him for his insatiable need to know everything, but I held back on the urge. My mother's eyes were concerned as she looked at us, not worried that Lucie was a threat, but that she was in trouble. My brothers' eyes were hungry as they watched Lucie squirm, just as curious as my father.

"The situation is being handled," I ground out, my hand resting on Lucie's lap. This was going about as well as I'd expected, although I'd anticipated my father would berate me a bit more for doing such a 'piss poor job' at existing. I stood second place behind my brothers in my dad's eyes, but it was a poorly kept secret that I was my mother's favorite. Our family's line in the sand was clear as we stood off.

"Are you handling it? How can I expect you to be a proper leader if you cannot handle whatever the situation is?" There it was, the sky-high expectations he demanded of me but not of my brothers. I took a deep breath to try and calm my growing anger.

"A proper leader cannot lead without knowing how to follow," I quoted his own favorite words to him. "The dean and security as well as our friends—"

"Your friends are helping?" he cut me off, the feel of a familiar argument building between us. He'd never truly approved of the guys, thinking they distracted me from being better and following in his footsteps. Not even Hudson was immune to my father's disdain despite our mothers' close friendship. I nodded once, and his disapproving frown appeared. "I see. Is that acceptable to you, Lucie? That my son requires the help of those *boys*." Lucie's face struggled to stay stoic, her lips pursing slightly. Knowing how observant my family was, they noticed the minute changes in her expression.

"Dante is an excellent leader, and our friends are irreplaceable," she countered diplomatically. My mom's smile was small but proud as she glanced at me. *At least someone in this family is proud of me.*

"I see." My father's tone held a significant amount of disagreement, but he didn't get a chance to argue because my mom cut him off.

"How about dessert?" She briefly looked around the table but focused on Lucie, trying to show her my family wasn't made up of complete barbarians. Lucie nodded, her dimples showing as she smiled. *I love those dimples,* I thought quietly as I stared at my girlfriend. She was too perfect and sweet to deal with my disapproving father and asshole brothers, but she was taking everything in stride, making me fall that much harder for her.

Dessert passed quickly, and no more questions were

fielded at Lucie as my mom kept focus on my brothers. They responded to her questions but kept their answers short, still unsure of Lucie. When we were finished, we all went into the living room, Lucie crowding close to me. I wanted to leave, but my mom wanted us to stay for just a bit longer, and her silent pleading cracked my heart. I purposely took one of the two armchairs that sat next to the sectional and pulled Lucie into my lap to make sure my brothers kept their distance.

"Awe, look at little Dante," Bas teased, "finally being a man." His words set my teeth on edge. Mom's lips thinned, clearly unhappy with the taunt, but my father looked unfazed. Lucie sank into me, her arm going over my shoulder so her side could press into my chest. Looking up, I gave her a soft smile, and in response, and she did something I didn't expect. She leaned down and gave me a lingering kiss, not caring that my brothers were trying to get a rise out of us.

"Do you need a room?" Miguel asked, eyebrow raising suggestively. Lucie blushed in embarrassment.

"Hey, leave her alone," I snapped. He didn't get to make her feel like she was doing something wrong.

"What, Dante? Afraid she'll see how soft you are and look for a real man?" Bas smoothed his hands over his shirt, wiggling his eyebrows toward her suggestively.

"Boys," my father called their attention, "that's enough. Let's not make Lucie uncomfortable." He didn't actually care if she was uncomfortable or not, but he didn't want his sons' behavior to tarnish his decorated image in the supe community. Also, the fact that he didn't like being reminded that I was such a disappointment couldn't be ignored.

"How do you like RSU?" My mom attempted to play

peacekeeper as she always did, redirecting tension and attention to less hot button topics.

"I love it so far. I have a really cool roommate. Straight A's so far," she paused, thinking of what else she could say, "the dean is nice." My jaw clenched at my father's expression, another piece to her puzzle to solve.

"You know Dean Renaud well enough to have an opinion?" He raised a single eyebrow, taking a sip of the scotch that he had refilled before sitting in the other chair. Lucie stiffened slightly, only noticeable to me since she was in my lap.

"He's working with me privately on my powers."

I kept a straight face, my elbow going to the arm of the chair and rubbing my fingers against my lips to hide my frown.

"Are you lacking in your powers?" Miguel leaned back, his hand swirling his scotch in a perfect rendition of my father.

Lucie realized how it sounded before shaking her head quickly. "No." She coughed lightly into her hand before continuing, "He said I would need extra lessons because I was progressing faster than the class was teaching."

"What powers are you working on with Dean Renaud?" Bas leaned forward with his elbows on his knees. As much as I wanted to intervene and end the near interrogation they were giving Lucie, she squeezed my shoulder just enough to say she was all right.

"Reality warping." She ended her statement definitively, not giving away that she was also working on her wish granting with him. Brows raised in surprise.

"Let's see it then," Miguel demanded skeptically. I had had enough, grilling her was pushing the envelope, but demanding she use her powers like a performing circus animal was too far.

"Not today, Miguel," I countered, my tone stern, "we need to be heading back. We have classes in the morning." I glanced at the clock to prove my point. It was already nearing eight, and it was still a half hour back to campus.

We were able to escape my parents' house with minimal issues from my father and brothers, all of whom gave a sharp nod to Lucie and myself before retiring to the den. My mother gave us both warm hugs and kisses on our cheeks before gushing about how much she liked Lucie. My poor firecracker's face was beet red by the time we reached the car.

"Well," she started, "that was, uh..."

"Yeah," I huffed out a tired agreement, looking at her after buckling my seat belt. "I'm sorry, Firecracker. I was hoping they wouldn't grill you like that, but clearly that was too much to wish for." She waved her hand back and forth in the air.

"It's all right, I didn't mind the questioning too much. It was more the fact that they all ganged up on you." I turned to face forward and started the truck. The music filled the silent lull between us. "What do they have against you?" she asked quietly, her eyes on my profile as I stared at the road. I sighed, hesitant to respond. "Dante, hon, you know you can talk to me, but you don't have to if you don't want to." My heart grew warm in my chest knowing she wouldn't push me. It was such a stark contrast to my father's or brothers' ever demanding behavior.

"It's all right, Firecracker." I ran a hand over my short hair, the length had grown up enough to stick up in places if I didn't wet it down in the mornings. "You remember when we had sex?" She hummed an agreement, her brows furrowing as she waited for me to continue. "There was a girl in high school who I had been dating, but it turns out she was also seeing someone else who was good friends with Bas. Well, when I found out, I broke it off, and she decided to tell him and Bas that I have a more..." I pressed my lips together trying to explain it. "Tender and gentle way of having sex. When Bas found out, he told Miguel because those two had always been close, and to them that type of behavior is soft, not manly." I took a shuddering breath, remembering all the hurtful words they had slung at me when they found out, telling me to man up or no woman would ever stay.

"Wow," she exhaled hard while staring out the windshield. "I didn't really like them, but that's just awful." She looked at me. "You know that doesn't make you any less of a man, right, babe?"

I smiled at her, the irrational worry that tightened my chest easing. I nodded before continuing. "I don't know if you noticed, but there are some differences between me and the other men in my family." She nodded. "It's because of my parents' relationship." The trees passed in blurs on the sides of the interstate after I merged onto the fairly empty road. "My parents fell in love when they were young. My father was going to be deploying soon, and when my mom fell for him, that was it. Their relationship flame burned hot for a while, but they were too different. He was a soldier quickly rising through the ranks while my mom is more of a gentle soul. He cheated on her. She was devastated, but she stayed because she already had us. They do love each other even if you can't tell." She listened patiently, her arm leaning on the center console.

"My father has high expectations of his sons, and my brothers were the perfect examples of what he wanted. They followed orders, were brash and 'manly,' and followed in his footsteps by going into the military. Both left strings of broken relationships and hearts along the way. Me, on the other hand..." I hesitated, remembering my mom's face when she found out about my father. I had only been six at the time, but I knew what had happened, and her heart was shattered.

"I wanted to prove to my mom that not all guys are like my father. They see the fact that I want genuine feelings and romance and love as less than what a man should be. I usually helped my mom around the house or with whatever she was working on for her job when I was growing up instead of playing out in the yard with my brothers. Despite being able to hold my own against almost anyone or that I've been the Kohl captain since my freshman year of college, I've never been able to earn their respect. When they found out about my sexual preferences, mixed with how I wanted to make sure my mom was happy, well"—I shrugged again, my eyes burning—"that was it. I wasn't ever good enough for my father or manly enough for my brothers. My mother's the only one who's ever been proud of me."

"Oh, Dante," Lucie's voice cracked. When I glanced over at her, her eyes were filled with tears that had just started to pour down her pale cheeks. I reached over, swiping my thumb over the wet tracks. Her hand trapped mine against her cheek, her lips pressing into my palm. "Your father and brothers are idiots if they think you're less than them just because you're not exactly like them. I want you exactly how you are, don't ever change." I smiled, my heart full again.

"Yeah?" I asked glancing over at her, and she nodded vehemently. "Whatever the lady wants," I teased, squeezing her cheek lightly before pulling my hand back to put it on the wheel.

"Good." She laughed, the dour mood from my family dinner melting away as we continued our drive. Her laugh warmed me from the inside out.

December 4th
Tuesday Late Evening
Lucienne

Excitement built as we neared the campus. Dante pulled into the parking lot near the library, taking a spot close to the front since it was starting to drizzle. I grabbed my coat from the back seat and bundled up. The door opened, and Dante held out his hand for me to take. I gave him a bright smile as I intertwined my fingers with his. The library parking lot was mostly empty, only the guys' cars and a few I didn't recognize were scattered around the spots. The library was now officially closed, but Muriel had left one door unlocked for me so I would be able to get in.

The heat of the library warmed my cold limbs; the weather had dropped significantly on the drive back with the rain starting. I left my coat on, walking with Dante through the front of the library. When he started to turn toward my room, I tugged on his hand. He looked at me in confusion, his green eyes covered in shadows ever since arriving at his parents' house. *Well that is about to change...*

"I need to grab a book for one of my classes before we go back." I tilted my head, and with no complaints he followed me. Our steps were hushed on the carpet, the library quiet, but my excitement and nervous butterflies, the good kind, started fluttering as we reached one of the study areas.

"Surprise!" Shouts startled both of us, despite me

knowing that they were there waiting. I laughed when I spotted everyone who had popped out of their hiding places. Everyone was decked out in 80's wear—neon colors, leg warmers, and side ponies with scrunchies as far as the eye could see. I wouldn't have expected any less after leaving Sadie and the twins in charge of Dante's surprise party. The birthday boy stood stunned as he looked around, his mouth hanging open. My guys stood near Elijah, Gabe, Sadie, Benji, and Austin. The entire Kohl team was decked out, and several familiar faces I didn't know the names of were sprinkled in the study area.

"What?" Dante stuttered. "How? Who?" Everyone laughed as we walked the rest of the way into the party. Sadie, as well as Logan and Landon, pointed at me, their sudden deflection making my cheeks heat.

"Her idea!" Sadie shouted. Her mouth was surrounded by neon colored stain that unsurprisingly matched the cupcakes and other desserts on one of the tables. Her eyes were wide as she jittered with a sugar rush. She was decked out in neon pink leggings under a bright yellow singlet with a bright blue belt around her waist. To match her belt, she had leg warmers and a sweatband around her forehead that were bright blue too. She had curled and teased her hair into a poofy 80's bob, the blue strands looking like cotton candy around her head.

"When?" He smiled at me, his shadows lifting into happiness.

"Last week when I found out your birthday was coming up." I waved a hand at my crazy roommate and my twins. They wore matching acid washed, high-waisted denim jeans, matching jean jackets and uglier-than-hell patterned shirts. Both were rocking neon yellow sweatbands. "I left these goobers in charge." I laughed as I looked around. "Can't say I'm disappointed either because this is awesome."

"Thank you," Dante whispered, leaning forward and pressing a quick, passionate kiss to my lips. I shucked my coat, tossing it over the back of an empty chair, and looked around the group while Dante went and thanked everyone for coming. My guys were all decked out, but Nik was one that made me laugh the loudest.

"Yeah, yeah, laugh it up, Babe," he grumbled. He was in his normal all black outfit, but on his head was a neon pink sweatband. I struggled to stop my fit of giggles, laughing so hard that I wasn't making any sound. My eyes were watering so badly I didn't see Cam come up behind me until the palm of his hand connected lightly with my ass.

"Shush, I had to bribe him with twenty dollars to wear that." He wrapped his arm around my shoulders. "If you keep laughing, he'll take it off, and I'll be out twenty bucks without getting to enjoy it." I struggled a bit more but was able to contain my laughter. Nik frowned at me, but it only lasted a moment before his lips twitched upwards. Cam was rocking a salmon pink suit, the pants short enough to show off his ankles, and a navy blue patterned polo underneath.

"Oh god, my eyes," I whined, running the heel of my hands on them. "That suit is horrid."

"This thing?" Cam posed like a magazine model; unfortunately, not even his sharp angled face and glasses could outshine the ugliness that was his outfit. "I think I look rather dashing, don't you, Doll?" I choked on a laugh, shaking my head rapidly.

"Pretty sure I will never unsee this." I gestured at his full outfit with my hands. He laughed before giving me a kiss and heading over to the refreshment table, Nik tagging along with him. Out of nowhere a set of strong, tan arms wrapped around my waist and spun me in a quick circle.

"Lemon Drop!" Landon exclaimed loudly in my ear. He set me down facing his brother and Hudson. Hudson wore a pair of ripped up acid washed jeans, a black t-shirt that had been cut into a crop top to show off his muscled stomach, and a black pleather jacket. He didn't wear a sweatband, but he had a piece of leopard print fabric tied around his forehead, the fabric trailing down his back.

"Hey, guys." I smiled, happy now that I was surrounded by people who cared about me and not people who wanted to grill me for answers.

"How was Dante's?" Hudson asked, his eyes filled with laughter as he looked at me. *Ass, he knows exactly what it was like.* I glared at him.

"That bad, huh?" I groaned at Logan's question and the empathy shining in his eyes. "Yeah, his dad doesn't like us much either, yet here we are!"

"Miguel was suspicious and demanding, his dad tried to figure me out like a puzzle, and Sebastian..." I trailed off, my head tilted, trying to keep my face straight. "He treated me like a piece of meat for sale." The guys' faces were hard as I finished.

"Well, I'll punch him next time," Landon suggested cheerfully, as if punching one of his best friend's older brothers was something he did on a regular basis. I chuckled, waving away their concerns.

"Let's go enjoy the party, Dante deserves to have some fun." I skipped over to the birthday boy leaving the others chuckling behind me. His wide, white-toothed smile focused on me as he scooped me up. "Having fun, babe?"

"Yes, ma'am." He kissed the tip of my nose. "Let me introduce you to the rest of the team." I bounced around the group making sure to greet Troy who stood off to the side of the party. I spent a good chunk of time repeating the names of Dante's teammates and friends in my head until I had them committed to memory. When I fell into bed later that night, I had a permanent smile affixed on my face.

23

December 7th
Friday Night
Lucienne

Sharp nails dug into my arms, his harsh scowl deepening as he held me hostage against the side of the school building. I was paralyzed with fear; all I had to do was scream and someone would come running, but I knew that if I did that he would retaliate ten times worse.

And who knew if I would survive a beating like that...

I shot up in bed, panting as my heartbeat nearly thudded out of my chest in its frantic pace. Sweat covered my face and neck and yet, somehow, I still was chilled, shivering under the blanket that hadn't been on me when I sat down.

"Shh," Logan comforted softly, a gentle hand rubbing circles on my back while Landon appeared from the bathroom with a wet washcloth clutched in his hand. "You're safe, Love. It's just us, chilling in your room watching movies on the laptop." Logan continued to talk to me in a soothing tone until I came down from my night terror. Landon patted my forehead and neck with the damp cloth, cleaning the sweat from my clammy skin.

"I'm all right," I muttered, redoing my ponytail that had half fallen out in my unanticipated nap. "When did I fall asleep?"

"About halfway through the movie; you were still for about a half hour before you started twitching and thrashing. You woke yourself up, though," Landon explained, tossing the wet cloth into the hamper in the closet.

At least I was able to get up, I thought. The guys had continued to be worried that another incident where I wouldn't wake up would happen, but since then I'd roused when they tried to wake me or I would scare myself awake.

Both of which sucked, but I'd rather be awake than in a nightmare-fueled sleep.

"Do you want to talk about it?" Logan took over, his hand shifting from circles to massaging tight muscles. I shook my head, still feeling too raw from the memory to talk about it. "Want to hear some funny stories to help take your mind off of it?"

"Yes, please," I mumbled. rubbing my cheek to try and hide the slowly building tears. I didn't want to cry. Not again. *Damn emotional rollercoaster and lack of sleep,* I grumbled, *making me all sensitive and weepy.*

"When we were in middle school, we taped an air horn behind the bathroom door one time when the guys all stayed over." Logan chuckled as he talked, remembering the story as he told it. "Nik was the poor unfortunate soul to go first; scared the shit out of him. So much so that he threw a jar of food at our heads."

"Aw, poor Nik." I laughed, trying to picture them as kids

all together, a smile curling my lips at my picture of little twin troublemakers and outgoing Nik before everything that had happened to him. *I wish I could have been there*, I thought wistfully.

"We had two really epic pranks we did when we were in high school," Landon jumped back in, his hands resting on my knees as he sat in front of me. "The first one was a bit bigger while the second one was more subtle but just as funny."

"How did you two not end up being arrested with all these pranks?" I questioned with a shake of my head.

"Oh, we did, but our dad's a cop, and we were juveniles. Lots of community service hours to make up for all of our shit," Logan explained. My brows shot up at his casual confirmation that they had been arrested in the past. I was just kidding when I brought it up, not expecting them to be serious. "Don't worry though, Love. We don't prank or get in trouble like that anymore. We actually like having a good future that isn't tainted by a record."

"Good, I would be so pissed if you two got in trouble for something," I playfully reprimanded. "Now tell me these so-called epic pranks, inquiring minds want to know." I practically bounced in place. Their story telling a big enough distraction to wash away the last remnants of my night terror.

"The first one, we let three piglets free in our high school labeled 1, 2, and 4. It took the entire day for the school to realize there were only three. It was great because we got to go home early. The second one was that we changed out the hand sanitizer dispenser at the school with lube. It was hilarious when the Principal used it and proceeded to just continue to rub it all over his hands. Before he realized what it was, the door handle to the office ended up slipping out of his hand, and it smacked one of the teachers, who was an ass, in the face. So, double score with that last one," Logan and Landon explained in a rapid volley of sentences, my head darting back and forth between them as they switched talking throughout the stories.

"You two are so mischievous!" I exclaimed with a laugh, lightly smacking both in the arm with the back of my hand. "No wonder Dante always looks like you two are constantly about to start something."

"We're not like that anymore!" Logan laughed as he rolled off the bed away from me. "But since it's late, I'm going to brush my teeth and all that pre-bed stuff real quick before we all hit the hay." He walked into the bathroom, the door closing quickly leaving me and Landon alone.

"I'm going to go grab a book from the library, Lemon Drop." Landon leaned forward to give me a peck before standing up. My brows dipping low must have caught his attention because he continued talking, only this time in a whisper. "When Logan has nightmares or trouble sleeping, I usually read to him, so I figured I could do that if you wake up with another one tonight."

My heart squeezed at the sentimental thought as well as the reminder that the twins had their own rough history to contend with. I knew they had told me they suffered from anxiety attacks, but I hadn't pushed for any answers, knowing they would talk about it when they were ready. Landon shuffled out of the room, leaving the door open right as Logan exited the bathroom.

Popping up off the bed, I made my way into the bath-room and brushed my teeth since I hadn't done so before my impromptu nap. When I emerged to my room, Logan was stretched out on the bed in nothing but his boxers, ready for sleep, while Landon still hadn't returned. I stretched up, and my back popped satisfactorily. Glancing down, I had noticed the bottom ribs of my rib cage starting to poke out against my shirt, undeniable evidence that the night terrors, resulting anxiety, and the eerie feel of Noah's eyes watching me were taking their toll. My eyes had permanent dark circles that were growing more purple and prominent with each night of sleepless tossing and turning. After several minutes of silence, Logan looked at his phone, furrowing his brow before looking at the door.

"What?" I asked as he got up, his shirtless chest holding my attention before he, sadly, covered it with a shirt.

"Landon isn't back yet. I'm going to go make sure he didn't get lost." He gave me a quick kiss. "Stay here. I'll be back in a bit."

Sitting down on the bed, I tried to settle in for a few moments of solitude. I was getting so used to the guys being around all the time that it felt weird to be on my own. After a few moments of silence, I flopped back onto the bed, my hair flaring around me on the sheets. I took deep meditative breaths to try and clear my mind so I could hopefully get some decent sleep tonight, but after a few minutes I didn't hear the twins' usual rambunctiousness. A deep niggle of fear wormed its way into my stomach as I sat up. My door was left open, but I still didn't hear anything, not even Bill and Troy's scheduled shift change. I slipped into the hallway that separated my room from the library. *This is a dumb idea, Lucie,* I mentally lectured myself, *this is how all the horror movie plots go.*

But I couldn't bring myself to turn around knowing that Logan or Landon, even Bill or Troy could be in danger. *I just have to be smart about this,* I reasoned, *I know the library better than anyone except for Muriel.* I slipped into the library, making sure to avoid any of the squeaky portions of the floor. I cursed when I went to check my phone. Alex put his foot down yesterday saying enough was enough, and now it was to be kept off. Bill was supposed to be bringing me a new phone tonight, but that clearly hadn't happened. I remembered there was a landline at the front desk, *now all I had to do was get there.*

I stayed to the edge of the library, the angle giving me an uninterrupted view of the room around me. Making sure to look down each aisle before continuing, the walk was slow going, and I still hadn't found my twins or my security. I struggled to breathe through the clawing panic in my stomach and chest. *Please let them be okay,* I mentally pleaded, swiping angrily at the tears that had spilled down my face. I was over this stupid fucking game Noah was playing. Finally reaching the front area, I quickly made sure Noah or anyone else wasn't around before darting to the desk.

"Come on," I whispered softly, typing out Alex's number. When I pressed the headset to my ear though, no sound came out. The phone's cord had been cut from the wall, the open wires sending me into a near panic attack. I set down the phone, rethinking my plan, but before I could think of anything solid or smart, I noticed a pair of legs sticking out from behind one of the stacks on the other end of the study area.

Oh no...

No, no, no.

I jogged over to the black combat boots, rounding the corner quickly. Bill was lying there, still as death. I knelt and checked his pulse, luckily finding it was strong and steady. Breathing a sigh of relief, I stood. *I need help.* I turned and bolted towards Muriel's office. She would have a phone and her magic. I made it to the desk, when two steel bands crossed over my chest, pulling me against a solid wall of muscle. I fought, doing everything I had been taught, but every move was countered with scary precision. When I got a look, the arms were darker than Noah's, distracting me just long enough for a cloth to press against my nose and mouth. The rag reeked of ether, and the suffocating scent gagged me. Darkness slammed down, dragging me under.

December 8th
Saturday Overnight
Alexandre

The phone continued to ring, and for the third time ended on his voicemail. I twitched, my hand running quickly through my hair. *Something is wrong...* Standing, I visualized the library, specifically Lucie's door, and pulled myself through the mental connection.

Her door was open, an immediate sign of alarm. Forgoing her privacy, I looked in to find it empty and my jaw clenched painfully. Doing something I hadn't done in years, I called upon my probability manipulation. The scales of good and bad luck stood before me in my mind. The large, tarnished metal contraption taller than me as I walked towards the right scale. A brief second of hesitation passed through me before I pushed it back and pressed down on the cool metal. Tipping the scales of luck in my favor, I started my search for Lucie and her boyfriends as well as her security detail. It was only a few minutes before I came across the Anson twins, collapsed in a heap in the darkness of the library.

"For the love of..." I groaned. *Hellions, both of them.* My eyes started scanning for Lucie's guard. A few rows over I found Bill, quietly groaning and shifting in a way that made me think he'd be awake again shortly. Realization set in that the twins had not knocked themselves out in a prank gone wrong, and I knelt to catch Bill's attention. "Where is she?" Panic and fear made my normally steady voice wobbly. He groaned, blinking quickly.

"I don't know, sir." He sat up, rubbing his head. "I came for shift change, and Troy stopped to talk to me. Next thing I know I'm here."

"She's missing, and Logan and Landon Anson are also passed out. I initially thought it was one of their crazy pranks or games, but that's turning out not to be the case." I helped him stand, trying to reclaim my calm exterior. "Are you all right?" I looked at his eyes while having him follow my finger before taking a pen light to test reactiveness. I didn't see any delay as I pulled out my phone.

"I'll go wake the boys and start searching." Bill turned quickly, running toward the twins. The phone rang for two cycles before Dante answered.

"Dean Renaud?" His voice was heavy with sleep.

I cut right to the chase knowing he and Lucie's other boyfriends would assist the security in the search. "Lucie is missing, and the twins were assaulted. They're okay, just knocked unconscious. Bill's taking care of them now." Shouting and rustling was heard in the background.

"Library?" he barked out. I gave an affirmative, continuing to look for Troy. After a few more minutes, I concluded that he wasn't in any of the stacks.

"Call Gerry, have him send as many security guards as he can. I need to locate Troy." It was his turn to give an affirmative. I visualized Troy's rooms, pulling myself quickly through the link. I had started closing the small space between me and the door when his voice reached me, and my steps stopped abruptly at his words.

"It's done. I'm leaving now." Troy shuffled inside the room before opening the door fully and starting down the hall. In his rush to get wherever he was heading, he slammed into my chest.

"Sorry, sir," he stuttered. Spluttering, he tried to right himself, but not before I caught the duffle bag he carried. Reacting instinctively, my hand shot out, catching him in his chest. He stumbled back, tripping into the Omnilock I opened. The seam sealed shut, silencing his shouts of protest. *Rather safe than sorry right now. I'll deal with that after we search the library.* I mentally tallied the lists of to do's before pulling myself back to the library.

Please let her be safe...

Hudson

We had split up, each combing a section of the library while Muriel had gone to the basement. She was the only one able to maneuver down in that maze except Lucie. *My princess.* My heart squeezed in fear. I rejoined the rest of the guys as well as Bill in the front entry. My heart stopped at the blatant worry on everyone's faces, betraying that we all feared the worst. A thunderclap startled all of us, and our gazes landed on Dean Renaud's face. It was harsh and stone cold while his ice blue eyes burned in fury as he straightened his suit jacket. My skin prickled under the feeling of his power wafting in nearly unrestrained waves. *When the dean catches up to Noah, he's going to be a dead man, no doubt about it.*

Gerry had just returned, breathless from scouring the library one last time, and we all turned to him expectantly. "Report," the dean ordered.

"No sign of her," Gerry huffed. Guilt ate away at his eyes despite the brave face he wore. My stomach knotted tighter.

"The phone line was cut at the checkout counter." Muriel's tinkling voice reached us as she stood up from behind the desk, a severed cord tightly gripped in her age-spotted hand. The floor seemed to drop from beneath me, finally accepting what I had been trying to deny, Noah had taken Lucie. "The phone was off the cradle; your number had been dialed." Her green eyes centered on the dean after having waved a hand over the phone, the keys last pressed illuminating in a soft purple haze. His jaw ground at the news, and another wave of power pressed against me near suffocating before he reined it in.

"Search the grounds, call in all off-duty guards," he directed at Bill who nodded before taking off. His attention shifted to Gerry. "Contact local law enforcement, especially the detectives on the case." Finally, he turned to us. "Help wherever there is something to do, search her room, contact Charlie and Abigail and find out if there is anywhere he could have taken her that they knw of." He yanked out his cell, hitting a button to speed-dial someone without even looking.

"Who are you calling?" I asked, not concerned that it might be a private call. His face was stern as he looked at me.

"The director of FSID," he said with finality.

Lucienne

Everything throbbed, and nausea rolled through me in thick waves. Taking steady shallow breaths, I was able to push back the urge to throw up, but only just. My head felt like it had gone up against Muhammad Ali in the ring and lost, miserably. My teeth ground against each other, unconsciously responding to the strain in my neck from having my head bowed down for who knows how long. Trying to move as another wave of nausea passed over me, the bite of a rope rubbed against my skin. I peeled my eyes open slowly to ensure I didn't lose my ongoing battle with whatever was making my stomach turn.

A wall of tears had collected behind my unopened lids, and my lap and the scuffed wood floor swam when my eyes finally opened. After blinking the unshed liquid away, I glanced around from under my lashes, wanting to be able to close my eyes in case anyone came in while I was surveying the area around me. My heart ratcheted in panic as I registered my surroundings, an empty room so small it was barely bigger than a closet. The walls were drywall, unfinished in some places showing the studs and wooden framing. The floor was a worn, older wood, scuffed and scratched, and the chair I sat in was cold metal. The sting of the winter air finally registered to my shivering body.

My breaths puffed out in front of me as I lifted my gaze. I eyed the door, deciding it looked to be a simple interior home door. Light-colored stain covered the plain flat surface, and the handle was a gaudy gold shining brightly against the drab of the space. The part that caught my attention was the large industrial-looking deadbolt. *Now what do I do?* I ground my teeth in irritation. The throbbing eased as I felt the fog lift from my brain, and I tried desperately to recollect what had happened and how the hell I'd ended up here.

Getting ready for bed with the twins? Check.

Attempting to find them or any of my security? Check again.

Make it to Muriel's rooms? Nope, no check this time.

Dammit, I huffed, *I got snatched like a class b horror movie victim.*

Frustrated at myself for being so careless, the anger overrode my panic and anxiety allowing me to focus on trying to escape. The rope that was wound tightly around my wrists and forearms was rough as it bit into my skin with each pull of my arms. I panted hard after a few hard tugs; whatever had been given to me was still lingering in my system, draining my energy. The thudding click of the deadlock sounded, my heart galloping in my chest as spots darkened my vision. *Stay awake, Lucie!* I mentally screamed at myself, shaking my head to clear away the impending darkness. Noah's cold face appeared in the crack of the door, his body covering the opening to keep me from seeing out into the other area of wherever we were.

"Hello, Babygirl," he greeted, a sneer taking over his face that had my blood running cold. Reality finally sank in; I was who knows where locked in a tiny room with the one person I knew would revel in the pain he wrought on me. I was at his mercy. "Nothing to say to the love of your life?" I remained silent, knowing that responding would only fuel him on. He knelt down in front of me, his hand resting on my bare thigh. My shorts had shifted up my legs in my attempts to wiggle out of my restraints. Swallowing back revulsion at his touch, I made sure to leave my face blank.

"I've missed you, Lucie baby," he cooed, his hand stroking my thigh softly before slowing. When he finally stopped his pets, his fingers dug painfully into my skin and muscles. "Of course, you were too busy with those freaks to be thinking about me," he ground out.

I held back a whimper at the pain, crushing my teeth together to keep the urge to spit on him at bay. Antagonizing him would be a bad idea despite how much I wanted to claw his eyes out and beat the smug smile that curled his lips up his face. I found a spot on the wooden door, a knot in the wood. Locking my eyes on that one spot, I focused my will power at ignoring everything else around me.

"I see you're still being feisty," he huffed, standing up. His hand gripped my chin, yanking my head up to look at him, the sharp angle tugging at my locked-up muscles. I looked at him, but I didn't see him, my eyes glazing over in an attempt to ignore to the rage I saw there. "I'll see how you are after a few hours." Nails dug into my cheeks as he hooked his fingers around my jaw, and my eyes watered involuntarily at the sharp sting. He stepped back, the cold air rushing into where his hot hand had been on my thigh and face. Slipping out of the room, he left me in my tank and shorts in the near freezing temperature.

He might think the cold would break me, but I refocused on that spot in front of me. He had no idea how strong my will had grown in the last seven months. *I will survive,* I chanted, losing myself in the knotted wood. *I bow down to no one...*

24

December 8th
Saturday
Landon

I couldn't sit still, my hands clenched tightly in fists to keep my daemon claws away. Logan and I paced back and forth in the conference room in the administration building, unable to sit still without my nerves pulling too strongly on my daemon side. My brothers all fidgeted in their seats; only Nik stood stoic against the wall, Grigori missing from his usual perch on his right shoulder. The hawk had taken off to scour campus and the surrounding woods as soon as we discovered Lucie had been taken. So far though, he hadn't sent any news to Nik via their familiar bond.

Dean Renaud strode into the room followed closely by Gerry, Assistant Dean Mastersen, and the two police detectives who had been working on Lucie's case. The woman, Detective Connelly, and the man, Detective Branch, both wore severe frowns, matching tactical pants, and the local human police department's polo shirt. Immediately following them were four men I didn't know. Out of habit, I squared my shoulders and watched them with suspicion. The rest of the guys did the same.

"Gentlemen," the dean called our attention, "these are the Special Agents from FSID assigned to Lucie's missing persons case." I growled at the phrase, and Cam snarled, flashing fang. Dean Renaud cut his hand through the air. "Enough!" he reprimanded. "We're all stressed, but we need to focus on the task at hand and not jump at every little thing." I stopped my growling, crossing my arms over my chest.

"Special Agent Mason Bronstad," one of the men introduced, his rough words clipped. As he shucked his coat he revealed he was covered in tattoos all the way down to his fingers, only his face seeming to be clear of the colorful artwork. "This is my team," he continued, gesturing to a tall, lean man with a beard and messy dark blond hair. "Dr. Ryan Tanner." Agent Bronstad's hand moved to a dark-skinned man with a small smile wearing a crisp white button up. "Special Agent Knox Jenkins, and finally, Special Agent Flynn Garcia." The last man wore a black leather jacket, black jeans, and had shoulder-length dark brown hair that he tucked behind a tan ear.

"You've already been introduced to my staff," the dean started, nodding toward the familiar faces in the room. "These gentlemen are Lucie's boyfriends." He held out a hand toward us as he performed introductions down the line ending with my twin and me. Agent Bronstad's icy blue eyes were even lighter and brighter than Dean Renaud's, looking like freshly frozen icicles. They were the complete opposite of my deep blackened blood red, or as Lucie liked to call them, my burned coal eyes. My jaw clenched at the pleasantries. *We need to be focusing on finding Lucie not making friends.*

"What's the plan?" Dante must have read the growing anger on my face. He glanced between the dean and the lead FSID agent.

"What did you learn from Charlie and Abigail?" Alex questioned. Agent Jenkins pulled out a small pad of paper and a pen ready to note what was said.

"Abigail has no idea where they could be," Hudson offered. He'd had to use his emotional manipulation to keep her calm enough to be able to answer his questions. The long-distance use had drained him, and his eyes now sported dark purple circles as he slouched in his chair.

"Charlie suggested we talk with Noah's parents; they live in the same area just a little ways outside of town," Dante added. "She said that when they started dating, Lucie didn't share much of what had happened until the end of high school and even then it was just bits and pieces. Said Lucie wanted to move on from that part of her life."

"Abigail is her mom?" Agent Jenkins asked, scribbling quickly on the paper. "And Charlie is her best friend?"

"Adoptive mom, and yes. They're both human," Dean Renaud informed him. Agent Jenkins nodded as Agent Bronstand started directing the investigation.

"Knox, go interview the boy's parents," he ordered. "Flynn, go look around her room and the library, see if you can get anything from there. Ry, contact Bren, tell him it's an emergency, and we need him here as soon as possible."

"What about us?" Dante questioned. Agent Bronstad fixed him an icy glare.

"Stay out of trouble and out of our way, kid." His condescending tone had me seeing red. My claws and horns shot out as my eyes darkened, and I heard Cam snarl again.

"I don't think so," Dante shot back, standing to face off with the arrogant agent. "Either you let us help, or we'll do it on our own." His tone was harsh, offering no room for argument. Dean Renaud eyed us with a curious look, but didn't disagree, showing he wasn't against our assistance. Agent Bronstand realized this as well, growling deep in his chest before answering.

"What type are you guys?" Dante listed off what we were and what our strengths were, Agent Jenkins and Dr. Tanner nodding with each new piece of information.

"Hudson, Dante, you two'll come with me," Agent Jenkins said, hitching a thumb over his shoulder, "your emotion manipulation may come in handy with his parents." Hudson and Dante shot up and followed him out of the conference room despite Hudson looking like death.

"You and you"—Dr. Tanner pointed to Nik and Cam —"go with Flynn. See if you can work together to find anything. I'll join you after I call," he told Agent Garcia. He left without speaking a word, Nik and Cam hot on his heels.

"You two"—Agent Bronstad waved toward Logan and me, as well as Gerry and the detectives—"and you should scour the wooded areas, try to see if he's holding her somewhere within the forest." I nodded and started to follow them out when Sadie's blue hair came flying into the room.

"Who are you?" Dr. Tanner asked politely, sending a glare to Agent Bronstad who looked irritated with the interruption and had opened his mouth to snap, I was sure.

"No time for that," she huffed, heaving a large canvas into the room behind her. The colors were dark, a single streak of light in the middle of the painting. I instantly knew what it was, one of her premonition paintings. I shot forward, taking in every detail, several destroyed walls, a single light bulb hung down. Finally, my breath caught when I noticed a figure seated in a chair. Long hair hanging down around the bowed face.

"Lucie." My whisper was filled with despair. *My lemon drop...*

"I just finished it. I listened to Dante's message immediately after and knew I had to come straight here." Her breathing was labored after having run here with the large painting.

"What is it?" Agent Bronstad finally spoke, his head tilting as he looked at her painting.

"Premonition painting," I supplied, letting Sadie catch her breath. "That's Lucie wherever she is right now." I was sure of it, I felt it deep in my gut.

"Sadie," Dean Renaud's voice caught her attention, "I want you to work with Professor Poll, see if you can trigger another premonition." He nodded to the assistant dean who led Sadie out of the room, leaving her painting leaning against the wall. "All right boys, let's get started." The dean gestured for us to head outside, and to my surprise he followed us. His determined face focused on the woods and the upcoming search. *Please let us find her...*

Lucienne

Time passed. I didn't know how long I sat staring at the door lost in my meditative breathing. My body had started to go numb to the amount of shivering I was doing. I wanted to be warm, but I would rather sit here and freeze than deal with anything Noah might do.

Unfortunately, my luck didn't hold, the lock's clicking loud and jarring after hours of silence. I refocused my eyes, attempting to catch anything through the crack in the door. The one thing I saw this time was sunlight, bright and shining through a window. The edge of the window was visible right before he shut the door, but all there was outside were trees. *That's not helpful.* I nearly growled until I realized that meant we were probably still in Washington, most likely near one of the forests or wooded areas. It was away from people and secluded, the trees giving cover to whatever structure we were in.

"Lucie baby." Noah's taunting voice pulled me back to myself. I made the mistake of looking at him, and his eyes lit up in pure glee. "There you are, Babygirl. Can't have you off daydreaming, now can I?" I just glared at him, fury burning in my veins. "Now," he paused, kneeling once more, his hand returning to my thigh. The heat from his hand shot through the numbness, near burning to my icy skin. "I have a few questions for you, and I expect the truth."

I scoffed, unable to hold it back. I felt the sting a moment later, the sound of skin against skin echoing in the barren space. My tongue darted out, tasting the copper tang of blood on my lip. My left cheek throbbed in pain from the slap.

"Ask your questions," I ground out, my teeth chattering. His cold anger melted into a facade of happiness.

"See, that wasn't so difficult, was it." I bit my tongue as he continued. "Now, my first question is what kind of supernatural are you?" I couldn't stop my brows from raising, unsure why he would even care. *Why does that matter?* I didn't say anything, knowing that if he knew it would be disastrous. After a few moments of silence, he held my jaw once more in a death grip, his thumb digging into my injured cheek. I couldn't help the cry that fell from my lips at the sparks of pain that radiated through my face. "What type are you?" he snarled, his eyes flashing dangerously.

"Go to hell," I bit out. He stood sharply, and I felt my

skin prickling under his hard stare. In an instant, his left hand whipped across his body before the ring on his knuckle bashed into my cheekbone.

"Watch your tone." My eyes watered from the pain, and his silhouette became blurry. My left eye throbbed and filled with spots, making me dizzy. "I'll be back."

The warm breeze from the area beyond the door flowed over me before the door slammed closed, leaving me in empty solitude again. The sharp noise echoed loudly against the dull thud in my head. I tried to focus through the dizziness even if only for a few minutes.

Why would Noah ask what type of supe I was? How long do I have before he figures out I'm a Djinn? With that thought, the feeling ate at me that I was forgetting something important. I tried to seize the thought, to hook onto it as an anchor to the present, but my head dipped as the darkness of unconsciousness pressed down on me once more. *Oh, shit!* I realized with a start. *How could I forget I'm a Djinn? Stay awake,* I screamed at myself, *I can do this, I just need to... try and warp it...* but darkness descended before I could find out why the rope wasn't shifting.

Dante

The car ride had been tense, no one talking as we drove from campus to Lucie's hometown. We arrived at a rundown apartment complex that looked just a few steps away from needing to be condemned. Agent Jenkins hopped down quickly and waved for us to follow.

"Where are we?" Hudson asked, his voice confused as he eyed the ragged staircase.

"Noah's last known residence." I felt a light bulb click at his words.

"Lucie had said that he moved into an apartment right after he turned eighteen," I informed the FSID agent. I hoped and pleaded that she would be here, but I knew that was too good to be true when we entered the one-bedroom apartment. It had been torn apart, a lot like Lucie's dorm had been. Holes littered the walls and doors, picture frames holding photos of a younger Lucie were smashed, blood splattered on the glass.

"Jesus," Agent Jenkins murmured at the destruction. "Try and find anything that could identify where she is." We nodded, separating into different areas, and started our search.

After an hour, we had thoroughly gone through anything and everything this asshole owned. Finding photos of a young Lucie beaten, naked, or sometimes both had me struggling to keep my breakfast in my stomach. I collected all photos of Lucie, knowing she wouldn't want anyone to have them, especially not this psycho. We were shaken as we got back into the black SUV, once again silent on our drive.

It only took a few minutes to reach Noah's parents' house. It was a single-story ranch. The siding was a pale grey, the white shutters and door doing nothing to brighten up the drab exterior.

Agent Jenkins knocked, but after several minutes of silence he started looking into the windows. We followed quietly, his steps purposeful as we rounded the back of the house. To our luck, the back sliding glass door was unlocked.

"Mr. and Mrs. Montgomery? My name is Special Agent Knox Jenkins with the Federal Supernatural Investigative Division," he called out. A wave of a pungent, stomach-turning odor permeated the air. Even after covering my face with my shirt, I could practically taste the wretched smell on my tongue. "Stay here," Agent Jenkins commanded forcefully before walking deeper into the house, his weapon drawn. I shuffled closer to Hudson, making sure we both stayed near the open back door, but not even the waves of fresh breeze could clear the air. Agent Jenkins returned a few moments later, his jaw clenched and fingers smashing numbers on his phone screen. The muffled ringing filled the space before a harsh, brash voice answered. "Yeah, Mase, we just got to the parents' house." More talking on the other end cut him off. Agent Jenkins' dark brown eyes centered on us. "The dad isn't here," he relayed, and more harsh commands cut him off as he huffed. "If you wouldn't cut me off, you would know already, now wouldn't you? We're not going to be getting any answers here." I felt my brows draw down in confusion, but my blood iced in my veins at his next words. "Noah's mom is dead; she was murdered."

25

December 9th
Sunday
Lucienne

"Lucie baby." The angry words pulled me closer to the surface. "Wake up." A blinding pain yanked me into consciousness. Dark spots flashed in front of my eyes at the intensity of the throb in my cheek. When the hand dropped from my jaw, my eyes focused, and my body finally responded. I was no longer seated in the tiny room tied to the ice-cold metal chair. Where I was at now was much worse, my stomach dropping in utter terror as I looked around. My wrists were suspended above me, attached to an anchor in the ceiling, and the balls of my feet were barely able to support my weight on the concrete floor. My shoulders ached with trying to keep my arms from dislocating my shoulder sockets.

"Hello, Babygirl, welcome back." I looked around Noah in unchecked panic, my heart beating erratically. The room I was in was bigger than the previous one, but not by much from what I could see. The walls were cinder block and held peg boards filled with a large amount of sharp shop tools. Grease stains littered the floor. *A garage workshop.* A table behind him was full of scary instruments, looking exactly like how it would in a horror movie. Only this time, it was real.

"Here," he bit out, stepping closer to me. A chunk of bread and a small glass of water were clutched in his outstretched arm, and he pressed the food to my lips. I clenched my jaw, unwilling to eat from my psychotic ex-boyfriend's hand. Anger flared in his cold eyes at my refusal.

"Fine." He chucked the food and glass at the wall, the explosive movements and shattering glass making me jump. "Ready to answer my questions?" His eyes re-centered on my face, excitement filling them at the sight of my fear. I dipped my head, not saying yes, but not disagreeing either. If I could string him along long enough, Alex and the guys could find me. I held on to that sliver of hope as Noah got started, circling around me at a languid pace. His fingers brushed against my skin, goosebumps rising in their wake.

"You *have* missed me," he teased as he sauntered back to face me. His twisted mind took my body's reaction of revulsion and fear to be arousal. "Maybe if you're a good girl, I'll reward you," he paused, and a look I knew too well morphed his features, "or if you're a bad girl, I'll punish you. I know how much you liked my punishments, Babygirl." Memories of him holding me down flashed in front of my eyes. *Focus!*

"What was your question?" I mumbled. *Stall him, distract him, anything!* My brain screamed at me, at war with my fear and memories.

"What type of supernatural are you?" I took a steadying breath realizing I would have to tell him the truth.

"Djinn," I murmured, knowing that the only option to survive was to be as honest as possible. If he knew the truth, and I lied... I didn't even want to think of his reaction, but I knew deep down what he would do. If what Alex had said was true, that he was working with someone at the campus, then he would know. The fact that his eyes lit up like a little kid's at Christmas, despite his stone-cold expression, meant he knew.

"Where are your tokens?"

I panicked momentarily until I realized I had taken my coin off in my bathroom so I could wash my face and brush my teeth. I had never once taken it off like that, not when I could easily tuck it into my shirt to go through my routine, but something had urged me to take it off. Whatever it was, I wasn't going to complain.

"Locked up," I answered honestly, hoping he wouldn't have any knowledge of my necklace. "In the dean's safe."

"And your necklace?" His fingers trailed down my neck and over the curve of my breasts. A shudder of disgust ran through me. His first two fingers hooked into the neckline of my tank and yanked down. To his disappointment, it was just skin, no gold coin or chain nestled between my breasts. It was a small miracle that the shirt still covered my breasts since I wasn't wearing a bra.

"I don't know where it is," I said quietly, not faking the fearful notes that filled my answer. He hemmed and hawed like this was an everyday interaction, his eyes still on my chest. I knew he could see how hard and fast my heart was pounding, my chest raising and lowering in time with its staccato beat.

"I see," he whispered, stepping closer. My throat closed, and the burning sensation built behind my eyes. His head dipped, his nose and lips hovering above my skin only a breath away. "You look good enough to eat, Lucie." Growling, his tongue shot out against the curve of my breast and the scar he had given me on my collarbone, leaving a trail of hot moisture against my pebbled skin. I shrank back from him, whimpering. *Please no...* "But that's not what we're doing, not yet anyway." His correction had my breath halting in my chest, spots forming in front of my eyes as my panic attack finally took hold. He kept talking, but I couldn't hear him over the sound of my pounding heart throbbing in my ears. I began to hyperventilate as he neared me shouting angry words, the fear overriding everything but the look of hate in his eyes.

A rough hand seized my throat and clamped; my breathing stopping abruptly. More stings and thuds sounded, the pain building throughout my body as he continued to strike. My eyes watered, the unwanted tears dripping onto his muscled forearm. After what felt like an eternity, but in reality was only a few terrible seconds, he let go and stepped back. My leg muscles had seized up under his hits, the nerves prickling with the force of a thousand needles even after he had stopped. My shoulders screamed in protest as I sagged. The weight of my entire body bearing down on the delicate joint, especially after being suspended for who knew how long, was too much to stand.

A door slammed somewhere behind me. Noah was gone, for how long I didn't know, but I was able to calm down a bit, the air no longer charged with negative energy. The sound of my ragged breathing filled the space as I gulped down as much air as I could, my eyesight and hearing finally coming back. I took a tally of my battered body—large throbbing red marks, cuts and lacerations covering my legs, face, and chest, and blood that dripped slowly into a pool on the already-stained concrete. But it was over.

For now.

Camden

"What do you mean she was killed?" My question was directed at Agent Knox who looked much too weary for my liking. We needed these agents at their sharpest to help bring our girl home. We had spent the last half day combing through everything in Lucie's room, the campus library, the wooded areas, her old dorm room, and nothing had turned up. The only thing we had managed to locate was her wish token necklace. I had the coin secured around my neck under my shirt, unwilling to let it out of my sight.

"Had been dead for at least a day based on decomp," he answered, hands rubbing down his face. The rest of the agents, Gerry, Bill, and the guys were scattered around the room getting caught up on what had happened between the different groups. Dean Renaud had called to say he was on his way with news.

"Any idea who did it?" Dr. Tanner's gaze was intent on his teammate.

"Daemon." I didn't mean to, but my eyes slipped briefly to the twins. The rest of the men around the room did the same.

"Fucking excuse you," Landon roared, darkening eyes glaring at everyone around the room as Logan's jaw clenched. "Just because we're daemons doesn't mean we fucking did it." I winced, it had appeared to be that way. Mumbled apologies circled around the room. Landon finally got control again before resuming his pacing.

"We aren't sure who did it or where the father is, but

right now we need to focus on finding Lucie," Agent Knox added firmly, looking to Agent Bronstad for orders as Dean Renaud stepped into the room.

"I believe I have a lead we can use," he stated, his tone cold. "I found out who the inside man was." His face was solemn as he looked at Gerry and Bill. "It was Troy." Eyes widened, and a few gasps filled the room at the news. "I caught him attempting to leave with a duffle bag after finding out Lucie had been taken. I've had him contained in the Omnilock since then, monitoring anything he did or said. He finally started screaming earlier this morning about how he'll give up information on what's going on."

Rage filled the room at the betrayal. He had been close with Lucie since before the semester had even started; she had told us about the time when the security system in the library had gone off for no reason after an update. It was in the middle of the night at the beginning of the summer semester, and Bill and Troy had been the responding security guards. I glanced at Bill, watching the warring emotions taking over his face. Anger and hurt battled back and forth as he processed what the dean had revealed.

"Cam, Nik," Agent Bronstad barked, taking command of the group, "go with Flynn and Ryan to research any way to locate her; spells, remote viewing, sensory scrying, anything. Bren won't be available for at least another week. He's currently in the middle of Tracking a wanted serial killer." I nodded, standing with Nik and the two agents. We waited by the door to hear the rest of the orders. "Dante, Hudson, twins, you're with Knox and Dean Renaud on interrogation. Observing only unless necessary." Everyone split up, determination surging through us despite our lack of anything useful yesterday.

I followed the two agents closely as we headed to the

library. It had been closed off pending further investigation into Lucie's kidnapping. I had heard the grumbles and complaints of the students as we walked across the quad, eyes straying toward us before continuing their whispering. I kept my eyes forward on Agent Garcia's leather jacket. Nik's power prickled against my skin, and it crackled seconds later in warning for the students who continued to stare, making it clear that we weren't in the mood to be gossiped about.

The heat of the library seemed oppressive, and I immediately regretted the thick sweater and coat that had seemed like a good idea in case we'd had to scour the wooded areas again. Shedding my layers until I was in a short sleeve shirt, I sat down at the checkout counter. My eyes closed, and I tried to connect with Lucie mentally. Yesterday, the connection was barely there, only a wisp in the wind, but today it was a bit stronger. I latched on tightly, refusing to let her go. I thrust myself through the connection taking no chances since I could lose it at any moment.

My body immediately started to ache, a bone deep throbbing burn in my wrists and shoulders. Lucie's eyes were half shut, and delirium overpowered other emotions. I tried to focus on what I could see from her position. A hazy picture of her body filled my mind, a grey dirty floor underneath her almost free-dangling legs. Unsurmountable fury filled me when I saw the start of a bloody puddle, red rivers dripping down her pale skin. I pulled back just enough to think properly, making sure to hold on to that connection.

"What?" Dr. Tanner was standing on the other side of the counter flipping through a book of spells, but my lip pulling back in anger had caught his attention. "See something?"

"She's been beaten, and I'm pretty sure she's being

suspended from her wrists," I ground out, catching Nik's and Agent Garcia's attention. "She's barely conscious, but more so today than she was yesterday. At least enough for me to form a connection."

"Describe what you saw," Nik's harsh demand was strong, his rough voice no longer soft or quiet. I relayed everything I could see, but in the middle of one of the statements I felt the connection flare.

"She's awake," I mumbled, already slipping into the link. I mentally prepared myself for what I was about to see and experience, reminding myself that I wasn't actually being hurt physically. Emotionally was a different matter.

"Let's try again, seeing as how you slipped away yesterday." A face that I recognized from the photos I had seen stepped into my line of sight. His eyes calculating and yet leering at the same time. "What powers do you have?" *Powers? Why would he be concerned with that when he considered us freaks?* I tucked the unanswered questions in the back of my mind and focused.

"Wish granting," Lucie's words were slurring together. The effort sent jolts of agonizing pain through my jaw, head, and neck. Something was wrong with her eyesight too. *One of her eyes is swelling shut,* I noted in disbelief.

"What else?" he demanded. My eyes finally noticed what he had leaned back against, and I couldn't stop myself from gagging. I didn't care how my body looked to the agents and Nik, I couldn't control the queasiness that came with seeing a literal table full of torture tools as our girl hung from the ceiling like an animal prepared for slaughter.

"Reality warping," she mumbled. Between the swelling in her face and her still tenuous grip on consciousness, her words came twisted, sounding more like re-all-tee wohp-ing. Noah's anger flashed dangerously close to the surface,

Lucie's delirium making it look like his eyes had blackened like Logan and Landon's. It lasted for only a moment before his dark-brown, almost black eyes were right in Lucie's face. The smile that curled his lips had my heart stopping. *Lucie!* I mentally screamed as he started, his fists and open-handed slaps making contact in quick precision.

Each hit had me screaming to the point that I didn't know what was Lucie and what was me. When I thought I couldn't take anymore, a fist clamped over my windpipe and arteries, squeezing with deadly accuracy. Air refused to fill my lungs while I was tied to Lucie through both remote viewing and sensory scrying. Her attempts to pull away from his choke hold were futile, and dark spots filled my vision as she neared blackout. When he finally released her throat, sweet air filled my lungs in ragged, choppy breaths, and I was pushed back from her as she lost consciousness.

"Cam!" Someone's shouting and shaking jostled my disoriented and sick body. I groaned, immediately rolling to my side and vomiting over and over until my consciousness had centered. "Jesus!" I heard someone bellow in the middle of my retching. When I could breathe finally, I rolled onto my back, somehow ending up lying on the tile floor behind the counter during my RV and sensory scrying. Opening my eyes, I met Dean Renaud's and my brothers' worried gazes, the agents standing off to the side still watching with serious expressions.

"I need to sit up," I coughed out, my throat raw from being sick. Dante and Hudson immediately hooked their arms around either side of me and gently sat me up making sure to turn me slightly so I could lean against the glass of the library offices.

"What happened?" Landon demanded, fear shining bright on his face. I swallowed hard trying to emotionally separate myself from the memories. I wanted to convey the information as accurately as possible, but I found it near impossible to keep the tears at bay. As soon as they started flowing, they knew. They paled significantly before I even started talking.

"Camden?" Dean Renaud's normally calm and commanding voice was soft and wobbly with emotion. I steeled myself.

"It's bad. It's really, really bad," I managed to get out before I choked on a sob. "If we don't find her soon," I sucked in a breath, "I don't know if she'll make it." Curses went up around the group. Logan and Landon lost control on their rage, quickly pacing back and forth while muttering obscenities to themselves. I worried my lip as I struggled to keep control of myself, trying to piece together the broken, jagged edges that had shattered at seeing Lucie in such a state. The coppery taste of blood filled my mouth, telling me I had punctured through my own lip in my emotional struggle.

"I know it's not easy, kid." Agent Bronstad squatted in front of me, his tattooed hand landing on my shoulder in a reassuring squeeze. "But we need to know what you saw."

"She's been strung up, hung from the ceiling by her wrists. He's asking about her powers. I could barely get anything through the pain. He's done a huge amount of damage already to the point that there's a blood puddle forming under her."

"What about where she was at?" Agent Bronstad continued his questioning, but even he looked sick. I couldn't take the chance of glancing around the guys or I would lose myself in my own emotions.

"She's in a single car garage, there was a wall full of

workshop tools," I hesitated only briefly before continuing, "he had a table set out."

"What was on it?" Agent Jenkins asked from behind the counter. Taking a deep breath, I pushed away another wave of nausea.

"Torture tools," I murmured. That's when Logan lost control for the first time in years, hands going up in hellfire that quickly spiraled up his arms and slowly engulfed his torso. Landon's hands were burning, but he was keeping more of a lid on it than his brother. I had to try and calm him down. "None of them have been used."

"I don't give a fuck!" Logan roared, his chest heaving. The FSID agents' eyes widened, and they moved to stand in a loose circle around the Raging daemon. Dante joined the circle, hands going out to calm him.

"Logan," he soothed, his voice firm, but not harsh. "Close your eyes." Logan snarled for a moment before Dante gave him an encouraging look. After a tense stand-off, his eyes closed. Landon stood outside the circle, his hands having stopped burning, his eyes worriedly locked on his twin. Based on the look on his face, he was mentally talking to Logan. "Breathe deeply and remember when we first met Lucie." Dante continued to guide Logan through his relaxation exercises until the hellfire was doused and his daemon side retreated. His shoulders sagged in regret, his eyes on the floor. Logan prided himself on his control after what had happened with his older brother Lance, and shame reddened his cheeks at this loss of control. When he got this bad, Dante and Landon were the only ones who could talk him down, Hudson's calming magic being a last and *very* extreme resort.

"Hey." Landon broke the circle, going up to his brother. "Let's go take a walk and get our heads cleared, all right?"

Without another word, Logan led the way outside, leaving his twin to catch up. Landon turned to us. "We might not be back until tomorrow unless you find something." We all nodded in understanding. I turned back to the agents and Dean Renaud.

"Now what?" Nik asked.

Question of the century...

26

December 10th
Monday
Logan

My body thrummed with nervous energy as we waited. The rest of the guys were seated within the room we were standing outside. I didn't want to come back until I had something of use. I wasn't helpful if I was busy feeling sorry for myself, so as soon as Landon and I left yesterday, we got to work.

"Any more information?" I heard Dean Renaud ask. The reigning silence in answer had me shuffling from one foot to another as I spun my phone in my palm. *Hurry up,* I pleaded.

"*They're going as fast as they can, dude,*" Landon's voice filtered through my head with his unwanted nosiness. "*You know they'll find her.*" I bit back the urge to snap at him because he was right, and I knew they wouldn't fuck me over, not with the position I held.

Well, used to hold.

"Do we know any other trackers or locators?" Dante's deep voice questioned next.

"Fuck, this is bad," Hudson muttered when there weren't any other responses. The vibrating buzz in my hand had my pulse skyrocketing, the numbers flashing on the screen sending my heart into my throat.

"*Ready?*" I mentally questioned my twin. Landon had a notebook and marker ready as I rattled off the location. The text that had come in was spelled to delete exactly one minute after arriving. When the coordinates were scrawled on the paper, I took the notebook and shoved into the room. My strides were purposeful as I tossed Lucie's location onto the table.

"We found her," I stated. Everyone surged forward and out of the room in a rush.

"How?" Agent Bronstad questioned, his eyebrows shooting up as he plugged the latitude and longitude into his phone.

"I called in a favor." My voice was even and cold, knowing the reaction my actions would cause among the group, but not caring, not right now. To me? Lucie's safety was worth more than my brothers being pissed off at me.

"We'll fucking talk about this later," Dante promised darkly, his eyes hard as he glared at me. I glared right back, feeling my eyes blackening slowly as we nearly sprinted to the parking lot.

"I don't need a fucking lecture. I did what I had to do," I fired back. Anger and irritation at his reaction mixed with the already negative emotions I had swirling around in my head. Dante opened his mouth to argue, but I sliced my hand through the air. "No, Dante, I did what I had to do to find Lucie. Her life is more important than anything they could ask of me." Dante growled, muscles pulsing and twitching with the urge to shift, but it was Dean Renaud who intervened.

"All of you, shut up!" he shouted, his power pressing dangerously against my ward. "Let's go get Lucie." We swallowed our qualms and hopped into our vehicles. Tires squealed as we took off in a caravan towards Lucie's location. *We're coming, Love, hold on.*

Lucienne

I faded in and out of consciousness, lost in a sea of pain and agony. My stomach clenched painfully in hunger, having only been offered bread and water three times. The first two I refused but finally gave in on his most recent attempt. I spent half the time trying to not throw up from his fingers brushing my lips, the other half trying not to throw up from my stomach rebelling at stale bread. I didn't have access to a window or any way to tell what time of day it was or how much time had passed since being moved to this makeshift torture chamber, but I knew I needed to eat, and so that's what I did. After he left that last time, all I did was focus on trying to breathe through the pain and pray Noah didn't come back out into the this makeshift torture chamber to beat the shit out of me again or ask me questions I didn't want to answer.

I lifted my head as much as I could, my mental and physical faculties sluggish and strained. I couldn't lean my head all the way back, welts and cuts on my neck searing in pain. Thankfully, I was able to lift it enough to see my hands above my head, but just barely. Calling on all my strength, I tried again to loosen the ropes and chains binding my wrists. I swallowed the screams of frustration that wanted to erupt from me, the restraint unmoving despite my best efforts.

I hung my head down, tears freely flowing from my good eye. My left one had swollen completely shut after Noah's third time out here. I wanted to fight, yet I also wanted to give up, to have it end, despite knowing that I couldn't. I had my mom, Charlie, my guys, and my friends at RSU. I had people who were fighting for me, who were looking for me. I just had to get out of here.

With renewed vigor, I looked toward my wrists deciding to try one last ditch effort to escape knowing I would probably permanently damage my hands and arms in the process. *If they aren't already,* I thought darkly. I mentally locked on my hands and wrists, visualizing what I wanted to do with my reality warping. I had attempted to use my powers on the rope and chains the first day out here, but nothing had happened, most likely due to the runes etched and branded into the restraints.

I took a deep breath, counting to three while imagining my wrists, forearms, and hands collapsing inwards to slide them out of the bindings. When I reached three, I pushed my thought to my limbs. There was no pain, no odd feelings in my arms, and at first I didn't think it had worked, but my feet were now flat on the ground, my body's weight bearing down on them.

I looked up.

My hands and arms had started to turn to pearlescent smoke. The wisps dissipated around the knots, reforming into a steady cloud. *I have to be going crazy. This is it. I've officially lost my mind.*

The longer I stared, the more I realized what I was seeing was actually happening. I focused on solidifying my limbs, and after some finagling I stood in the middle of this hellhole no longer hanging from the ceiling. My arms fell to my sides, and the burn from the sudden movement and rush of blood was so intense I wanted to scream. I held my breath until the pain subsided enough to think. As the pain dulled, hope surged in my chest. *I can escape,* I frantically thought, turning unsteadily on my near useless legs. There was a closed garage door behind me, and I nearly did a little dance. *Pay attention!* my brain shouted. *He could be back at any minute.* With that, I focused on shifting into smoke.

It was difficult to get my entire body and head to shift and stay that way. I jumped at any little sound, fearing Noah was on his way out. But my luck held, finally, and I was able to filter through the edge of the metal garage door into the outdoors. I didn't solidify, keeping focus on staying in smoke form as I drifted away from this place. As I floated farther and farther, reaching the tree line at the end of the drive, I turned and looked to see where I was.

It was a small house, practically the size of a bread box, where the living space looked as big as the single car garage where I had been held. There was caution tape on the door and a construction sign in the yard to keep any unwanted visitors away.

Shaded and blocked by the large wooded area, I finally took in the space around me. It was dark, but I couldn't feel the cold bite of the winter air or my injuries when I was smoke. It was like I was wrapped in my own bubble, safe from the elements and what had been done to my body. Unfortunately, I was losing my mental hold on this new form, the throbbing in my head growing steadier and more intense with every foot that I floated deeper into the trees.

I shifted back, stumbling into the frozen brush, my injuries flaring to life at my body's change back to its corporeal form. I whimpered to myself, biting down on my tongue to keep from crying out. I couldn't bring Noah's attention to anything suspicious. I stood and started to run, solely focused on one thing and one thing only.

Survival.

Nikolai

We had been ordered to wait in the vehicles on the very edge of the property, tasked with interfering only if Noah evaded them. The twins' claws and horns were out while the others shifted and fidgeted in the wait, Dante struggling with controlling his urge to shift. My fingers brushed against the small pouch of spelled objects and potion orbs, ready to throw if Noah made it past the Agents and Dean Renaud. Though I likely would not need it. He would not make it past us alive based on the expressions I could see us all wearing. Grigori shifted on my shoulder, hunkering down in case he needed to launch himself at the psychotic asshole we knew waited in the house.

After an excruciatingly long five minutes, Dante's phone rang. He did not even say anything after accepting the call, and a couple seconds later, he hung up.

"They got him," he relayed. That was our cue to approach. We took off, running as fast as our legs would carry us towards the little ramshackle building. Masculine screaming could be heard all the way outside. Agent Bronstad and Agent Garcia clamped down on either side of his thrashing body. I stopped in front of him as they exited the front door. His eyes widened slightly in surprise before falling into a mask of arrogance.

"Nikolai Volkhov," he sneered. I ground my teeth together to stay in control, dedicating all my focus to keeping my tone steady.

"Where is she?"

He laughed, the maniacal sound betraying how crazy he truly was. He did not answer, just continuing to laugh. I gave up and stormed into the house but immediately skidded to a stop. The abrupt movement caused the rest of the guys to run into my back, piling into the small space behind me. Dean Renaud was standing with his back to me. His feet apart, fists down and clenched tightly at his sides. Power, nearly unrestrained, pulsed dangerously around him.

"She's not here," he ground out through clenched teeth, his face turning so I could see his profile over his shoulder. "The garage is empty." I tiptoed around him feeling my brothers following towards the open door at the other end of the hall.

"Oh god." I immediately clamped a hand over my mouth. Cam's description of what he saw had not seemed to fully form in my head until I was standing in the room. Grigori's gaze darted around the room taking in the scary as fuck instruments that had sent Logan into a frenzy yesterday. Blood spattered over the cinderblock walls and workshop tools. But what caught Logan's attention the most as he knelt was the large drying blood spot.

"What are you doing?" Hudson's voice was shrill as Logan dipped a single finger into the puddle.

"It's not fully dry, not fully cold either," Logan explained. At his explanation, Grigori's eyes shifted to look around, his frantic change in perspective making me sick. Bloody Lucie-sized footprints started, but then seemed to disappear.

"Where are the rest of the footprints?" I pointed toward the dried markings.

"Did he move her, knowing we were coming?" Landon offered, looking sickly green.

"Or did he do something more permanent?" Cam whispered the question no one wanted to ask. Dean Renaud must have heard the words because immediately after, he lost control. A wave of pure power knocked us flat on our asses, and the dean roared.

"She can't be dead!"

Dante was the first to recover, his wide eyes betraying his faux calm exterior. He was as bewildered as the rest of us at the dean's reaction. Collecting himself, Dante did as Dante did best, talking down an overly emotional supe back to relatively normal levels. Hudson was standing off to the side, waiting on standby in case Dante was not able to talk the dean down from his emotionally explosive state. While it would have been faster for Hudson to use his emotion-altering power, it was considered bad form to influence others. If push came to shove, Hudson would do what he needed to so no one would be put at risk.

Unable to keep looking at the space, I pulled back from Grigori's eyes, darkness descending until I was no longer seeing. I ignored my familiar smacking the side of my head in irritation, unhappy I was not using him to his full potential. As I stood there though, a strange tingle of magic brushed against my skin. It was not coming from the dean as Dante talked to him but coming from above us. Feeling outside of me, my sensory perception sharpened until it locked on the rope and metal chains that had held Lucie up.

"Runes," I whispered, my throat sore from the building acid in my throat. "How did she get out of rune-etched bindings and how did Noah get them in the first place?" I asked no one in particular, no one paying attention to my whispers as I heard the dean straightening his suit jacket and ordering the group of police who had shown up.

"Spread out, start searching." The officers hesitated for a moment, reluctant to take orders from someone who was not in law enforcement, but Dr. Tanner confirmed the directive given by Dean Renaud. Finally outside the house, I reconnected with Grigori to see their flashlight beams bouncing through the trees. My brothers and I started toward the woods, but the dean and Dr. Tanner stopped us.

"If we don't find her tonight, you can assist in the morning, but tonight you need to sleep," Dr. Tanner instructed firmly. "Go back to campus. If it will help you sleep, go check in with Knox and Flynn, and they'll show you where Noah's being held." We wanted to argue, but we knew they had pushed a lot of regulations out of the way to allow us on this investigation. Clamping down on the urge, we got back in our cars and headed back to the university. Once we were back on campus, we immediately went straight to talk to the agents. No talking occurred between us, but we moved as a team, all arguments and high tempers from the last few days forgotten and forgiven. Once we were back on campus, we immediately went straight to talk to the agents.

Agent Jenkins and Agent Garcia were waiting for us, Dr. Tanner having called them when we left. They led us down a hallway and into a room on the left, leaving the door open. It was an observation room, one wall holding a large two-way mirror. The asshole sat handcuffed and shackled to a large metal table that was bolted to the floor. I knew from their conversation the other day that Troy was in the room next door, but he had not talked yet.

"Can I murder him?" Landon asked, his voice serious as he looked to the FSID agents. They chuckled, their laughs resigned, before shaking their heads.

"No," Agent Garcia spoke for the first time since arriving, "unfortunately." We stood in silence, staring, unbeknownst to Noah, and attempting to process what had happened.

"Where is he?!" Sadie's voice radiated around the hallway, her face stormy as she stomped into the room. Her cheeks were pink in anger, her eyes wild behind her purple framed glasses. "I'm going to murder that motherfucker." She paused like she had an idea. "No, scratch that. I'm going to maim him, then murder him. Slowly." She nodded manically, her face transforming into one that any daemon would be proud of.

"Who are you?" Agent Jenkins asked, his dark brows rising at the angry little faerie. She whirled on him, as if finally realizing there were other people in the room. Her hands landed on her hips, her attitude in full swing.

"I'm Lucie's roommate and one of her best friends." She squinted at him suspiciously. "Who are you?" More eyebrow raises from the two agents, and Agent Garcia's lips twitched.

"FSID Special Agent Knox Jenkins and one of my teammates, Special Agent Flynn Garcia."

Her head tilted back, and she eyed them for a moment longer. When she reached whatever conclusion was going on in her crazy head, she nodded, satisfied with the answer.

"Now, where the hell is that little piece of douchery?" She turned her attention to me, and I pointed through the two-way mirror. She stormed up to it, her nose pressing against the glass. "Would it be frowned upon if I set him on fire?" Despite the dour mood that had filled the room with Lucie still missing, her question had me smiling, just a little bit.

"Yes," Agent Jenkins groaned, "you're just as bad as these guys are." *Well, I cannot say I blame her,* I thought, turning back to the bastard handcuffed to the metal table. *Do not worry, asshole, you will get what is coming to you...*

We will make sure of it.

27

December 11th
Tuesday
Hudson

Crunching leaves, pines, and branches were constant as we continued our search. The police had gotten far throughout the night, reaching the university's property line inside the forest. According to the agents, Noah had most likely been camping out at that house since locating Lucie. Four-wheeler tracks were deep within the soil after days of the same ride being taken. A camo painted four-wheeler had been uncovered under a tarp of fake foliage. It explained how he was easily getting on and off campus.

Since the police and agents had scoured the property around the house, we were now working from the property line toward the campus. Grigori fluttered between the trees flying in a wide s-pattern to give Nik a literal bird's eye view. I didn't really recognize where we were, all the trees and bushes had blended together in an hour of endless greenery. We continued to randomly call out Lucie's name every few minutes, desperately hoping she would hear us.

Another half hour passed before Grigori let out a squawk and dove. We all took off at a sprint, converging on the location in which Grigori had descended. It was a small clearing, a little frozen over pond was surrounded by large worn stones. Grigori perched on one of the rock formations, his eyes focused on what looked to be a patch of fog.

"We know this place," the twins announced at the same time as we broke through the trees. Logan, Landon, and Agents Garcia and Jenkins were to my right while Dante, Cam, Nik, and Dean Renaud were on my left. Agent Bronstad and Dr. Tanner followed a few steps behind the group.

"I do too," Nik added, his head tilted as he looked at his hawk. "Why did you bring us here?" Grigori squawked, but Nik didn't seem to understand.

"How do you know this place?" Dean Renaud asked them, his eyes darting around the space curiously.

"Lucie brought me out here after our debate, wanted to help me relax. Brought her mom's hot chocolate recipe to help soothe my throat," Nik said quietly, his gravelly voice thick with emotion. My heart squeezed at the thoughtfulness Lucie always put into her interactions with us.

"This is where she hid her locked box with her wish tokens before she brought them to your office," Landon supplied, looking over at the dean whose brows shot up.

"She hid them outside?" His tone was disbelieving. Logan nodded, heading for one of the stone formations.

"She had it wrapped in fabric and tucked into this little alcove with those rocks covering it to make sure it was wedged in," Logan explained, looking at the small opening in the middle of four rocks. I had to admit, I was impressed. This was a location almost no one would know of, especially considering the grass and dirt were undisturbed. We walked closer into the clearing, curious as to why Grigori had brought us here.

"I don't understand," Agent Jenkins started, spinning in a circle looking around. "I don't see her, does anyone?" Everyone shook their head except for Agent Garcia who squatted down and pressed a hand into the grass.

"Do you feel it?" His question was quiet. A round of no's went up. "This clearing is a ley line nexus." My jaw dropped, and a few gasps went up. The ley line nexuses were well documented and typically guarded to keep anyone from misusing the power. This one had clearly been missed during the search for the world's nexuses. "But this one isn't normal"—his brow furrowed—"this one had enchantments wound around it, stemming from the wards of the campus. It keeps anyone with ill will or negative intentions out while calling to those needing help or asylum." Agent Garcia stood, dusting his hand on his pants.

"So, it isn't a surprise Lucie found this place?" Cam questioned, eyeing the space with new interest. Agent Garcia nodded. I found my eyes drifting around the space. There was something odd, but I couldn't place my finger on it. I took a few steps away from the group, the odd patch of fog catching the light at just the right angle for me to see the pearlescent shift. My heart leapt in my throat.

"Guys!" I shouted, stepping closer to the cloud of smoke. If I was correct, this was Lucie right here. They started forward, almost going past me into the cloud. "Stop!" I demanded. I was greeted with odd expressions questioning why I was acting strange. "See this?" I pointed.

"Yeah, it's a patch of fog. If you hadn't noticed, there's a lot of that here," Agent Bronstad smarted. I glared at him before explaining.

"That's not fog. Dean Renaud"—he glanced at me —"you've seen Lucie when she's called upon her wish granting, correct?" He caught where I was going with this, the fire in his icy eyes burning with intensity.

"Will one of you please explain what's going on?" Landon demanded, frustrated he didn't understand.

"You know the myth about the genie and the lamp? When the person rubs the lantern, the genie comes out in a smoky haze?" Dean Renaud started to explain, walking in a very slow circle around the two-foot diameter cluster of pearlescent smoke. "When Lucie's token is used, she does the same." Dead silence answered him.

"Though only her arms, legs, and lower torso turn to smoke while her hair turns black and her eyes get all pearly," I added. "I don't know how she did it, but that's Lucie." Flynn stepped forward, staring intently at the smoke.

"She might be able to shift into smoke, she's still young and coming into her powers." I felt my heart leap.

"We don't know how injured she is though," Dr. Tanner warned. "If what you explained, and what we saw at that house is any indication, we can't force her to shift back. Not until we have her in a stabilized area where we can have life-saving precautions on hand."

"I can open the Omnilock and have it close around her. We can take her out when we get to the hospital wing." Dean Renaud worked quickly, and within a few minutes we were sprinting behind the twins back toward campus. *Thank fuck we found her.* I pushed my worries about her injuries to the back of my mind. Focusing on the positive was the only thing holding me together at the moment.

December 12th
Wednesday Afternoon
Dante

Lucie's smoky cloud hung in the air, contained to a quarantined room in case, for some reason, she tried to float away. My griffin pressed and urged in my mind, his pacing and whipping tail made me twitchy and irritable. He wanted to take charge, to demand we force Lucie to shift back, that we go to the rooms where Troy and Noah were being held and get the answers we needed regardless of how we got them, but I couldn't do that. So, I pushed back, I denied those animalistic instincts to maim the two men who had hurt Lucie, and I paced as I waited for the agents to tell us what the next step was. Submitting to their positions as federal agents went against the very core of what I was, but I had to, for Lucie.

Finally growing anxious from pacing, I sank down to the ground with my back against the wall. I hadn't slept despite having been awake for the past 48 hours since before we found her. Staring without seeing, my eyes glazed over as Dr. Tanner, Dean Renaud, and the university's doctor discussed the best course of action to take to help Lucie since she had yet to shift back on her own. Shuffling footsteps caught my attention, but I didn't bother to look up at who it was from my seated position on the tiled floor.

"Dante," Agent Jenkins' voice surprised me. I finally looked up, finding his worried eyes focused on me. "Come on." He jerked his head to the side. I shook my head, opening my mouth to explain that I couldn't leave. *Not yet, not until I knew Lucie was okay.* He knelt, no qualms about his crisp black slacks touching the tile floor. "Dante, I know what it's like to worry about teammates and people you care about being in danger. The wait to make sure everything's all right is full of 'what ifs,' 'what could have beens,' and 'now whats,' but the truth is that there is nothing you can do right now. You need a distraction, and I know damn well you haven't slept. Half your face is purple in dark circles. I want you to come watch Noah's and Troy's interrogations until the doctors have a plan to share."

"Will they let me know when they plan to do something?" He nodded. I sighed, knowing that if I sat here, my dad's and brothers' voices would echo through my mind, bringing all my insecurities to light, more than they already did on a regular basis. I stood and followed him to where they were keeping Noah and Troy. The head agent was leaning against the wall when we reached the hallway. I stepped into the empty observation room, Agent Jenkins and Agent Bronstad taking seats opposite Troy.

He still wore his security uniform, his hair pulled back in his signature ponytail at the back of his head. His olive skin held a sickly tint to it as he eyed the two men. Neither FSID agent spoke for a moment; instead, they stared at him with completely stony faces. The monitor in the corner of the observation room showed a dual screen video, one facing Troy, one facing the agents.

"So, Troy," Agent Jenkins started, his tone not quite friendly, yet not cold either. "Why don't we start with you telling us what happened?" Before he started talking, the door to the observation room opened, Dean Renaud stepping inside with Dr. Tanner.

"Dante." The dean nodded his head in greeting, and Dr. Tanner smiled warmly.

"Have we figured out what to do about Lucie yet?" I couldn't hold back my anxious question. Dr. Tanner laid a hand on my shoulder to stop the stream of questions that were surely about to come spilling out.

"We're not going to force a shift until 48 hours is up. We don't want to risk any issues with rushing it. We aren't sure if her body is essentially in a hibernative state or if it's healing itself. If she doesn't change back by tomorrow afternoon, we will be forcing it." He looked me in the eye, his warm brown eyes intense on mine. "I promise, I will personally do everything in my power to make sure she's all right." I took a shaky breath, nodding my head before turning my attention back to the interrogation.

"So, you didn't know that Noah was previously violent with Lucie?" Agent Jenkins asked, his tone suggesting he doubted him.

"No, I didn't," he pressed. Dr. Tanner scoffed, sending a quick text to Agent Bronstad. His ice blue eyes scanned, nodding ever so slightly in response as he read the message.

"What was that?" I didn't understand what had just happened.

"Oh, I'm a walking lie detector," Dr. Tanner supplied. "It's why I'm here, actually. Usually I'm in the interrogation, but Lucie's health comes first. I *am* a doctor, after all." I nodded, really intrigued with that power. It wasn't common, most people who had truth or deception-based powers would get a vibe or a hint but couldn't straight out know.

"Why did you help him?" Agent Bronstad took over questioning, his tattooed forearms on the steel table.

"I thought her boyfriends were hurting..." Dr. Tanner knocked once on the glass.

"Lie," Agent Bronstad cut him off. "I want the truth." His words trailed off in a growl. I could see the gears turning in Troy's head as he stared at the agents, but before he could come up with another lie, both men stood. "We'll be back in a while."

"Come on." Dr. Tanner nudged both the dean and me out into the hallway. We followed Agents Jenkins and Bronstad down to Noah's room, us splitting off into the observation room.

They followed the similar procedure only this time they didn't say anything, just sitting in silence, staring. I watched with fascination; I hadn't been as interested in something like this since I had started playing Kohl. Noah tried to stay still and stoic, but after we passed the one minute mark, he started to squirm. After the two minute mark, he finally spoke.

"What do you two want?" he sneered as they continued to stare. Agent Bronstad glared coolly at the psychopath across from him as he leaned his forearms on the table.

"Why'd you ask Lucie about her powers?" Noah's face cracked, just barely, but I saw it. A sliver of uncertainty widened his eyes before he slipped back into his apathetic mask.

"Because I wanted to see if she was valuable," he played off, shrugging. Dr. Tanner's brow furrowed, head tilted.

"What's happening?" I realized something was going on telepathically. Dr. Tanner looked similar to how Hudson does when he communicates.

"He's not lying, necessarily, but there's a weird note to it. Like it isn't the full story." I turned back to the piece of shit who had hurt our girl, paying particular attention to his body movements. His face was stone cold, eyes closed off, but his fist tightened just enough.

"Why would she need to be useful?" Agent Jenkins took over questioning. The scumbag shrugged but didn't answer. "You know supes who would find her useful, it's not just for yourself." At his words, Noah paled. *Bingo*. Despite the surge of victory at finding out what he was really up to, the worry in my stomach grew at the fact that there were others who viewed Lucie as a hot commodity.

"Maybe, maybe not," Noah shrugged again, finally answering the question, "even if there is, you won't find out who. And by some miracle you do, well, let's just say you're outnumbered." His smug smirk had me growling, my muscles twitching painfully to shift as I felt my griffin pacing in my head.

"What does that mean?" Agent Bronstad scoffed. "We're supposed to believe a single human with the help of one supe has an army behind him?"

"Believe whatever you want, not my problem." The interrogation came to an end after that as they both stood at the same time, but as they reached the door Noah spoke once more. "Lucie will be mine; she always will be."

Unable to listen anymore without fear of ripping him to shreds, I stepped out of the room to meet Agent Jenkins and Bronstad in the hall. Dr. Tanner and Dean Renaud talked softly in the observation room. I had to take my own advice. *Deep breaths and soothing thoughts.* It was odd to be on the receiving end of my relaxation coaching since normally only the twins needed it.

"He was telling the truth when he hinted at having friends." Dr. Tanner's voice startled me, having been lost in calming the urge to shift. I frowned, unsure what to make of that.

Agent Bronstad took charge. "Right now though, let's focus on getting Lucie healed and finish questioning Troy.

We can interrogate Noah again later." I stayed in the hall, unsure if I could handle any more confessions. A sharp ringing sounded in the quiet space, echoing against the tile. Dean Renaud excused himself to take the call, leaving me alone in the empty hall. My dad's and brothers' harsh criticisms going 'round and 'round through my thoughts.

28

December 13ʰ
Thursday Morning
Lucienne

I felt weird and there was an incessant beeping in the background. All I wanted to do was continue to swim in this nightmare-free sleep, but when I tried to roll over, my body refused to move. I groaned, the rumble of my chest and throat burned and throbbed. *What the hell?* Peeling my eyelids open, I was only able to open my right eye, my left pulsing in lightning sharp pain if I tried too hard.

"Lucie?" Alex's voice sounded strange—breathy, wobbly, and something else I couldn't place. When my eyesight finally focused, I saw the fear etched in his face. *Where am I?*

"Alex?" My voice cracked from disuse. My brain was fuzzy as I tried to process what was going on, but the ache that held my head in a vise-like grip wouldn't allow me to focus.

"Oh, thank goodness," he sighed, the relief in his voice

bringing tears to my eyes. Whatever was going on was bad if he had been that scared. "Do you know where you are, Lucie?" I finally looked around me, recognizing the thin papery gown I wore and the white walls that surrounded me.

"Hospital room," I breathed a chuckle, "told you." His brow furrowed in confusion. "Habit." I smiled as far as my battered face would allow. The longer I lay there, more and more memories came back to me, the fog in my brain slowly lifting. *Kidnapped, Noah, torture chamber, shifting to smoke, running until I collapsed.*

"Hopefully this won't happen again," he ground out, catching my attention. "We have him in custody; he can't come after you again." His words echoed in my brain, a few moments before it finally registered.

"I'm safe?" I sobbed joyfully. He nodded. I grabbed his hand from edge of the mattress, trying to show him how appreciative I was. He squeezed back gently, taking care not to aggravate any of the bruises or the wrappings on my wrist. When I finally got control of myself, I realized it was just me and him. "Where are the guys?"

"They're sleeping, but they should be awake soon. I had to dose them all with sleeping draughts because they'd been awake for several days refusing to leave you. Professor Calypso is using her sleep manipulation to wake them, and they should be here soon. I hate to do this, Lucie, but do you remember what happened?" I tried to nod, but my neck was covered in bandages in different places, making it impossible to shift my head up and down. I hummed an assent to his question instead. "When you're feeling better, the police and FSID will need your official statement and recount of what happened, but not until you're ready."

"All right." The emotional waves of everything came

crashing down at that point, and I fought back tears. The weeks of psychological bullshit, his physical abuse, the utter fear and terror, and now, finally, hope and relief all flowed through me releasing in sob after sob. Alex shushed and cooed comforting words in a soft voice, kneeling to look me in the eye, his thumb brushing gently against my knuckles. It took several tries, but I reeled in the emotional tremors that wracked my body, the sobs quieting to sniffles.

Ten minutes later, Alex had successfully calmed my mind with different topics of conversations. I tried my best not to laugh because it was extremely painful on my bruised and tender torso. My lips were cracked and still slightly swollen, making my words sound weird to my ears, but I had fully regained my mental clarity. The delirious state I had been lost in during the five days at Noah's hands, and then the forest's harsh weather, was completely gone. I had just asked something that I had been thinking about for the last couple of weeks when the door burst open, my guys stumbling in and crowding the bed.

"I'll see what I can do, Lucie." Alex gave me a small smile before excusing himself from the room. No one said anything, we just stared at each other. More tears built, and with the inability to control them, they poured in waves down my cheeks.

"Love." Logan's voice cracked, his hand hovering over my face wanting to wipe away the tears, but afraid of hurting me. I leaned as comfortably as I could into his palm, the familiarity of his skin against mine bringing a fresh wave of tears. I couldn't hold the intense emotions back any longer, not when I could have died without telling them.

"I love you guys." The words were heartfelt and brimming with the emotions I had tried to ignore for a long time. "I'm in love with every single one of you." I hiccupped a sob at the end. "I almost gave up; I almost broke." Their faces now glistened with tear tracks as I confessed how hard it had been. Knowing I needed to get this out, I continued, "But I couldn't live with myself if something happened to me and you guys never got to hear how I really felt about you."

"Fuck, Lemon Drop," Landon huffed, his voice thick, "we love you too." They all passionately agreed, bringing even more tears despite my efforts to push them back. I didn't want to be a blubbering mess any longer.

We spent the rest of the day together once they had informed my mom and Char I was safe, talking about light-hearted topics and purposefully avoiding any and all discussion about Noah and what had happened the last week, but the impending interviews I knew I'd have to face sat over me like a dark cloud that not even my guys could take away.

December 19ᵗʰ
Wednesday Early Afternoon
Lucienne

Sinking down onto my mattress, I took several breaths. *Fuck, this is a lot of work,* I mentally huffed while eyeing my suitcase with disdain. The wrappings and bandages covering various injuries of my body made moving difficult, restricting a lot of movements especially in correlation with all my bruises.

To be honest, I looked like I had been run over by a truck that then backed up over me before driving off to ensure it hit me on the way. Hell, I felt like that too, but I was alive, and Noah was in jail, and to me that was all that mattered. Well, other than the fact that my guys and my friends had been there for me through this whole shit show.

Speaking of my guys, the twins were flopped back on my plum comforter, Dante and Hudson were on their way back over after helping Sadie move her stuff back into our dorm, and Nik and Cam were both seated on the ground at the foot of my bed.

"You okay, Doll?" Cam asked, his hand straightening his plastic frames. I nodded as much as I could with the thick pile of gauze taped to the sides of my neck.

"Yeah, just exhausted." At my statement the twins jumped up off the bed and stood in front of my closet and dresser.

"What else do you need, Love?" Logan eyed my open suitcase on the floor in front of me. I shook my head, a small smile curling my lip at their eagerness to help.

"Nothing, hon, I got everything. I just got winded at the end." Logan nodded before kneeling and zipping my bag closed. Landon tucked my messenger bag on top of it after Logan had stood it upright, both sitting on either side of me on the bed when it was done.

"I can't believe we aren't going to see you for a couple of days," Landon whined, his lip pouting out at the end and making me giggle. "Can't we just come with you right away?" I rolled my eyes. We had had this same conversation several times already. The guys were planning on coming to stay for a portion of the winter break at my mom's house with me. Sadie was also going to come for a day or two with Benji and his boyfriend Austin, but only after our Yule celebration on Friday.

"You guys have to go see your families, then come over. That was the plan, remember?" I quoted the plan for the fourth time today. Hudson's laugh met my ears as he entered my room, followed closely by Dante.

"He still bitching about the fact that we aren't going to

your house right away?" Hudson asked, shaking his head at the whiny daemon. "Dude, it's only until the weekend. I think you'll be all right." Landon huffed, and flopped backward still pouting.

"Aw," I cooed teasingly, "don't be like that, babe. You wouldn't want to make me feel bad, would you?" He lost his pout in a laugh.

"Cheater." He scooped up my hand gently, his thumb tracing circles on my skin. I looked at the clock realizing Charlie would be here soon to take us back to our hometown. Groaning, I stood, my muscles having tightened up in the few minutes of sitting down. *Definitely need to do some light stretching after I get home.*

"We might be separated for a few days, but we can text, and talk, and video chat," I listed off as I glanced around the room. Despite my teasing toward Landon, I had to agree with him. I didn't want to be away from them after just getting them back. We hadn't been separated for any length of time after I had been released from the hospital on Sunday.

Landon grumbled but didn't argue as he and Logan stood. Dante and Nik took my bags and filtered out of my room and into the library with the rest of us behind him. I ignored the stares and whispers from the other students. I had been excused from classes and finals and hadn't been back around the other students since Noah had kidnapped me. This was one of the first times they had seen what I looked like after everything. I knew the gossip and rumors were going around like wildfire, but I couldn't bring myself to care. It was the start of the holiday break tonight, and I would be spending almost the entire time surrounded by Sadie, Charlie, and my guys, so the curiosity of my fellow classmates couldn't dim my excitement or happiness.

When we reached the curb, Charlie's car was pulling up, her head bouncing to music we couldn't hear. I gently hugged and kissed each of my guys, Dante piling my bags in the trunk before turning to me.

"Be safe, stay out of trouble, make sure..."

"Make sure to do my stretching and exercises from Dr. Ingress," I finished for him, a wide smile pulling painfully at the cuts on my lip. "I know, babe, I will." He nodded, happy with my promise. I turned and opened the passenger door, looking over my shoulder one last time before getting in. "I love you guys." They lit up, echoing the sentiment as I got situated in my seat. My heart was filled as Charlie started the drive back to my mom's house, my phone already dinging with text notifications from them all. My smile permanently on my face for the rest of the drive, I couldn't help but think, *It'll be the perfect holiday break...*

EPILOGUE

I lay facing the stone ceiling on the lumpy cot, the bumps digging painfully into the large bruises that covered my body. Three other inmates had cornered and jumped me a couple days ago during yard time. Gritting my teeth in rage, I started to see red. *They'll pay for laying a hand on me.* Internally growling, I felt my skin tingling as my anger grew. Taking several deep breaths, I calmed. *The plan is well underway,* I thought, taking solace in the reminder.

Lucie's beautiful face came to the forefront of my thoughts, her dark blue ocean eyes and lush pink lips. I felt myself growing stiff in the scrub pants I had been given at intake and booking. To pass the time, I thought through all our memories together, how we had met, how her skin reacted under my fingertips, how her eyes widened in fear when she angered me. *She never learned,* I thought in disappointment, *always trying hard to aggravate me instead of just following my directions*. I did everything for her—love her, provide for her, pleasure her. *And now she has those damn freaks vying for her attention*. Gritting my teeth once more, I fumed. Those freaks would not have *my* babygirl.

The train of thought was interrupted by soft steps, and my lip curled.

Right on time...

SMOKE AND MISTLETOE

BOOK 3 OF THE BEST WISHES SERIES

Coming December 2019

ACKNOWLEDGMENTS

Jake, my amazing husband, who supported me and cheered me on even when I doubted myself!

My PA Katie and closest friend Jare for keeping me sane when things got overwhelming!

My beta readers-Michelle, Jessica, and Cassie—you guys are awesome and are the best, forever #AJsAlphabets!

Finally, for all of my readers, this wouldn't be possible without you.

ALSO BY A.J. MACEY

Best Wishes Series:

Book 1: Smoke and Wishes

Supplemental Point-of-View Stories: Smoke and Wishes: Between the Wishes

High School Clowns & Coffee Grounds

Book 1: Lads & Lattes

The Aces Series:

Book 1: Rival

ABOUT THE AUTHOR

A.J. Macey has a B.S. in Criminology and Criminal Justice, and previous coursework in Forensic Science, Behavioral Psychology, and Cybersecurity. Before becoming an author, A.J. worked as a Correctional Officer in a jail where she met her husband. She has a daughter and two cats named Thor and Loki, and an addiction to coffee and swearing. Sucks at adulting and talking to people, so she'll frequently be lost in a book or running away with her imagination.

Stay Connected

Join the Reader's Group for exclusive content, teasers and sneaks, giveaways, and more:
A.J. Macey's Minions